Silence

Josie Henley-Einion

Legend Press
Independent Book Publisher

Legend Press Ltd
Unit 11, 63 Clerkenwell Road, London EC1M 5NP
info@legendpress.co.uk
www.legendpress.co.uk

British Library Cataloguing in Publication Data available.

ISBN 978-1-9065580-3-1

Set in Times
Printed by J. H. Haynes and Co. Ltd., Sparkford.

Cover designed by Gudrun Jobst
www.yellowoftheegg.co.uk

Legend **Press**

Independent Book Publisher

This book is dedicated to Alyson Henley-Einion

Alys, for being there even when I wasn't.
For not giving up on me even when I did.
For telling me the book was worth it.
For allowing me this big romantic gesture.
And for so much else, I owe you.

Penetration (`p_nI\tr_I__n) *n.* *1. the act or an instance of penetrating. 2. the ability or power to penetrate. 3. keen insight or perception. 4. Mil. an offensive manoeuvre that breaks through an enemy's defensive position.*

Silence *() n. 1. complete absence of sound. 2. the fact or state of abstaining from speech. v. 1. make silent. 2. (silenced) fitted with a silencer.*

PRISON COUNSELLOR KILLS EX-CON

Jacqueline Harris, 35, prison counsellor at Newpark Women's Prison, has been arrested for the suspected murder of Francis Little, 37, who previously served time at Fenton. Jacqueline, who is known as 'Jack', claims that Francis was 'raping' her lesbian lover Jemima Albinelka, also 35.

Today, Ms Albinelka was unavailable for comment but a neighbour, who sees them regularly walking hand-in-hand to the car and once spotted them kissing on their doorstep, says this was inevitable. "They are always at it," said the neighbour, who does not wish to be named. "I hear them arguing all the time, they have parties till the early hours, and now this. It's disgusting."

A police spokesperson this morning confirmed, "A woman was arrested last night for the suspected murder of a homeless man and is currently being held at the South Valley Station while our officers conduct their enquiries."

Valley Gazette comment, see page 22.

Chapter One – 1988

JACK

O yez, o yez. Now hear this. Shout it from the rooftops, darling.

She is mixing – a mix here, a mix there – in her element. She is a mixture herself: a crazy mixed up kid. Looking out over the crowd to check they still like it. Not that she cares what anyone thinks of her art, but to be out of a job again would be difficult. To be a paid DJ is tough call enough, but for a dyke in Maddeston, North Warwickshire, there is really only one place to work. She doesn't fancy hauling her arse over to cardboard city Coventry and slumming it with the rest of the dregs. Though looking out over the crowd, she isn't sure this place is any better. She leans into the microphone.

"DJ Dance Jack comin' at you with the b-b-*best* sounds of the eighties. Get yo' dancin' feet on the floor for some *Ride On Time*." She eases the dial up for the first chords of the extended dance track and leans back to light a roll-up.

There has always been the possibility of passing for a boy and getting into warehouse work. She is tall and young enough to be beardless. Not yet grown into her skin, she is like a spring-born fawn – leggy and awkward with a potential for greatness. (Oh where are you now, you butch beauty?) Time will come for her to flesh out and slide in with the ranks of sad old bull-daggers at the bar, snarling over a piece of fresh meat.

As a gay club, its members at least keep the style that everywhere else lacks, between New Romantic and Acid Jazz, although there are still the sheep. Jackie sighs as she sees the regiments of miniature Jimmy Somervilles and Alison Moyets. Something catches her attention, flighty like a ruffle of feathers, and draws her eyes to a figure standing near the DJ box. Jack squints through the haze of stinging smoke and poppers to take a look and there she sees a straight woman quickly looking away. How does she know this girl is straight? Is it the long blonde look, the handbag and Silk Cut cigarette, the polished fingernails curled around a glass of white wine (*I didn't know they sold wine in this beer swinging club!*) or the tentative biting of lips as lustful eyes follow the butchest dykes on the floor?

No, what gives her away is the fact that she is unconsciously twisting her wedding ring, tugging it on and off her thin finger as if indecision were the worst thing in the world. Jackie feels a tightness in her boxers and with it feels every single moment of the last few months without a lover. The local girls have been warned off her, have learned to call her 'Jack-the-lad', and she is suffering for it.

The *Ride* over, she sets a long-playing twelve-inch of *Like A Virgin* on the spinner. Knocking the lit end of her roly against the side of the box, she leans over and nods to the woman. "New here, babe?" The straight woman laughs a reply, but her eyes dance with interest, flickering over the DJ's lithe body. As she comes closer Jackie can see beneath the makeup that she is older, at least in her thirties. This makes Jack feel good – like a young stud.

"See anythin' you like?" She smiles and then turns away to twist the dials before she hears an answer. Jack sets up another twelve-inch – Billy Joel's *Uptown Girl* – to play unattended for a while, and drops down out of the box to come close to the straight.

Jack wants to be sure the woman knows where she's coming from. She looks pointedly at the ring. "You going back to your husband tonight?"

"Not tonight..." Playful lips draw out the words like an expert, but the tremor in the woman's hand and voice give her away as a newcomer. Far from putting her off, it only serves to spur Jackie on all the more. They draw closer together and as their bodies move in time to Billy's agenda, Jackie risks leaning forwards to give a soft, teasing kiss on the woman's cheek. She groans in Jack's ear. "Do you know, the last time I slept with a woman I was eighteen."

Jackie laughs, "Do you know, same here!" It's a lie, of course, for she is only recently eighteen, but, hey, why pass up the chance of a good line?

"What's your name?" she asks.

"Jackie Harris. Jack. What's yours?"

The woman, whose name Jack learns and forgets again within a few seconds, buys herself another drink and waits for closing time at Jack's insistence. They spend the next few hours eyeing each other and flirting with body language until finally the last dancer stumbles out of the club. Jackie then allows her into the DJ box while she packs up.

"So, have you always been a lesbian?" the woman asks carelessly. Jack stiffens. Is she taking the piss? But the knowledge that she hasn't felt flesh against flesh for some time helps in shrugging off her belligerence. She doesn't have to like the woman to shag her.

"Just about as long as I can remember," she growls.

"Oh. I just wondered. You know, I've always wondered what it's like to be a lesbian."

She is turned away and the woman can't see her face. Of the myriad terse replies she could have given, Jackie chooses a mild one. "Oh yeah?" She faces the flighty bird. "Well let's just see if you can take it, babe."

Leading her by the hand out of the deserted bar, she says, "I got a room just up from here." Jack stumbles into the after-club crowd in the street. Each club has its own clientele who stick together in small groups around the communal courtyard created by the focal-point of a burger van. The van pumps out its fetid stink, enticing drug-hungry ravers to risk their lives for the sake of a food fix. The January freeze attracts even vegetarian hippies to hang around the back of the van. A group of skinheads appraise the couple, at first thinking Jackie to be one of them due to her haircut and dress; they then snap to attention as they notice the club from which she has emerged.

"Hey!" They hear the shout as she grabs the straight woman again and hurries past. "Hey, you two – off for some lezzie licks!" Jackie speeds up as she senses the fright escaping from her companion – it wouldn't do to lose her now she's so close.

"Run!" she whispers harshly, and as they run they hear laughter and thudding footsteps behind. Had she been alone she might have faced them down. Cowards mostly and she has enough bravado to pull it off – although she remembers the time she was mistaken for a gay man and set upon by a gang. When they had realised she was female they laughed at the mistake and kicked harder. She shudders at the memory of the cracked ribs and crushed pride as she throws herself down stone steps to her basement room, key at the ready.

Breathless, they lean against the door as it closes behind them.

Jackie thumbs the light switch and the bare bulb flicks on dimly to reveal damp walls and stained carpet. Wide-eyed, the straight woman turns shakily towards her. Jackie laughs unsympathetically. "You wanted to know what it's like to be a lesbian. This is what it's like."

She pulls her close again, not caring how harshly she kisses, how hungry she is, whether she's hurting. If this straight thinks another woman would be soft all night then she is about to have her preconceptions blown out along with her cobwebs.

The kiss leaves both of them wanting more and Jackie pushes her over towards the bed, tearing at straight clothes and straight sensibilities. Far from putting the woman off, she is pulled down on top of her, gaining power all the way. They struggle on the bed, the woman wanting, wanting, and yet trusting that somehow this wild girl will manage as she seems so confident. The lie she'd told Jack about sleeping with a woman at eighteen had been a half-baked attempt to make the little dyke realise she was serious. And this might be the culmination of so many nights of fantasy in a cold bed, so many false starts and failed attempts. There is no way she is going to let go now. But Jack is holding back, not in a timid I-don't-know-what-to-do kind of way, but in a teasing, I'm-going-to-force-you-to-beg way, so that in the end she has to say. "Please…"

"Please, Jack…" she insists.

"Please, Jack, just do whatever you do. I need something, I need –"

Jackie sits up abruptly. "I know what you need: you're straight. I know what straight women want." She speaks with venom, almost hatred, and for a moment the woman is frightened. Jack turns away, suddenly cold. Although she knew this would happen it still feels like a rejection, an indication that she herself isn't good enough. And yet, why does she continue to pick up straights?

She sighs and opens the top drawer of a scuffed cabinet, the second of two pieces of furniture in the room, including the single bed. The drawer is stiff and opens only halfway; she reaches in and draws out the contents. Placing several items on the bed, Jack turns back to the woman who watches greedily like a child at a chocolate counter.

Now Jimmie, don't get coy on me. You may not want to face it, but I'm not pulling any punches with this one. Skip it if you need to, but you won't know 'the truth, the whole truth and nothing but the truth', will you? You'll only know your own sanitized version of the truth. And if you want to know the real me, as you say, then this involves a fair amount of penetrating thoughts.

Jackie's cynicism is abated and her sense of fun returns as she sees the look on the woman's face.

"Regular, medium or supersize?" she quips as she lays out the dildoes in a row. "Or I've got a vibrating one somewhere around here…" she ducks under the bed but the woman grabs her wrist to haul her back up.

"That's fine," she whispers excitedly, "that's ok. This one will do." The woman's hand hovers slightly over 'medium' – a blue-coloured solid latex model, also Jackie's favourite – as if she were afraid to touch it directly. "I hadn't realised I'd get a choice," she laughs.

"Of course you get a choice!" bursts out Jackie, sweeping the two rejects off the bed and dragging a leather harness from the back of the same drawer. "I'm not a single-size one-hit-wonder, you know," she continues conversationally as the fascinated woman watches her deftly strapping the dildo over her boxers and wiggling it into place. "I have a full set of unmutated chromosomes, size *and* stamina and can keep on going all night if required. How can anyone compete with that? There! What do you think?" She pulls her jeans back over her hips and shifts the bulge to display it at its best, strutting up and down in front of the amused older woman. In the arrogance of youth, she adds, "Once you've tasted the best, you'll never go back."

Jack nudges an ancient cassette player with her toe and turns the volume down as it springs to life with Meatloaf – it's now approximately 3am.

She is still swaggering around the small room while the woman shifts impatiently on the bed. "Stop posing and come here, you teasing little bitch." Despite the macho exterior, Jackie likes to be called a little bitch and likes being ordered around, so she obediently goes over to the bed and allows her jeans to be tugged down again. She lifts the woman's long denim skirt and expertly pulls off her pants. They kiss as before, passionately pulling at each others' clothes. Only this time there is something hard between them, something sliding against Jackie's diamond and rubbing against the woman's open wanting until neither of them can bear it any more.

Jackie pulls back to watch it go in. She enjoys this: like a reversal of the rabbit-out-of-a-hat magic trick. She pauses for a moment to check it isn't hurting (having shagged a few young, tight girls) but the woman is groaning, pushing up to her. Jack grins and grabs the cheap headboard for the ride of her life.

Let's play a game of peekaboo. Now you see it, now you don't. A gasp, a flash of shiny latex, dark-nippled breasts bursting out of a tight teenage bra and spilling onto your face. Oh Jack, oh God Jack! There's more where that came from, so much more – always hard, always ready. What more could a woman ask for?

At some point they roll over so that the woman is on top sitting up and holding Jackie's shoulders, while Jackie lies on her back. She watches her hair flying wild and screams getting wilder. She is overwhelmed as wave upon wave of orgasm shake the woman's body. Then over again, Jackie on top, more gentle this time, slower and sweeter. Then hard again, taking her cue from the woman's movements; and again; and again.

This woman grabbing the leather belt of the harness-like reins and pulling Jackie down and into her, demanding more, demanding a constant hard, fast rhythm. *Oh God, when will she ask me to stop?* Jack makes it a personal policy not to stop until she is asked to do so. She tries to be as un-male as possible, given the circumstances.

Her concentration is beginning to lapse and she becomes aware again of the replaying Meatloaf tape.

She realises she is hungry, thinking, 'have I got any food in?' when, almost from outside herself, Jackie begins to feel something she wouldn't normally allow in company. She feels the wave of an orgasm beginning in her own body. Don't get me wrong – all this humping, pumping, rubbing action turns her on no end, but usually leaves her feeling frustrated and having to finish herself off when alone afterwards. But this insatiable straight woman has turned a corner in Jackie's sex life. She has shown that if you just keep on going for long enough and stop trying so hard then there are glories to come.

When the woman notices the surprised look on Jackie's face and realises that she is coming, she too begins a swift ascent into bliss. Gripping the headboard behind her, she pushes her hips up and out and calls out for Jackie to use her, to go as hard as she needs. In that brief achievement of immortality, in the throes of ecstasy it seems that their souls entwine somewhere a metre or so above their bodies, and Jackie knows then that she'll never be the same again. Their simultaneous yelling drowns out Meatloaf's voice and the complaining thuds of Jackie's neighbour. Then a crunch as the headboard finally gives way and a crack as it hits Jackie on the back of her head. She slumps on top of the stunned woman, a dead weight.

Dropping the broken headboard, the woman extricates herself from Jackie's body and in her panic almost flees the bedsit. But she turns back just to check the girl's pulse. Relieved to find her still alive, the woman sits on the bed at a loss for the next action. The *Karma Sutra* doesn't say what to do when your lover falls unconscious. She notices an old pop bottle filled with water next to the bed, takes a swig first to check that's all it is, and then splashes some into Jackie's face.

Jack sits bolt upright, blinking away the water from her eyes. "What you do that for?" she whines, then lies back down rubbing her face.

"You were out cold," the woman says. "Sorry, love. It looks like you're going to have a lump on your head. Maybe you'd better get to hospital?"

"No, I'll be all right. What happened, anyway?" Then she notices the broken stumps of bedposts and begins laughing.

"Don't worry, this bed's knackered already – it came with the room." She reaches over to her jeans on the floor and pulls out a leather tobacco pouch. "Want me to roll you one?" The woman declines and fishes around in her own clothing pile for her packet of fags. What to do with post-coital embarrassment – light a fag. Jackie rolls a small, tight, fag quickly like she's been practising all her life and lights up one-handed, while she pulls at the buckles on the leather strap around her hips.

"Here, let me help you." The woman balances her newly-lit Silk Cut on the side of the cabinet and reaches over to prise the buckle open. Jack leans back to watch her peal the harness away, her unbuttoned shirt falling to the side to expose a creamy honey-coloured stomach. The boxers have ridden down and red wheals show where the buckle has been held tight against bare skin.

"Why do you pull it so tight?"

Jackie blows out smoke before replying. "It slips if it's loose and I don't get good control."

The woman pulls it all the way off and exposes Jackie's vulnerability, but Jack doesn't move – just lies there watching her face.

"Well you certainly know how to use it, anyway." The woman smiles up at her and as their eyes meet there passes a moment of intimacy, deeper and qualitatively different than all that has passed before. Jackie feels a stirring within her again but, unsure of her energy levels, she breaks eye contact and lets it dissipate. The woman goes back to her cigarette and Jackie pulls an ashtray out from under the bed, placing it on her bare stomach for both of their use.

Now don't be sad, 'cos two outta three ain't bad.

"Turn the tape off, will you?" Jack nods towards the cassette player on the floor. "The neighbours'll complain."

The woman stands up and finds the 'stop' button, then returns to the bed and Jack. Turned on her side, she begins to run the fingers of her free hand along Jackie's legs and stomach while she uses the other to smoke. She strokes questioningly at Jack's hair – perhaps she's only just noticed the quality of it, being so short it's not obviously Black. Amazing how many people completely miss the significance of Jackie's large mahogany eyes and luscious lips. Light skin is everything, after all. But the race issue obviously doesn't bother this woman as she becomes all PC and dismisses it. Perturbed that she hasn't actually 'been a lesbian' after all, she cups her hand over Jackie's crotch. "Are you sure you don't want…?"

"What?" Jackie snaps, shrugging away under her touch.

"Me to… er…"

Jackie laughs cruelly. "And what exactly *would* you do? You're straight, what would you know?" She stubs out her roly petulantly, hands over the ashtray and turns her back. "Anyway, I need to get to sleep. Got college tomorrow."

The woman considers this, smoking quietly for a while, then, "What are you studying?"

"Doing my A-levels next year," Jackie mutters, half-asleep already. "And then university." She is pleased to feel the effect this has on the woman – a change in the quality of air around her. She knows that she's shocked her. Not only showing her age, but her intellect. The woman finishes her cigarette and lights another. Jack can almost sense what's going through her mind: she's afraid. Perhaps she has a son or daughter near Jackie's age, perhaps she is a teacher, policewoman or doctor, one of those professions that can be lost at a hint of illegal or immoral behaviour. Or a social worker – now that would be funny! Jack often thinks she'd like to rattle her own social worker's cage a bit.

Jack has lost count of how many women she'd invited to play a bit-part in the story of her life. Could it be that a higher percentage of these were blonde? Is it necessary to count?

Most people don't realise Jackie is as young as she is; she has a job and her own place (albeit a dump) and carries herself with an air of arrogance not considered decent in a newly eighteen-year-old girl. Having already led a full life, she has the outward appearance of a youth of at least twenty.

However, her mind is that of a child and her social skills need a lot of work. What was that I said earlier? – what more could a woman ask for? Well, a more winning personality would be one thing, a modicum of tact and respect. But for now, while still physically attractive, she doesn't feel she needs these bonus attributes. As long as the girls are flocking, Jackie is fucking, and that's all the extra-curricular activity she's interested in. Not relationships. Not long-term lovers. Not anyone encroaching on her space for more than one night at a time. She has fought hard for this place and she is still fighting. Those who stay for more than one night do not stay for long. There is no argument as to her ability to satisfy in bed, but all who leave do so feeling strangely frustrated.

As she lingers on the brink of wakefulness, Jack feels a slight, birdlike, peck on her cheek and the other side of the bed lightens as the woman moves away. She wakes alone at eleven, sees £40 on the cabinet under the ashtray that still holds two Silk Cut stubs and half a roly, turns over and falls back to sleep. She is smiling to herself: another £40 towards the motorcycle fund. She dreams of a big fat purple one, throbbing viciously between her legs; a Harley or something classic like that will be an appropriate means of escape from this dire life she leads.

Are you going to say now that women don't pay for sex, Jim? They pay with a lifetime of drudgery; they hand over their self-respect with hardly a second thought. £40, then, is very little compared to forty years or more of housework. Talk to your mother about that one.

***

The English class notice her absence but no-one comments. Jackie often skips Fridays. They know she is working her way through college but most of her classmates prefer not to mention it. Perhaps they feel guilty in their middle-class familial homes.

Perhaps they are jealous of her freedom. Perhaps they just can't make her out – she is an anomaly: the intelligent street urchin. Such a cliché that few people believe she can exist. Whatever it is, it blocks any possibility of intimacy while at college, though she often catches the posh girls looking. Jackie doesn't care because she isn't there to make friends. She is there for one thing only – to get an education. She isn't going to be a DJ for the rest of her life. She is going to get somewhere, be one of those professional, suited women – teacher, doctor, social worker, educational psychologist – that have so far dominated her life.

Meanwhile, why not be a gigolo? She gets her kicks; she gets the rent paid; she gets through college. Jack knows the looks won't last – beardless boys are only good for a few years; might as well use it while it's there.

She's not a gigolo anymore, though. A counsellor is a prostitute of a different kind, although she is not even this any longer. Let those without sin cast the first stone. She never asked for the money, she never stood on street corners and plied a trade. The money was the weight of the woman's conscience and it's surprising how heavy consciences can be.

Oh, Jim don't you judge me now. Don't tell me that you haven't prostituted yourself at some time in your life. Pretended to like someone for the sake of a job; gone against your better instincts and compromised for the sake of a quiet life.

What I'm trying to do here is to avoid making Jackie out as a victim. She may have been victimised, but she never considered herself a victim – of the care system, of abuse, of life; she never once sat down and sobbed 'oh poor little me'.

No, she got out there and survived. Like you. So why am I making her out to be such a bitch? Needless to say you've realised by now that I don't like myself very much.

Dearest Jim, you said you wanted to find out who 'I' am. But I must warn you that there is not just one story. The story of a life is a patchwork quilt: each oft-repeated scene a brightly shining piece of material, its edges clearly defined; those that are not so well remembered are the frayed pieces of indeterminate colour; and the thread that weaves between the patches is made of the stories we tell ourselves about what and who we are. On this thread the life-story depends because if it unravels, the patches fall apart, along with the life. Every day a new patch can be added, but as we get older the patches have to be forced to fit into the whole and the thread becomes thicker and stronger, filling in more gaps between patches.

It's all about choice. You might argue that choice is restricted by opportunity, but there are ways of forging your own opportunities. Look at Jackie now. At every point in her life she had the choice to deviate from the route. And had she not gone on, had she just said 'all I gotta do is stay Black and die' then she may still have ended up singing the jailhouse blues. *Aint that right, sister! You say it how it is.* Fate and free will are slippery customers. We are born; we become who we are; we try to be different; at some point in our lives we do something that makes people who knew us when we were younger say, 'ah, I always said she'd do that'; we become our parents. There's no point in hiding from your past as the faster you run from it, the more likely you are to trip and fall flat on your face.

I know you've read in the papers about Jackie. All sorts of distorted, exaggerated vignettes of her life have been on public view. Jackie Harris the sex fiend; Jackie Harris the murderer; Jackie the victim; Jackie the criminal; Jackie the Ripper (can you believe that one?); Jackie Harris True Crime Friday Night Special. All flash in the pan, of course. Sell a few papers; get a month or two's coverage; move on to the next sensational story. Slightly more than the allocated fifteen minutes, but by next year she'll be all but forgotten.

This is a story of a different kind. This isn't written by some hack-journalist simply regurgitating the same old tripe that's already been said, adding a few of their own salacious details to sell more copies. This is the truth (or as near to the truth as memory will allow). I have to write it well for my own sake, and yours. I don't have to sell it. If I manage to finish it before I die then maybe I'll see it published. I am a journal-ist, the opposite of the journalist. A hack has to sell but doesn't have to write well.

Unfortunately for Jackie (or perhaps fortunately, depending on how you look at it), she didn't know her origins. She never found out who her parents were or anything about their race, identity or circumstances. Her mother may as well have been the Queen of Sheba or the Wicked Witch of the White West. Or she might be shagging her own sister/aunt/mother. And if you're destined to become your mother but you don't know who your mother is, does that make you free or more constrained? So why not claim Maya Angelou, Alice Walker or Joni Mitchell for a mother; Bessie Smith, Billie Holiday or Gertrude Stein for a grandmother; Oprah Winfrey or Jodie Foster for a sister?

I was so proud of my arse when I was slim and beautiful. Now it just blobs away behind me and follows me around like a lost puppy. Too much sitting down and not enough sex. I'm getting too old for this.

Chapter Two

JACK

The clang of metal prison doors reverberated around the yard, setting my teeth on edge. Keys rattled in the lock as I pulled my coat collar closer to my neck and shoved the annoying wiry ponytail inside, scant protection against the late afternoon drizzle. Head bowed, I trudged to the outer gate. I blinked into the rain as I glanced up to see who was on gate duty. Old George wasn't too bad, but Tommy could be a real smarmy bastard.

"Just my luck," I muttered to myself as I recognised the massive frame moving inside the portacabin gatehouse.

"Hello darling," Tommy growled, leaning out of the half-open window as I passed. I felt the heat escaping from the cabin and saw the steam of his coffee but did not linger on the way through the gate.

"Oooh, ignore me then, see if I care," he guffawed. And, frustrated at still getting no response, he ventured to stick his prematurely balding head out into the rain to bark after my retreating back, "See you next week, my love!"

I restrained myself from retorting or even looking back as I knew it would incite him to further attempts at intimacy. He probably said that to everyone leaving the prison, inmates and staff. Given the weather, I estimated just one second of him staring at my backside (I was glad to be wearing the long coat) before he ducked back inside his kennel.

I headed towards the waiting Skoda that I would recognise

anywhere. Not because of its distinctive pattern of rust, nor the nodding Scooby-doo on the dashboard, nor even the '*I'd rather be riding a bike*' bumper sticker on which I'd cleverly altered the 'b' to a 'd'. It's the angel sitting in the driver's seat that does it. Reaching out a numbed hand to open the passenger door, I flung my briefcase onto the back seat and slid into the relative warmth and comfort of the car I shared with my partner, Jimmie.

Despite her butch-sounding name, Jimmie is a picture of lesbian chic. Short-but-not-too-short, wispy blonde hair, pale blue eyes and a fresh-faced, mildly freckled complexion; I wondered several times a day at the fortune of landing such a good-looking lover. As Jimmie revved the engine and turned the rattling heater up a notch, she could well have been an angel sent from heaven.

"Oh God," I groaned, "what a day! I'm so glad it's Friday."

"Tough week?" Jimmie enquired vaguely, her attention elsewhere as she revved and reversed the car. "This thing's like a tank," she muttered, wrenching the gearstick.

"Tough day, tough week, tough *life*," I intoned, looking back at the imposing building we arced in front of. "That place gives me the creeps." I dug around in my briefcase for my E45 cream and rubbed some on my hands. The cold weather always brought out my eczema.

"Why work there then?"

I ignored the question, as it was one I so often asked myself and for which I could find no answer except that I was compelled to continue. "Still," drawing myself up as the Skoda lurched forwards into the rain, "thank God I've got the weekend off. Home, James, and don't spare the horses."

"You always say that," complained Jimmie.

"Ok then: lead on McFluff if you prefer." I snickered at Jim's annoyed expression. "Well you should change your name then, to something more feminine. Like *Jemima* for instance..."

"Shut up, *Jacqueline*!" The car swerved as Jimmie leaned over to poke me in the ribs. Both of us object to the use of our given names, even in jest.

No doubt Tommy chuckled to himself, "Women drivers!" wishing that he could be the one to show us how a real man motored.

Okay, he's a stereotype. So what? There will always be some people who live up to the image or it wouldn't have arisen in the first place. Possibly Tommy had a sensitive side, maybe he cried at Bette Davis movies before cycling off to his macramé and quilting night classes. But somehow I don't think so. And anyway, this story isn't about him.

Jimmie's driving settled down once we were on the main road and the Skoda was behaving itself. "Are you sure you're ok to drive?" I asked, always aware of her bad leg. She shrugged; she knows how much I hate driving. It's her car after all, technically; her mobility allowance. I would drive if we were going a long way, like the impending visit to parents for the weekend, but I'll always be a biker at heart. And my knees will never allow me to forget that fact. By the time we were halfway home, the conversation had turned to the evening ahead.

"Do you want to stop off for some grub? Before we go to The Claires?" asked Jimmie, always aware of her lover's need of sustenance in times of trial.

"Hmm, have we got enough cash for a pizza?"

"Have a look. My purse's in my bag." Jimmie flicked her eyes away from the road for a brief moment to nod at her hippy patchwork handbag on the back seat. I strained against my seatbelt to reach the strap of the bag, nearly dropping it as a high-pitched rendition of *The William Tell Overture* blared from within.

"You've changed the ringtone *again*?" I protested, fishing in the bag for her mobile.

"I've set a different tune for specific numbers," she explained, as she searched for a spot to pull over from the busy road. "I know who that is."

I looked at the display on Jimmie's phone and groaned. "Do you want me to answer it?"

"Here," she said impatiently as she swung the bulky car into a mini-sized space, grabbing the phone and thumbing the green button as the nearside wheel mounted the pavement.

"Hello?" she chirped brightly, frowning at me and dragging on the handbrake. "Yes, tonight? Hang on…" Jim put her hand over the end of her Nokia and turned to see me pouting like a child. "Jack… we need the money."

I threw up my hands, "Ok, fine."

"I won't be starting till eight. We can go to The Claires early. I can –"

"Ok," I said. "Fine. Do the shift if you want."

"Jack…" Jimmie pleaded and I sighed, softening my tone. "Sorry love, I just think it'd be nice to have a night together for once."

"We'll have tomorrow night."

"Tomorrow night we'll be at your parents'," I muttered and then looked up to meet my lover's eyes. "You do still want me, don't you?"

Jim always melted when I displayed rare signs of insecurity. "Look. If you really don't want me to…?"

"No, it's ok," I said, looking out of the window at an irate pedestrian trying to manoeuvre a pushchair through the gap between the Skoda and a shop front. "I just needed to know you'd turn it down if I asked you to. Take it – we could use the money, like you said."

Jimmie released a breath, trying and not succeeding to hide her annoyance, and returned to the phone conversation. "Yes, I'll do it. Sorry to keep you waiting. Yeah. See you at eight then." She pressed the red button and handed the mobile back to me. "Full steam ahead to Pizza Land?" She looked over her shoulder and began gradually reversing into the stream of traffic. "Oh shit. Now I've got to get out of this tight hole."

"I thought tight holes were your speciality, darling." Jimmie glared at me before her face cracked and she laughed. I laughed too, even as I gripped the edges of the seat as the Skoda swerved away from oncoming traffic. I'll never get used to her driving, any more than she'll get used to my sense of humour.

***

We still had to go home to our two-bedroom terraced shit-hole so I could get changed, but buying the pizza cut down the amount of time before we would be ready and out again. Jimmie slopped two slices onto plates while I went upstairs to throw off my professional suit and drag on jeans and white t-shirt. Just another kind of uniform. The jeans were tight and I considered digging around for some jogging bottoms but thought maybe I should make an effort to look reasonably smart for a social occasion.

Jimmie didn't need to change; she wore the same embroidered jeans and frilly tops whether she was working at the night shelter, hanging out at home or visiting friends. I sometimes envied her for this simplicity although I never envied her femmie clothes.

She was already munching in front of the TV, stripping the pizza topping away and nibbling at it, when I arrived back downstairs for my slice of action. It was congealing on a plate next to my mug, both of which were balanced precariously on top of a full A4 envelope on the corner of the computer desk. "Oh thanks," I said, picking up the mug and taking a sip.

Jimmie glanced up. "I presumed you'd want tea," she said as she chewed.

I nodded, non-committal. I could have really done with a

decent coffee but we couldn't afford such luxuries. Still standing I took another sip and looked at the TV. She was watching some crap as usual and I hovered over the computer. "Mind if I do some writing while we eat?"

Jimmie shrugged and I leant down to switch the computer on. I had a bite of pizza while the computer was warming up, then wandered off through the galley kitchen into the toilet at the back of the house.

The computer was still not loaded when I got back and I sifted through the pile of books, letters and paraphernalia on the desk to find my puzzle book. Jimmie noticed me ferreting for a pencil and smiled. "I'm glad you like the puzzles," she said. It was her that got me hooked on them, her and her *Logic Problems* magazine. "Remember your pizza though," she chided.

"Yeah, yeah," I said, already colouring in a couple of squares on the Tsunami grid. I put the book down again and took a bite of pizza, looking up at the now completed screen. I double-clicked the Word icon and opened the most recent document. I stared morosely at my title page.

Breaking Down
Jacqueline Harris

I had to change that title or people will think it's about a car mechanic. I double-clicked the word 'Down' and changed it to 'Out'. I then sat back and looked at it again.

Breaking Out
Jacqueline Harris

Not much better but it would do for now.

I skipped to chapter five which I knew needed work and began to read the opening line: 'She was mixing – a mix here, a mix there – in her element...'

Jimmie finished what she wanted of her pizza and got up to throw the rest away. She paused on her way to the kitchen. "Are you going to eat yours? Before it gets cold?"

I minimised the screen self-consciously before I answered.

"You can talk," I said, but I picked up the plate and looked at the envelope that it had been resting on. "Is this new?"

I looked at Jimmie, who frowned for a moment before answering. "Oh yeah. It arrived this morning. Sorry I forgot to tell you. The postman woke me up. And I put it on the end of the desk and then went back to sleep again. Sorry." She drifted off into the kitchen and I heard the toilet door close.

I sighed. I couldn't be annoyed with her when she was so knackered all the time. And that was a long speech for Jimmie, who usually speaks in such a halting way that most people interrupt before she's finished her point. The only time I hear her being really articulate is when she's passionate about politics. I wonder if this is why she writes: she needs it more than I do as a mode of expression.

I turned the envelope over and recognised my own handwriting, not unexpected but disappointing nevertheless. I took another bite of pizza and chewed distractedly, looking for somewhere else on the desk to rest the plate. In the end I balanced it on my lap and rubbed my hands on my jeans to rid them of grease before attacking the envelope. I peered inside and read what I had anticipated.

Breaking Down
Jacqueline Harris

I pulled out the covering letter, which was a standard rejection without even the pretence at interest in the novel. After reading the letter I was about to toss it aside in disgust when I noticed that it had two pages. My heart leapt despite itself and I flipped the first page over only to find a blank sheet of headed notepaper. Maybe someone had carelessly taken two sheets from the printer instead of one. An idea occurred to me and I slipped the blank sheet into my own printer. Opening up a new document, I began to type.

Esteemed Jacqueline,
We are eternally grateful that you chose us as a publisher to

receive your novel. Your style is beyond comparison to any unsolicited manuscript previously received. Our editors were moved to tears on reading it and found themselves unable to return to work for several weeks.

However, it is with great regret that we find ourselves unable to publish your masterpiece. We are a publisher of trashy junk read by illiterate morons. Your work has inspired us to upgrade our list and perhaps include literary works in the future. But for the moment we feel that, were we to publish your novel, we would fail to sell any of our other titles.

Being unable to find another work equal to yours would halt our production and inevitably put us out of business. It is therefore with deep regret that we find we must return your manuscript to you. We hope that you will find a publisher more worthy of your intellect.

We will be forever in your debt for giving us the opportunity to review such a work of genius.

Yours regretfully,

With satisfaction at a job well done, I took a sip of cooling tea while my printer whirred and shook, and the new rejection letter appeared. I clipped the two sheets together, mine at the top. Impaling the letter on my Stephen King style rejection spike that hangs on the wall behind the computer, I smiled as it stabbed through the heart of yet another company of ungrateful bastards. That spike was very useful for taking out frustration. Of course, I haven't got anything like that here; they barely let us use cutlery let alone murderously sharp spears.

***

A visit to The Two Claires was our standard Friday night entertainment. This is so for a whole sector of the Valley lesbian scene, who prefer domesticity to clubland. Although living in a private house of usual size, The Two Claires have the benefit of a huge knocked-through lounge that can host numbers of standing guests and several prized places on the sofa. This lesbian haven has achieved such notoriety on the scene that ingénues have been known to think that 'The Two Claires' is the name of a public house. The Claires had, in fact, considered running a pub but neither had any business sense, as Claire Tilley's failed hairdressing shop demonstrated.

We didn't have parties ourselves since, during our housewarming barbeque, our new neighbour had called the police with complaints about noise and lewd behaviour. The music hadn't been particularly loud and the 'lewdness' had been a couple of women openly holding hands as they arrived on the doorstep. The police arrived and told us to turn it down which we did, but it kind of put a damper on the day. The neighbour then stood in his back garden and watched us and our guests with a smug expression.

We haven't had many visitors since and we haven't played music very often. Jim only practises her trumpet when she knows he's out, but that doesn't stop him complaining. The Claires don't have this problem as their neighbour on one side is deaf and on the other side the house is vacant.

The Two Claires have two cats, Dart and Sheba, both rescue cats from abused backgrounds but otherwise have nothing in common – as unalike as the Two Claires themselves. However, much to the couple's dismay, Dart appears to be heterosexual. If she detected a male presence, she would pounce onto the unsuspecting bloke and proceed to tart herself all over him. Considering the fact that Dart would normally have nothing to do with other cats, including Sheba, I argued that she indulged in what should properly be described as bestiality.

I generally object to labelling people, especially in terms of sexuality, which I see as a fluid state. This makes me unpopular among certain quarters of the lesbian community, and I have on more than one occasion been accused of not being a 'real' lesbian – especially when I admit to having had a relationship with a man in the past (however unmanly he was). The objection is not so much that I'd had sex with a man, but that I refuse to say that I hadn't enjoyed it.

As far as Jimmie (and the rest of the Valley lesbian scene) were concerned, I'd had a relatively amicable split with my ex, although we hadn't stayed in contact. Only Claire-O knew the truth, and I didn't know until recently whether she told her partner what had really happened to my 'husband'. I would not pretend to having wasted five years of my life in a so-called heterosexual relationship. I could have explained, of course, that my wife was a transsexual and our sex could hardly be referred to as hetero. Going on past experience, though, I found that this usually opened a whole new can of worms. I left their narrow minds to make assumptions on who penetrated whom in our marital bed and who wore the tux at the wedding.

The 'lesbian fascists' (as I call them, sometimes to their faces) not only dictate correct modes of sexual behaviour, but proscribe on areas such as dress code, hair length and general demeanour. They do not accuse Jimmie of unreality, however, and I often wondered about this. My lover's cheeky grin and engaging disposition gave her that 'boyish' air (and of course the fact that half the scene – including the men – will admit to fancying her, and the other half are lying), and therefore she gets away with being so feminine.

"What is a 'real' lesbian anyway?" I asked into the air that night, during yet another discussion on whether a local MP was gay. "At the end of the day, if you're a woman and you fuck women – then you're a lesbian."

"Ah, but what is fucking?" Jimmie countered with a smile, "but a patriarchal construct. Designed to keep women in their place under men. Penetrating them with the ideals of a heterosexist society."

To which I replied, "Oh fuck off, Germaine fucking Greer." The conversation then veered again to the MP.

I know what you're thinking but let me assure you that this exclamation came from an ironic stance, not an ignorant one, as Ms Greer is all for penetration from what I can gather.

That Friday, Jimmie stayed for long enough at The Claires to have a cup of strong tea, and for her tiny share of the pizza, so speedily devoured, to settle down. Then she headed off for her shift at the night shelter, leaving me to the wolves. At that time, Jimmie worked twelve-hour shifts, contracted for three per week but more often working four or five, at a direct access night shelter for homeless people. She'd been doing this for a few months, before that clerical work following factory work and, before that, her own unique concoction of benefits only understood by the higher echelons of the Department of Social Security.

Jimmie is a musician by vocation, playing the trumpet beautifully in an all-female blues band called 'Girls In Blue'. They gig weddings, women's parties and various social functions. The Girls organised a couple of festivals and had recently cut a CD with funding from the Arts Council. They always seemed to be on the point of breaking through into the big time. As I said, Jimmie rarely practised the trumpet at home as the neighbour objected. Banging on the walls, banging on the doors, shouting abuse through the letterbox was the general level of complaint. Maybe now I'm gone, Jimmie will finally decide to move out. The Girls mainly practise together at Liv's house. Liv is the drummer and Jimmie's ex-girlfriend. I loved to watch Jimmie play but rarely got the chance. Don't know now if I ever will again.

Jimmie was right about us needing the money. Debts from my marriage and Jimmie's years on benefits after university meant that we were still living in a scrappy terraced rented house with shitty neighbours and little chance yet of a mortgage. And, although well-paid by the hour, counsellors rarely find full-time work, so my job at the prison barely paid the bills. We hadn't had a holiday in the five years we'd been together and scraped around for treats like pizza on a Friday night. In my darkest hours, I wondered how much better off I'd have been had I stayed a DJ and not bothered with university at all. I was the professional suited woman that I had set out to be, but somewhere along the way I'd forgotten to ask destiny to ensure that my finances were in order.

I drifted through the conversations, overhearing but not joining in, waiting for a spot on the sofa.

"…decided to have an *L-Word* night, ordered the box-set DVD of the new series from America. But like a thick tart didn't think to check the DVDs were compatible and everyone was sitting there when she found out they weren't."

"So what did you do?"

"Changed it to a *Xena* night instead."

"…think we might have the ceremony but I doubt if her family will come. Good excuse for a party though."

"If you've been together for twenty years, what's the point in getting married?"

"Legal stuff, she says, but I think she just wants a new dinner service."

"It's not really *marriage* though, is it?"

"…they're going to have a wake-up call when the kids start growing up. We've been under the radar for so long, now all these lesbians are having children and soon it'll be in their faces, in their play-schemes and their schools, in their comfortable homes."

"You make it sound like a terrorist network."

"That's how the papers'll see it, you wait. Few years' time and it'll all be the scandal of thousands of lesbian parents. They're quite happy if we stay in our boxes and they can label us as weird but as soon as we start acting normal like them, setting up a family, using the same facilities, then they'll complain."

"...I said to him, if you're my alternative darling I'm glad I'm a dyke."

I sat in the corner of the sofa nursing an empty glass and watching the party unfold around me. No-one spoke more than a few words to me and I wondered not for the first time if these people only put up with me because I was Jimmie's lover. What I didn't realise was that they were mostly repelled by my glowering bulldog impression and preferred to leave me alone.

Claire-O, who was my friend from long ago, came and sat next to me on the sofa handing me a glass of gin and a concerned look. "You in the dumps, girl?"

I took the gin and sipped, smiling gratefully. "Not now you're here."

"Jimmie's job getting you down?" I sighed and picked at the corded fabric on the sofa arm, not meeting Claire's eye. "You're not getting it much, are you?"

I laughed. "You know me so well!" I swallowed a larger gulp of gin and flashed my eyes at Claire, waiting for the inevitable.

"Well, you know I'd do what I could but..." Claire shrugged, grinned and nodded over to her lover who was holding court in the other corner of the lounge. A large group of young women surrounded her as she talked animatedly, "...so there I am in the back room of the newsagents and still haven't found the magazine I wanted. I came out again and asked the girl at the counter – she said, 'look up'. 'Aaaah,' I says, and went back in. Well – they're all on the top shelf of course, aren't they? I'd forgotten about that. So I'm stretching up and jumping and still can't reach. It's a patriarchal conspiracy, isn't it! Only men and tall people are allowed to read them. So what did I do? I asked for a stepladder of course. Then this guy comes in just when I'm climbing up the ladder and you should have seen the look on his face..."

"Does Tilley really read porno mags?" I looked at Claire-T with a new level of respect.

"No!" Claire-O laughed, and then amended her comment. "Well, I don't think so anyway – who knows what she gets up to when I'm at work? No, she's probably only saying that to wind up those two dinosaurs in the corner. Look at them pulling a face. Honestly, anyone would think that to be a lesbian you have to renounce sex!"

I looked and saw that Claire was right, there were two women in the corner scowling dangerously as Claire-T's story slipped from the bizarre to the ridiculous. I kept my tone low as I said, "They're gopping, man. Who'd want to shag them anyway? They're just jealous because their own nude pics were turned down by the ugly sisters."

As if they'd heard my words, the two women in question abruptly stood and marched out of the house. Claire-T wound up her story and laughed fit to wet herself. I laughed too, momentarily feeling that I might belong here after all. I fervently hoped that I didn't belong with the ugly sisters.

The look on Claire-O's face as she watched her lover said it all: adoration, admiration. I couldn't remember the last time Jimmie had looked at me like that. I was happy that my friend was still in love after – what, thirteen years? – but seeing Claire like this somehow made my own situation sadder. I covered up by flirting.

"I know you're happy on a ball and chain. But hey, if ever you're interested in some *real* action, sister, you know where to find me. Meanwhile, you'll have to settle for the soft-focus-touchy-feely-sisters-in-the-woodlands."

This is our favourite game: one of us will quote from a lesbian film and the other one has to guess which. But Claire wasn't playing tonight. She saw through the facade. She did indeed know me so well and was worried. "Listen, you look after yourself, ok? How're you getting home tonight?"

"The bus I suppose." I looked at my watch and stood up. "I'll catch the ten o'clock." I sighed, gulping down the weak gin and handing back an empty glass. It may as well have been water, the effect it had on me.

Claire stopped me, frowning again. "I mean it, you know. I got a premonition something bad's going to happen. I wish you weren't going home on your own. How about staying and asking one of the girls to give you a lift?"

I didn't need to consider this option for long before discarding it. "I'm fine, honestly. Have a good night." I leaned forward to kiss Claire softly on her cheek, smelling the familiar hair oil and feeling the brush of her breasts.

It didn't hurt so much anymore to settle for this, but I was reminded of the long years of yearning for Claire's touch as I stumbled through the crowd. As I swept past Claire-T, I couldn't resist a quiet dig. "How non-PC of you, Tilley."

She turned to me and sneered. "I could hardly compete with the larger half of *Little and Large*, could I? The most politically correct couple in the Valley: a disabled lesbian and a lesbian of non-white origin. Tell me – did you settle on Jimmie deliberately because she makes you look good? 'Cos someone should tell you it ain't working."

"You know nothing of my origins!" I answered hotly. She really knows how to wind me up.

"No, and neither do you from what I've heard."

I think I actually raised my fist but whether I would have used it or not we'll never know because at that point Claire-O appeared at my elbow and steered me out into the cold night. I immediately regretted not staying for another gin and almost turned back but, as I left, a burst of laughter came from the crowd within and my paranoia went into overdrive. I couldn't go back in there in case it was me they were laughing at.

Claire knew that I had been in love with her when we were kids, and I knew that Claire knew. Tilley knows too, and this really gets her goat. But none of us spoke about it. Claire and I preferred to flirt lightly and skirt around each other nonchalantly while Tilley glowered silently. I walked to the bus shelter, not far from The Claires' house, thinking about tomorrow.

Tomorrow morning Jimmie would be home around eight, she'd need some sleep before we set off north to her parents for their anniversary party. I would drive and we'd arrive late-afternoon, change clothes, stand around being polite, sleep and come home again. The usual kind of family thing, but at least Jimmie's parents aren't offensive and even allowed us to sleep together, unlike some partners' parents I've known.

In fact, I think that Jimmie's mother quite likes the kudos of having a lesbian daughter. She's a Women's Studies lecturer at a northern university and an incredibly intelligent woman. I can see where Jimmie gets her political sense from, if not her looks. I can't remember what Jimmie's dad does because he rarely gets a chance to speak, but he's ok by me if he loves Jimmie.

The bus pulled in just as I meandered up to the shelter. A group of hoodies jostled me as they got off and I hurried to a seat, glad when the doors swished closed and the bus pulled forward. I glanced back out of the window and saw them looking over their shoulders at me. One of them made a lewd gesture and another mouthed what looked like 'fucking dyke'. I turned back and rubbed my eyes; I could have been imagining it. Then I felt eyes on me again and became aware of hostility from the other passengers. Another set of young people sat sullenly staring at me and didn't look away when they saw I'd noticed. I pulled my coat tightly over my chest, and folded my arms in an unconscious defensive stance.

I was reminded of Claire-O's premonition and reached for my mobile phone. An older model to Jimmie's, it was nevertheless functional and I was glad to hear my lover's voice through the static.

"Hi Jack. You ok?"

"Yeah, fine. Just on my way home now – on the bus."

"Oh, right. Wanted a bit of company."

"Yeah, how's it going down there?"

"Quiet. Not many in tonight. And most of them are in bed already."

"Good for you, you'll get some studying done then. Won't be long before I'm in bed myself."

"Yeah. You'd better get some sleep. You'll be driving tomorrow."

"I know. So who's on with you?"

"Babs."

"Oh, lucky you! I wouldn't fancy spending the night with my manager. Couldn't she find anyone else to cover?"

"No. Friday night, you know…"

"Can you talk? Is she there?"

"Yeah, but…" I heard a door close. "I'm in the laundry room now." The laundry room, which doubled as an office and place to store workers' belongings, was compact and warmer than the rest of the shelter. It also had the benefit of a very noisy dryer so that one could have private conversations from inside, if the conversant on the line didn't mind the feeling that there were aeroplanes taking off in the background. And there was a window overlooking the main hall so that workers could keep an eye on the residents while in there.

I've never actually been to the shelter but Jimmie's very good at detail. She can't talk about any of the clients due to confidentiality, but she's gone into the whole layout of that place so I could draw a map or walk around it myself with my eyes closed. "God. It's a nightmare you know! I've only done one shift with her before. When I was new. She's had me sorting through the cupboards, reading all the files… I don't know if I'll get any rest at all tonight."

"Oh poor you." I tried not to sound amused as I generally felt that she was onto a cushy number with this job at the shelter, which from what I could tell only involved a few hours' work in the whole night. "Hey, here's my stop – hang on a sec." I jumped off as the bus slowed at the end of our street and I began walking up the steep incline to our darkened home. "You still there, Jim?" I asked, already breathless from the climb.

"Yes. I'll walk you to the door, shall I?"

"Thanks. Ok, so tell me a fantasy."

"What?"

"Go on, tell me something I can think about tonight while I'm missing you."

"Do you ever give up?"

"No, and I hope you'll shoot me if I ever do."

"I can't... Christ! I'm blushing already. Babs is just out there."

"You're in the laundry room?"

"Yes, but –"

"Are you leaning against the washer while it's on a spin cycle?"

"You dirty little –" but Jimmie didn't finish her sentence as she was interrupted by my raucous laughter. "Aren't you home yet?"

"Yeah," I sighed, "just putting the key in the lock now." As I sneaked the door open, I heard the familiar scuffling at the adjacent door – the neighbour's house – and took the phone from my ear just long enough to swing the door fully open, rush inside and slam it before the neighbour appeared outside to shout whatever abuse was on the menu tonight. I double-locked and bolted the door and then returned to Jim. "Right, all set now. Goodnight then, sweetipie. Try and get some rest."

"Yeah. G'night then... Jack?"

"Yes?"

"I love you."

"Love you too."

Ending the call, I walked through to the middle room. We barely used the front room as it was on the colder side of the house. The middle room wasn't much warmer but had a friendly, 'lived-in' atmosphere and a more comfortable sofa. The old settee in the front was the one that came with the house and was mainly used as a filing system rather than a place to sit.

Every now and then I tried to tidy the front room to make it look like a 'best' room and create a good impression on the unusual occasion of visitors. I'd polish the old double-headed axe that I'd found at a car boot sale and hung over the fireplace, reclaiming it as a labrys – the quintessential lesbian symbol. I'd clear out the boxes of junk that just seemed to accumulate in every corner, but inevitably the clutter amasses and multiplies so that on entering the house I would be confronted with disorder. I can't blame Jimmie for not throwing things out as I know that it's me: I have problems letting go.

I like to have a big old clear-out once in a while but it hadn't happened for some time. When I was younger I didn't live anywhere for long enough to gather that many possessions or that much fluff behind them. The clear-outs would happen every time I moved.

This isn't the first time I've walked away with a single bag and left most of my belongings behind. It probably won't be the last. As one of my old foster mothers used to say: you can't take it with you when you die.

I plugged the phone into the charger that sat next to the PC on the cluttered desk we shared. My hand hovered over the keyboard. Now that I was home, I didn't feel ready for bed at all. I felt alert and restless. Perhaps the encounter on the bus, the unsatisfactory ending of the phone call or the suspended thought of Claire's 'bad thing'. Whatever it was, it wouldn't leave me alone and I knew that if I forced myself to lie in bed then I'd be awake all night.

I set the CD player running, turned down as low as it could go so the noise of the disc spinning was louder than the strains of Bessie's voice.

I've got the blues, I feel so lonely
I'll give the world if I could only
Make you understand

I crept into the galley kitchen tacked onto the end of the long, thin house, reached into the back of the undersink cupboard and felt through various bottles of cleaning fluid. My hand brushed and then gripped the cold neck of a glass bottle. I drew it out and poured myself half a tumbler of strong vodka. Sipping at this thoughtfully, I walked back into the middle room.

Baby won't you please come home

The computer screen flashed momentarily and then commenced a low hum to indicate that it was ready. As I straightened up, I noticed a coaster was in a skewed position and I moved it to line up with the corner of the desk. I was reminded of how amused Jimmie used to be to see me do something like this; amid a pile of dusty clutter, which I will make no attempt to rectify, I will be irritated by some small straight-edged item that doesn't align with the edge of the desk. It's my own distinctive form of Obsessive Compulsive Disorder. My world can be falling down around me but I will be satisfied to control the immediate minutiae. Containment is important to me.

However, while funny to her the first year or so together, I know from experience that it's the little idiosyncrasies that begin to aggravate a lover to the point of contemplating homicide. Like the way she doodles on my work when she's on the phone, or taps her pen against her teeth when she's thinking. Sometimes the way she talks really gets to me. And don't ask me about those bloody jangly bangles. We all have our foibles.

As the ancient machine whirred, I rubbed some more E45 cream onto my sore hands and ruminated on Claire's premonitions. She'd always said that she could see things coming and I had believed her because some things were just too much for coincidence.

The problem with saying there is a 'bad thing' about to happen is verification. A bad thing for whom: for me? For her? For someone we know? For the world? The environment? There is always something bad going on. At any point in time there is a war, a rape, a murder, a death, a deceit, a lie. So to say she had a premonition of a 'bad thing' is really leaving the options quite open. She could just as easily said that a good thing will happen. Because at any point in time there is a peace, a love, a life, a birth, a virtue, a truth. The bad thing could already have been prevented in that I didn't knock Tilley's block off on the way out of their house. So if you think about it, what I was about to do may not have been the 'bad thing' at all.

JIM

"Was that Jackie?" Babs asked as I emerged from the laundry room. I returned my mobile to the pouch habitually attached to my jeans.

"Yeah. She's just off to bed. Saying goodnight." I had always been open about my lesbianism in the job. It was a voluntary agency and the housing charity had an extensive Equal Opportunities Policy. Most of the staff made an effort to be politically correct.

"Was she ok with you taking on the shift?"

"Think so. Want a coffee?" Babs nodded. I strolled into the large church kitchen. The shelter was a church hall during the day, the campbeds and bedding folded away and deposited behind a curtain. I spooned out two coffees and sugared Babs' excessively. I looked up to find that the shelter manager had followed me into the kitchen. She was now leaning on the worktop. Looking at me. My sleeve rode up as I reached to drop the spoon into the sink. Deep stainless silver sink. My wristband clinked on the side of it. I pulled the sleeve down self-consciously and covered my wrist.

Babs was still looking at me. She could be quite talkative and obviously wanted to talk now.

"I envy you, Jemmy."

"Please call me Jimmie. Or Jim."

"I did, Jem. You seem to have a really solid relationship. You know, most husbands would complain about being left at home all night."

You don't know the half of it, I thought. But I kept my irritation to myself. Why do so many hetty women assume that? Is a lesbian relationship more communicative, more intimate than a heterosexual one? Simply by dint of being two women? Sometimes it is easier to put up with the nasty comments than the patronising ones: at least you know where you stand when you're being spat at. People who refuse to call me by my chosen name? Who insist on reworking it into a format with which they are more comfortable? Don't get me started. Babs can get irritatingly patronising about disability issues as well. Thank God she's never actually met Jack because then we'd have race to contend with as well.

"You never told me how you two met." Babs took her coffee and looked at me expectantly. It was going to be a long night.

"Well. We first met at the agency. Where Jack worked before she got the job at the prison."

"Oh, were you a counsellor there too? I thought you were only just doing your certificate now."

"No, I was…" I realised that I'd dug myself into a hole. "Actually I was a client." I watched Babs' expression change, recover, then change again. Amused, I perceived her conflict: her realisation that I had had counselling, yet she was not permitted to judge me on this openly. Jack had worked in a sexual violence survivors' agency. I had already told Babs this. But from each of these realisations she recovered. Then another shocked look appeared, along with the inevitable question.

"You mean she was your counsellor?"

I laughed. "No. No, nothing like that. Jack would never do that. It's breaking all the rules. No. I was seeing one of the other counsellors. I didn't go there for long anyway. Just a few sessions." I was tempted to add, "I wasn't abused". I decided not to. Let the woman make her own assumptions.

"We chatted a couple of times in the reception area. She

encouraged me to become a counsellor myself. Didn't do anything about it until this year though. Anyway. Then a few weeks later I was doing a gig. You know I play in a band?" Babs nodded and made an encouraging sound. I continued, "And Jack was in the crowd. She came up to me afterwards. Said she liked my piece. We got chatting. She invited me out the next day. We had a few drinks. Then we were together."

"Just like that?"

"You know the joke? About where do lesbians go on their second date?"

"No, what do you mean?"

I sighed. "Women traditionally want commitment. Yes? And men are traditionally commitment-phobic. So in a heterosexual couple, there is a lot of skirting around before a commitment is made." I could see that Babs was getting lost here. Probably not someone who contemplates sexual politics on a daily basis, however PC she tries to be. "So anyway. A lesbian's second date is a visit to the estate agents. That's the joke. It fails miserably when you have to explain."

"Oh I see," said Babs. Light dawned. "You mean you moved in together."

"Something like that." I took my coffee and moved over to the work desk in the corner of the shelter hall. It had taken a bit longer than the second date to persuade Jack that moving in together would be a good idea, though I was too tired to go through the ins and outs for the sake of Babs' nosiness. I picked up my textbook recommended by the course tutor. I hoped that the manager would take this as a cue to end the conversation.

I leaned back in my chair and looked up at the windows under the high ceiling. From where I sat, I could see the waning moon surrounded by a brightly illuminated cloud mass. I had a sudden yearning to play my trumpet. Slowly. Painfully. Pointing at the moon. The snoring of one of the old men dragged me back down to earth. Reminded me that I was here to do a job. The large hall was cool and all the residents were snuggled into blankets. I went into the office/laundry room again and warmed my hands on the dryer as it spun residents' clothes. I often grinned at the irony of how years of feminism had led me to a job where I was washing men's clothes, cooking for them, cleaning and tidying up after them. I reached for an old jumper from my bag. It fell, dislodging my book. It was going to be a long, long night.

JACK

Impatient while the computer still whirred and rumbled, I wandered through the cold kitchen and into the even colder toilet/shower-room. Condensation settled on the walls, window and porcelain, and showers were excruciatingly miserable in the winter. I peed and splashed my face with cold water. Wiping mist from the mirror, I stared into my reflection.

"When did I get so old, fat and ugly?" I asked myself out-loud as I poked at my jowls. "The only recourse is vodka."

I'd taken to talking out loud to myself when Jimmie wasn't around. Perhaps a sign of age or possibly impending madness. If we'd had a dog then at least I'd have an excuse to talk out-loud. But I can't have pets; I've told Jimmie it's an allergy and let's leave it at that for now.

I poured another large one and checked the remains in the bottle. Surprising myself at how little was left, I returned it to the undersink cupboard. Why I kept it there was a mystery, as I wasn't hiding it from Jimmie or anyone else. But then, maybe I was hiding it from myself.

Setting the full glass on the windowsill next to the computer desk, I bent down to switch phonelines so that I could use the internet. My knee banged against the solidity of Jimmie's trumpet case, which she stored there along with boxes of unsorted clutter. I brought out the case onto my lap and paused before opening it. It felt strangely like invading my lover's privacy – like reading a diary or sniffing underwear. Would Jim be angry or embarrassed at the knowledge that I sometimes took out the trumpet and caressed it on the long, lonely nights?

I opened the case and there it sat, brassily beautiful. What else would embarrass or anger Jimmie, I wondered: the collection of erotic books and magazines, my sordid past, the anonymous conversations I had begun holding over the internet with people I had never met? The fact that I'd prefer a single cup of good strong coffee to the endless gallons of wish-wash tea that got foisted on me?

I remembered the first time I had seen Jimmie play the trumpet. The half-closed eyes, pursed lips, swaying hips. Claire-O had commented that she could have sworn Jimmie had Black blood as no White girl could play like that. I had turned to my friend and muttered, "Black or White, she can blow my trumpet anytime." Claire had replied that Jimmie had recently split with her lover, the drummer in the band, and that I should go for it.

So lust had brought us together, but what had kept us going? Was it just pure habit? Surely not the puzzles?

No really, we have lots in common: counselling, writing, music. Sometimes I know she can be irritating and she tends to speak like a robot, but she's very kind and she's one hell of a looker. Don't get me wrong, I'm not someone who goes just by appearances. But I'm telling you anyone would be hard-pressed not to admit she's fucking gorgeous. What worries me sometimes is why on earth she stays with me.

I sighed again and put the trumpet case back under the desk. I took a swig of vodka and started up the internet, dear Bessie still giving it some in the background. I tapped into the sex chatline live sites, finally noticing the effect of the alcohol firing through my veins, and further thoughts of Jimmie's admonition ceased to trouble my mind.

If I should take a notion
To jump into the ocean
'T ain't nobody's bizness if I do, do, do do

Chapter Two and a half
(You didn't expect me to be conventional?)

JIM

"Dearest Jim," she says. "I'm not going to be around to tell my story so I'm trusting you to do it for me. I know you'll do a good job. Look on the computer: you'll find all sorts of things there that aren't in the manuscript."

It took a while. I couldn't face reading her private files. Not only due to the guilt at metaphorical breaking and entering. Albeit with permission. It was the dread at what further betrayals I might find; Jackie's mistaken belief that I cannot be hurt is breathtaking. I may be unable to show emotion but I am not unable to feel it. This, I think, is where I lost her. After reading her life-story I understand a lot more about her. I have come to accept that her protective self-centredness is part and parcel of who she is. And something I cannot change. However, this doesn't soften the blow when one discovers deceit in one's lover.

Much of the online conversing between Jack and Pie has been lost to the ether. Now it only exists in a summarised form in their collective memories. But a few of the earlier sessions remain on the computer – Jack managed to copy and paste the text and in this way save them. The emails that weren't deleted also remain. Of course, it all might have been recorded and holed up in a vault somewhere, saved by an obsessive paedophile-chasing policeman. What do we know about the Web? How can we protect our privacy when it is so regularly violated? But that is a discussion for later in the book. For now, I'll give you a taste of those first tender moments.

Welcome to the chat, JackieJack!
cosmonaut left the chat room.
 Angelique: Kamelot, yes, I see , nice
 men_mars82: im not bad. i dont think we did, unless you had anothre name
PUSSYLICKER left the chat room.
 bbq2scot: I am from Australia Lokking for a lovely loyal pretty wife
 Kamelot: GOODBYE EVERYBODY
Americano75: JackieJack, hello.
JackieJack: hey.
mister1: SimonX, hello
SimonX: hey mister
JackieJack: I'm sort of new and not sure what goes on here.
A2765865 left the chat room.
Kamelot left the chat room.
 bbq2scot: I AM FROM AUSTRALIA ANY LADIES WANT TO GET MARRIED
 mister1: SimonX, why dont sleep now in USA is night
 Americano75: JackieJack, want to talk privately? Click my profile and we can chat.
 SimonX: mister1, becuase i am not at this time sleepy...
 Mika: SimonX, LOL
JackieJack: Er... ok – got it.
Welcome to your private session, JackieJack and Americano75!
JackieJack: hello?
Americano75: hi. What you up to then?
JackieJack: Just surfing around, dude
Americano75: same here – not much going on in slutland

JackieJack: no. Americano, what's 75?

Americano75: birth year

JackieJack: ah, makes you 30?

Americano75: soon...

Americano75: so how old are you <please don't say seventeen>?

JackieJack: 34 in body; 17 in mind.

Americano75: good answer! lol

JackieJack: always quick, me :)

Americano75: :)

JackieJack: i must say i'm disappointed with the level of slut-talk on this site. i mean for the name you'd expect more.

Americano75: I am happy to oblige... what are you wearing?

JackieJack: ??!

Americano75: is that shorthand for a bikini?

JackieJack: no, i just thought you might have said something original.

Americano75: Ah, what's on your mind?

JackieJack: grrrls

Americano75: but not on your body, right?

JackieJack: you know me so well already!

Americano75: so what you do to get the girls?

JackieJack: it was so easy when i was younger.

Americano75: that says it all.

JackieJack: :(

Americano75: don't be blue Jackaroo.

JackieJack: haha

Americano75: where are you?

JackieJack: UK

Americano75: OK

JackieJack: where you?

Americano75: US

JackieJack: shoulda guessed.

JackieJack: i like this spontaneous poetry.

Americano75: we got rhythm

JackieJack: where in US? what time is it over there?

Americano75: Sanfran, sunny afternoon.

JackieJack: cool

Americano75: what time for you?

JackieJack: around midnight <yawn>

Americano75: am i keeping you up?

JackieJack: i can keep on going all night, babe

Americano75: lol

JackieJack: jus' singin' the blues, bro'

Americano75: want to try some blues?

Americano75: woke up this morning, blues spinning around my head...

JackieJack: woke up this morning, blues spinning around my head...

Americano75: <cheat> looked in my mailbox, I may as well be dead.

JackieJack: God that's depressing! Can't think of something more cheerful?

Americano75: your turn

JackieJack: Got me a girl, got no place to go...

Americano75: Got me a girl, got no place to go... <:)>

JackieJack: found me an alley, found me a blow

Americano75: !! Now that's slut-talk.

JackieJack: and why the hell not?

Americano75: why indeed.

JackieJack: if i'm too old already for a blowjob then i may as well slit my wrists here and now.

Americano75: now confused. Are you morf?

JackieJack: morf??

Americano75: male or female?

JackieJack: yes

Americano75: LOL! Good answer again. Same here.

JackieJack: seems like we hit it off quite well

Americano75: yup, so it seems

JackieJack: shame you're the other side of the world...

Americano75: too true, blue

JackieJack: what made you think i was female?

Americano75: your name – men don't call theirselves Jackie.

JackieJack: ah

Americano75: netiquette – if they don't want to give their gender then don't ask. (but i always do)

JackieJack: so...

Americano75: ...?

JackieJack: you morf?

Americano75: aha... that would be telling

JackieJack: tease.

Americano75: oh yes please!

JackieJack: now now, naughty boi

Americano75: <drool>

JackieJack: i could get used to this.

Americano75: you logging on again tomorrow?

JackieJack: you gotta go?

Americano75: soon... just thought i'd mention the food'n'sex site. it's pretty cool if you're into that kind of thing...

JackieJack: :(can't tomorrow. got to drive a long way from home and not looking forward to it. Maybe Sunday?

Americano75: how far is a long way in the UK?

JackieJack: too long for me to drive! England is quite big, you know, contrary to popular opinion.

Americano75: ok, touchy subject – say no more.

JackieJack: sorry. had a tough day today as well.

Americano75: want to talk about it?

JackieJack: just work stuff.

Americano75: what's your job?

JackieJack: i'm a therapist

Americano75: !!

Americano75: seriously?

JackieJack: yes

Americano75: well well, who'd a thought?

JackieJack: who indeed?

Americano75: good luck with it. i'm glad i work from home.

JackieJack: what do you do?

Americano75: this and that. Mostly internet business

JackieJack: sounds dodgy

Americano75: dodgy?

JackieJack: illegal

Americano75: not at all! Occasional hacking involved, but mainly very boring virus work – sort of net doctor.

JackieJack: how exciting.

Americano75: you don't sound v impressed.

JackieJack: you don't make it sound impressive

Americano75: ok, I'm a spiv wiv a crackin' good liv

JackieJack: you been watching too much imported *Eastenders*

Americano75: so i hack computers and you hack minds

JackieJack: i don't usually put it that way, but you could say that I hack *into* minds.

Americano75: what was the problem?

JackieJack: difficult client.

Americano75: say no more.

Americano75: well, i'd better let you get your beauty sleep... sweet dreams, chicadee

Americano75 left the chatroom.

JackieJack: hey, i didn't get your email

KILLER COUNSELLOR WAS FOSTERED

Jacqueline Harris, the prison counsellor arrested for the suspected murder of vagrant Frank Little, was a troubled youth who went through a string of foster homes until she was sent to Hillbank halfway house, a Leicestershire institution now closed due to allegations of abuse, at sixteen. Her bosses at Newpark Prison, where she worked as a counsellor, did not know of this history and, if they had, would they have employed her?

Valley Gazette reporter Viv Diggen tracked down one of Harris's foster families. "Jacqueline was always very active," says Mrs Appleton, 73. "I remember her working hard at school and being involved in all sorts of sports. Her only problem was that she just had this attitude with authority." The Appletons no longer foster but still have contact with many of their 'children'. "Jacqueline was one of those that left and didn't bother to stay in touch," says the woman who was mother to her for nearly nine months.

For the full story, turn to pages 16 & 17.

Chapter Three – 1984

"Jacqueline!" Pause. "Jacque*line*!!" She sits, grinding her teeth, staring at the open copy of Shakespeare's complete plays. She is waiting for the foster mother to call her 'Jack' or 'Jackie' like she asked. But it doesn't happen and she wonders why she expects it. Instead there is a thud, stomping on the stairs and a crash as her door is thrown open. The red-faced, middle-aged, out-of-breath woman stands exasperated in the doorway. Jackie ducks automatically as if anticipating a smack across the head. The foster mother ignores this.

"Why don't you come when I call?" Jack stares blankly at the desk, not knowing where to begin. 'Dumb insolence' is what they called it, but if she tries to reply then they call it 'answering back'. "I shouldn't have to come up here every time I need to speak to you. There are five children here, you know – not just you – and I've another due any minute. Now come downstairs and help me prepare the tea."

Jack slouches to a standing position and moves towards the door, not looking up. Mrs Appleton steps aside to let her through and sighs heavily at this child's attitude. Already tall and leggy, Jack is almost the same height as the woman but usually keeps her head bowed and her back stooped so as not to press the point.

The food is laid out on the large dining table and all that it needs really are a few finishing touches. The foster mother has not called Jackie because she wants help, but wants her downstairs, cleaned up and ready with the welcoming committee for the new girl soon to arrive. Jack feels a finger prod her back and is tersely but not unkindly told to entertain the kids in the lounge. There are two toddlers in the foster home and twin boys of eight years who behave like toddlers, and then Jackie. Now this new girl is due and all that she knows is her age and name.

At fifteen, Claire is two years older than Jack and will usurp the position of oldest resident. She is unsure how she feels about this. On the one hand, it could ease the pressure on herself to be the older, responsible one. Another female with whom to share the household tasks could only be a bonus. On the other hand, what if she turns out to be a bitch? What if she bullies Jack and makes fun of her like so many other older foster siblings have done? Changing families is something she should be used to since leaving her long-term foster parents aged eleven, but after two years of moving from one home to another, she still feels twinges of nervousness at the thought of new arrivals.

Her anxiety finds its way to the surface in the form of getting high and silly: messing about and making the kids shriek; winding the boys up to perform; and tickling the toddlers enough to make them sick. It isn't long before she is being shouted at again. The foster mother is canny enough to resist sending Jackie to her room because of course this was what she wants. Instead, she forces her to sit quietly in a corner of the hall, so that when they arrive Jack will be the first to see them.

She is often told she is too bright for her own good. Whatever that means she can never figure out, for as far as she is concerned she is too bright for everyone else's good. At school she was put up a year as she was educationally advanced and then put up another year, but still found herself bored with the level of work given. And when she is bored she cannot just sit still and wait for the others to catch up. Luckily, as a small child, she attended a progressive school, where teachers encouraged pupils by allowing them to read or work on other projects once their given task was completed. She was in for a big shock, then, when it came to the next school.

On entering the comprehensive, Jackie soon turned from every teacher's dream to every teacher's nightmare. Not only was she expected to share attention with twice the number of children, but she was forced into a regime of study-to-order. Her first foster mother had always taught her to question everything – to see both sides of the argument – yet she had learned in school that to be good was to sit quietly and copy everything down unquestioningly. There came a point, however, when she couldn't keep the questions inside her mind and she began to resent the wasted years of sitting quietly. Not only did she contradict everything said in the classroom, but she found herself increasingly getting into fights in the schoolyard. This was often sparked from the jealousy of other students when they realised that she was younger than they and yet in the highest streamed class. As a result, they were constantly trying to catch her out on some piece of folklore knowledge she might not know, usually of a sexual nature.

At home she became intractable and argumentative. She fought on the streets and came home bloody-mouthed but refusing to speak about it. How could she repeat to the Baptist Mrs Appleton the filthy names they had called her? Her behaviour did not alter the results of her schoolwork, however, until she was finally threatened with withdrawal from classes. When she realised that her education might suffer, she did manage to pull herself together for a short while. Then something happened which no amount of angelic intellect could diffuse and she was taken back into care. They decided to change her school, humiliatingly putting her back down a year. Bilgeworth Comp was supposed to give her a 'clean break' so that she would have a second chance. She is now on her third or fourth chance – she's forgotten which.

Shadows through the frosted glass, low voices and scuffling feet. Two adult-sized figures silhouetted against the front door making Jack think that the girl has not come. Maybe she's done a runner and the door will be opened to two social workers. She half-stands as the bell rings, still unsure what the rules in this home are – should she answer herself or let the foster mother be the hostess?

The woman comes bustling through, wiping her hands on a teatowel, and scowls at Jack. So she should have answered the door after all. They stand talking for a moment and Jack tries to peer unobtrusively over the cold shoulder to see who the social workers are – she knows most of them in this district.

"Well, come in then…" the foster mother stands back to let them in and then Jack realises that the girl has come after all. "Claire O'Malley, this is Jacqueline Harris." She feels herself being pushed forwards and in the awkwardness of adolescence, is unsure whether to shake hands, wave, or hang back shyly.

"Well, say something then, girl! God, you can't shut her up normally." The foster mother laughs a little too loudly and smiles conspiratorially at the social worker, leading her through to the lounge. "Time to stay for a cuppa tea?" And Jackie finds herself alone with Claire.

The girl, she knows, is fifteen. But Jack thinks she could be twenty if a day. She is well dressed, well made up, bejewelled, wears a fur-collared coat and gloves (not woolly gloves, but the grown-up velvet kind) and carries a clutch-bag. She holds herself with an air of amused disdain, a smile playing around the corners of her lips as her eyes trail up and down Jackie. Jack realises that her own mouth is slackly open and she closes it, swallowing dryly. She has never seen a Black girl so well turned out; the only coloured kids she's lived with are babies and in all the foster homes she's lived in, she'd never before seen a child with dreadlocks. Claire's braids are tied back and make her seem exotic, like an American. But her voice is British.

"You seen something you like?"

Jack ducks her head, flushing furiously, and coughs. Maybe this girl didn't hear the foster mother properly when she said Jack's name. Claire thinks she's a boy. It often happens – Jack wears her hair trimmed as short as they will allow, to keep it tidy and out of her eyes, and sports jeans, t-shirts and trainers. She feels Claire's velvet finger under her chin, lifting her head to look into her eyes.

"Don't be scared, sweetie, I don't bite."

At the touch, or from falling into the deep pools of eyes, Jack feels her knees give way and her stomach sink to the floor. It is all she can do to keep standing and with a great effort she opens her mouth to speak.

"I'm a girl."

Claire smiles, cups her hand around Jack's cheek and whispers, "I know." And with those two words the last vestiges of Jack's dwindling self-assuredness fall away. Claire walks on through to the lounge without looking back and Jackie drops heavily into the chair.

Over the next few days Jack finds herself in the situation where she feels the floor drop from beneath her several times an hour in the house and, on occasion, at school when she catches glimpses of Claire in the upper school yard. They must share a bedroom until the foster parents have cleared out the box-room for Claire, as she has arrived at short notice. This means that Jack is subjected to Claire's taste in music (which, excepting Culture Club, consists of bands Jackie has never heard) and a bewildering array of perfumes, feminine clothing and cosmetics, not to mention the brief flashes of shining ebony flesh that take her breath away and leave her feeling raw and confused.

What it is about Claire that fascinates her so much, she can't say. Jackie has never found herself attracted to another girl before, not really. She knows the words, of course; she knows what it means. In all the years of being a tomboy, she has sustained many insulting remarks. She has been called 'lesbian' and more offensive names, and heard stories in the playground of what happens between women. But she has always denied it with a clear conscience. She has thrown insulting names back and fights anyone who dares call her something she is not.

But now it must be true. Somehow, others have seen something in her that she hasn't seen herself. She often enjoys being mistaken for a boy because it means she's afforded more freedom and respect than is appropriate for a girl, but does this masculinity mean that she must be not fully female? Does the rejection of skirts, makeup and long hair stem from a desire to be practical as she has always said, or does it point towards something more dark and sinister? She knows all too well the place in society for women like that and she doesn't want it. And she hates Claire, even as she loves her, for making it so.

But if Jack is not a proper girl, then what does that make Claire? Surely she is as feminine as one can get; yet she seems to enjoy and encourage Jackie's adoration. After all, it was Claire that started it that day in the hall, Claire that offered to brush Jackie's hair, taking delight in cursing and tugging as she did, Claire that reached out to say goodnight on that first night.

Claire treats her with amusement, like a toy. She knows that Jack follows her around like a sullen puppy and she plays with this. One minute Jack will be her special confidante, being allowed a sniff of this perfume, a try of that hair gel, being asked for an opinion on a blouse or pair of shoes, sharing sweets and lingering looks. The next she is rejected while Claire lavishes attention on one of the babies or boys, ignoring Jackie as she sits forlornly watching from the corner of the room.

And then, just when Jack is despairingly wondering if she will ever feel happy again, Claire turns to her and says, "Let's go to our room. Got something to show you, sister."

They then sit in the room they share, listening to Claire's Culture Club tapes and talking about previous foster homes they've been in.

You come and go; you come and go.

Claire explains that red, gold and green are Rasta colours, and explains a lot more about Culture Club. She also plays Bob Marley and some heavy-beat reggae music. Jackie is interested as she's never really been aware of any music outside of the standard 'top twenty' charts. Years later, Jack attributes her continued interest in alternative music to Claire's influence.

It only takes three days (a lifetime to Jack in love) to realise that something is odd about the way Claire speaks to Jackie. She generally speaks with a broad Mancunian accent, calling the other children in the house, and anyone younger than herself, 'chuck' and sounding like a member of the *Coronation Street* cast. But she doesn't call Jack 'chuck' – she calls her 'girl' or 'sister' – and she sometimes speaks in a different voice that Jack finds hard to place. There is something lyrical about the intonation, the grammar and vocabulary changes, sounding almost American.

At first Jack is pleased – interpreting the words literally she is surprised at how fast Claire has accepted her as a sibling and possibly an equal. But she becomes nonplussed when she overhears Claire speaking to the only other Black girl in school and realises that they are using the same language. When Claire talks about 'being Black', which she does often enough to notice, her voice also changes. Eventually Jack comes to understand this way of speaking as 'Black Speak' and she guesses that Claire has developed it from films, TV, and with her friends as a way of preserving her identity.

On the fourth day of Claire being in the house, they move her into the box-room and Jack is left alone in her own room again, which suddenly seems far too big and quiet. They still spend a lot of time with each other, Claire most often coming into

Jackie's room as her own barely has space for the bed and cosmetic collection.

Claire keeps her promise to 'sort that hair out' and spends long minutes brushing while they talk. The easiest place to do this is with Jackie sitting at the dressing table in her room – somewhere she doesn't usually spend much time. But Jackie relishes the feeling of Claire touching her hair and will put up with sitting in front of the mirror. She generally doesn't look at her own reflection, but focuses on watching Claire's face or hands reflected in the mirror.

Claire often comments that Jack's hair is like her own little sister's. Foster care custom means that you don't talk about another child's real family, but Claire has mentioned it so often that Jack is sure she wants to be asked.

"Where is she, then? Your sister, I mean."

Claire stops brushing but keeps her hands on Jack's head. "She's with my Nan."

"How old is she? What's she like?"

"She's a cheeky little bugger like you." Claire smacks Jack on the side of the head lightly and continues brushing. "When I'm older, I'm going to have loads of kids, at least seven. And maybe I'll foster too."

Jack doesn't have an answer for this as she's never wanted kids herself, and the thought of what she'd have to do to get them is just sick. Claire brushes on as they sit in companionable silence for a while, listening to Bob Marley's *Three Little Birds*.

Claire quietly hums until she encounters a tangle, causing the usual laughing frustration. Claire pauses and looks at Jack's reflection in the mirror. "The curse of the Black woman's hair."

Jack turns her head around to face Claire, suddenly feeling cold. "What do you mean?"

"You got Black woman's hair, girl."

"But I don't understand. I'm *not* Black."

Claire throws her head back and laughs, then squints at

Jackie with a solemn expression. "Serious? You really don't know? I knew it! Man, all this time I thought you were a coconut and you're not even that."

"Co-coconut?" This is beginning to get too much for Jackie; she can't work out whether Claire is insulting her or not.

"Some Black people behave like they White, you know? Black on the outside, White on the inside – coconut. But you're not that because you're not even Black. That's funny." And she laughs again.

"Claire, this isn't funny. What are you saying? I'm not Black."

Claire stops laughing and looks serious again. "Oh you Black, sister. You Black." She spins Jack around to face the mirror again. "Take a good look. You got Black eyes, you got Black lips, you got a deep, Black voice, you got Black hair. Hell, the only thing about you that isn't Black is your skin. Ain't that ironic?"

Jackie stares at her reflection in the mirror, poking at her blotchy pink skin with a trembling finger. Her voice reduced to barely a whisper, she repeats, "But I'm not Black." And for the second time in a week the world around her shatters.

Claire may have realised that she's opened a whole can of worms because she continues to brush in awkward silence. Jackie's hair bristles and sparks as her brain smoulders and whirrs under Claire's long, brown fingers. Bob Marley sings on, oblivious to Jackie's confusion. Incongruously, the song he sings is *Don't Worry, Be Happy*.

After she's finished brushing and tied Jack's hair back with a tight band, Claire takes the cassette player and makes for the door. She turns to look at Jackie before leaving and Jackie turns wide, frightened eyes back at her. Claire shakes her head sadly. "Had a premonition something bad was gonna happen, but I never thought it would be this. I can't believe no-one told you."

That's it. *Someone* must have known. And if Claire has seen it then it must be obvious to trained eyes. Probably her previous foster parents knew. And no-one has said. No-one has *ever* said. Until this day, nobody has sat her down and said, "You are Black." Why? What is it they were protecting her from? Of course, if they didn't want her to know she was not theirs then it would be difficult to explain how she was of mixed race within a totally White family. Living in a White village, going to a White school in a predominantly White county – she had not seen very many Black people at all.

Now so much else makes sense to her, some of the nasty things other children have said to her, some of the overheard conversations of her parents or teachers; so much that she's put down to being abandoned she begins to attribute to her race. But what is her race? Like Claire said, she isn't Black on the inside, or on the outside – so why did she call her Black? Why call her *Sister*?

Jackie has never before considered her racial identity – in the arrogance of the dominant culture, she never even knew that she had one. Now the inherent racism underlying that culture begins to make her reconsider her whole life up until this point. *That's* why she has gone bad. That's where the belligerent, aggressive, *criminal* element inside her comes from. Her Black genes. Prejudice against other people is a revolting thing, but there is no escape from prejudice against yourself.

Jackie has never thought of herself as racist against Black people until she realises that she might be one of them. Now that she knows, she doesn't want it. She can't be proud like Claire; she can't assimilate it into her identity. She wants to excise it – if she could get a knife and cut the Black gene out of each piece of her DNA then she would. Everything that has gone wrong in her life she now blames on those Black genes.

If she hadn't been mixed race, then maybe her biological mother would not have abandoned her. If she hadn't been mixed race then her adoptive mother would not have rejected her. If she hadn't been mixed race then she wouldn't have got so much hassle from other kids, then she wouldn't have got into fights, then she wouldn't have got into trouble.

Of course with hindsight it's easy to laugh at this naïveté – the adolescent that does not go through *some* form of identity turbulence is a rare animal and will grow into a bland adult. But this is what initially goes through Jack's head on discovering her ambiguous race. It does not occur to her to attribute her abnormally high intelligence to her Black genes, or her beauty and charm (which can be overpowering when she chooses to show it). Nor does it occur to attribute her dark moods and arrogance to her White genes.

***

Over time Jack will learn to accept what she cannot change and, with Claire's help, learn a great deal about a Black heritage. She will develop a certain amount of pride in her origins although she will never talk the talk as Claire does so well, only managing an occasional self-conscious phrase. But on this day, the momentous day when her sexual and racial identity become intrinsically, inseparably linked, she wants more than anything to know why Claire calls her *Sister*.

Claire has changed the tape again, and Jack hears the echoes of Boy George's pained voice coming from the box-room as she lingers in the hall. Going into Claire's room, Jackie reaches behind her back and knocks on the door belatedly. She stands in the doorway and waits for Claire to finish applying eye shadow and turn to her. Claire holds the small brush from her face, raising one eyebrow questioningly and devastatingly. Jackie doesn't know where to begin.

Precious kisses, words that burn me.

Lovers never ask you why.

"Well?" Claire says at last.

"There's something I don't understand."

Claire laughs. "Is that what they call an understatement?"

Jack smiles, relieved that Claire isn't angry about her reaction. She decides to brave it out. "Why did you say I was Black when I'm mostly White?"

"*Mostly* White! Oh, I like that." Jack shrugs, indicating that she has no other way of explaining herself. Claire puts the makeup slowly back into its case and gestures towards the bed. "Ok, sit down."

Jackie slouches over to the bed, aware of how she is moving, wondering if she walks like a Black person. The way she feels now about Claire, if Claire wanted her to be Black then she would be, even if it means feeling so bad. As she sits on the bed, a feeling of delicious dread descends on her as if she were about to do something she knew was wrong, knew that she'd enjoy, but didn't quite know how to. Almost the same feeling as smoking her first cigarette, except that had made her sick.

Claire steps over to the bed and sits next to her, taking her hand. "You are White, yes I can see that. You know, I'm a mix too – I'm mostly Black but I got some White. Did you ever hear what 'Claire' means?" Jack shakes her head and Claire grins, showing big, brilliantly white teeth. "It means 'blonde'. Funny that, ain't it? But it's different for me, of course – one look at me and you know where you are. But listen, girl. You got Black blood. And as soon as them whitie crackers see that, you may as well be Black as midnight. You may as well be Black as me. Now you got two choices – you either hide it and forever hope that no-one notices or…"

Her voice trails off because Jackie has looked up and is staring into her eyes. She rarely makes eye contact and even more rarely allows anyone to see her cry, but here Claire sees tears collecting in the corners of her eyes. Jack ducks her head again and blinks, laughing at herself, then looks back up at Claire's face. "I don't want to hide it. I want to…" and she leans forward, their lips brush and Claire turns away.

They never mention that moment and it is the closest Jackie gets physically to Claire in the whole time they know each other. Jackie is moved on again several months later and thinks that this is the last she'll see of Claire O'Malley. Life is full of these little ironies, and Jack would never have guessed at the age of thirteen that she would meet Claire again in the following decade – at which time she herself would be married and Claire would be living with a woman.

You come and go; you come and go.

***

Jimmie, you might think it isn't such a big deal to be mixed race and that maybe Claire went over the top in her warning, but we are talking about the early-eighties in a suburban midlands town. Later on in life, Jack discovers there are some advantages to being able to slip in and out of a minority group at leisure. Being mostly White means that one can stay in the closet when around White racist people but still pull out the race card when political correctness lands positive discrimination in one's lap. And as a practised chameleon she can change herself at will to fit any given situation.

You think that I am writing this intentionally so that you will despise Jackie's character? You think that she has no integrity? *Au contraire.* What actually happened was that she realised that she didn't give a flying fuck what anyone else thought of her. She knew who she was inside and she knew that nothing that other people said or did could alter this, so why not manipulate their expectations to her advantage?

***

Remarkably little happens in the months following Jack's

identity discoveries, except one day that Claire may have forgotten but Jack never does. The boys are on a weekend home visit and the foster mother has taken the babies out to the park on this Saturday morning. Jack and Claire have opted to stay at home and offered to do the washing up as a persuasion tactic. Claire has promised Jack that she will show her a trick.

While washing up, Claire has brought her cassette player downstairs and is playing the Culture Club tape in the background. They both sing along since Jack knows the words as well as Claire by now.

And I keep on loving you, it's the only thing to do.

Jack puts the dishes away quickly while Claire goes back to her room to get something. "This is one of my Nan's teacups," she says proudly as she comes back into the kitchen, holding up a cracked and rather ordinary-looking flowered porcelain cup. "Boil the kettle, then." Claire places the teacup reverently on the kitchen surface as Jackie fills the kettle and flicks the switch, hiding her disappointment as she had thought it would have been more interesting.

"It has to be tea *leaves*, not bags," Claire is saying, annoyed that she can find nothing like leaves in the foster mother's kitchen.

"Well, why not just tear the bag open?" Jack suggests.

Claire's face lights up. "All right, Einstein. You do it." Jack shakes half a teabag's worth of dust into the cup and Claire peers in dubiously. "Not sure this is going to work, but here goes." She pours the water over the tea, filling the cup halfway. "Now, you swill it around three times, take three sips and then tip the water and turn the cup over."

Jack purses her lips at the scalding bitterness of the tea, desperate to spit the bits out, but Claire insists she swallows. When it's done and turned upside down on the draining board, Claire looks at her excitedly. "Now, you have to think about what you want to know."

"But I don't know what I want to know."

Claire sighs, exasperated. "Well, just think about your future then."

Jack closes her eyes for a second, then turns the cup up and holds it close to her face. What she sees gives her such a start that the cup flies from her hands and smashes on the tiled kitchen floor.

Claire shrieks. "Oh my God! Look what you've done, you stupid…" Jack barely hears the cursing as Claire throws shards of china into the bin, muttering about needing the dustpan. Eventually Claire notices that Jack is still standing and staring at the floor where the cup landed. The quick thinking that follows her into adult life takes over and she steers the now convulsing girl towards a chair, putting the kettle on again for a cup of sweet tea, this time made with a bag.

"What did you see?" Claire asks as she sits Jack down. "What was in the cup? What did you see, Jack?" But Jackie can only shake her head, staring into space. She never tells anyone what she saw in the cup, and eventually Claire stops asking.

Jackie never mentions it again, but what she saw haunts her for a long time afterwards and to this day has made her wonder about fate and destiny. The dead man lies on his back, his face glistening as white as the surface of the porcelain cup, blood pooling from his head. It may have been only tea leaves, the blood not real but dust, but this image is burned onto the inside of Jack's eyelids from that day on.

But they're always there like a ghost in my dreams.

***

It was inevitable I'd be a writer, really, considering all the things I've been and the places I've seen. Female and Male and Female again. White and Black and White again. Gay and Straight and Gay again. Child and Adult; Victim and Criminal;

Manic and Depressed; Bizarre and Conventional; Celibate and Promiscuous; Feminist and Misogynist; Dominant and Submissive; Intense and Light-Hearted; Perpetrator and Recipient; Extrovert and Introspective. Yes, Jim, I can fairly say that I've lived a full life in a short space of time.

Perhaps you don't realise how painful it is for me to write this. The eczema on my fingers is getting worse – the doctor says it's due to stress but what would she know? I'm sure that I'm allergic to something. And I have that cough again. I'm not a hypochondriac; she understands my situation but keeps on telling me that I'm ok. She's not increasing my meds just yet. I've told her she has to be honest with me. I don't want her hiding the truth to protect me – I've had enough of that already. My skin is raw and cracking – each key press is agony and yet I must write. I must. One doesn't notice how much one uses a thumb until it's covered in sores.

In and out of every available orifice, I've been inside some dark holes but this one has to be the pits. They say I shouldn't complain. You get three hot meals a day, time to think, a full library, classes and a gym. You even get sex so long as you're not too ostentatious about it. What more could a woman ask for? Well, freedom would be one thing.

The only thing keeping me sane is writing this book. And so I write on, and on.

Chapter Four

JIM

I was at the shelter again on Sunday, not having spent a night in my own bed for some days. Chatting to Pete, my co-worker for the night. We did the initial safety checks before opening the shelter. I mentioned the family party.

"They're ok with you and Jackie then?" Pete asked, surprised.

"Yeah. Why shouldn't they be?" This approach had always got me by when faced with any form of possible prejudice. Those who would not have been 'ok' were too embarrassed to pursue the matter. I generally don't put myself into situations where people are likely to feel that they are justified in being severely abusive. Of course, I wasn't out to the clients in the shelter. That would be asking for trouble.

"What about Jack's family?" asked Pete, possibly ignoring my spikiness.

"She's not in touch with them. None of them. She doesn't really talk about her childhood. Or any of her past."

"That must make things difficult?"

I shrugged. "It can be sometimes. But I respect people's privacy. I get the feeling that something pretty horrible happened to her years ago. Maybe one day she'll tell me about it. I'm not going to push it." I walked off to check the fire door. Hoped that Pete would take this as a signal to drop the subject.

We completed the checks. All doors locked. No empty alcohol containers. No suspicious packages hidden in the toilets. The dinner was incinerating slowly in the kitchen. I looked at my watch. "Time to open up?"

Pete picked up the allocations book and the two phones. He offered one to me and we walked to the main door. I gripped my stick in one hand, my wristband in the other. But the bangles had already made a noise.

"Honestly, you with those bells," said Pete, "you're like Lady bloody Godiva."

"Hardly," I said. But I laughed anyway.

For safety reasons, every time the door was knocked, both workers had to answer. There were no security cameras. Not even a peephole. The shelter had been temporarily housed in the church hall. Temporarily for three years.

"Wait –" I turned back just to double-check that the laundry room door was locked, to see that nothing important was left out on the desk. "I did a shift with Babs the other night," I explained to Pete. I imitated Babs' voice: "Constant vigilance!"

Grinning, I unbolted the front door. Then straightened my face. I stood back, leaning on my stick. I heard the scuffle from outside: the residents vying over first place in the queue. If they fought openly then they wouldn't be allowed in. But there was always a scuffle.

Pete held the book open and the door opened outwards. This felt strange. I never got used to pulling it closed. I put my arm across the gap, barring the way. Let the residents in one by one. "Ok, ok," I called in what I hoped was a commanding voice. I opened the door. Allowed the first one in.

"John, ok?"

"Yer." I looked at Pete. He nodded and eyed John over his spectacles. The tall, grey-bearded man lumbered past into the hall. Quiet and unassuming. And yet always managed to hold his place. Pete wrote the name down, waved him through. I turned back to the door.

I sighed and turned back to the queue. "Frank. How's the

stomach?" Frank had been sick Friday night.

"Fine now, thanks. How're you?"

"Fine. Go on then."

And so on to the end of the queue. Six residents in all. John Rollins; Ian Smith; Frank Little; Billy Williams; Shannon Haf; Joe Spoke. Space for two more should any present themselves before ten. That was locking-in time. Not much work for Pete and myself tonight.

The real graft came when someone new turned up on the door asking for a bed for the night. A speedy assessment would be done on the doorstep. The criteria were simply: between the ages of 18 and 64, claiming benefits, no permanent address. But there were rules of residence. These included no violence or threat of violence; no drink or drugs on the premises; obvious things like no theft or sex on the premises. A set of these rules had to be given to new residents to read through and sign.

My book of this week was *Lord of the Rings*: I am a big Tolkien fan. The kind that reads The Book once a year. Twice if it's a dull year. I've been doing so since a child. My original copy has fallen apart. I still keep it in a box. The copy I had with me that night was a hardback that Jackie had bought last Christmas. It was inscribed, 'For my lover from Jacxx'. I was delighted by the film when it came out. Although I was somewhat perturbed at seeing plastic toys of my personal heroes on sale by the million. I said to Jackie, it would be like her seeing Maya Angelou and Bessie Smith dolls on the shelves in Woolworths.

Despite having bought me The Book, she can be very disparaging of Tolkien. When she sees me reading it she says I'm 'away with the fairies'. But it's not that at all: it gives me great inspiration as well as being a fantastic read. She's never read it herself, preferring her thrillers, true crime and Fay McMullins. I've told her she should give it a go. The battles would be just her cup of tea, all that blood and violence.

I checked my watch again. Five to ten. Jack usually phoned around ten. Says goodnight. Then the night would drag on. I would visualise my lover snuggling down between the sheets. Snoring till dawn. I took my phone out to check it had a signal and nearly dropped it as a sudden loud banging rained on the door. Pete looked up, closed the message book and slipped it under the allocations book on the desk. Both of us rose from our seats wordlessly. I grabbed my stick from the behind the desk where I habitually left it.

Pete slid the chain across before opening the main door. This is a precaution usually used after lock-in. The sudden banging had unnerved Pete as much as me. It was lucky that he chained the door – the ex-resident trying to gain access was a known violent character who'd been banned previously. He was also roaring drunk and could hardly stand. A shaking hand reached through the gap. Pale fingers fiddled ineffectually with the chain.

"Dave, you know you can't come in tonight…"

"Oh please, it's cold out here. Please…"

"Take your hand out of the doorway. We're shutting the door."

"Please just let me in, just to warm up and then I'll go, I promise."

"You know we can't do that. Your ban won't be lifted until next month. Now I suggest you go." Pete inched the door forward. Tried not to trap the man's hand, but the hand didn't move. "Dave…"

"Can you bring me a blanket then, or a cup of tea?" Somehow he had managed to pull the door from Pete's hand. It opened wider again. An eager face appeared in the gap. "I promise I won't be any bother. Just a cup of tea here on the doorstep."

"No, we can't. We're not allowed to."

"*Please*, just a cup of tea!"

"You know we can't, Dave. You know the rules," I interjected, trying to speed things along. It was already lock-in time. I put my hand on the door, tried to ease it shut again. Trying to get them to go away by being nice is always the preferable option. At first, it had almost broken my resolve to turn homeless people away like this. I knew they had nowhere else to go – it made me feel like the heartless bitch that they called me. But I soon learned that people were banned for a good reason, no matter how pleasant they seemed on the doorstep. Once over the threshold it was a different matter. I did not need Babs' wrath if an incident happened tonight.

Pete looked at me. We exchanged nods. It was time to end it. If presenting clients became aggressive on the doorstep then the police might need to be called to remove them. If it was going to happen then this would be the time.

"Dave. I'm shutting the door now." I brought the door towards myself carefully. Leaned my head against it so I could see the gap – I didn't want to trap his fingers or anything else. He might make a complaint.

"Can't I just – can't I...?"

I had succeeded in shutting the door. I kept my left hand on the handle, quickly slid the bolt across with my right. Pete had his key out ready to lock. Suddenly there was an ear-splitting bang against the side of my head. For a moment I was convinced that I'd been struck. I felt pain jolting my hand. Jarring my arm and shoulder. I let go of the door handle as if I'd had an electric shock.

"What the fuck was that?" I asked Pete. "It sounded like an explosion. Do you think he's got a gun?"

Pete laughed. Though he was trembling slightly himself from shock. "I think he just kicked the door."

"Kicked the door? Is that all? Christ. My arm's just about to fall off." I noticed that Pete was staring at the closed door. He didn't give my arm a second thought. I turned and looked at the door again myself, cradling my elbow with my right hand. "Is he still out there?"

"No." Pete shook his head. He began to walk through to the main hall. "I think he just kicked the door and went. Is it all right, your arm?" He paused. Turned to me as if noticing my pain for the first time. "Do we need to write an incident report?"

"No. I'll be all right." I shrugged my shoulders. I felt the left one fall back into place. "I'm not left-handed."

"Not your *good* arm, then?"

I smiled a crooked half-smile. We walked on through to the hall. I noticed Frank hanging around the desk in front of the office/laundry room. "Shit!" I hissed to Pete, "the laundry room wasn't locked."

Pete looked up ahead to assess the situation. Then he said, "I'm off for a piss."

I walked quickly up to the desk. I said "hi" breezily to Frank on my way past. I went into the laundry room. Frank was still hanging around the open door. I moved some clothes from the washer to the dryer. Then went to my bag as if an afterthought. I pulled out an apple. Nothing had been taken.

"Ok?" I asked Frank on my way back out. I raised my eyebrows at him expectantly. "Did you need something?"

"No, no. I only noticed you were reading *Lord of the Rings*. It's a good book, that."

"Yes. It is," I said distractedly.

"Coffee?" Pete stalked into the kitchen without waiting for a reply. I leaned my stick behind the desk and sat down heavily in my seat. I noticed that The Book had moved. It was at a slight angle. Perhaps someone had picked it up and replaced it in a hurry. This irritated me. I don't like people messing with my things – especially my Tolkien things. But I accepted that it was my own fault. I had left it out on the desk.

"Who was at the door?" Frank asked, conversationally.

"An ex-resident who's banned."

"Who?"

"Do you remember Dave?"

"Dave… oh yeah, big bloke with ginger hair."

"No. The other Dave. Short and annoying."

We laughed. Frank was alright. One of the ones you could have a laugh with. If he was a Tolkien fan then things were looking up on the conversation front. Just as I was about to chat some more, my mobile vibrated in my pouch. "Excuse me," I said to Frank and went back into the laundry room.

JACK

I leant back in the computer chair, stretching my aching muscles as I waited for Jimmie to answer the phone. I had been working at the computer for several hours and was ready for a break. I stood up and wandered into the kitchen to put the kettle on. The mobile rang on.

"Hi babe. Sorry about the wait," Jimmie's cheery voice chirped into my ear. "Are you off to bed?"

"Soon, I'm just having another cuppa. Everything ok there with you?" I moved away from the kettle as it began to boil and stood over the computer desk again.

"Yeah, fine. Quiet night. You know: no problems. Did you get that thing done?"

"Yeah, just about. Although I've worked so long on this frigging machine that I think my eyeballs are going to drop out."

"Sorry. You didn't have to do it, like, *tonight*."

"Well, you need it for the weekend and I'm busy all week, aren't I? Anyway, do you want to hear it?"

"Yeah. Go on then."

I placed the mobile next to a computer speaker. "Right, here goes…" I called and clicked 'play'. The music that played sounded like *Girls In Blue* but with a subtle electronic backbeat, the vocals surreally lengthened and an overtone of crackly static to lend an air of authenticity. I let it play for thirty seconds and then clicked 'stop', picking up the phone with breathless expectation. "Well? What do you think? Do you like it? Do you? Not bad for free software, what you think?"

Jimmie laughed. "Ok, ok you big kid. Yes, it sounds fab. Have you done the whole song?"

"Yes, but I thought you could listen to it all when you get home. I mean, I could try emailing it to your phone but I'm not really sure how to do that…"

"No. That's fine. I'll listen tomorrow. It sounds great."

"Well, it's not brilliant. Just a rough first cut, you know. It needs tweaking a bit but I can do that maybe Wednesday night…"

"It's fine. Really. I just wanted something to show the girls on Saturday. It's only a sample."

"I'm dead impressed with this ProDJ thing. Think I might try some mixing later."

"Get to bed, you! You told me yourself that you were tired. You've a full day tomorrow."

"Yeah, yeah. Just having a cuppa and then I'm off up the wooden hill to bedfordshire."

"You're a nutter. Listen. See you in the morning. You take care ok?"

"You take care. I miss you."

"Miss you too. Gotta go now. Love you, bye."

Jimmie had already rung off when I replied, "I love you."

I made my cup of tea and, feeling a nervous kind of hunger, put a pasty in the microwave. I sat at the desk, playing the song again a couple of times and feeling *good*. It was the first time in years that I had truly created something from beginning to end and I had forgotten how fantastic it felt. It's not like writing; music is more of a sense of creation. Giving birth. Besides which, I never *finish* any of my damn writing. My eczema had subsided over the past few days while I was working on these cuts. I was buzzing; I was extreme. There was absolutely no way I was going to sleep now.

A compulsion forced me to open Internet Explorer and go online again in search of... what? I had met someone on a chatline on Friday night and we had really hit it off. It wasn't being unfaithful (although I did feel a twinge as I realised that I was not going to tell Jim what I was doing). At that time, I could not know how the relationship with 'Pie' would progress. As far as I was concerned, this was just harmless fun. There was so much in my life that I didn't discuss with Jimmie – confidential issues at work, my childhood and past, the fact that I had the occasional drag of a cigarette when necessary – and I knew there were issues that Jimmie did not discuss with me. Why not just add one more private thing?

I had convinced myself that this was ok by the time the computer had connected to the website. I stationed myself at the desk in my sloppy PJs and bare feet. Scrolling down a long list of 'sex and...' chatrooms, I got right to the bottom and then began to inch up slowly, reading out-loud as I did so.

"Sex and slavery – no thank-you. Sex and seduction – hmmm. Sex and... eurgh! Skip a few... Sex and frottage. Sex and... ah, here it is." I clicked onto the 'sex and food' site and logged in as BRITISHBEEF, chortling to myself at the pun. "Right then, Americano75, let's see if you're there yet."

Chapter Four and a half

Chocolate69: i like it with lots of cream...

Leah: not much of a cucumber fan myself

Welcome to the chat, BRITISHBEEF!

Chocolate69: hi leah, you like corgette?

Babyblue left the chat room.

StrangeFruit: hey Pie, where you been hiding?

Marsbar: hi everyone.

Leah: grapes?

AmericanPie: been busy – had a lot of work on for once, lol. How's the site, Strange?

Chocolate69: grapes? bizzarre!! Whatever pulls your pipe

StrangeFruit: pie: going ok, could do with your help again, tho' masterhacker that u r :)

Leah left the chat room.

AmericanPie: lol, glad to be of assistance.

Eatme2000: anyon wnt some hard provate talkk ?

Welcome to the chat, Fishslice!

BRITISHBEEF: AmericanPie, have we met?

Chocolate69: eatme, clickme!

StrangeFruit: think eatme is typing one-handed. lol

AmericanPie: Beef – don't know, who are you?

BRITISHBEEF: would you be Americano75 ??

Fishslice: anyone here from previous food'n'sex sesh?

AmericanPie: aha, Crackerjack?

BRITISHBEEF: JackieJack.

Fishslice: hey creamy, how's the houses?

CUMALOT: LIK ME TO STIK IT UP YA?

AmericanPie: Beef, wanna get outta here?

Welcome to your private session, BRITISHBEEF and AmericanPie!

BRITISHBEEF: hey babe

AmericanPie: hey. feeling blue tonight?

BRITISHBEEF: not so bad, btu got a busy day at workk and not looking forward to it.

AmericanPie: you should look forward to your life more

BRITISHBEEF: thank-you, Operah ;)

AmericanPie: just call me the therapist's therapist.

BRITISHBEEF: hmm. got one oft hose already. tat may be the problem...

AmericanPie: what?

BRITISHBEEF: nothing. so want to talk food'n'sex ??

AmericanPie: why British Beef

BRITISHBEEF: well, i'm British and er, eat me I suppose. Nto very originla i know.

AmericanPie: you having problems with your keyboard?

BRITISHBEEF: sorry, trying to eat.

AmericanPie: what are you eating? British beef?

BRITISHBEEF: ha! No, just beef pasties.

AmericanPie: ?

BRITISHBEEF: don't have beef pasties in sanfran? It's a sort of pie.

AmericanPie: I'm sending you a link to a site that sells American pasties.

BRITISHBEEF: Oh. Oh! OMIGOD!!! I can't believe it, is that true? I've seen pictures of strippers wearing those tassely things but never knew they were called pasties.

BRITISHBEEF: Language is a strange thing. We think we speak the same language but we find out that we don't at all. Pop and crisps.

AmericanPie: Pop what? You lost me again.

BRITISHBEEF: Case in point. Pop and crisps are party food from when I was a kid. Before it became normal everyday stuff. In America you'd probably say soda and chips.

AmericanPie: I know chips means fries to you, but I never heard of pop as a drink.

BRITISHBEEF: It's simple enough, it goes 'pop' because it's fizzy.

AmericanPie: Same with beef pie. To me a pie is a desert.

BRITISHBEEF: What is American Pie anyway?

AmericanPie: Usually apple pie, but American Pie was a way of life that was over before it was named. It's about the death of culture. A kind of anti-culture.

BRITISHBEEF: I see. Hence 'bye-bye'.

AmericanPie: Yup. So what's your favourite pie?

BRITISHBEEF: I like pork pie. I'm a savoury fan, sausages, black pudding.

AmericanPie: Black pudding? Isn't pudding a sweet?

BRITISHBEEF: Don't ask. It's a British thing. Long thick sausage. Very phallic.

AmericanPie: My kinda sexy.

BRITISHBEEF: woo.

AmericanPie: :-)

BRITISHBEEF: would you like a cream puff?

AmericanPie: always :)

BRITISHBEEF: have you noticed how easy it is to make food and sex puns?

AmericanPie: yeah, think that's the point of these sessions – doesn't take much imagination.

BRITISHBEEF: how about 'I like my coffee like I like my men – strong and black.' ?

AmericanPie: weak, sweet and milky for me.

BRITISHBEEF: lol. what about the number of endearments that are food-orientated?

AmericanPie: ?

BRITISHBEEF: sugar, honey, chicken, sweetiepie...

AmericanPie: you say the nicest things.

BRITISHBEEF: lol

AmericanPie: beefcake...

BRITISHBEEF: !

AmericanPie: just visualising you eating pastie. hmm, sexy...

BRITISHBEEF: pah!

AmericanPie: what you look like, anyway hon?

BRITISHBEEF: big muscles; tattoos; short spiky hair; punky makeup; piercings. you know the kind of thing.

AmericanPie: lar!

BRITISHBEEF: is that a compliment?

AmericanPie: I'll say it is. when's the next flight?

BRITISHBEEF: haha

AmericanPie: serious, babe.

BRITISHBEEF: you coming to visit me?

AmericanPie: ah, I was talking about *you* flying over here.

BRITISHBEEF: sorry, left my broomstick with my ex-lover

AmericanPie: now there's an image...

BRITISHBEEF: don't even go there. what about you? What you look like?

AmericanPie: slim, long hair, exotic tinge to skin, nose too big, general sanfran look.

BRITISHBEEF: uhuh.

AmericanPie: is that good?

BRITISHBEEF: good enough for me, darling. but not too thin, i hope?

AmericanPie: what is too thin?

BRITISHBEEF: if you snapped in half when i put my arms around you – that's too thin.

AmericanPie: i'm no supermodel.

BRITISHBEEF: that's all i need to know.

AmericanPie: got a coffee grinder, got no coffee to grind...

BRITISHBEEF: my baby got some coffee, but she ain't no

nevermind.

AmericanPie: my baby done up and gone

BRITISHBEEF: now i live my life sittin' in the sun.

AmericanPie: (not)

BRITISHBEEF: you don't sit in the sun in sunny sanfan?

AmericanPie: don't go out

BRITISHBEEF: ?

AmericanPie: dont really need to go out. Working from home and have food 'n stuff delivered. benefits of the internet age.

BRITISHBEEF: exercise?

AmericanPie: <shrug>

BRITISHBEEF: visitors?

AmericanPie: not really – no family, friends over net.

BRITISHBEEF: sad?

AmericanPie: no, happy. you saw the kinda place I live, you wouldn't want to go out either.

BRITISHBEEF: can appreciate that. lived in some shit places myself.

AmericanPie: Always lived in UK?

BRITISHBEEF: far as i can remember, but moved around a fair bit. you always lived in sanfran?

AmericanPie: moved here as a teen from Flick Knife Valley, Alabama.

BRITISHBEEF: sounds like something from a horror movie

AmericanPie: believe me, it is

BRITISHBEEF: you know it's funny, but sometime I think u r my previous lover come back to haunt me.

AmericanPie: how do u know I'm not, then?

BRITISHBEEF: do computers connect to the other side?

AmericanPie: u mean the other side of the atlantic?

BRITISHBEEF: I mean she's dead.

AmericanPie: ah. That wouldn't be me.

BRITISHBEEF: so what's wrong with Alabama?

AmericanPie: !! what's right, Beefy?

BRITISHBEEF: ah.

AmericanPie: did you know that in Alabama it's illegal to own a vibrator but not a gun?

BRITISHBEEF: !! no

AmericanPie: uh-huh. same is true for Texas and Georgia.

BRITISHBEEF: what about a vibrator that's shaped like a gun?

AmericanPie: you are soooooo naughty!

BRITISHBEEF: you better believe it.

AmericanPie: i suppose one could always use a gun...

BRITISHBEEF: yeah, but don't point it the wrong way or you might get more of a blast than you bargained for!

AmericanPie: (:0 you're scary.

BRITISHBEEF: not afraid of earthquakes in sanfran?

AmericanPie: only when having sex, lol

BRITISHBEEF: ;) how do you meet partners if you don't go out?

AmericanPie: over net, like you...?

BRITISHBEEF: you're my first

AmericanPie: ah – a net virgin

BRITISHBEEF: <blush>

AmericanPie: nice! yeah, that works – keep blushing

BRITISHBEEF: ha, sorry – can't keep it up.

AmericanPie: don't usually have that problem myself

BRITISHBEEF: time for me to go, i think.

AmericanPie: shy all of a sudden?

BRITISHBEEF: no, just tired, sorry. hey – give me your email address you bastard.

AmericanPie: you can check out my website, i'll patch it to you now.

BRITISHBEEF: patch? oh – i got it. ta

AmericanPie: ta?

BRITISHBEEF: thanks.

AmericanPie: until next time?

BRITISHBEEF: counting the hours...

Chapter Five

JACK

"You look a bit hungover, are you ok?" Annette's usually unfurrowed brow showed concern as I eased the door behind me closed.

"I'm ok, just a bit tired. Monday morning, you know."

"Ah." My supervisor smiled a slightly irritating knowing smile. "Coffee?"

"I'll love you forever if you do." I laughed.

"That won't be necessary! Just for as long as we're working together is fine." We both laughed as Annette poured me a cup from the percolator in the corner of her office. I took the cup and my shoulders relaxed. "Thank God someone can make a decent cup."

"We all have our drugs. Mine is coffee."

"At least you don't get strip searched when you arrive at work every morning."

"Do you?" Annette seemed surprised.

"No, no I didn't mean that." I was silent for a while, wondering why supervisors always seem to take comments seriously. But then, Annette was only echoing my interaction with my own clients. That was the point, after all – as a supervisor Annette was a trained counsellor herself.

"Something on your mind, Jack?" I looked at her. "You left a message on Friday for us to bring the supervision session forward. Said you had something urgent to discuss." Annette sipped her coffee, watching me expectantly.

"Oh," I said, distracting myself by looking out of the window. "That." Annette's office overlooked a play-park and was the other side of town to the prison – if one knew where to look it was possible to see Newpark's distinctive grey stone walls from the window. "Thank you for agreeing to see me so early by the way. It was important to see you before the sessions today."

"That's ok." Annette waited for me to continue but I could not think where to begin.

I blew on my coffee for a moment and looked at the now familiar walls of the supervisor's office which were plastered with postcards, photographs of landscapes and motivational posters. As a compulsive reader, just glancing at a poster on the wall meant that words already read dozens of times previously still filtered into my conscious brain.

SUCCESS

Arriving at our destination may be the aim but how we make the journey is the measure of success

Annette coughed. "Something about… a client?"

Startled out of my contemplation of the wall, I spoke almost involuntarily. "Larissa." I looked down at my hands as I said the name, then met Annette's eye for a second before looking out of the window again. I felt annoyed at myself now for behaving like a client but at least I wasn't avoiding the issue.

"Ah," said Annette. "Go on." I coughed and crossed my legs. "Larissa Thomas," she said. "We've discussed this client before."

"You remember that I thought she was making a play for me. I mean, that she seemed to be flirting with me in session."

"Yes."

"Well, it's got worse and I've given her plenty of warnings. I think it's time to end the sessions with her; I don't think she's going to get anything more out of working with me while she continues on this track."

"But…"

"But what?"

"Well, breaking a contract is always a difficult business. But you don't usually need my approval to end counselling with a client. You've been doing this long enough now to judge for yourself. I sense that you need my approval here. Am I right?"

"Not approval as such, but I'm worried that there are other issues involved. I've been honest with you from the start about this client. I just…"

"Go on."

"I feel that my judgement might be clouded." Annette did not reply so I continued. "I had initially found her attractive – found myself attracted to her – and maybe she picked up on this or maybe… well, whatever. I have wondered about my motivations in continuing and in ending," I concluded lamely.

"So what do you need from me?"

"I need you to tell me to break the contract, I suppose. I need it to come from a higher authority than myself."

"I see." Annette steepled her fingers together and looked at me for a moment. I looked at the wall again.

DETERMINATION

The will to succeed can overcome the greatest adversity

I knew that she wasn't going to do this. Annette drew a breath to speak. I looked back at her. "If I were to tell you to do something and it turned out to be the wrong thing for whatever reason, who are you going to blame?"

"I know…"

"It needs to come from you, Jack. You should be able to rely on your own judgement. Now, what do *you* think you should do?"

"End the contract."

"So end the contract. But not because I say so – because *you* say so. And be sure that you let the client know this."

"Ok."

"Are there any issues with your other clients at the moment? How many do you have now, ten is it?"

"Eleven now, since I started a new one last week. But it will be ten again after Larissa."

"Be careful of burnout."

"I will."

"I wonder if I could talk with you about this issue of you being attracted to clients; how do you feel about that?"

"It doesn't happen that often."

"But occasionally it does. What do you think it's related to?"

"I'm not sure really. I know that whenever I myself have been the client I have tended to fall for my therapist. It was the same with college: I always fell for my lecturers. And when I was a teenager, it was the social workers I fell for..." I laughed. "A pattern, I think."

"It is a pattern for a lot of clients. As you know, it's the power differential. As a counsellor it is something you should expect, that a client will feel that he or she is in love with you. It is something you should be careful of."

"Yes. I know, and I am."

"There is no need to be defensive, Jackie. What I am saying is that as counsellors we are expected to be able to deal with this situation professionally. Do you feel that you deal with it professionally?"

"Well, I haven't shagged any of my clients if that's what you're saying."

Annette sighed. "I'm not suggesting that at all."

"I can't help how I feel. If I see an attractive woman then I'm attracted to her."

"It's not how you feel; it's how you behave that matters. You can bring your feelings to me and if you acknowledge them then we can deal with the situation without it getting out of hand." I looked down at my lap and was quiet. I felt like I was in school and being told off by a teacher. Annette spoke again, more gently, "How do you feel about what goes on between us?"

"What do you mean?" I looked up suddenly and met Annette's eye and then it was the supervisor's turn to look away.

"How would you feel if I said I was attracted to you?"

"I-I don't know. I hadn't thought about it." I felt confused now. "Are you?"

"I only wanted to demonstrate to you what a minefield this is. Whether I am attracted to you or not is not relevant because our relationship is professional, and if I were then you would never know." Again, the irritating smile. But this time I thought I detected a slight tinge of sadness, or was that my imagination? I used to be quite good at picking up when someone had the hots for me but now I'm not so sure. It just doesn't seem to happen as much as it used to.

The supervision session ended and I finished my coffee. It was time to drive over to the prison and see my first clients of the day. I turned to speak to Annette as I was about to walk out of the door, but could not think of anything to say. The supervisor had got to her feet and was pouring herself another coffee, leaning over the percolator, her short greying fringe falling into her eyes. Annette emptied the coffee pot and flicked the hair from her face. She looked up and was surprised to see me still standing at the door.

"Was there something else?"

"No." I drummed my fingers on the door. "I'd better go."

"Next week then."

"Yes, bye."

Ok, so maybe that wasn't the *best* scene of me at work to use as a demonstration of my professional abilities. It is, however, relevant to the story and is the best I can do at the present time. It would be easy to invent some triumph or success with a client; manipulate some true event to cast Jack as the hero. But as I have mentioned before, this book is the ultimate truth and nothing else. And I have to admit that in my current state of mind I can think of little positive to say.

I know that there were successes; there were accomplishments on a grand and a mundane scale, times when Jack could have been guru therapist and started her own cult. But these have temporarily slipped from recollection.

Here is the problem with life writing: what to leave in and what to take out. I could simply relate every moment as it happened had I another lifetime in which to write and you a lifetime to commit to reading. But time is pressing on.

This particular day is scorched into memory for a number of reasons. It might be that I consider this day as when 'it all began' (drum-roll here); it may be because of the overriding memory of Lara as she was then; it may be just the accumulation of significant events happening all in that one day. For whatever reason, it is important that this day is in the book.

Skidding to a halt at Newpark's gates at nine-thirty (my first client group was at ten but getting inside the prison could take half-an-hour or more), I parked the Skoda and grabbed my briefcase before swiftly rearranging my coat and hurrying towards the portacabin.

"Morning, George!"

"Mornin' my dear. Good weekend?"

"Fine. And yourself, how's Mrs?"

"As well as can be expected, thanks. Weather cold enough for you?"

"Think so, wouldn't know it was September, would you?"

"Soon be Christmas."

"Oh don't get me started – anyway, have a good day."

"I'll try, bye then."

I waved over my shoulder and rushed through the yard to the first set of doors. No matter how much of a hurry or what kind of mood I was in, it was always necessary to perform the 'good morning' ritual with George.

The doors opened from the inside and the first smell was metal: a stinging taste in the mouth like blood. The next doors opened and then came the standard prison smell. That combination of school disinfectant, hospital vomit and madhouse fear mixed in unique proportions to give Newpark its own distinct flavour. The prison officer escorting me into the central part of the complex was Annie, sullen enough to ignore my polite 'hello'. She had been recently demoted due to some slackness on the job and attended to her duties with the reluctance of an inmate.

Claustrophobic corridors opened out into a large, bright room, still poorly ventilated but not so much of an assault on the olfactory sense. This room was a decompression chamber between the outside and inside worlds and there was often a wait before the two prison officers who had to escort me further were free to do so. The staff rooms were off to the right and straight ahead was the last set of locking doors before access to the prisoners themselves. The first time I made this trip I almost panicked and ran. Although it still gave me the creeps, I was much more used to it now, only occasionally wondering how quickly I would escape in the event of a fire.

As I waited with the tight-lipped prison officer, a staff door opened halfway and voices rose to echo around the chairless, airless room. I recognised one of the voices as Mr G, the prison Education Officer, the civilian head of staff, and the other, quieter voice, as John – an officer of junior but promising rank.

"So you'll get those figures to me then? Jolly good, good lad. Right then, ah – Miss Harris here again, our resident counsellor!"

"Not resident, I hope!" I laughed and thankfully noticed John smiling warmly over Mr G's shoulder.

"Yes, yes of course. Lovely to see you and may I say you look splendid today. Quite a picture, in fact." Mr G had a curious manner of being simultaneously dismissive and overly attentive which crawled the flesh of the women he attempted to charm. As he was my boss, however, I preferred to humour than annoy him. "When are you going to let me take you out for that drink, then, eh?"

"Well..." I stepped away from him slightly but he leaned closer.

"Now don't tell me you've found yourself a young man since I last saw you."

"No, I –"

"Well, what is it then? Don't be a dark horse. Do you think I am too old for you? Is John more your style?" At this comment, John coloured from collar to fringe and took a few steps towards the inner door, rattling his keys purposefully. He seemed more embarrassed than me; I simply put my head down and followed him through. Mr G turned to his own office, calling after us, "I *will* have that drink, Jackie," and Annie only smirked.

Inside at last and installed in my counselling room – which doubled as an archive room. A tiny sealed pane looked over the prison garden, walled on all sides to give the impression of *Secret Garden*, but the glass was frosted and made me feel that I was sitting in a toilet while I waited for the first client to knock. If it hadn't been for the viewing window to the side, the shelves of box files would have been too overpowering. It was not the first time I had worked in a cupboard, though this one had the feel of a goldfish bowl. According to the textbooks, the counselling room should be a pleasant environment, the perfect colour scheme and temperature, and without distractions.

Clients were escorted by prison officers in the same way that I had been. The officer then had to wait outside the room whilst watching through the viewing window. John usually stationed himself in the further corner of the room when he was on escort duty, rather than stand right outside the door like the other officers. There was a safety buzzer for emergencies as with any decent counselling arrangement, but there would be no need to use it in this environment where privacy is lacking. I always felt that bit happier with John around. It really was little to do with his tall, muscular appearance and boyish charm, although that always helps. In many ways, he reminded me of myself at that age.

The first two scheduled clients were Jane and Mary, both long-term petty offenders and both long-term counselling clients with a whole host of problems. Something meaty for a Monday morning. Just after twelve o'clock, I emerged from the cupboard thirsty, blinking and desperate for a pee. As I had a break before seeing the next client at one o'clock, I often sat in the library to write up notes and sneak a few bites of lunch. Officially I was meant to stay in the counselling room or sit in the staffroom, but neither option was particularly appealing.

I often bumped into Gail, one of the prison tutors, on these lunchtime retreats. Gail, who taught creative writing and drama, was something of a therapist herself and was motivated to hang out in the library for the same reasons as me: neither felt that we had much in common with the rest of the prison staff. And they felt the same way about Gail and me, seeing both counselling and drama as a waste of time and a perk for the prisoners. I was always pleased to see Gail; she would not necessarily have been someone I would choose to socialise with, but she was an ally in an otherwise hostile work environment.

Although I knew that Claire Tilley visited the prison once-a-week as a voluntary beauty and hair technician, Tilley's day was a Tuesday, which I rarely worked. Claire-O often commented on how we should arrange to meet at work but both of us knew that the only thing we had in common was the love of Claire-O, and had very little else to talk about.

Gail was browsing the Shakespeare section when I arrived fresh from the toilet block. "Looking for something particular?"

I asked as she sneezed at the dust rising from the shelf.

"I was wondering how many copies of *A Midsummer Nights' Dream* we have." Gail shook out her curly ginger hair and gave a tinkly laugh. "Thinking about staging a production for Christmas."

"Really? Here?"

"Well, it would have to be a very bastardised version, of course."

"Who would be Bottom, I wonder? I can just see Mr G with donkey's ears." At this we both laughed belly-laughs.

I slid a copy of the Bard's Complete Works from the shelf in front of me and turned to an appropriate page, reading from the text: "'Pat, pat: and here's a marvellous convenient place for our rehearsal. This green plot shall be our stage, this hawthorn-brake our tiring-house: and we will do it in action, as we will do it before the duke.' I love this play, it was one of the first I read when I was a teenager. Much less depressing than *Romeo and Juliet*."

Gail, coughing from all of the laughing and dust, removed the remaining relevant copies from the shelf.

"So you're serious about getting them to perform it?"

"Well, it might not get performed, but it'll be a good one to rehearse."

"Who could be Titania, I wonder?"

Gail opened her mouth to answer, but another voice cut in, making my head swivel round to look at the speaker. "One guess."

The name slipped involuntarily from my lips for the second time that day: "Larissa."

"At your service." Lara pushed herself from the shelf she had been leaning against, her golden hair falling into place over her shoulders, and sauntered towards me. She spoke directly to me with her rich Kensington tongue just as if Gail were not there. "I've played Titania before, you know, in school."

Not breaking eye contact, Lara's voice became husky as she quoted:

"'I pray thee, gentle mortal, sing again:
Mine ear is much enamour'd of thy note;
So is mine eye enthralled to thy shape;
And thy fair virtue's force, perforce, doth move me,
On the first view, to say, to swear...'

"...what was the next bit?" Lara lifted the book from my limp hands and read the lines again. "Oh," she laughed, "it should have been: *I love thee*. I'm a little rusty obviously. Could do with some practice; I'm sure you could help me." Her smile left me in no doubt that rehearsing a Shakespeare play wasn't what she had in mind.

Gail's cough broke the spell and I realised that I was blushing. "I'd better go and have a fag before my next class starts," she flustered.

Lara looked down at Gail as if noticing a stain on the carpet. "Puck off, then. Ha ha." The laugh was mirthless and Gail winced.

I caught myself. "No. No, don't go yet. Let me help you carry these books; I need to do something before my next client anyway." Taking the book from Lara's grip, I piled a few of Gail's copies into my arms and walked out without looking back.

Lara called after us, "Don't be long, now."

Gail asked in a whisper as we left the library, "Who's your next client?"

"She is," I replied.

In the staff room, Gail busied herself with the books and her files before sitting down with a sigh next to Annie and getting out the pack of Embassy from her handbag. Annie saw the cigarettes and began fishing around in her own bag. I stood in the corner of the room until she finally noticed me there and cleared one of the chairs. "Sit down! No need to feel out of place. God, how long have you been working here?"

"About two years." I sank gratefully into the seat and eyed the open packet of cigarettes.

"That long, huh?" Gail nonchalantly lit a fag, offering her lighter to Annie, who took it with a grunt, all the while unaware of the pain she caused me. "You know, that woman: Larissa Thomas? She's the bane of my life." She blew the smoke out of her mouth sideways – away from me. "I can't get her thrown out of the classes because she's always so well-behaved. But she's – she's arrogant, superior – she's…"

"… a pain in the arse." I finished the sentence as Gail took another drag. Annie nodded in vehement agreement as she lit her own B&H. "You don't have to blow the smoke away from me, you know," I said. "I'm quite happy to inhale passively. In fact," I reached for the lit cigarette, "do you mind?"

"Not at all!" Gail offered the packet. "I didn't know you smoked."

"I gave up. No, really – I only need a drag and it'd be a shame to waste a whole one."

Gail handed over her half-smoked fag with a bemused expression. I took a long pull with closed eyes and then gave the cigarette back to my colleague. "Thanks."

"That's ok. At least you didn't leave a lipstick mark. What was the thing you had to do, then?"

"What? Oh, nothing. I just had to get away from Lara for a while." I smoothed my trousers down, hoping that Gail and Annie hadn't noticed my trembling hands.

But Gail was already puffing away again and barely looked at me as she spoke. "Larissa Thomas, it sounds like a stage name, doesn't it?"

Annie piped up, "It probably is. I mean, she may be well-educated, she may be beautiful, but she's still a criminal. She's no better than the rest of them, really."

Gail shifted uncomfortably. "Well, we shouldn't be

judgmental, but… well she's always going on about how she's a businesswoman and she was running a *bone fide* escort agency. It's like she thinks she's above everyone else here, including the staff."

"Escort agency, my arse! She's just a common prostitute, that's all," Annie sniffed.

"I'd say she's a rather *un*common prostitute," I said, aware that I was quoting *Sister George*, but knowing that it was wasted on the other two. I suspected that they would never have seen the classic lesbian film. "Well, back to work then, I suppose." I walked out of the staffroom and headed for my counselling cupboard, feeling as if I were walking to the city of doom.

HARRIS THE SCHOOL BULLY

Killer Jacqueline Harris was a bully in school. *Valley Gazette* reporter Viv Diggen has interviewed several of her old school mates from Maddeston Comprehensive in North Warwickshire. Sandra Reed, now 36, tells of Jackie's lesbian advances towards her during games lessons when they were both 14. "She was always looking at other girls in the showers," says Sandra, mother of two.

"I'm not a lesbian and I never was but everyone knew that Jackie was. She would make moves on other girls and then if you were upset she'd get really nasty. One time she waited for me till school was over and tried to follow me home." Other previous students, who do not wish to be named, have said that Jackie was very tall for her age and used this to her advantage.

HARRIS ATTACKED ME

Jacqueline Harris, who killed homeless Frank Little in a frenzied bloodbath last week, has been revealed to have had a violent youth. Reliable sources expose her as a karate expert having achieved medals for fights, and famous in her hometown for using her skills outside of the competitive arena.

Michael Flannery, 37, remembers her as a hot-tempered teen. "She's got a thing against men. She always did have, even at that age. We were fostered together and she never liked me. When I learned karate too, she attacked me and the instructor had to pull her off. I'm not surprised something like this has happened. She's a menace. They should lock her up and throw away the key."

For more on the Jackie Harris story, including details of her first lesbian affair, turn to pages 16, 17 & 18.

Chapter Six – 1985

Jack is heavy on schoolwork, always has been. Teachers know to give her more than the other kids or they will have trouble halfway through the class. She speeds through tasks such as sums, reading and spellings but finds it difficult to do colouring particularly fast. She hates colouring. Colouring tasks are given to other children who complete their work first though she wasn't given colouring in primary school because the teachers knew her. But at Maddeston Comp she's given separate work without even having the chance to start the class tasks.

It doesn't exactly put her behind, because she works like a demon when she gets back to the foster home, studying anything she can find textbooks on. But with no mentor-figure for support, she finds herself with little structure and goes through phases of being obsessed with obscure pieces of knowledge. From Shakespeare to Shinto; Freud to Von Daniken; photosynthesis to Latin; Aristotle to Asimov. She has also found some books by Maya Angelou that are slowly creeping into Maddeston's library.

Jack has recently been studying philosophy. She is intrigued by utilitarianism: for the good of the people. This viewpoint suggests that we should behave in a way that is best for the greater good. To please the majority of the people rather than focusing on a small minority. It reminds her of school – the teaching will focus on the middle-ground intelligence, with the occasional pause so that those who need time can catch up. Those of higher intelligence are not in the majority and so, from a utilitarian point of view, will not be catered for.

What makes her laugh is the refutation of utilitarianism with the example of Christians, Romans and lions. The Romans threw Christians to lions; they made a spectacle of it and had a party while they watched. This is a perfect utilitarian scenario: thousands of Romans are happy; several lions are very happy; one Christian is not happy. Jackie laughs at this because the Appletons of Bilgeworth had forced her to attend church with them. Whenever she thinks about the Christians and lions story, she imagines Mrs Appleton standing in the middle of the arena glaring at a group of lions who cower in the corner.

Philosophy, ancient languages, politics, parapsychology. She laps up every last drop. But school is another story.

Jackie has never really been a young child. And now more than ever, she doesn't feel like a child. It seems preposterous that, given the strength of her adult feelings over the last few months, she should now yet again be reduced to the position of an inferior being.

Claire is gone; will I ever feel anything again?

Jackie entertains herself by drawing caricatures of her vindictive French teacher inside France on the map of Europe that she's been given, then annihilating them with colour. While the other children complete the French comprehension task, Jackie colours. While the other children chant the conjugating verbs, Jackie colours. Sitting at the front of the class and slightly to the side of her compatriots, Jack is nearest to the teacher and nearest to the door. France is green, England yellow, Wales and Scotland red, Belgium pink. While she colours, she conjugates the verbs in her head while the others say them out-loud, and in the gap between each verb she conjugates them in Latin as well just for good measure.

The map completed, Jackie looks down at her handiwork. She removes the lid from the black felt pen that she hasn't yet used and hovers the tip over the middle of England. Locating her estimate of Maddeston on the map, she stabs with the tip of the pen, creating a black dot on the yellow. The pen slips and she thinks that she's probably got Birmingham instead but shrugs as, the way things are going with the Bacons, her current foster carers, she may be back there again soon enough.

Jack begins to replace the lid but stops, her attention caught by the sight of the ink bleeding around the dot. Birmingham is growing, its tendrils slowly creeping into the surrounding area. Satisfied with the effect this has, Jack stabs the pen at her approximation of London – where she knows Claire has gone – then watches as the inky smear that is London grows in the same manner. Like a neuron sending out its axons to connect with another cell. The strands of both cities creep closer to each other, beginning to look like motorway diagrams, and Jack waits with bated breath for a strong branch from Birmingham to join with an equally meaty one from London.

She is startled from her reverie by the scraping and dragging of chairs that accompanies the end of class. Jack makes no attempt to move as the others push past her, some deliberately bumping into her, some sneakily thumping her in the back or kicking the chair. Instead, she looks again at the map, disappointed to see the tendrils that had been progressing well *have* halted just slightly short of each other. Eternally reaching across the great divide.

***

Some people keep a diary; I made a quilt. It started with my first baby blanket – the one that I was found with. My only connection with my real mother. It wasn't much, just soft and blue. Yes, blue. Either she was uncannily predictive or simply unprepared. It came with me everywhere as a baby and eventually began to fall apart. Of course I didn't know as a child why it pained my foster mum so much to see me clutch this blanket. I only knew that the smell and feel made me comfortable and I screamed when she tried to take it away. I kept it in a box from the time it developed holes and I learned how to sew on it. My first ever stitches are on that blanket. I found out years later that it was The Blanket and it had had The Note pinned to it and this was when I began to make my quilt.

The quilt is not that special really, just a jumble of rags. It's important to make something look less than it is when you are in care. That way you can be protected. No-one is going to steal a bunch of rags but they might read a diary. I never found a better code than smell and feel – these things are lost on people who don't hold the memories. If I wrote down: I love Claire I want to kill myself, then someone could read this no matter how secret I kept the book. The quilt could lie out in the open for all to see and only I would know the significance of each patch of cloth. Of course there is always the risk of someone taking a loved possession and destroying it out of spite but the quilt mostly stayed under my pillow. Back then it was small enough.

***

During PE, there are the usual accusations. Jack walks with her eyes cast down for the majority of the time anyway, but in the showers she is likely to bump into the clothes rails. If she looks up for a moment then the shrieking begins. "Miss! She looked at me, Miss. She's always staring at us." It is made even worse by the fact that the PE teacher believes them and keeps taking Jack into her tiny office for 'a quiet word'. This then starts up the rumour that she fancies the bloody teacher, whose own sexuality has already been put in question by the students' active imaginations.

Jack doesn't have a shower. She's had a verruca for the past four months and is not in any hurry to get rid of it as this gets her out of completely undressing in front of the other girls.

Strangely, as they are so obsessed with whether she is looking at them or not, they seem to feel that they have every right to stare at Jack.

She can't go anywhere to get away from Sandra Reed and her sidekicks. Now the girl stands over her menacingly as Jack tries to change her PE shirt into her school shirt while keeping a towel draped around her shoulders. "What you got a towel for? Look at her, under a towel when she's not even wet!"

Jack glances up, tears stinging her eyes, and sees the sneering expression on Sandra's face. She quickly looks away, focusing instead on the embroidered 'S' and 'R' on the girl's PE shirt collar. SR like the toothpaste, she thinks as her eyes drop again to the floor.

Sandra makes a grab for the towel but Jack holds on tight, eyes still down. Both pull and Sandra's friends also join in so they eventually rip it away from Jack, who is left feeling exposed in just her sports bra and skirt. Her gaze involuntarily follows the towel up into the air and then down onto the floor. Sandra stands on it. The wet floor combines with the dirt on her trainers to render it a muddy rag.

The rest of the class look on, too scared to confront Sandra or too interested in seeing Jack's response to think of calling the teacher over. Sandra and her friends laugh when they see Jack's bra. "What do you put in there?" they ask. "Gnat-bites!"

Jack grabs her shirt and stands up as she pulls it on. She is actually nearly a head taller than Sandra, but it never occurs to her to strike back. Sandra recoils, momentarily frightened, as Jack towers over her. Then she glances at her friends and sneers again before kicking the towel at Jack. "Aren't you going to say something, then, weirdo?"

Jack doesn't answer but ducks down to retrieve her towel. Then she hears the familiar voice of the PE teacher: "What's going on here?"

Sandra's tone changes abruptly. "Miss, she tried to touch me.

Look, she's trying to see up my skirt. It's not fair, miss, we shouldn't have to share the changing rooms with a pervert."

Jack stands up quickly and grabs her bag. She remains silent as she pushes her way through the crowd. The silence destroys her.

***

It isn't a long walk back but Jack prefers to dawdle. She waits around inside the school for the rush to die down, not wanting to be among the crowds outside the gates and in the adjoining street. She has learned from bitter experience that this is when the majority of the bullying occurs. And, unlike in the changing rooms when a teacher might turn up at any time, outside of the school they get physical. Sometimes she manages to stay in the school library but today she has been ousted by a vigilant librarian. There are only so many places to go and eventually she gives in and leaves the premises. Contrary to current opinion, Jackie actually loves school. Without the pupils and teachers it is a vibrant place, full of potential.

A practised, slow-paced walk takes Jackie to the bench at the park entrance within five minutes. She puts her schoolbag on the fag-butt strewn gravel and sits with it between her knees. Getting the folded-up leaflet out of her bag for the twentieth time that day, she reads the words that she has already memorised. 'Karate Klub, open to all ages 5-adult. Tuesdays 7-9pm at the Sports Centre. 50p per week. Qualified black belt instructor. Come along and try!' On the back of the leaflet, handwritten in large, curved, bold script: 'Why don't you give it a go? Just for me.' Jackie traces Claire's words with her finger. She's had the leaflet for several months, the paper worn at the folds, the ink faded. The 'm' of the 'me' has been all but obliterated.

She remembers Claire's attempt to persuade her to try karate or some other self-defence sport. "It'll stop them from trying anything on with you. And it'll give you self-confidence. You know you have to do something about your painful shyness."

"But I can't go along to something like that, where I don't know anyone!" Jack countered. And Claire rolled her eyes – like, that was the point.

Now that Claire is gone, Jackie wonders why she didn't ask Claire to come with her. It would have been so easy to do, but it just didn't occur to her until it was too late. The day she came 'home' to a Claire-less house, she found this leaflet on her bed, sitting on top of Claire's favourite t-shirt. An early Christmas present. Since then, every Monday evening she prepares herself to go the next day, packing a bag with gym kit and trainers. Then on Tuesday she finds some excuse to miss it. But today is different, she is sure of it; today she'll make it. When she next sees Claire she will be a karate champion and Claire will be so impressed that she will forget that she likes boys and will let Jackie…

She looks at her watch, still not yet four o'clock. She sees a long dog-end on the floor and picks it up. Straightening it with one hand, she fumbles in her pocket for a plastic lighter and flicks it until it lights up with a tiny flame. After several attempts, Jackie manages to light the second-hand cigarette and leans back for a few puffs. It makes her cough but she continues wrecking her lungs just for the sake of looking cool on that bench. Just in case any nice girls walk past and think she looks sexy.

At five o'clock, Jackie finally saunters into the madhouse foster home. Mrs Bacon has long-since got used to Jack turning up whenever she feels like it and most of the time she isn't even acknowledged. That suits her fine and she stomps upstairs to change out of the military-style school uniform. She eyes the sports bag in the corner of her tiny bedroom. It seems to speak back to her. "You're never going to make it; you coward; you silly little girl." "Shut it!" Jack gives the bag a boot on the way out of the door and slams down the stairs two at a time.

"What's for tea?" she asks as she enters the kitchen.

"It speaks!" says the foster mother in mock-surprise. "Beans on toast or sandwich, take your pick." The little kids are already scoffing at the dining-room table; Jack usually waits for second-sitting as she finds the slobbering puts her off her own food. "You'll have to make it yourself, though. I'm busy getting ready for tonight."

"Tonight?"

"Yes, Mr Bacon and I are going out. To a foster parents' meeting. We did tell you – it's been on the calendar for weeks." Jackie looks at the calendar tacked to the back of the kitchen door and sees some scrawl on today's date that could be anything.

"Who's coming round to look after the kids?" she asks, with an ominous sinking feeling.

"Well…"

"I can't! I'm going out."

"No you're not! You're just saying that…"

"I've got karate, look –" Jack produces the leaflet from the back pocket of her jeans.

"What? Since when…? Well, you could have told me."

"Do I have to tell you my every move? You should have asked me about tonight. Not just assume that I'd be here."

For a moment, Jackie thinks that her foster mother will explode with rage, but then, with practised calm, Mrs Bacon breathes out slowly. "I'm sorry that I assumed, but you are usually in of an evening. Still, I suppose it's good that you're going to do something sociable for once instead of having your head in a book. I'll go round next door and ask Nancy if she can come and sit here for a couple of hours – seven till nine is it? – OK, can you just… just get yourself some tea and I'll be back in a minute." Mrs Bacon bustles out of the back door distractedly, leaving Jack alone and triumphant in the kitchen.

Ha, that showed her.

But as she ushers the kids into the sitting room and sits down at the table with her bread and beans, the feeling of victory subsides. Jackie realises what this means: she will have to go. There's nothing for it unless she wants to wander the streets for two hours on the cold, bleak, February evening.

At six o'clock she goes to her bedroom and tries to read. She has lately got into John Wyndham but can't settle even on her favourite *The Day Of The Triffids*. Jack's own writing talent is beginning to develop. In a grubby exercise book hidden between the mattress and the bedbase are the opening paragraphs of *Detour To The Dinosaurs*: a science fiction novel about a fourteen-year-old girl genius who invents a time machine. In her naïveté she doesn't imagine that any of the story will expose her own character. She pulls it out to read a portion of this:

I pulled the centuries lever and the machine lurched forward. Experiencing a momentary panic, I wondered if all the pistons were in the correct order. My mind went over the system checks again as I drank in the scenes before me. Here a brontosaurus, there a pterodactyl, I pulled the lever further to speed my descent in time until I felt the bitter chill of an Ice Age. This was my destination, as this was where I knew I'd find the Key of Ages...

Currently unable to think of anything else to add to this masterpiece, Jack returns it under the mattress and pulls out the other thing she hides there: a porno mag she has stolen from an older male foster-sibling who has now left. Although she is not at all interested in the girls in the changing rooms, there is nothing to stop her from looking at women in magazines. Jack knows they'll have been paid to pose and this somehow justifies her voyeurism. She is also intrigued to find that grown-up women don't always have pubic hair. The stories are very short and they are written for a low reading-age, unlike her own. She finds her favourite passage:

When my husband is out at work, I like to meet my neighbour for a coffee. She is a bored housewife just like me and we get up to all sorts of things together! My husband doesn't like me to have sex toys so we have to find our own fun. Here we are in the shower together with a loofer, and there is always a cucumber in the fridge. But what I like best of all is when she puts her tongue right up...

Jack feels a bit guilty about reading this stuff. She knows that men openly ogle women in the street and on 'Page Three' but is aware that if she were caught looking then she'd be in big trouble. Seeing men, and boys in school, claim the right to look, touch and comment as much as they want makes her angry. This anger is not for the benefit of the women and girls on the receiving end of the unwanted attention. It is anger that the world is such that men can demand this privilege and Jack cannot. She redresses the balance by possessing this illicit magazine. She is desperate to get herself an education in sexual behaviour and will do so by any means. Jack is learning to objectify women, picking up some very useful tips. This is also her first instruction in what a woman wants and in the kind of things that lesbians do. One might understand why she has problems in later life.

The children are bathing and bedding, and Mrs Bacon flustering and blustering, and Jackie is growing more nervous. She turns over onto her stomach and crams the magazine back under the mattress. The bag is laughing at her again and takes a few more kicks before it is quiet.

At six-thirty she hears Nancy coming in through the back door and ventures down. The woman could be Mrs Bacon's sister for the resemblance and only differs in her choice of slippers. Nancy sports fluffy pink models, which she feels no shame in wearing into other people's homes. She has brought a bag of knitting with her and settles down on the sofa, picking up the remote control as if she's a permanent resident.

"Going somewhere nice?" Nancy keeps her eyes on the screen, though the comment is directed at Jack who skulks in the doorway. "Just to karate." Nancy nods in a way that says to Jackie that Mrs Bacon has already told her the whole story.

"Right then." The foster mother is business-like in her dispensing of kisses to Jack and the other two older children who are still up. "Mr Bacon is meeting me there, and we should be back around ten-thirty. I'll expect *you two*," pointing at the two boys, "to be in bed before I get home. And, Jacqueline, try not to be too late after your karate thing finishes as I don't want to put Nancy out any more than necessary."

"It's all right Beryl, don't you worry about me. You just enjoy yourselves and don't think on it at all."

Mrs Bacon flaps around for a moment and then is gone. Jackie looks at Nancy, who meets her eye and nods. Then Jack goes up to get her bag. "I'll be off, then."

"Right you are. Have fun."

She is out of the door and down the street before it starts again: "Don't know why you're bothering. You know you won't be any good. Everyone'll laugh at you; you'll look like a fool, you always do. Why don't you just sneak back in and go to your room. Chicken, you always were."

"Shut up." Jack shoulders the bag and digs her hands into her pockets, embarrassed that she's spoken out-loud and glad there is no-one around to hear her. She doesn't want to turn into one of those sad people who mutter to themselves as they walk along the street.

The bus arrives quickly and she bounds on before anything can stop her. She puts her coins into the automated collector and rips the ticket out of the dispenser. Only three stops to the sports centre; she could walk it but that wouldn't be wise in the darkened avenues of Maddeston.

Arriving early, Jackie wanders around the playing fields for a few minutes; watches a five-a-side game being played in one of the lit Astroturf cages; kicks an empty can around the car park. At five-to-seven she walks in through the main door and it strikes her then that she doesn't know which room the karate class is held. The spotty young man behind the reception counter is reading a *Star Trek* novel and looks annoyed at being disturbed. "In the main hall, can't you see the poster?" He points to a large colourful poster tacked onto one of the double-doors that lead into the main hall of the centre. *Karate Klub 2Nite*. "Uh, yeah. Sorry." He shakes his head in melodramatic exasperation and goes back to his book.

The screeches of trainers on a hard shiny surface assail Jack's ears as she creaks open the swing door. She glances around the hall, trying not to look like a newcomer. Shrugging off her bag, she kicks off her trainers with the others and joins in with some warm-up exercises.

It all seems familiar so far; like school PE sessions. The stretches give Jack time to catch her breath and to look around the room at the others. The students are mostly teenagers, some younger children and some adults, all male. The instructors are men. She sees a few of them look curiously her way and then look away again. They don't seem particularly interested and she assumes that they have mistaken her for a boy, as usual.

After the warm-up, the lead instructor demonstrates basic punches and kicks, commanding the class to perform ten of each. The exercises progress, punctuated by orders to 'KEEP YOUR GUARD UP' and 'STAY ON YOUR TOES'. Then he calls to the other instructors and divides the group up. Jack is shepherded in with the beginners. She receives some sideways glances but she doesn't speak.

In a row, they snap punch, reverse punch, lunge, cut and thrust, kick sideways, frontwards and spin. It is all done into the empty air, with an instructor, an older teen, pacing back and forth in front of them. When they are finally released, Jack's arms and legs ache and she is glad to sink to the floor to watch the more experienced groups sparring. She marvels at the grace and agility of the fighters and thinks that it seems to be more like dancing than the sort of scrapping that she's done in the street. Wishing she'd thought to bring a bottle of water, Jack rests against the back wall of the sports hall. An instructor saunters over.

"Hello mate, first time?"

"Uh, yeah," says Jack, in what she hopes is a deep voice.

"How d'you like it?"

"S'okay."

"Think you'll come again?"

"Maybe."

"Well you've got potential, I'll give you that."

"Eh?"

"I was watching your kicks. Long legs, you see. You'll be good with a bit of training."

"Thanks."

"What's your name?"

"Jack. Jack Harris."

"I'm John. Want to have a go at some sparring?"

"Er..."

"Don't worry, nice and light. Look, borrow these gloves."

Before she knows it, Jack is standing on a mat surrounded by boys and receiving glancing blows from John. Shouts of encouragement come from the crowd. She tries a few moves and lands a punch. John nods, smiling, and gestures for her to keep going. By the end of the class she is exhausted, elated and feeling heroic. She strolls back to the bus stop on bouncing heels, wondering why she didn't try this long ago. It's only when the adrenaline wears off that she notices the searing pain in every single muscle and limb, abdomen and even in the arches of her feet.

Jackie feels so different; Claire was right after all. Not only did she enjoy the exercise, but she easily slotted into place among the other Karate Klub members. She was not the youngest, or the most unfit, and she actually drew some admiring looks due to her height and muscular figure. She wonders whether things will change if they notice she's a girl, but for now it feels good to belong.

Nancy finishes off her row and packs the knitting back into her bag. "Uh, what are you making?" Jackie asks more out of politeness than interest.

"Just a cardie for my granddaughter. How was karate?"

"Fine."

"Meet any nice young men?"

Jackie smiles, shaking her head as she thinks about the spotty bloke at the reception desk, the instructors and students in the hall. She wonders about her life surrounded by nice young men. "Did the boys go to bed ok?"

"Yes, though I'm not sure they're asleep yet." Right on cue, there's a thud from the room above them. Jackie looks up. "Well, I'd best be off then. You can get yourself to bed I expect."

"Sure I can. See you then." Jack settles down in the armchair, enjoying the freedom of being alone with the remote control for once. She flicks through three channels before finding a film with a sexy blonde. After she hears the click of the back door shutting behind Nancy, she lifts her left leg over the arm of the chair and puts her hand down the front of her jeans, thinking of Claire.

***

"One, two! One, two!" Jack has got into a routine of exercises morning and evening and her muscles are building up. It makes her feel good and it stops her thinking too much which can only be a good thing. If she finds the doubts getting to her then she conjugates verbs aloud while doing the routine. Now she's been to the Karate Klub a few times, she has become a regular. She realises that new students turn up every week, sometimes coming back, sometimes not. Eventually someone turns up at the Klub who also goes to Jack's school and she's recognised. It doesn't take long before someone tries to goad her into a fight in the schoolyard.

"Girls don't do karate; don't your tits get in the way? Oh wait, she hasn't got any!"

Jackie balls her fists and turns her back. The jeers follow her. "She's too chicken. Bet she's not really doing karate. Bet it's all crap."

Jack grinds her teeth. She is learning to control her temper. Karate is not street fighting. She's being instructed in the martial arts, the first rule of which is not to start a fight, to avoid if possible fighting outside of the arena.

Word has begun to get around. Jackie is no longer providing entertainment by losing control. She is calm and confident and the bullying has subsided. There are sometimes still whispers and hostile looks and there will never be any real friends, but at least Sandra Reed has stopped attacking her. That demonstrates to Jack what cowards they are.

At the Klub, things get awkward, but only until another girl joins. And another. Girls arrive in pairs or with their parents, asking for self-defence classes. John slaps Jackie on the back as he tells her that she was the catalyst – girls have been enquiring about joining but none wanted to be the first. Again, she is a hero.

Now that Jack isn't being bullied, she is no longer seen by teachers as a troublemaker, and in all but a few lessons is treated almost with respect. It isn't long before her schoolwork begins to pick up again. And all because of karate; all because of Claire.

But still no word from her. She said she would write; maybe

she's lost the address. Maybe she will be back in care anyway, soon enough. From what Jack has heard about Claire's mother she is pretty flaky and will get fed-up with having a couple of teenage daughters around. So Jack concentrates on getting on and building herself up, to look her best for when Claire returns to the Midlands. Jack is sure she would spot her if she did.

As she gets older, Jack is more likely to be the eldest in her foster home, although other children come and go. One in particular she remembers as being particularly brutish. Mikey Flannery is hostile to Jack from the instant he arrives. When he finds out what she does on a Tuesday evening, he decides that he wants to try karate as well. And he is certain that he will be better at it than a girl. He follows her to the bus stop, blathering all the way about how he already knows plenty of moves. His father is apparently a karate champion and Mikey is convinced that it won't take him long to get to the top.

In the sports hall Jack is relieved to lose Mikey to the boys' changing area and she sits for a moment in peaceful contemplation before entering the main hall. Mikey sulks in a corner because he's been put with the beginners and Jack smiles to herself as she joins one of the middle ranks. Weeks later she is surprised and grudgingly impressed to find Mikey still tagging along. He is due to move on soon but talks tall about how his father is going to buy him a karate suit and get him into tournaments.

Mikey has been training at home, as does Jack, and he occasionally attempts to entice her into sparring. Jack is clear on the golden rules of safe combat: never start a fight; practise only in a safe area; don't attempt a manoeuvre unless you're capable of following through. On his last night at karate, Mikey asks the instructor if he and Jack can spar. He lies that they've discussed it on the way over and is believed. Jack doesn't bother disputing it.

As they set-up, Mikey smugly whispers, "Gonna thrash you."

Jackie smiles. "Bring it on."

His first hit takes her off-guard as she was blocking his left hand – Mikey being left-handed. She steps back, away from his conceited grin and rubs her chin. "Gotcha," he says.

"You're supposed to pull your punches not hit with full force."

"Oh sorry," he says with mock-sincerity. "Did I hurt you? I thought I was being gentle."

They bow and begin again. She blocks him successfully and gives him a few hits, pulling her own punches so that she doesn't injure him. But he gets a couple of kicks in and he is still giving it full-strength. A small crowd has gathered to watch the battle. "Stop!" she shouts and steps out. He throws another punch after she has stepped away but she blocks it and holds his fist. She calls to the instructor. "He's not controlling his power."

The instructor speaks to Mikey, who mutters and shrugs sullenly. The instructor turns to Jack and says, "You go to fifty percent force." She smiles because now she has permission to hit him half as hard as she is able.

Mikey and Jack step back in together and the sparring continues. He is tiring now because he has thrown himself into it early. She leads and blocks all his attempts, then begins to thrash him. At fifty percent she can hurt him, hurt his pride but leave him alive. She has him on his knees within minutes and then walks away to the girls' changing area. When she returns he is gone. He catches an early bus and she doesn't see him again until the following day when his case is packed and ready to go.

Mikey has a slight bruise under his left eye and a murderous look on his face. The expression tells her that she'd better watch out if she ever meets him in a darkened alley. And she knows that he doesn't fight fair.

***

Jack is fifteen, almost sixteen and still no Claire. She has moved to Hillbank. She has to give up the hope that Claire will some day get in touch. Hillbank is near enough to Maddeston for Jack to continue with the Karate Klub, but as it's over the border in Leicestershire, she has had to move schools again.

There have been other crushes, but no real loves. Not like Claire. Karate is big now in Jack's life. She has the kit, is on the tournament circuit and doing public demonstrations – something she would never have dreamt of doing in her shy days. She wins trophies for karate and prizes in science, bestowed on her by new teaching staff who can't find a reason to deprive the star pupil of her stardom. At last, the fresh start that she was promised.

Now she is preparing for 'O'-levels, locked in the eternal struggle of revision. She took English and Maths last year and this has reduced the pressure slightly, though she is still taking nine separate subject exams.

A few weeks before her first exams begin, a new member turns up at karate. New members come and go sporadically and Jack usually takes no notice, but Heidi is different. Softly spoken, she appears shy at first but is a brown belt, and when Jack sees her in action it is obvious that she is an accomplished fighter. She is much older than Jackie, in her late-twenties, and seems sophisticated, feminine yet strong. Long, ash-blonde hair tied back in a ponytail, dazzling blue eyes, and pale cheeks that blush just a hint when she is exerted. A contrast to Jackie's very black, very short, tightly curled hair, brown eyes, heavy eyebrows and dark complexion. Total opposites. Jack feels sure that Heidi would not be interested in someone like her; yet when it comes to the break she seems eager to talk.

"I just moved here from Cheltenham. Got a job in Coventry, you know, but can't afford a place in the city so Maddeston's not too bad for travel."

"I've lived in North Warwickshire since I was eleven." Jack

doesn't elaborate further.

"Are you at college?" Heidi has made the common mistake of thinking that Jack is older than she actually is. For a moment, Jackie considers lying to impress but knows she will find out sooner or later and what would she think of her then?

"School, just doing my 'O'-levels."

"Oh." Heidi looks away briefly and Jack feels let down. But then Heidi looks back and Jackie notices she has kind eyes. "What's your best subject?"

"Science. Well, Physics really. But I'm studying languages too."

"So, what do you want to be?" Her eyes are more than kind; they are like pools of knowledge that you could lose yourself in.

"Be?"

"When you leave school?"

"Oh, yeah – be." Jackie feels a fool – it's the most obvious question anyone could ask and she's cocked it up. "I haven't really decided. I don't think it's fair for someone to have to decide, you know, at my age. Just concentrating on getting to college really. So what do you do? For your job I mean?"

"I'm a copy editor. Nothing amazing but I like it."

"No, that sounds good. Interesting."

Heidi laughs. "Only interesting for geeks like me."

Jackie doesn't get a chance to say, "I'm a geek too," because the instructor calls them back to their separate lines. She looks over to Heidi who smiles and winks, making her heart pound more than necessary.

Heidi is there on Friday and becomes a regular smiling face. They sometimes talk, Jack telling her how the revision is going, Heidi talking about her new job, the people in the office. It seems strange to Jackie that she should have found a friend who was almost twice her age, but then it might be stranger still to find one her own age. Heidi doesn't seem to have a boyfriend or indeed any life outside of work and karate – or if she does then she's careful not to mention it to Jack.

The exams begin with a vengeance. It isn't long before Jack is sitting two or three per day and falling exhausted on a pile of more revision when she gets back from school. She's mentioned to Heidi that she lives in a children's home, and tells her how difficult it is to concentrate with a house full of noisy teenagers, most of whom couldn't care less about schoolwork. Heidi is sympathetic. "You could come round to mine to revise if you need some peace," she offers, scribbling her address on the back of a bus ticket. It's an offer that Jackie has no intention of refusing.

***

"Didn't you really mean it?" Jack stands unsure in the doorway of Heidi's small flat when the woman opens the door with a surprised smile.

"Oh, of course I did. But I hadn't realised you'd come round today." It's Saturday morning, the day after the invitation was extended.

"Uh, ah. I could go if…" Jack turns away, trailing her bag.

"Don't be silly! Come in now you're here. Have a coffee?" Heidi opens the door wide so that Jack can slip past. She draws her hand through her long hair and looks away as their bodies brush. Jackie stands awkwardly in the middle of the flat and Heidi looks briefly out into the dirty, carpeted hall before shutting her door again. "So, coffee…" she says distractedly and wanders over to her kitchenette.

"This is cool," Jack says approvingly, looking around. It is a single-room apartment above a pizza place and video arcade. Everything that would normally appear in a house all packed into one place: kitchen in the corner, study next to it, bookshelves, an armchair. Bed. Jackie quickly looks away when she sees that the bed isn't made.

"How do you like it?" Heidi asks, turning from the kettle to face Jack.

"I like it!"

"Thanks." Heidi laughs. "But I meant your coffee."

"Oh! Oh, milk and one sugar, please."

"Here, you can sit here…" Heidi clears magazines from the single upright chair and removes some dirty crockery from the desk. Gesturing Jack towards the study space, Heidi finishes off making the coffees before placing herself gingerly in the armchair. "It's broken," she explains to Jack's quizzical look. "So, what are you revising today?"

"Uh, literature? Shakespeare."

"Oh cool! What text? *Romeo and Juliet*'s my favourite."

"*Macbeth*."

"Ha!" Heidi stands and punches the air, shouting, "'Unsex me now! Turn my milk to gall'…."

"O-kay…." Jackie says slowly, unsure of how to react.

"Lady Macbeth, don't tell me you don't know that bit!" Heidi sits down again abruptly and then winces as the chair makes a loud squeak.

"Yes… no, maybe? The only bit I really know is 'out out damned spot' when she keeps washing her hands 'cos she thinks there's blood on them. After she killed the king, you know. Oh yeah, and 'tomorrow and tomorrow and tomorrow.' And, and something about the crown not fitting. I remember that from when I read it first, when I was about nine or something…" Jack trails off as she realises that she's rambling and Heidi is looking at her with a smile.

"Oh, but you must have seen what a great woman Lady Macbeth is? I mean, she's the strength in the relationship, isn't she – she's the one that actually does the killing because Macbeth can't face it. And she's just, well – she's such a strong female character, you don't get many of those in classic texts."

"No, I suppose not…"

"It's excellent that you're doing Macbeth! Something to get your teeth into. There's so much in it – power, treachery, magic – it's an eternal story like so many of Shakespeare's plays. It's a shame you're not doing 'R and J' 'cos I've still got some of my old essays hanging around somewhere…" she looks distractedly at some boxes of papers under the desk. "Still, we're going to have so much fun today. Here, give me the book and I'll find the best bits for you. Have you brought any past papers?"

Jackie empties her bag out onto the floor and hands over books and her folder to Heidi who takes them eagerly. She is perturbed and just slightly uncomfortable at the woman's reaction to her being there. What did she expect from Heidi's offer of 'peace and quiet to revise'? In her mind's eye she recalls the fantasy she'd had of sitting in a tidy study while Heidi wanders around the flat doing her own thing – possibly practising some karate – and occasionally bringing her drinks and encouragement. She hadn't considered that Heidi's flat would be so small. This tiny space forces intimacy, and she hadn't expected this involvement, *intrusion*, into her studying. She isn't used to anyone showing more than a passing curiosity in her schoolwork and really doesn't know how to react at all.

As Heidi enthuses over Macbeth and its themes and symbolism, Jack becomes infected by her passion and realises that discussing the text has given her much more insight into it.

"Well," Heidi says, as she stretches and stands up, "I suppose I'd better offer you some lunch."

"Oh," Jack looks at her watch. "I hadn't noticed the time. I should go really; I've done enough on Macbeth now I think."

Heidi looks crestfallen. "Do you have to go? I mean, are they expecting you back at home, I mean, the… you know."

"No, they're not. But I don't want to intrude on you."

"It's nothing, don't worry. So long as you don't mind toast and something. It's not *haute cuisine*. If you came around one evening we could have pizza, but they don't open till six."

"Well, if it's no trouble…"

"What other subjects have you got left? I speak French, you know."

"You do?"

"*Mais oui.*" Heidi laughs her musical laugh again and Jack feels her heart flip over. "Look over in that box next to the TV; there's some French films in it on Bet Amax. I'll whip us up something quick and then we can watch one if you like."

"Yeah, that would be great. Sure you don't mind?"

"Hey, I wouldn't offer would I?"

Jack dives into the box, pulling out first some martial arts videos, *Kung Fu*, *Karate Kid*. "Hey *Monkey*, I used to watch that! I loved it: Pigsy and Tripitaka. Only I could never work out whether Tripitaka was a girl or boy."

"I think the character was male but played by a woman. Why, did you fancy her?"

"No!" Jack ducks back into the box, sorting through the videos.

"Oh – " Heidi quickly reaches over Jack's shoulder and grabs a case out of her hand, " – not that one!" She turns away but not before Jackie has noticed a blush rising to her cheeks.

Jackie picks out something that looks like a children's film. She opens the case and fumbles with the video for a few minutes before admitting that she's out of her depth. "They haven't got a video at Hillbank."

"Oh sorry, silly me, I should have thought." Heidi sets the video up and switches the TV on while Jackie watches. "It's easy once you get used to it. Mind you, most people have VHS these days, which is a shame in my opinion. Here," she hands Jackie the remote control and goes back to preparing the meal.

Jackie stands up and steps back from the TV, knocking the backs of her legs against the bed. She spins around the room for a moment and then realises something with a strange sick feeling. The TV is angled in such a way that the only position for seeing the screen is from the bed itself. She doesn't do sitting on beds with people. The last time she sat on someone's bed was when she tried to kiss Claire, and that hadn't worked out too well.

Heidi stands in front of her with two plates of cheese on toast. "Do you like brown sauce? I don't have any red, can't stand the stuff myself."

"Oh, er, yeah. Brown's fine."

"Good, oh here –" she hands both plates to Jackie and leans around her to tidy the bed. Then she takes her plate and sits down. Noticing Jackie's confused hesitation, Heidi chuckles slightly. "It's not so bad, you know – just think of it as a sofa with no back. When you're a student you'll use your bed for lots more things than sleeping."

The opening titles of the film begin and Jack perches herself on the edge of the bed, the plate awkwardly balanced on her lap. Once she has eaten the toast, Jack feels her back aching from the strain of sitting without support. She inches backwards self-consciously and is soon leaning against the wall next to Heidi, who looks at her with an amused half-smile but doesn't comment. The film is a funny one and, although Jack struggles to follow the dialogue, it relies quite heavily on visual humour so she's able to laugh along with Heidi. When it's over, she realises they're snuggled quite closely together and draws herself away, embarrassed.

"What's wrong?" Heidi reaches up to put a hand on her shoulder. Jack stiffens and her hand drops. "Don't you like me?" Heidi asks. "I thought you did."

Startled by her directness, Jack looks her briefly in the eye and then looks away. "I don't know what you mean. I don't want you to think… I mean, I'm not…"

"Not what?" Heidi asks, amused again.

"I'm not, I don't want you to think that I'm…"

"What, for heaven's sake?"

"A lesbian."

"Oh," Heidi laughs. "Is that all? No, I won't think you're a lesbian. Unless you want me to?" Again the direct look, and then she stands up and picks up the plates. "*Comment que tu pense le film?*"

"Oh, *tres bien. Oui.* I'd better go."

"So soon?" Jackie starts to shove her books into her bag. "Ok, here let me help." They both grab a book at the same time but Heidi relinquishes it as Jack pulls rather too forcefully. "I'm sorry, have I upset you?"

"No, it's ok."

"The lesbian thing, you know. We get it all the time in karate – you'll get used to it. People are always accusing me of being…"

"No. It's ok. Really."

Heidi reaches up to put her hand lightly on Jackie's cheek. "It's no big deal, you know. Don't worry. I'm sorry – I keep forgetting how young you are. You're so tall and you seem so mature. It's just…" Her voice trails off as Jackie looks at her. Heidi seems about to speak again but doesn't.

"I'll be sixteen in October. I'm not a child." Before giving Heidi a chance to answer, Jack turns to the door and leaves.

***

Whether Heidi expects her to come back or not, Jack doesn't know. But Sunday morning finds her walking through an almost deserted Maddeston town centre towards the pizza place. After spending most of Saturday evening torturing herself over the ambiguous comments Heidi had made, the close contact, the intimacy that rose so quickly between them, she has to know. She just has to know.

She kicks around some takeaway litter for a time, trying to muster the courage to walk up the stairs next to the closed pizza place. Jackie notices some boys crowded in the arcade. One looks out at her curiously and she rushes past, up the stairs before having time for a second thought.

Now she stands outside Heidi's door deciding whether to knock. She's in a dilemma – can't go back down to face jeers from the vid kids, can't knock and face Heidi answering. What if she isn't there and Jack has to go away again like a fool? What if she is there, but doesn't want to see her? What if someone else is with her? Her heart pounds inside her chest, but she propels herself forwards and knocks. She has to be the one to make the first move, she can't be so passive.

A groan from inside tells Jack that Heidi hasn't yet got out of bed. Maybe she should go now, like a coward, and Heidi will answer the door to empty space. Blame kids knocking and running. But what if Heidi sees her going down the stairs and knows it was her? No, stand your ground, be a man.

Movements from inside the flat and the sound of scraping at the door. Heidi is putting the chain on – it is the town centre after all. The door opens a crack and her face appears: eyes red, hair mussed, beautiful. "Oh, it's you." She closes the door and for one painful moment Jack thinks that is it: she's been dismissed. Then she hears a grinding noise and realises Heidi is taking the chain off so that she can open the door fully. They look at each other wordlessly and then Jack pulls herself together.

"I'm sorry I got you up. I hadn't realised…"

"That's OK – I'm not sleeping too well. The pizza place is noisy at night, especially on Saturdays. Well, are you coming in or what?" She stands there in winceyette pyjamas, teddy-bears dancing a pattern across her breasts.

"Maybe I should go…"

Heidi reaches out and grabs the front of Jackie's coat, pulling her inside. "Don't you dare, now you've got me out of bed." She shuts the door behind Jack and leans her against it, their faces close.

Time to take some action, time to be forceful like in the films. Jackie pushes her away and spins her around so that it is Heidi leaning against the door. Ignoring the stunned expression on her face, Jack leans in and kisses her fully on the lips. The first time she has given an adult kiss although she really doesn't know what to do once their lips meet. But Heidi responds readily to the kiss and then laughs and pushes Jack away. "You *really* need to learn how to kiss, love."

Frowning in consternation at this unexpected turn of events, Jackie slumps down in the armchair, remembering at the last minute that it isn't up to rough treatment. She feels herself falling as the back of the chair gives way and sprawls on the floor ungracefully, with Heidi standing above her laughing uncontrollably. Jackie struggles to get up, but then Heidi kneels next to her and cradles her head. "It's ok, you know. It's alright to be vulnerable."

Heidi bends down and kisses her gently, lots of small kisses, murmuring between each one, "I can teach you," "I can show you how," "If you'll let me." Heidi's hands are on Jackie's face and in her hair, stroking and holding her; the long hair falls downwards, tickling Jack's neck. Jackie reaches clumsily towards Heidi's body; arms around her back she tries to pull her close but the woman moves away again. Standing up, Heidi takes Jack's hand and pulls, forcing her to stand. Ignoring the broken chair, she leads the girl to her still-warm bed and sits her down.

Jackie lets Heidi undress her like a child. This is all too easy, too quick. Her fantasies haven't got further than the kissing, but more through ignorance than lack of wanting. She doesn't need to explain that this is the first time: Heidi must know. But when Heidi puts a hand on her breast, she gasps; and when Heidi puts a hand between her legs, she cries out. It's too much, too much to bear. She grabs the woman's wrist and pushes the hand away. "Let me do it to you, show me. Show me the best way," Jack demands. "I want to learn."

It turns out that what Heidi wants isn't that difficult to provide. Jackie has been masturbating for four years already and the technique is second nature to her, the only difference being that it is someone else she is rubbing and not herself. She likes the way that Heidi gasps and clutches her; she likes the things Heidi whispers in her ear; she likes the warm toast smell of the bed, the slimy feeling as her fingers slide rhythmically in time with Heidi's hip movements. It's over too quickly for Jackie and she keeps her hand in place as Heidi stifles her cries in a pillow. After a moment, the woman looks up lazily at Jack and laughs.

"What's funny?"

"You, so shy and then this! I thought it was your first time?"

"It is."

"Well you must be a natural then," sighs Heidi, sitting up. "Haven't had one that good since... well, I don't know." She leans in to Jackie again and kisses her languorously at first, then becoming more insistent. Jackie responds, getting the hang of it at last and moving her mouth around in similar patterns to Heidi's. She feels Heidi's tongue with her own and pushes deeper, braver. Jackie pushes Heidi down onto the bed again, and the woman lets her climb on top, still kissing. Jack's thigh falls into place in between Heidi's open legs and she moves against her, trailing her hand up and down Heidi's ribs, hip and thigh as she's seen men do in films.

They kiss like this for a time, Jackie moving against Heidi, sure that she's doing something right as it feels so good. Heidi seems to be enjoying it too and her breaths begin to come shorter and faster. Heidi then whispers in her ear, "Will you do something else for me?" and Jack pulls back slightly concerned. Heidi laughs and kisses her quickly, "You're so cute when you pull that face! I just mean, will you..." then Heidi seems embarrassed. "I want you to go down on me."

"Go down where?"

Laughing, Heidi explains what she means by using gestures and light dawns for Jackie. "Ah, you want me to lick you out?"

"Oh yuk, that's a horrible expression! That sounds like something you'd hear in the schoolyard."

Jackie shrugs. "It's only words," Jackie says after a while. "I won't call it that again if you don't like it. But I've never done it before so you'll have to tell me how." Jack still looks concerned and hesitant.

"Don't worry. Let's just say that the lesson for today is over." Heidi begins to do up the buttons on her pyjama top and Jack takes that as a cue to collect her clothes.

As she walks down the steps and out into the day, a silhouette appears from the video arcade. She rushes past, wiping her face with her hand, not wanting any confrontations to dampen the high she feels. She's out on the street when she hears the familiar voice call to her.

"Aincha gonna say hello then?"

"Mikey," she says, before she turns.

"Yeah. The very same." He walks up to her and his smug look takes her back nearly a year. "How about finishing that fight we started?"

"I already finished it. But we don't have an instructor here to hold me back." She looks over his shoulder and sees a dribble of curious vid kids looming. She nods to them. "Now you wouldn't want me to batter you in front of your friends, would you?" He follows her line of vision and then looks down, a shadow of doubt crossing his face. She moves closer as she knows she's got the upper hand. "That's right. If you remember: *I* beat *you*. And I wouldn't refrain from doing it again so just stay out of my way."

She is close enough to notice he's learning to shave and she smells trashy aftershave. But she doesn't realise that he can also smell her, until he suddenly looks up, an entirely different expression on his face. "You smell like..." he begins. Then it's Jack's turn to look frightened. She backs away and he calls after her, "Fucking lesbian! Hey, dyke, who've you just shagged?" She runs away from Heidi's flat with laughter ringing in her ears.

HARRIS TRIED TO 'RAPE' ME

Jacqueline Harris, who killed a man she claims was raping her lesbian lover, has been a sex pest in the past. Last week *Valley Gazette* reporter Viv Diggen revealed that Jacqueline, known as 'Jack', preyed on young women while she was still at school. It has now been confirmed that she attacked a woman when she was seventeen.

The woman, who does not wish to be named, was a friend who trained with Jack in karate. They fought together a number of times but once, it is claimed, during a fight Jack pushed the woman onto the floor and began tearing at her clothes. This despicable behaviour is something that might lead to a charge of sexual assault. However, Jack relied on the fact that her victim would be too embarrassed to report the incident.

Who knows how many other victims have fallen prey to this evil sex attacker? How did someone like this come to gain a position of power in a women's prison? *Valley Gazette* is calling for these questions to be answered and for more stringent controls on employment in the prison service.

Chapter Seven – 1987

There is no happily ever after. Inevitably the age difference will impede the progress of the relationship. They do have a blissful few months over the summer, where Jack discovers the joys of cunnilingus. She also discovers that Heidi has a vibrant social life that she hadn't spoken about. She has a vast array of lesbian friends, most of whom are wary of Jack, which makes things difficult. They seem particularly panic-stricken if Jackie ever turns up to Heidi's flat in school uniform, which she does on a few occasions. When back in school for 'A'-Levels, there's no uniform, for which Jack is grateful. She mostly wears jeans or sports clothes. Although Heidi doesn't make a comment, Jack suspects that the uniform had actually turned her on.

She still lives at Hillbank and hasn't told the workers about Heidi – they think she's out with school friends. She's unsure what the reaction would be if her keyworker knew that Jack's 'friend' was in fact more than ten years older and she knows they'd ban her from going there if they realised she had a lover.

Jack and Heidi rarely go out together, as Heidi doesn't like the idea of taking her to bars and clubs even though Jack insists she'd be able to get in with no trouble. She can pass for a boy most of the time and she's sure she can pass for eighteen. Hadn't Heidi herself thought that Jack was much older? But Heidi is firm; more often than not, they spend time in the flat and Jack meets Heidi's friends singly or in small groups. This is often a bone of contention between them, Jack wanting to go out more. Their arguments become more tempestuous as the weeks draw on, both under pressure from the other to change.

"Why can't we be like *normal* couples?"

"What is a normal couple, then Jackie? You mean heterosexual?"

"No. I mean when both are the same age."

"Oh, so if I was *your* age, we'd be snogging in bus shelters freezing our arses off. Is that what you want?" Heidi sneers.

"And if I were your age," Jack counters, "we'd be going out to restaurants for dinner."

"I bought you dinner!" Heidi shouts indignantly, indicating the empty pizza box on the floor.

"What do you want, a medal?" Jack screams and storms out before Heidi can answer. She regrets it immediately after the door has slammed behind her but is too proud to turn back. Instead, she stomps down the stairs and turns to enter the video arcade. If Heidi cares enough, she'll know to come and find her. There aren't many kids in the arcade and no Mikey thank goodness. The weather is good and the evening light so most of the older kids are in the park drinking cans of lager and cider. Jackie fumbles in her pocket for coins and then changes her mind and wanders out into the street, unsure of her next move.

"Hey, are you ok? It's Jackie, isn't it?"

Jack looks around, startled, to see a woman smiling at her. She's trying to place the face when the answer is provided for her.

"Judith, Heidi's friend." The woman holds out her hand as she introduces herself and Jack takes it distrustfully. "Hey, don't be so suspicious! I was just on my way to see Heidi but maybe I'll talk to you instead." Jack looks at her. "Well, you must have something to say for yourself. I've never seen you out; is she keeping you cooped up in there all to herself?" Jack smiles and looks down shyly. "Ah, I get it – you've just had a row, haven't you? Never mind, your old pal Jude'll look after you. Tell me all about it." She puts an arm around Jack and leads her away from the front of the pizza place.

Judith is a not particularly close friend of Heidi's and doesn't seem at all phased by Jackie's age. Jack soon learns that she hates being called Judy but doesn't mind Jude and, at twenty-eight, is older than Heidi by five months. She works in a warehouse as a forklift truck driver and is training to drive HGV lorries, which impresses Jackie. She remembers now that Jude visited briefly once when she was lounging on the bed; she appeared to be delivering some merchandise. Although they didn't speak, she had looked over curiously at Jack and their eyes had met. Heidi was clearly uncomfortable with Jude there and ushered her out quickly. Jackie had wondered at the time if it was drugs but, as there were no other indications and nothing forthcoming, she had forgotten about it.

Jude steers them towards the West side of Maddeston and away from Jack's bus stop. Soon Jack begins to feel uncomfortable. "It's getting late; I should go back."

"Oh, sorry, I hadn't really noticed the time. Where do you live?"

"Uh, back that way." Jack points her thumb over her shoulder, reluctant to give an address to a stranger and not wanting to tell her that she lives in a children's home.

Jude looks at her for a moment. "You know, you should come out with us. Don't let Heidi be so possessive – there's a big scene out there; you could have some fun."

"I'd like to, but I don't know where to go."

"No problemo, I'll show you. How about this weekend, there's a club in town... but, well, it's a bit out of the way, not very obvious from the street. Why don't you meet me at the pub first and then we can go together."

"Where would you want to meet? I mean which pub?"

"You mean she hasn't even taken you to the pub?"

Jack shakes her head dumbly; she doesn't want to give the obvious reason that Heidi thinks she's too young in case Jude also changes her mind. It turns out there is only one gay pub on the north side of Maddeston, quite near to the club which makes 'a proper little village' according to Jude. Although Jack is not really sure what she means by a village, she's provided with the name, directions and a time to meet Jude on Friday night.

***

"Where did you go yesterday?" Heidi demands when Jack turns up after school the following evening.

Jack shrugs. "Nowhere really, just walked around for a bit and then went back home." It isn't a lie, but she feels bad about neglecting to mention Jude's involvement. "I'm sorry I…" she shrugs again. "I'm sorry," she finishes lamely.

Heidi purses her lips but accepts the apology. "Come in." She pulls her through the flat and pushes Jack's coat halfway off. "Just kiss me." And when Jack has obeyed, "Now, where did we leave off last time?"

Jackie smirks; it's alright again. "I think we were stuck on a particularly stiff obstacle in the clitoral region."

"Ah yes, maybe you need some more practice on that one…"

But the truth is that Jackie is now bored. She never panted after Heidi and lately the only time her passion is truly aroused is when they fight. If Heidi notices that Jack isn't coming as often, or coming around as often, she doesn't say anything about it. And Jackie herself just presumes that this is what happens with relationships. She's heard about how the spark can go between people but has no experience in how to end it.

The first step as far as Jackie is concerned is to make some other lesbian friends. Jude hit the nail on the head: Heidi has no right to keep her away from them. And Jackie is so naïve that she doesn't understand why Heidi is doing this.

***

After school on the Friday in question, Jack is nervously scrutinizing her scant wardrobe for something appropriate to wear. She knows she's likely to end up in her usual jeans, t-shirt and leather jacket but is panicking as to whether this will be acceptable. She remembers Jude as wearing jeans and a checked shirt when they met, but is that what she wears out? Jack doesn't have any checked shirts, but she does have a plain white one – her old school shirt in fact. She always buys men's shirts because she feels more comfortable in them – girls' blouses feel too fancy, even the uniform type. She is glad that in Hillbank she is allowed to buy her own clothes; it hasn't always been that way.

The decision made, Jack showers quickly and slips back to her room in a towel. She has her own room: another perk that comes with age and length of stay. When she first arrived, she had to share a four-bed room with sectioned-off bedspaces. This lack of privacy is imposed on all newcomers. Jack's keyworker says this is so they feel part of the group and not isolated, but Jack suspects it's more to do with the risk of newbies topping themselves or running away. She longs for her own flat where she can be as isolated as she chooses. She opens the wardrobe door again and hangs the towel over the mirror on the inside so she doesn't have to be confronted with her own nakedness.

The evening is a brisk one and she feels the wind through her thin shirt. She fumbles with the broken zip of her jacket at the bus stop, eventually giving up and clutching it closed. Hopping up the steps, she is glad to feel the warmth of the bus.

Jack has an affinity to buses. She feels this is because she was found at a bus stop. She's known this since she was eleven and a foster mother told her the whole story, even giving her The Note. She obviously thought a child has the right to know. Before Heidi, she would often hop on the bus just for the ride, going up to Bosworth to look at the battle site, or even as far as Leicester itself.

The diesel fume smell makes her think of Jude. Jude, the lorry driver. A strange feeling of excitement boils in the pit of her stomach. She's out at last! And maybe Jude is interested in her, or was she just being friendly?

At the pub there isn't much of a crowd and Jack feels slightly let down. But Jude comes lurching out of a corner, smiling broadly. "You made it!"

Jack notices Jude is wearing a white shirt and jeans, and she congratulates herself on getting it right for once. "Come and meet the gang. Oh – what'll you have to drink?"

"Er…" Startled, Jack realises that she hasn't thought about this bit. "Beer?"

"Good choice! Two pints of bitter please, Louise!" Jude yells over to the barmaid who nods. "Come on, sit down. Lou'll bring them over."

She leads Jack towards a tightly packed table and reels off a list of names that she promptly forgets. But everyone seems to know who she is. "So this is Heidi's little friend, is it?" "Love the jacket." "Where's she been hiding you, then?"

Jack has an overwhelming feeling of hands reaching to grab her, although they are only smiling and looking. She almost breaks free and runs, but Jude has an arm firmly over her shoulder and is manoeuvring her towards a stool. She sits and tries to answer their questions. A pint is delivered into one hand and a cigarette into the other. The bar slowly starts to fill up and the rest of the evening goes by in a blur. It isn't the first time she has drunk alcohol, but the first time so much, so quickly, and in company. She enjoys the looseness it gives her.

Jackie has forgotten they are meant to be going to a club so when Jude stands up at 10.30 she thinks it's time to go home. She starts to say goodbye to everyone but is greeted by surprised stares. "You're coming with us, aren't you?" Jude says. "To the club?"

"Oh! Oh, yeah." Jack laughs nervously.

They walk as a group through Maddeston town centre, attracting catcalls and shouted obscenities. Jackie is appalled that none of the women shout back or react at all. "Just ignore them," Jude says when she senses Jack stiffen next to her. "They'll get over it."

One skinhead breaks free from a bunch and comes very close to Jack and Jude, hissing, "Lezzie perverts," in their faces and spitting at them. This is just too much for Jackie. As he backs away, laughing, she walks right up to him and delivers two smart punches – one in his face and the other in his abdomen. He is so surprised that he doesn't have a chance to block them and rolls on the floor at her feet while the rest of the gang stare. "Anyone else want to try?" shouts Jack, feeling the familiar rush of adrenaline as she sinks back into a defensive stance. Apparently no-one does and the lad on the floor gets up quietly and joins his mates who skulk off muttering darkly.

Jack turns back to her new friends expecting applause and is disappointed. Jude beams approvingly and some of the other women call out encouraging words, but for the most part the sea of faces remain unimpressed. Confused, she falls into step with them as they continue on silently. They arrive at the club and Jude pays Jackie's entrance fee – another thing she hadn't expected. Jude leaves her at a table to go to the bar and Jackie looks around for the toilets. When she looks back at the table she finds herself face-to-face with one of the women from the group. Sharon, is it? She is short and slight, with a blonde perm, feminine features, a pink blouse and a mean expression.

"You might think you're really clever for that, but you don't know what you've done."

"Pardon?"

"They *will* retaliate, you know, only it won't be you that gets it. Oh no, you'll be safe enough. It'll be someone like me. I hope you're pleased with yourself."

Suddenly contrite, Jackie realises that she's right. It had been a foolish act of bravado, showing off in front of Jude and the others. She should have been more disciplined and perhaps would have been if she hadn't been drinking. "I'm sorry. I didn't think... but surely if we all stood together?"

"Do you think we've not tried? Do you think it doesn't happen all the time?" This comes from one of the others. There is now a small crowd around her; over half of those who earlier had been so eager to get to know her now look at her with disdainfully disapproving expressions, and some downright hostile. Muttered phrases fill her ears: "Thinks she's so hard," "Making it worse for us," "Some kind of hero." Jackie's eyes sting and, though determined not to cry, she feels like bolting out of there.

"I really, honestly hadn't thought of it like that. I'm sorry."

Jude is back with the drinks. "Come on you lot, leave her alone. How was she to know we don't fight back? Here, love." She hands Jackie a bottle of expensive-looking beer and stands next to her against the crowd.

"What an entrance, eh?" Jude smiles when they have dispersed. "They won't forget you in a hurry!"

Jack isn't sure whether she means the skinheads or the lesbians, but isn't about to pursue the matter further. She swigs the beer in silence, forgetting to thank Jude for buying it. In fact, she realises later that she hasn't bought herself a drink all night. Jude watches her contemplatively for a while and then starts up a shouted conversation.

"So, what's Heidi think about you coming out with us?"

"Haven't told her."

Jude laughs. "You and her...?"

"Don't want to talk about it."

"OK." She nods to the dance floor. "Want to dance?"

"Uh," Jack panics. "I don't really dance."

"Oh come on!" Jude takes Jack's beer and puts her own drink down with it. Grabbing Jackie's hand she leads her out into a space among the swaying bodies. Women and men dancing, but not dancing together; rave music and Kylie; sweat and a smell like bleach. Soon Jack is feeling dizzy and breaks away to sit back down again.

"Are you tired?" Jude asks. Jackie looks at her watch and sees it's 11.30 – where has the last hour gone?

"What's that horrible smell?"

"Poppers, amyl nitrate, they sell it behind the bar here." Jack looks bemused. "It's a kind of drug – but legal. You're supposed to sniff it, gives you a high."

"Makes me feel sick, not high."

"You're not supposed to just smell it. You have to stick the bottle right up your nose, quite disgusting really but each to their own poison. I prefer alcohol." Jude raises her bottle and finishes it off in one swig. "Want another?" Jack shakes her head, indicating her half-full drink. "It's mostly the men that do poppers – relaxes your muscles," she finishes, in a stage-whisper.

"Why would that…?"

"Relaxes *all* your muscles. Including your anus." Jack is revolted but Jude shrugs and goes off to the bar. "Like I said: each to their own."

She comes back with another drink for both of them and Jack feels mildly irritated now that she's got two to drink up. "I didn't want one," she has to shout right into Jude's ear due to the sudden increase in volume in the club.

"What's this crap music, anyway? Kylie? Who the hell listens to Kylie these days?" shouts Jack.

"Don't you know she's a gay icon?" asks Jude with an amused expression. "This song is like an *anthem* for the blokes. Look at them." She sweeps her arm towards the dance floor, taking in the bare-chested dancing queens.

"Well, they've got no taste, then," mutters Jack to herself.

"Think you can do better?" asks Jude, still amused. "They

need a good DJ here. If you want a job, me and the management here, we're like this," she crosses her fingers and winks. "Know what I mean? Course, you'd have to show your gratitude if I got you the job."

Jack is not sure what Jude means by this; maybe she'd want a cut of the wages. She smiles and nods, "Yeah, maybe." They continue drinking and watching the dance floor, conversation now impossible. Jack leaves the rest of the old beer that has gone flat and starts on the new. She keeps checking her watch, aware that the night-bus will leave at 1.30 and she has to be on it.

"Got to go somewhere?" shouts Jude eventually.

"Just don't want to miss my bus," shouts Jack.

Jude puts her beer down and turns her face to Jackie. The kiss seems to come out of the blue and Jack is so surprised that she barely responds. "Come on," murmurs Jude. "I know you want it; you've been flirting with me all night."

"No I haven't!" Jack pulls back indignantly and Jude laughs.

"Oh, you're going to let me buy you drinks and then not give me anything in return?" Jack is astounded. "Let's get out of here anyway, go somewhere quiet." Before Jackie can object, Jude grabs her hand and leads her out of the club.

"I live just down here, not far," says Jude, pointing towards a dimly-lit street littered with cans and takeaway detritus.

"I should go…" Jack turns away, realising that she doesn't actually have any idea of how to get back to the bus station; she should have been more observant on the way to the club. At least there aren't any skinheads around now; it's close to midnight and that in-between time when pubs are closed but clubs haven't yet kicked out.

Jude is walking on, pulling Jack's arm, and she allows herself to be led. "Here it is, told you it wasn't far." Jack looks down the steps at the basement flat and knows with a sick feeling that she won't be able to say no to whatever is going to happen in there. Jude pulls out a key and sways slightly at the door as she inserts it into the lock. Jack stares at her: she has drunk a lot of beer but hasn't shown any sign of being intoxicated up until this moment. She wrenches the door open and Jack is pushed roughly in.

The first thing she sees is a single bare light bulb dangling from the ceiling, glaring brightly as Jude switches it on. Then she looks around and sees a very basic bedsit, much lower down the scale of 'cool' than Heidi's flat. Jude shuts the door behind them and steps over the stuff on the floor.

"You like it?" Jude turns to Jack expectantly.

"Yeah. It's pretty cool," says Jack.

Jude shrugs. "Not much, I know. I'm moving out soon, though. So if you're looking for somewhere in town I could put in a good word for you with the landlord. You'd have to show your..."

"...gratitude," Jack finishes the sentence for her, beginning to understand now what this means.

Jude leans down the side of the bed, pulling something from out of the shadows. "Hang on a minute – needs a wash." Jack tries to see what's in Jude's hands but can only make out a kind of leather belt. She watches as Jude opens what at first she had taken for a built-in wardrobe but turns out to be a door leading to a tiny cubicle containing a grimy toilet and sink.

Jude re-appears holding up a lurid peach latex object like a trophy. "There, clean as a whistle." She notices the look on Jack's face and her tone changes to a defensive one, "It was only fluff! Been behind there for ages, you know."

Panicked, Jack's eyes flick to the door, but Jude is standing between it and her. "I don't... I can't... I don't like..."

"Oh, stop being such a silly little tart and put it on." Jude flings the dildo and belt at her. Jack feels relief as she realises that Jude wants her to wear it, not be on the receiving end. Then she feels angry. "Why are you asking me to do this? What about Heidi; I thought you were her friend?"

"Friend? She's my ex. Haven't you worked that out yet?"

Jack looks at the device in her hands, her mind reeling. "Did you? Did Heidi…?"

Jude laughs again. "No. Heidi doesn't like it, does she? She's ashamed of being a lesbian."

"What do you mean, ashamed?"

"She doesn't like to be *seen*; she doesn't like people to *know*. It suits Heidi down to the ground to go out with you."

"Why?"

"Well, let's face it, you look just like a boy."

Jack throws the apparatus onto the bed and marches towards the door, pushing Jude out of the way. But Jude grabs her on the way past and holds on with a surprisingly tight grip. "Look, I'm sorry. I didn't mean it like that. I only want you to put it on so I can see what you look like in it. You can't deny you'll look good. You'll like it, I promise. Hey, you can wear it over your jeans if it makes you feel more comfortable."

Jack looks at her watch and then back over at the bed. "Really? Over my jeans?" She is curious. In answer, Jude kneels down in front of her and reaches for the belt. It is a complex affair and Jack is glad she's being shown how to do it. Straps go between her legs and connect to the belt at the back and a large metal ring at the front holds the thing in place. She feels suddenly very turned on as Jude tightens the buckles on her hips and straightens the dildo. Even through the jeans she can feel the base of it as a solid pressure against her pubic region. Jude holds onto the dildo as she stands up and pushes her body up against Jackie.

"There. What do you think? Feels good, doesn't it?" Jack gasps as the woman gives a practised tug, pulling the straps even tighter. "I said you'd look good in it and you do. You look fabulous. Come on, give us a twirl." She lets go, steps back, and pulls a cigarette packet out of her back pocket.

Self-consciously, Jack steps from side-to-side. The dildo

droops slightly and bobs as she walks. She laughs and stomps up and down, enjoying the effect. It strikes her as a very odd appendage and she doesn't think she would ever be able to wear it without laughing at its ridiculousness. She is reminded of the fantasies she had as a child about growing a penis: unsure of the function of these exotic items, her childish brain had nevertheless recognised the significance of possessing one. Now that she does indeed have one, albeit false, she is glad that it isn't a permanent fixture.

In her reverie, she's forgotten where she is and that Jude is watching her through a cloud of smoke. "Want one?" Jude offers Jack a fag from the packet and, although she can already feel the rawness in her throat she knows she'll regret it in the morning, she takes one: just to see what it feels like to smoke as a man. "So." Jude steps close again to light Jack's fag, their eyes meet.

"So?" asks Jack, blowing smoke away from the woman's face.

"How does it feel?"

"Weird. But... kind of good."

"You like it now," Jude smiles. "You're gonna love it later."

"Er... I'd better go!" Jack tugs ineffectually at the buckles. "My bus..."

"Fuck your bus." Jude moves right up against Jack, who finds her back is pressed against the wall. "You're going to fuck me," she says conversationally. "I know you want to; I can see it in your eyes."

"N-no I don't. I should go, really..."

"OK." Jude steps back again abruptly. "Go on then, little girl. Come back when you're all grown up." She flicks one of the buckles loose and the whole thing drops to the floor around Jack's ankles.

Jack is too stunned to answer and doesn't move for a second. Jude folds one arm across her chest, hand cradling her elbow.

141

She holds her fag up in the other hand and raises her eyebrows expectantly as she takes a drag of the cigarette. Jack steps out of the belt, feeling like she's being dismissed by a teacher.

She finds her way to the bus station more by chance than skill and hangs around for half-an-hour waiting for the bus shivering. There are a few other people there and more turn up just before it is due, but they are mostly couples and groups of girls so she doesn't feel threatened. She starts to contemplate the evening. One thing that predominantly bothers her is that someone as mannish as Jude had wanted to be fucked. She feels that she will never understand women, especially lesbians

***

Jack stays in on Saturday to get some homework done. Going to Heidi's to study is no longer productive as whenever they are together they either have sex or argue, and little else. When she turns up on Sunday afternoon, Heidi is sulking. "I waited up for you Friday night. And last night," she says, attempting to sound light as she puts the kettle on.

"Oh, I had stuff to do."

"What stuff?"

"Oh, things. Homework projects. My keyworker wanted to talk to me and told me to tidy my room. I can't stay long." She's in trouble about staying out late on Friday night, and the home are insisting that she appears for mealtimes and goes to bed at a reasonable time. She daren't refuse as she knows that, only sixteen, they can easily tell her it's time for her to leave. Whereas that would mean she could get her own flat, she's not sure she would be able to continue going to school without any earnings. She thinks of the DJ job at the club but dismisses it again as this will mean 'showing her gratitude' to Jude.

"Did you get it done?"

"What? Oh, mostly." Jack shrugs, realising she is being

evasive but unsure of what else to do.

"Well. You're here now." Heidi hands her a cheap instant coffee and they sit on the bed. Jack feels odd. After Friday she feels removed from Heidi; it has previously just been the two of them and now it seems half of the lesbian scene has become part of their relationship. She has a hundred and one things she wants to talk to Heidi about, to ask her and discuss, but the fact that she's lied means this is impossible.

They watch the TV for a while and barely speak. If Heidi has noticed that Jack is preoccupied then she doesn't say anything, although Jack catches her watching her thoughtfully on a couple of occasions.

"I suppose I'd better go." Jack stands up.

Heidi seems distant when they kiss goodbye and in a way Jack is glad that she hasn't lingered. She doesn't come back until Wednesday after school and finds Heidi even more distant.

"What exactly did you do on Friday, then?" Heidi asks once Jack is inside the flat.

"I told you: stuff. Why this obsession with Friday?"

"Because someone fitting your description was seen outside the club beating up a skinhead. That wouldn't have been you by any chance, would it?"

Jack looks at her, startled. She opens her mouth and closes it again. She considers lying but thinks better of it. Instead she nods and looks down guiltily.

"I'm not totally devoid of friends, you know, whatever Judith might have told you," Heidi says grimly.

"I never thought…"

"And do you mind telling me when you started fucking her?" Heidi's voice rises to almost screaming pitch.

"I didn't!" Jack counters indignantly.

"Oh come off it – you were seen leaving the club together."

"So?" They are standing in the middle of the flat, facing each other. Both have their fists raised instinctively. "Just because I was with her doesn't mean anything happened."

Heidi's voice becomes softer and she drops her hands. "Jack, she's notorious for it. She preys on younger women; she takes pride in converting heterosexuals. She is totally unashamed, gives lesbians a bad name."

Jackie has all sorts of questions related to this last speech and she could calm down and discuss things but she doesn't feel like it. She feels like she wants a row. "Well at least she's proud of who she is," she flings out. Before she can block it, Heidi delivers a stinging slap to her face.

Stunned for a second, Jack goes to hit back but Heidi is prepared and blocks it. She tries to deliver a few blows, but all are blocked by the brown belt. She breathlessly moves in to grab Heidi who rebuffs her. They fight, neither managing to land a blow, for a few minutes, then Jack catches Heidi off-guard and throws her onto the bed. Panting with exertion and anger, Jack climbs on top of Heidi and kisses her roughly. She realises she's more aroused now than she has ever been during any of their gentle lovemaking. Heidi tries to push her off but Jack holds her down, fumbling with the zip of Heidi's jeans. "What the fuck are you doing?" screams the woman, shoving Jack to one side and sitting up.

Jackie calms down immediately and stands. "I'm sorry…"

"Get out."

"I didn't mean…"

"I said get out of my flat." Heidi isn't looking at her but is sitting on the bed staring at the floor. Her tone is menacing enough for Jack to know she's serious.

"Ok," she says, affronted. She slams the door behind her and never goes back.

Walking through the town centre, Jack considers what just happened. She was out of control and this scares her. She knows what she had wanted to do – she had wanted to fuck Heidi, wanted to break through her prissy boundaries, and if the woman hadn't stopped her then she would have gone ahead and done it. She feels agitated. Still turned on and still angry, there is only one place she can think of to go.

The club is closed but still recognisable and Jack easily finds the side street that she had staggered down a few days previously. The house is more difficult to find, but after walking up and down the street for a while, she notices the railings with peeling paint and an excess of litter in the yard. She tiptoes down the steps and knocks gingerly on the door. No answer comes so she knocks again. What if no-one is home; what if there is a whole gang of them in there?

The door opens a crack and then wider, and Jude stands there looking blankly at her visitor. "Well, I'm back," says Jackie, hoping she will remember her.

A smile slowly creeps across Jude's face. "So you are," she says and steps away from the door so Jack can enter.

***

And there you have it, Jim: my formative years. But as Jude didn't try to make a quick buck from me, I won't go into any salacious detail about her. Suffice to say I showed enough gratitude to get the job and the bedsit. You can fill in the blanks yourself. I have very little idea where the dildos came from, though. Jude didn't leave anything under the bed except fluff bunnies and a couple of interesting magazines. All I remember is that I went on a bender one afternoon in Birmingham and woke up the next day with a stinking hangover, a pile of new dildos and a whacking great hole in the motorcycle fund. I think someone slipped some acid into my drink or something because since then I've had flashbacks about a girl with long blonde hair. But that really could be anyone.

Chapter Eight

JACK

Although I arrived at my counselling cupboard a few minutes early for the session, I found John and Larissa waiting expectantly outside. John shot me a look of apology and Lara's smile blasted me with full-on charm.

The door swung open and Lara sauntered in, stationing herself on her usual seat. I was glad that she sat down immediately as she's almost a head taller than me, even in the flat prison shoes she so disdains. Lara habitually wears heels in 'outside' life and I can imagine that she's an imposing figure. In fact, I try not to imagine as often as possible.

"Can you stay close to the window?" I murmured to John as I passed through the doorway, looking back at him to meet his eyes.

"If you need me to," he said with a nod.

I closed the door. "So, Larissa." Lara immediately took a tin of cigarettes from her cleavage and popped one in her mouth, offering the warm open tin to me. She knew I would refuse, as always. I had long ago stopped asking clients to refrain from smoking during session and I even provided ashtrays, but somehow Lara had picked up that cigarettes pained me and seemed to enjoy the power this gave her over her counsellor.

"What is it with that woman?" began Lara petulantly. "She farts around in her own little world without noticing that everyone thinks she's ridiculous. I mean, how many of this lot would want to do Shakespeare for heaven's sake?"

Ignoring the question, I drew a breath and tried to be strong. "Larissa, there's something we need to discuss…"

"Call me Lara won't you, Miss? I've told you, only the screws and scum call me Larissa. You're a friend. Shakespeare is all very well, you know, but some of us would rather do Madonna or Robbie Williams."

"*Larissa*," I repeated, managing to maintain eye-contact and finally grabbing her attention for long enough to get the message across. "The counselling relationship is not a friendship – I would like you to understand this. But please, you don't need to call me 'Miss'. Jackie is fine. Up until this point we've had open-ended sessions without a finish date, but in any counselling relationship there comes a time when it should end. Either naturally or because a decision has been made to do so…"

"What do you mean 'naturally' – you mean if one of us dies?" Lara laughed. My stern expression turned her laugh into a cough and she modified her tone in an attempt to be more serious. "Well, you know, Miss, I won't be here for much longer anyway –" She broke off as she noticed me involuntarily raising my eyebrows. "You knew I was due for release? They told you, didn't they? I'm being let off early for good behaviour – funny that, isn't it?"

My head was swimming as I tried to assimilate this new turn of events into my planned speech. "Yes, yes – of course. You threw me for a moment with talk of death. When was your release date again?" I was really rattled.

"Not long now, Miss. Couple of weeks, Miss." Lara stubbed out her cigarette and grinned cheekily as her accent changed again. She slipped between high class and the gutter so often that anyone listening would be hard pressed to work out which one was put on. Without prior knowledge of her background, an observer might consider Larissa Thomas a 'rags to riches' case rather than a 'riches to rags'. I knew from counselling sessions that there were times when the woman herself was unsure where the real Larissa stood.

Knowing that Lara was leaving the prison soon – a piece of information that Mr G had not passed on – allowed me to breathe again. Letting her go would be easier. I knew I would be copping out by not telling the client why the sessions were ending, and was irritated that I had brought the subject up with Annette, who would expect a full report.

"So, as it seems that this will be our last session, is there anything specific that you'd like to discuss or shall we review?"

"The last one? Oh, that's a shame, Miss. I've really enjoyed our little chats."

"Well, that's not really…"

"You've been a big help, you know. Getting me to see my inner self and all that shit. What do you think of Robbie Williams?"

"Robbie…?"

"Compared to Shakespeare." Lara sang softly: "*I'm a burning effigy of everything I used to be, you're my rock of empathy my dear…*" She checked my reaction to the song then began to slowly unbutton her blouse. "But, you know, it was always something else that I wanted from you. You must have known…"

I glanced quickly at the window. John was reading a book, dammit! I wanted him to rescue me; I wanted someone else to make the decision for me.

Lara's unbuttoning exposed firm breasts held in a lacy purple bra. I gasped as she pushed herself up from the chair. I had half-expected something like this to happen but didn't expect my own reaction to be so drastic. "Holy Shit!" I cried and stumbled for the door, but Lara got there first.

"Don't fight it," Lara murmured, taking my hand and guiding it towards her erect nipple, which poked through the lace of the bra. I snatched my hand away and Lara's face became hard. "If you don't do it, then I'll tell them you did anyway."

I lunged past Lara for the door, swung it open and slammed it behind me. Lara's laugh reverberated inside my head long after it had ceased to vibrate the air around me.

"Fuck! FUCK. *Fucking* fucking fuck."

I paced the few square feet in front of the door, unaware of anyone around me, only of how close I had come to losing it completely.

"Fuckety fuck fuck. Fucking fuck."

"That's a lot of fucking," said John with a smile. I looked up, suddenly embarrassed, and noticed the serious but compassionate look in his eyes. "She got to you too, did she?"

I looked down and held the bridge of my nose between finger and thumb, letting out a laugh that was more relief than humour. "Just a bit, yeah."

"Session over?" I nodded silently, still looking down and sidestepped as John leant past me to reach the door. He knocked softly and waited a beat before opening. I lifted my head to see Lara sitting calmly in the client chair, blouse fully buttoned, just about to light another cigarette.

John held the door open and gestured for Lara to exit with an exaggerated arm movement. She stood up, slipping her cigarette tin into her cleavage, and swept majestically through the doorway. "Some people," she said to no-one in particular, "some people just can't take a joke. Oh well." She looked directly at me and winked. "Catch you later."

I watched as John and Lara walked down the corridor, back to the cells. "Not if I can help it, you won't."

Later in the Education Officer's office, I explained the incident. Of course John had reported that something had gone amiss, but Mr. G wanted to know from the counsellor if it was anything to worry about. I related Lara's behaviour and my reasons for cutting the session short. I nervously rubbed a new patch of eczema between the forefinger and middle finger of my left hand while I waited for his response.

"That *is* interesting," he said, tapping a pen on the desk and not meeting my eye. "I've heard of a number of reports from male prison officers of Larissa performing those kinds of antics, but never from any of the female staff." He coughed and his eyes flicked over me as if he expected an explanation for this.

"Well, it's a – a known phenomenon that... er – that a client can develop feelings for a therapist, but..."

"Yes, yes of course." He waved the pen in a dismissive manner. "And I realise that you would not have had a – ha ha – a *hand* in the proceedings, but we do have to take things seriously under the circumstances. You say she told you that she'd make a complaint if you didn't... er – didn't..."

He seemed more interested in finding out what exactly Lara had wanted me to do than in what actually occurred.

"Yes. Her exact words were: 'if you won't do it, then I'll tell them that you did anyway'." I felt exposed going over this with my superior, very different to addressing personal issues with Annette, but I knew that I had to in case Lara carried out her threat. "We were discussing this being her last counselling session at the time. Perhaps she was trying to hold onto me – this is also a common occurrence."

"Her last? Oh yes, she's being released soon." He squinted out of the window, distracted.

I know, you bastard, I thought, but smiled.

"Well, I won't detain you any longer, Miss Harris. I'll mention it to the governor, and I'm sure he'll tell the POs to keep an eye on her. I'll let you know if she does make a complaint." I was about to rise from the chair when he added, "I take it that you won't be making a complaint yourself? That might..." he lowered his voice an octave, "delay her release."

"No – no, I won't make a complaint against her." I rose and looked questioningly at the Education Officer before leaving. He waved his hand without meeting my eye and I took it as a dismissal.

Outside the office, I wondered whether his coldness towards me was because he'd finally got the message that I didn't want a date, or more because of the nature of the incident. I reflected, not for the first time in my life, that people sometimes behave towards me as if I have the word 'lesbian' tattooed on my forehead.

The remainder of the day's work passed by on autopilot with no more clients, just paperwork and then the drive home. I found myself pulling up outside the stone-fronted terrace almost unaware of how I had arrived there. I looked up to the bedroom window and noticed the curtains were still closed. Quietly, I unlocked the door and crept through the unused front room. I eased the joining door open and found my lover snuggled under a duvet on the sofa, sipping a milky drink and watching children's television.

I laughed at the sight and dropped my bag down next to the sofa. Jimmie yawned and stretched like a cat, blinking at me with tired eyes. "How was your day?"

"So-so. Couldn't you sleep?" Jimmie's hair was stuck up in all directions and I noticed that under the duvet she was wearing the t-shirt and shorts that passed for pyjamas. I ruffled Jimmie's hair lovingly and she put down her drink so that she could hug my hips. I tried to pull away but Jimmie clung on tighter. "Hey, hey. I've got to go for a pee; don't squeeze too hard or you might get more than you bargained for!" Jimmie reluctantly let go and I popped the button on the kettle as I went on through to the toilet. I came back out rubbing cream on my eczema.

Jimmie pulled the duvet over to make room for me as I plonked myself gratefully down on the sofa. "Kids' TV, huh?" I asked, nodding to the television, "that bad, was it?"

"Not really." Jimmie shrugged. "I woke up around one. I could have dropped back off again. But if I'd slept all day then I wouldn't be able to sleep tonight." Jimmie often stayed up late on her nights off, doing college work or just reading, because to sleep all night would be to break the routine. But when she had several days off in a row she could afford to sleep whenever she wanted to. Tomorrow was a college day.

"Three nights off in a row – it feels like a holiday. But I will be working over the weekend again. Sorry. Lucky it fell like this really. If I'd been put down for duty tomorrow then I'd have had to swap with someone. I'm running out of favours."

"Tomorrow… college?" I frowned, trying to remember Jimmie's changeable routine.

"The gig. You know, the gig tomorrow!"

"Oh yeah. The women's festival thing."

Jimmie shook her head and sipped her drink, muttering, "Sometimes wonder if we're on the same planet."

I refrained from responding to this. Instead I leaned over to my bag and drew out the local newspaper I'd bought that morning on the way to Annette's office. After a few minutes of flicking through photographs of smiling sticky faces, lost cat stories and local politics, I arrived at the jobs section.

South Valley Women's Aid require
Female Development Worker – 30hrs
(3yrs funded by National Lottery)
and
Child Outreach Worker – 20hrs
(2yrs funded by Children in Need)
Salary £21,921 (point 31)
(pro-rata for part-time posts)

Closing date: 24th September
Interview date: 10th October

"Got one!" I yelped and threw the paper into Jimmie's lap, causing her to nearly spill her drink.

"Wha...?"

"Women's Aid job – perfect! Better pay and they're usually workers' collectives so no more shitty bosses. You know, Women's Aid jobs used to be like gold dust. *Plus* if it's part-time, you can still go to college."

"Used to be?" Jim squinted at the advert. "I saw this in the *Big Issue* last week. It's a bit far away? Isn't it?"

"Not really – only the same as the shelter but in the opposite direction. South of town, instead of north. Besides, it doesn't give the location, only a PO Box number."

I bounced into the kitchen full of plans. "You could sort out going to college and everything; the fact you're training to be a counsellor would make them want you more. I'd help you with the application of course. Look, the interview date is my birthday. Claire would say that's an omen."

"One problem."

"What?"

"We'd have to get another car. We can't both work day shifts."

"We'd manage," I said. "We'd sort something out. I might even think about getting a motorbike again. That'd be cool; imagine me turning up at Newpark on a bike!"

"I'll think about it." Jimmie tossed the paper to the floor and reached for the remote control.

Stupefied, I nearly spilt scalding water over the edge of my mug. "*Think* about it? What is there to think about? Send off for the forms and apply for the job." I left the tea stewing and looked around at Jim who shifted uncomfortably on the sofa. "What? I thought you didn't like working in the shelter. The people you work with piss you off, the residents piss you off, the pay is crap and the hours are abominable."

She laughed and shrugged. "Put like that it doesn't sound too good!"

"And plus…"

"What?"

I didn't want to get into the safety issues of the shelter. We'd thrashed that out before but I still didn't understand why she continued to put herself in danger. Especially considering her past. "So what's stopping you from applying for this job? Or any other job for that matter?" I carried my mug back through to the lounge.

Jimmie scratched her head doubtfully. "I don't know... Better the devil you know. I suppose. Anyway. I wouldn't be able to do the job. I mean, if they're paying so much. They'll expect a better person than me."

"Don't talk rubbish – better person indeed! Don't sell yourself so short, Jim. Look at you, look at all you've got going for you. They'll snap you up, mark my words." Jimmie harumphed and I blew on my tea for a few moments before continuing: "Or at least look at the other jobs. Come on – you're in a rut. Surely you don't want to work in a night shelter for the rest of your life?"

"You know why I'm there, Jack. It suits me. With college and everything. And at least it's better than factory work."

"For fuck's sake, Jim! You're worth more than this. Anyway, what do you mean it suits you? Does it suit *us*? I mean, do you want to spend half of your week sleeping separately?"

"Let's not get into this now. Please. I'm tired. I don't want a row. Let's just drop it." Jimmie stood up and, stepping over the paper, let the duvet fall to the floor as she went through to the kitchen. She leaned on the counter for a few moments before heading for the bathroom. "I'm going to have a shower."

"At least think about the Women's Aid job," I called after her.

"I already said I'd think about it," snapped Jimmie and shut the door. I waited a moment to see if she'd come out again to apologise, then heard the shower run. I tidied up the lounge, placing the paper carefully on the table and bundled up the duvet to take upstairs.

Once there, I changed out of my work suit and into home uniform: jeans and jumper. Sitting on the bed, I suddenly felt drained of all energy. I got my quilt from under the bed where it falls when we're asleep and held it up to my face. I let myself fall sideways and lay on the pillow on Jimmie's side of the bed, noticing the still-warm sleep smell. The wind picked up outside, rattling the window frames and I could hear the swish of the dreamcatcher that hung from the curtain rail. The door clicked, the house creaked, somewhere a wind-chime tinkled. Everything in my home made a noise in synchrony with the wind outside. Even so, I felt the familiar drift of sleep taking control of my conscious thoughts and I let it happen.

Walking down a long white corridor, I'm in Hillbank again. I'm hungry: it's supposed to be dinnertime but I can't find the dining room. I can't find anyone. Doors everywhere all locked. I can't get out. I can't go anywhere. I've got bare feet – I must be having punishment. I must have tried to run away. I'm supposed to be in my room; if they find me they'll take my clothes. I'm in my pyjamas. People will see me. I need the toilet. I can't go in the toilets in Hillbank: I know what will happen. People are coming. I have to hide. Voices. It's Lara! Lara and Mr G. I must be in Newpark, not Hillbank. But why am I here? Where are my clothes? Lara has seen me – she's laughing. I have to run. Run now. I can't move; my legs won't move. Lara has come for me; she's going to get me. She's going to do it to me in front of Mr G. No! No, I can't! Annette is there – Annette, save me! No, she's frowning, she's disapproving. Why? It's not my fault. Angry. I'm so angry. I shout; I hit; I slash them all; smash them to pieces. They laugh. They're laughing at me. I'm angry. I'm angry. I can't get out. Doors all locked. Smash the doors. Falling now. Falling into the river. It must be Hillbank after all: there's no river at Newpark. The water is warm. I go under. I can't breathe, I'm going to drown. I've escaped and now I'm going to die. But the water is warm, warm, so warm.

There's Jim! She reaches me, she grabs my pyjamas and pulls me out of the water. Jimmie has saved me. I'm so happy, I'm so grateful. Thank you Jim, thank you. But she turns away, sneering and then I know. I hear the sirens. They've come for me. Jimmie is going to hand me over to them – she didn't save me. She hates me. I run away from her, but my pyjamas are heavy with water. I see the police cars coming with their blue lights and sirens. The sirens are so loud, I can't think straight. I shout. Turn them off! Turn off the sirens; I can't hear what you're saying. I'm on top of the car, smashing the blue lights. Trying to turn off the siren but it gets louder and louder…

I woke up thumping the pillow. Still groggy from sleep, I thought I could hear the sirens of the police cars I had been dreaming about. For one manic moment, I thought that the police were outside, coming to arrest me for something I couldn't remember doing. Then I sighed and slumped down into the pillow as I identified the sound of Jimmie playing her trumpet downstairs. Waiting for my heartbeat to calm down, I turned over and rubbed my eyes. I got up from the bed and glanced out of the window. Just checking.

"You didn't do your job very well, did you?" I flicked the dreamcatcher with the back of my hand and it spun in a slow circle. "Supposed to keep the bad dreams out and only let the good ones in. Where are my good dreams, eh?"

As I went downstairs, Jimmie stopped playing and looked up. "Wondered where you'd got to. Sorry if my practising disturbed you. Next-door went out. I took the opportunity…" she broke off and peered at my face. "You OK? You look awful."

"Thanks." I went into the kitchen to put the kettle on. "Feeling a bit rough; maybe I'm coming down with something."

"Oh, love…" Jimmie stood behind me and laid her hand on

my shoulder. I stiffened. I couldn't shake off the image of her sneering expression from my dream.

"I'm ok, just give me a minute. Don't let me stop you practising. Come on – you know I like to watch."

Obediently, Jimmie went back to her music stand and continued to play. I watched for a while. Self-consciously at first Jimmie teased the notes from her instrument. She closed her eyes and was soon lost in the slow whining, almost human sound. One step further into the blues and she would be oblivious to my voyeurism. But I knew that Jimmie never went that one step.

The sight and sound of Jimmie playing her trumpet had always had the same effect on me, since I had first witnessed it that night we met at Claire-O's do. An unquenchable yearning in my heart; an overflowing of something akin to joy; an unmistakable animal need to make love to the woman.

Old jaded dyke that I am, it's still enough to bring tears to my eyes.

JIM

"What?" I held my trumpet. Slightly in front of my chest. My fingers still caressed the valves. My lover stared frankly at me.

"You know what."

I continued to practise. I hoped Jack had noticed a twinkle in my eye. A smile playing around my lips. I wished I could do more. I know she loves me. I know that now more than then. She understood. But it's hard for someone in her position. It took long enough to get this close. I appreciate her need. This is why she went with someone else in the end. Anyone would.

She came back with her cup of tea and watched me some more. She had always been so patient. I finished the practice. I cleaned the trumpet. I put it in the case. She was still watching.

"Want to go to bed?" she asked.

"I'm really tired." I said.

"That's ok," she said. "Just for a cuddle."

I shrugged. Non-committal. I could go to bed – I was certainly tired. Dog-tired. Most of the time. We curled up together. Like The Two Claires' cats. She put her hand over me, from the side. Always from the side. I don't mind her touching me. I can handle that. Just don't. Go. There.

Stroke me. Gently. Kiss my back. Touch my legs. Kiss my ears. I'm fine. I can do that. Touch me. Touch me in those places that he didn't. So touch my back but don't hold my neck. Don't cover my eyes. Run your fingers through my hair but don't put them in my mouth. Stroke my cheek. Taste my tears. Don't hold me down. Don't expect.

After more than twenty years I still get flashbacks. Jackie understood. These things stay with us. Follow us through life. She was never impatient. She never said, "Aren't you over that yet?" Although I think she thought I would be in the end. She believed she could save me. She did save me. She saved my life.

Yes. I was raped. A long, long time ago. He got away. It's a long story. And now I've been raped again. It won't go to trial. People say I'm crying wolf. I say neither of them were wolves. They were both men.

I was thirteen. I was on my way home from school. I was with my friend. Why didn't you run? Why didn't you scream? I did run but he had her. I came back for her. I'd stayed late for a trumpet lesson and was carrying my trumpet case. Why didn't you hit him over the head with it? I was brought up a pacifist – the thought never occurred to me. What were you wearing? My school uniform. How short was the skirt? Not short. I had a long coat. It was winter. It was dark. Why did you take that shortcut through the park? It was late; I wanted to get home. Why didn't you fight back? We were too scared. He was too strong. Why did you stay with him? I don't know. I don't know. Why did you stay after he killed her? I don't know. Leave me alone.

All these questions. Each one pointing the finger at me. It was my fault. Because I didn't fight back. Because I didn't scream for help. Because I chose that route. Because he killed her and not me. Because I was there. Because of how I look.

I didn't ask to be born beautiful.

And now I've been raped again. And now the questions again, and the doubt. Double doubt. Are they trying to say I was having an affair with Frank Little? The thought repulses me. No smoke without fire they say. Lightening doesn't strike twice.

How can there be doubt that I was attacked? I was missing for years. My stay in the psychiatric unit lasted an eternity. There was no doubt then. Now time has gone by. Now all that is left are invisible bruises. The silent scars that follow me through life. There can be doubt. The underlying assumption now: if there is doubt about this time; perhaps last time…? Or the other line of presumption. I am a victim. I attract attack. What exactly does this mean? People who know one thing about me. One thing. Decide who I am. What I am.

I'm no victim. I never was. I survived the attack. I survived the trial. I survived the vilification. I survived the eating disorder. I learned to walk again. I learned to speak again. I get through every day. I work. I have a life.

So that night. Yes, I let her touch me. I touched her. I am a lesbian, after all. That big question. Are you a lesbian because of what happened to you? Yes. No. I don't know. Who knows? Why is it important? Are you a writer because of what happened to you? Are you blonde because of what happened to you? Equally ridiculous questions but still get asked.

Afterwards, she said, "We forgot to have dinner."

"You get yourself something. I'm ok."

"I can whip up a protein shake?"

"That sounds good." I turned over. I looked at the clock. She went downstairs and I heard her in the kitchen. Faffing with the blender. She puts double cream in the shakes. She thinks I don't know. But I always knew. I can taste it.

The thing is, it wasn't about food. It wasn't about eating. It wasn't about feeling full. Or staying thin. The problem was my mouth. The feel of something solid in my mouth. If I could have told them this. Then along comes Jackie. Jack of the liquidised Mars bars. And saves my life.

I owe her my life. The least I can do is tell her story. The time for silence is over.

HARRIS FORCED TO LEAVE HALL

Jackie Harris, the counsellor who killed, was kicked out of her halls-of-residence while at university. She attended Birwood University in the West Midlands during the early-nineties and at this time was well-known among the other students as a sex fiend. A source inside the University has revealed to the *Valley Gazette* that Jackie was forced to leave because of the unwanted advances she made on other students at the all-female hall.

Harris, who killed homeless Frank Little in an unprovoked attack last month, was notorious within the student community as a predatory lesbian. She nevertheless managed to gain her degree in Psychology and go on to obtain work at Newpark Women's Prison in North Valley.

For more stories of Jackie's lesbian lovers while at Birwood, see inside pages 16, 17 & 18.

Chapter Nine – 1989

"I have a full set of unmutated chromosomes, size *and* stamina, and can keep on going all night if required. And this baby – " she flicks the tip, "– won't get you pregnant or give you any horrible diseases."

Apart from changing her patter slightly, Jack hasn't altered much in the last two years, and here in a new space, in a new town and with a new life, she finds plenty of opportunities to practise her technique. She isn't your typical first-year university student on many levels but in some ways she fits right in.

I won't say that she had a *lot* of sex, drugs and rock 'n' roll that first year at Birwood University – certainly less than the other students give her credit for – but she can't recall many lectures. The quilt patch for this year is a smoky haze of parties, breasts, joints and cunts of all shapes and sizes. She doesn't remember any of it being non-consensual but then she doesn't actually remember their faces either.

Having applied to stay in an all-female catered hall, she finds her bedsit-sized room much cleaner and brighter than the basement shit-hole she's lived in for the last year of college. However, the reality of actually *living* with all of these females – i.e. sharing bathroom and breakfast table with them – is more mundane and problematic than the vivid fantasies she's been having all summer. The other two unclosetted lesbians in the three-hundred strong hall of fresh young things get together in the first week. Both have long hair and lipstick and both steer themselves very obviously away from Jack.

Joining the LGB group at the Students' Union, Jackie enjoys being the darling for a few weeks before her newcomer status wears off. She continues to go to meetings, hoping that she might find some like-minded individuals after all. It doesn't take long to realise the distinction between mature students and immature students, and so most of Jackie's conquests are imported into the hall rather than insiders. Still, a few of the girlies will tip-tap to her door after a night on the Mad Dog 20/20. They stay for long enough to scare themselves into straighthood and then ignore her the next day. Sad? Oh no, it is the happiest time of her life.

Towards the end of the second term she becomes somewhat cynical and begins to wonder what doing it more than once with the same person would be like. And so she finds herself thinking, 'here we go again' as she feels thighs tighten over her ears and muffled shrieks become mere whimpers over the sound of *Walk on the Wild Side*.

However, the anonymous encounters are not so anonymous these days as Jack often finds herself bumping into prior lovers in the most obscure places. Birwood is an even smaller town than Maddeston. She's not used to the sensation of seeing a face so recently squeezed against her breasts peering over the frozen food section in Safeways. The night that she sits in the pub for a quiet pint and looks up to see a row of women, all of whom she's slept with, is the night she decides it's time to put a stop to it. She can't get away from the feeling that they're comparing notes.

She doesn't go to pubs very often these days: alcohol has lost its appeal somewhat since her eighteenth birthday. Cannabis, now, is the new material. Jack takes to it as easily as coffee and cigarettes. Most of her nights out are spent in the basement bar of the students' union where the spliffs pass freely around. This is where the LGB gang meet and where Jack has found a precarious niche. One night she announced her new status.

"You celibate?" shrieks Fiona, a shaven-haired mature student who wears check shirts and smokes roll-ups. She's one of the few women in the group that Jack hasn't shagged.

"Don't sound so surprised. I've done it before." Although she doesn't mention that the last time was not deliberately so.

"I know what it is; she's run out of people to shag. That's all."

"Oh, har har." Although that could almost be true.

"Let's see how long she lasts, then."

"Wait till the next blonde bombshell comes along."

"You lot, you've got no faith. And anyway, I don't always go for blondes."

"Oh yes you do!"

"It's like being in a fucking pantomime." She turns her back on them – still laughing – and takes a long drag on the joint she holds, refusing to pass it on. "Nope, not until you apologise."

"W-well, I-I respect your decision anyway." Jackie raises her eyebrows at the depth of expression in Richie's pale blue eyes. He hardly ever speaks and Jack passes the joint over to him without a word. "You – you can't be too careful these days," he takes the joint, puffs quickly and passes it on, then looks up to meet her eyes again. "I mean, you know, what with – with the disease and all."

"Yes," she says quietly, although this hasn't entered her mind. "Yes, I suppose so."

Richie smiles briefly and studies his long, clean fingers. Jackie looks at him afresh. She has always thought him boring as he is so small, meek and quiet and she lost patience with his stutter long ago. But he is the only one out of all of them who doesn't take the piss. He looks up to find her still watching him and she smiles and turns back to the larger group.

"What's going on this weekend then, you lot? Anything good?"

"Oh, now she's not shagging, she'll deign to join us, will she?"

"Shut the fuck up, will you? I wish I'd never said anything."
Jackie petulantly lights a roll-up for herself and leans her head
back to blow smoke at the ceiling. "'Sides which, you probably
wouldn't have noticed anyway. Didn't I come with you last
week to see that Ruby character on the cabaret?" A few titters
from her companions make her look. "What? What did I say?"

But they won't tell her, only a few sidelong glances at Richie
and, "Do you remember what you said about Ruby on the
night?"

"I said a lot about her. Him." She wonders why they are
looking at Richie – maybe Ruby is his boyfriend.

"You said, if she was a woman you'd shag her –"

"– and if she was a man you'd shag him anyway!" At this
they all break into gales of laughter, much more than at the
news of Jackie's celibacy, and draw the attention of the other
people in the bar who stare openly at the screaming queens and
dykes sitting at the corner table. Jack notices that Richie's pale
skin has reddened and he is studiously ignoring the rest of the
group. He blushes easily, his freckles deepening and joining
together. She can see even his scalp reddening through his short,
thinning, light-ginger hair.

She can't believe that they are making such a big deal out of
some stupid comment she made when she was half-cut. "I only
said that because I'd never seen a drag queen as good as her.
The club I used to work in had a regular drag act who looked
like Fanny Craddock on a bad day. I wouldn't shag him if he
was a man, and anyway, I wouldn't shag him now because I'm
celibate ain't I?" She glances at Richie again and a thought
enters her mind, but she dismisses it immediately as the
memory of Ruby's brazen act comes full frontal in her brain,
obliterating all other thoughts and feelings.

The others laugh so hard at their own joke that nothing Jack
can do or say will persuade them to part with it. She can't get
anything out of Richie either. "Just – just leave it," he says, not

meeting her eyes this time as if guilty.

Jack gets up in disgust to go to the toilet. She makes a mental note to find out more about this Ruby.

Jack is not entirely happy with her social circle. The childhood feeling that she doesn't fit in has followed her into adulthood. All the time she spent focusing on 'when I get to university' seems to have been a waste as she now comes to understand that, no matter where she goes, she will always be an outsider. Other non-white students could be homophobic, other karate club members could be homophobic and racist, other gays... well, she really *hates* the word 'gay' and this kind of says it all. Nevertheless, for want of anything better to do, she hangs around with the gay group and finds herself trolling over to the cabaret again with them sooner than expected.

Nudges, winks and knowing nods accompany the announcement of the billing for the night as Ruby's name is mentioned, but Jackie just smiles and sips her diet coke. She has dressed for the occasion – no use in ignoring one's appearance even if not on the pull. The leather trousers squeak and creak as she shifts in her seat, sweat already beginning to trickle over her itchy skin.

There are a few acts to sit through before the notorious Ruby's stint. She takes some time to observe the audience: mostly a combination of slightly effeminate men and butch women that might be reviled in public but inoffensive in a gathering of equals; pockets of muscle boys and lipstick lesbians that had already begun to arise in the late-eighties; and the occasional outlandish costume that must be donned on the premises unless worn by the truly suicidal.

The drumroll, the fireworks and the opening bars of *I Will Survive* precede Ruby's appearance on stage and bring clapping and stamping from the assembled queer folk.

Last time Jack saw the act, Ruby wore a dark wig, vampish lipstick and long black sequined evening dress, looking like

Morticia Adams. This time, she is a blonde, dazzling, Marilyn Monroe. Jack whistles quietly to herself at the sight of those long, shapely legs and bites her lip, reminding herself that this is a man. But what kind of man is it that wears these clothes rejected by feminists as oppressive? His deep voice, perfect for the sultry bluesy songs he sings, washes over her as she sits staring at him moving over the stage. He doesn't camp it up, doesn't make himself ridiculous as other drag artists tend to do; he simply is himself, as an artist, singing. At the end of the opening song he waits for the crowd to cool down. Then he begins the usual between-songs banter.

"You may have noticed tonight a change in costume," (cheers) "which I'm wearing especially for someone I know," (shouts of 'lucky him!') "and to mark this occasion I am going to sing a new song," (cheers, whistles, then calm as the music starts and he whispers) "for Jack."

Startled for a moment, Jackie thinks she had heard her name. But then she shakes herself: there are a million Jacks in the world and this one is surely a man. She grounds herself with a sip of coke and opens her tobacco tin while the crowd whoops at the ambiguous lyrics.

"Running wild; lost control.
Running wild; mighty bold.
Feeling gay, reckless too.
Carefree mind all the time, never blue..."

Jackie laughs to herself at the thought of Marilyn Monroe singing those lyrics, totally unaware of how they might be interpreted years later. Or was she? Ruby finishes the song to wolf whistles and catcalls. Jack looks up and thinks she sees the drag artist glance in her direction, but tells herself she's imagining it – the lights must be so bright that anyone on stage would only see shapes and shadows. She is saying something now about people being cold and lonely and the opening bars of a slower song begin. Ruby wanders through the crowd, stopping at tables to sing directly to people before moving on. Jack thinks she can identify the tune but the lyrics don't mean anything to her. Then when the chorus starts up, she suddenly recognises the song as one her first foster mother had often sung when she was small.

"*Every baby needs a da da daddy, to keep her worry free
Every baby needs a da da daddy, but where's the one for me?*"

Ruby is frighteningly near to Jack's table and, for one awful moment, she thinks she's going to sit on her lap. Instead she leans against the table and smiles at Jack to sing the next line: "*Every baby needs a da da daddy, could my da daddy be you?*" A musical interlude begins and Ruby lingers there, looking at Jack through the false Monroe eyelashes. She moves the microphone away from her mouth and speaks softly, "You still don't know who I am?" Jackie sits bolt upright, but he's already moved on before she has a chance to speak. He's singing again and walking back towards the stage. He hasn't stuttered, but she has recognised the voice as Richie's.

***

Blagging her way backstage is easier than she'd expected. She has a suspicion that the smiling, nodding stagehands are expecting her. They eye her leather jacket knowingly as she squeezes her way through the thin corridors at the back of the club. The dressing room (actually a toilet with a paper star blue-tacked over the 'ladies' sign) is along a corridor and upstairs. Breathless, Jack knocks hesitantly. "Come!" calls an amused voice. She opens the door and is greeted by a smell of sweat and hairspray. He is still wearing the costume. Close up she can see that he is shiny with sweat and somewhat dishevelled but very riled up and excited. "Well?" he squeaks, "did you like it?"

"Yes," she manages. "What… why did you…?"

"Oh, not just for you, darling," he turns away as he speaks, looking into the mirror. A length of wood is balanced over the sink in front of him and holds pots and bottles of cosmetics, along with a quart bottle of vodka. He picks this latter up and takes a swig. "I needed to change my act; it gets stale after a while. Always good to keep ahead, you know. And you gave me the idea, talking about blondes."

"I don't think *I* talked about blondes."

"But you liked it, didn't you?" He stands up to face her.

"Well, yes," she admits, stepping back slightly.

His eyes take on a knowing look. "Oh, you're thinking about me being a man, aren't you?" She looks down, ashamed by his sadness. "I'm going to have the operation, saving up, and then soon you won't have to think about it."

Jack looks around the room, trying to think of some way of changing the subject. Talk of sex changes makes her uncomfortable. "What happened to your stutter?"

He waves his hand. "It comes and goes. On stage it's never a problem." He then turns back to the mirror and pulls the wig off. Jack stares at him. Without the hair, he looks like Richie again, just like Richie in makeup. She feels sorry for him because he looks so sad, gazing at himself in the mirror. He raises his voice to a false cheeriness and says, "Well, better get this shit off." As he is wiping his face, he seems to notice Jack again as she leans against the sink next to his makeshift dressing table. "Do *you* ever wear any makeup?"

In answer, Jack picks up black eyeliner, scrawling under her eyes and giving herself Cleopatra points. She smiles at him and he smiles back. Then she uses the eyeliner to paint on a small moustache and pouts at herself in the mirror. When she turns back to him, he's staring in awe. "Fucking hell, that's it!" he shrieks.

Taken aback, she drops the pencil. "What?"

"You could do it; I think you really could!"

"Do what?"

"Be a drag act. Come up on stage with me and be a drag king."

She thinks she's misheard him. "A dragging? What's that?"

He sighs. "A drag *king*, you idiot. My, we really are provincial here, aren't we? Like a drag queen? But a woman who dresses as a man."

"I can't sing…" she begins, panicking.

"Neither could I; you can learn how. Loads of drag queens mime along to songs anyway. It's the image that counts." He is looking her up and down appraisingly. "You wouldn't have to change much about the way you dress, but maybe keep some clothes just for the stage? And you'd have to wear… *it* of course. Or at least have a convincing bulge."

"It?"

"It, you know, your strap-on. Don't look so shocked, everyone knows."

"Everyone?" she says hoarsely. "Fuck."

"You're the talk of the town," he laughs and finishes wiping his face.

"Fuck, shit. Shit. Fuck. *Fuck*."

"Now now, less of the Anglo-Saxon. Would you unzip me?" He turns his back to her and braces himself against the wall. Jack's hands hover for a moment, as she looks at his tight behind, and then she sighs and takes hold of the zip. As she drags it down, the folds of cloth open out and she sees his milky white skin. Again she feels an erotic surge and bites her tongue. *He's a man; he's a man.* But what she wants to do more than anything is to put her hands around his waist and pull him roughly towards her.

The zip pulls right down to his buttock crease and she is surprised to notice that he wears plain old M&S Y-fronts underneath the ultra-feminine attire. She turns away as he slips out of the dress and when she turns back he's wearing a Harley Davidson t-shirt and doing up the flies on his jeans. "There." He holds out his arms in an open gesture. "Better?" She shakes her head, smiling. He smoothes back his hair and takes her arm. "Fancy a t-takeaway?"

***

Jackie rehearses a couple of times with Richie but her heart isn't in it, and he becomes exasperated. "If you're not going to bloody concentrate," he says, tossing his head so the wig twists comically, "then you may as well piss off." She shrugs and shuffles over to where she dumped her helmet and coat earlier. He seems to be a lot more moody lately and Jack wonders if it has anything to do with the hormones; she wouldn't fancy a double dose of PMT herself.

"Listen," she begins, when she finds him petulantly smoking in the ladies. "I'd like to try it, really, but I've got the end of year exams coming up and… well, I can't say I've done much work all year so I ought to be revising or they'll kick me out."

"Oh poor you," he sniffs, and takes a long drag of his fag.

"I'm sorry. I know it's difficult for you." He has told her that his being at university is to do with his gender reassignment therapy. Part of the rules for transsexuals being granted an operation is that they have to hold down a job or some kind of position within the community for three-years. It makes sense to study a three-year course rather than chance one's luck in the job market. Jack thinks that the idea of 'rules' is barbaric. How many 'real' men or women don't hold down a job or valuable position in the community?

He is leaning against a sink and looking down at the tiles; she is standing in front of him trying not to look at her reflection in the mirror. He reaches under his long skirt and produces from a dubious source a packet of Consulates. She blinks a couple of times but takes the proffered filter-tipped cigarette without comment. He laughs as he flicks his lighter. "It's OK, I've got a secret pocket. These dresses, you know, I don't know how you women do it."

"Me, women? Well, *I* don't. I don't think I've ever worn a dress like that, nor do I want to. You know, you're more feminine than most of the women I've ever met."

He bows his head to her in mock-deference. "Thank you."

"No, I mean it. You should pass your gender test with flying colours." He looks tense and doesn't comment so she quickly goes on. "I've often wondered myself where they put their hairspray bottles; I mean those clutch bags can't hold much, can they?" He looks amused and is suppressing a laugh. "Maybe they stick it up their... well, that would explain the walk, wouldn't it? And I always thought it was the high heels." She makes an attempt at slinking up and down in front of the sinks, impersonating the worst kind of girlie thing she can imagine. But it's virtually impossible in her jeans and combat boots, and she just looks like a duck with a sore arse. She turns around to see Richie gripping his stomach and pressing his lips tightly together, a bubble of air trapped behind them. Suddenly the dam bursts and he dissolves into fits of giggles. She smiles; she's got to him at last.

When he's recovered, he looks up at her. "You, my dear," he points with his fag and a flake of ash falls. "You should be a bloody comedian." He leans forward and kisses her on the forehead. Then he leans back again so she can see from her reflection that he's left a maroon smudge. He looks at her appraisingly for a moment and then turns away. "Go on, get back to your fucking revision." He waves his hand dismissively. "And come back when the exams are over."

***

Riding the bike is one of the rare occasions Jack feels totally free. Like she is flying – a strange dichotomy of power and vulnerability, but best of all: alone. In a catered hall there are few chances to be totally alone. Even in bed in the middle of the night there is still an oppressive sense of other beings on every side. The night sounds of sex, arguments, toilet flushes; the invisible hormonal gasses leeching into the room to overpower the unsuspecting. During the exams, Jack spends time in halls studying, either in her room or in the small library, and when she isn't studying she's either taking an exam or eating, sleeping or trying to relax. It isn't surprising that after a week something snaps and she finds herself sneaking out of the halls at midnight to ride her bike.

She doesn't know where she's going and she doesn't care. Out of the town she snakes the back lanes, gets lost, finds her way again and comes back into town. She passes the nightclub where she first saw Ruby; her head turns but she doesn't stop. Back in halls she feels refreshed and invigorated and heads for the showers. It is 1am and very few people are around. She walks back to her room wet and naked, carrying her clothes and bike gear. When she gets to the room, she finds the door ajar. Confused, Jack pushes the door open and steps inside. What confronts her makes her catch her breath. She drops the gear and switches on the light so that she can see properly.

The room is trashed. Every single item has been pulled out, ripped, stamped on or some other violation done to it. It's normally in a mess but this is total frenzied chaos. And just in case she might not have noticed, someone has left her a message to reinforce their feelings. Scrawled across the wall in two-foot high neon spray paint lettering are the words 'lezzi cunt suker'. Jack sighs. This is the end of a long campaign. They have not managed to oust her throughout the whole year and so do this in the last week of her stay here.

More disappointed than angry, she still manages to raise a smile as she feels superior to the student who can't spell. She finds a towel, luckily reasonably clean, and dries herself. Then she hunts around for some clothes. She settles on the leathers as the only undamaged items of wear. It's obvious that she must report this now to the Wardens. She can't get into bed anyway as it's covered in tomato chilli sauce – her own tomato chilli sauce she notices, as the empty bottle is among the debris on the floor.

The essay container is on its side, contents strewn across the room. It's possible that the person who did this is actually an essay thief, a fellow student who's jealous of Jack's ability and wanted to steal her hard work, destroying the room at the same time. She sifts through the papers and finds that the model answers are damaged but mostly present. So, it was simply a trashing and not a burglary.

Another thought occurs to her and she scrambles under the bed, reaching for her locked box. It's still there and the lock is untouched, but she opens it anyway. There are her most treasured possessions, the leather of the harness starting to crack from exposure to moisture and the bright blue dildo shining as ever. The plastic wallet containing The Note is also intact. She locks the box again and crams it into the bottom of a sports bag. She pulls her quilt out from under the pillow, wipes off a smear of chilli sauce and wraps it tight before adding it to the bag along with a variety of other items salvaged from the wreckage. She hoists the bag on her shoulder and strolls off down the corridor. She leaves the essays as they are. She will sort them out in the morning. Whoever has done this is quite possibly still around, watching for her reaction. For her own integrity she has to be seen to be amused. It's not the first time she's moved on in a hurry and left the majority of her possessions behind. It will not be the last.

She knocks on the Assistant Warden's door and waits. No point disturbing Warden Wilson tonight; he'll only be grouchy. She knocks again. It occurs to Jack that she has spent a fair proportion of her formative years knocking on doors and waiting for something to happen. She yawns just as the door is opened and the dishevelled young English tutor catches her with her mouth fully open: not a pleasant sight in the early hours. Alicia looks at her expectantly for a moment and Jack ceases yawning and coughs. "Er, sorry to disturb you, but someone's broken into my room and I can't stay there – I wondered if there were any spare rooms or something and then I can sort it out in the morning."

Alicia blinks at her for a second as if she hasn't understood what Jackie is saying. Maybe she doesn't sound panicked enough; maybe it doesn't sound like an emergency. "I said that someone's broken into my room. My whole room is trashed and I've got nowhere to sleep."

"Someone broke into your room?" squeaks the tutor. "Well, who?"

"If I knew that then I might tell you, or I might just go round to their room and trash it back," Jack says testily. "You can come and see it if you want."

Alicia looks back into her flat and then at Jack again. She picks up her keys and comes out of the room, wrapping a dressing gown tightly around herself and running a hand through her hair. "Come on then."

Jack sighs. She had thought that maybe the tutor would be happy to leave it till the morning but, no, this is going to be another lengthy questioning session. They arrive at Jackie's room, the door still ajar as it won't shut properly. Alicia looks at the broken lock with something akin to shock. "This kind of thing doesn't happen here," she says.

"Oh really?" asks Jack. "Well, it looks like it does now."

Alicia glances around the room and then back at Jackie. "Is it usually…?"

"I'm not the tidiest of people, but I keep my notes in order," Jack nods towards the essay box, "and the spilled sauce is new."

"Is anything missing?"

"Nope, not that I can tell. But a lot of stuff is ruined; it'll have to be replaced."

"Are you insured?"

"Are you joking?"

"Well… do you want to call the police?"

"Do you think that'll do any good?"

Alicia shrugs and then looks at the wall, noticing for the first time the lurid writing. Jack follows her gaze and then looks back at her, noticing Alicia's cheeks reddening. "Sorry you had to see that. Maybe now you'll accept that these aren't just random acts that could happen to anyone. I'm being targeted."

"Yes. I can see that. I'm sorry."

"Don't be sorry, just help me."

"Well," she turns to leave the room, stepping gingerly over the crushed glass and litter, "we ought to call Mr. Wilson. We can sort out the lock tomorrow, but I'll find you a bed for tonight. Is there anything you need to take from this room?"

"It's all here," Jack gestures to her bag. They leave Jack's room and she follows Alicia in silence down the corridor and onto another floor.

"This one is empty," says the tutor, selecting a master key from her huge bunch. She opens the door and Jack walks in, plonking her bag on the bed. She looks around the bare room. In size and layout it is exactly the same as the one she's just left. Alicia hovers in the doorway and Jack turns to thank her but she waves her hand dismissively. "Come and see me tomorrow after breakfast and we'll sort out your room."

"I've got an exam tomorrow morning."

"Oh, better make it before breakfast then." And she shuts the door.

"Fine," says Jack and slumps on the bed.

She lies on her back and looks at the ceiling. Then looks around the room. A thought arises. At least this is the ideal way to have a clear-out before the end of term.

***

"Well, at least they didn't try to make you pay for the damage," says Fiona when Jack recounts the events the following Friday in the basement bar.

"They couldn't do that, could they?" asks Jackie, shocked.

"A private landlord would," says Fiona. "Happened to a couple I knew back home. Had a brick put through their window and stuff written on their door, all sorts. Came time to move out and the landlord withheld their deposit."

"Landlords always withhold d-deposits from students; they're n-notorious for it," Richie says, blowing smoke sideways and patting Jack on the knee. "Never mind d-darling, at least you don't have to clean your room now!"

Fiona looks hurt. "These weren't students. They were a respectable gay couple." This is greeted by gales of laughter from the others and Fiona turns away in a huff. Richie ignores her.

"When are you moving out, anyway?"

"Oh, a couple of days. I've got a room set up over summer in the mixed hall. Stupid really that I can't just stay in the room I've got till next term. I feel like a nomad."

"You know you can always come and s-stay with me," says Richie. "If you can't face going back there."

"Thanks."

"So, you want to go shopping tomorrow?"

"What do you mean?"

"Well, I don't expect you've got many clothes left?"

Jack looks at him, frowning slightly.

"How did I know? Hey, it's happened to the b-best of us."

***

That night, Jack turns up on Richie's doorstep with a bloody mouth and grazed knuckles.

"Don't ask me, I don't want to talk about it," she says and dumps her bag in the hallway. "I hope that was a serious offer, about me staying?"

"Is that all that's left?" He looks at the bag in amazement.

"No, I've left a load of stuff there. I'll move it properly the day after tomorrow."

"Need any help with it?" Jack shakes her head and he continues. "Look, I'll put the kettle on and then we can clean up your face."

Jack is sitting on the toilet with the lid down and Richie is leaning over her, dabbing the side of her mouth with damp cotton-wool. "I can do this myself, you know," she says defensively.

"What you need, darling, is some TLC." Richie stops dabbing and looks her in the eye. "Look at you, got blood on your face…"

"Yeah, I know. I'm a big disgrace…"

"Waving your banner all over the place," Richie finishes and they both laugh. Their faces close, Jack almost feels as if she's going to kiss Richie. Instead she stands up and checks her face in the mirror.

"You sure you're OK for me to stay here?"

"As long as you want," he says.

***

Shopping with Richie is more fun that she thought it would be. Generally when she needs new clothes, she finds a clothes shop, picks up a few shirts or trousers, buys them and leaves. Maybe half-an-hour tops. While she shops like a man, Richie shops like a woman.

"Oooh, look at this! Isn't that gorgeous? What do you think? In the blue or purple? Oh but *this*, now this would go well with…" and so on until Jack's feet are sore and her head is spinning. After two hours he still hasn't managed to buy anything more than a pair of fluffy mules, whereas she's been carrying around the same bag of cheap jeans and shirts all morning. And yes, it's fun to be out with Richie, to be laughing and joking, to watch him being so publicly outrageous, and to witness the public being outraged.

Richie promised to buy her lunch, which is a veggie burger in a newly established burger bar. And halfway through, he drops his bombshell. "I thought I'd ask you to m-move in with me. Permanently I mean."

Jack chokes on her burger and he passes her the large carton of diet cola. "I told you, I've got it all set-up. I'm moving tomorrow – I get housing benefit and everything."

He seems disappointed. "Well, I've got to find a co-tenant, that's all. And I j-just thought… you know."

"Sorry." She bites into her burger again and hopes that this is an end to it.

They finish the meal in silence. When it's time to go, he turns to Jack and says, "Well, I hope I'll see you over the s-summer?"

"Yes, I'll visit. Anyway, I thought you were going to help me rehearse for my big performance?"

He brightens. "You mean you still want t-to?"

"I thought I'd give it a bash. No singing though." She turns to go.

He laughs and waves her off. "Come round to the club tomorrow after you've moved!"

As Jack had rightly pointed out, so little is salvageable that she manages it without even having to call a taxi. She simply borrows a supermarket trolley and pushes her few bags and boxes from one hall to the other. She is still annoyed that she has to move, but understands the reason. Very few students decide to stay over summer.

Most of the students go home once their exams are over, only the hardy few stick it out till the very last party, and they are now in trains, buses and parents' cars nursing hangovers and contemplating whatever summer job they have lined up. Those students that don't have homes or don't want to go to them, a mix of mature and overseas students along with a few like Jack, are currently moving into the one hall that continues to function over the summer, or they already have private accommodation.

The room in a self-catering hall is larger by comparison, and now Jack will have to learn to cook for herself again. She peruses the kitchen, noticing the lockable cupboards and large gas stoves. It is quite filthy but better than some she's seen. The view is more pleasant than from the previous hall: instead of looking out over a car park and main road, she can see woods and the side of a hill. "Well, here we are again," she says to herself out loud. "Just as soon as you get used to one place, it's move along please."

Later, she wanders over to the club and finds Ruby in mid-rehearsal. Instead of interrupting, she sits at the empty bar and watches, grinning. When the rehearsal is over she claps and Ruby makes extravagant bows.

"Thank you darling," says Richie, pulling off the wig and tossing it onto his bag in the corner of the stage. "Fancy a coffee?"

Over fags and a milky coffee in a greasy spoon opposite the club, Jack recounts how she pushed the trolley through the small town centre, receiving stares from the non-student population. "I felt like a bag lady!"

"Isn't that just what you are?"

"*You're* an old bag, not me!" She digs him in the ribs.

"I wish, darling. I fucking wish. You know what that refers to, don't you?"

"What?"

"Bag – as in, old bag for an old woman."

"No, never thought about it."

"It means a womb; it's the one thing I'll never have no matter how perfect the outward appearance."

She is silent for a moment, thinking this through. "Well, do you *want* a womb? I mean, do you want periods? You must be mad." He cocks his head and looks at her wryly. "Oh, I didn't mean…"

"That's ok. My psychiatrist says I'm perfectly sane." They laugh.

"What I meant was –why would you want a womb? Do you want children, and to be pregnant and all of that?"

"Not really, no. But it's the one thing that women can do that men can't. It's why there has been so much persecution of women down the ages. You've heard of the theory of hysteria? The wandering womb?"

Jack turns her laugh into a cough. "I'm sorry, it's just I find it ironic, you know, a man teaching me about feminism."

Richie looks pained. "Could you do me a favour and not refer to me as a m-man?"

"Oh, sorry. Erm…"

Jack sips her coffee and looks around the café for a moment. It's half-empty. She will usually go to the Students' Union where a coffee is half the price but now that term is over the SU closes early and it is already late-afternoon. She looks out onto the street at the shoppers hurrying home and realises how different it looks without the students. Students make up around twenty per cent of the Birwood populous and during term time it takes on a vibrant, almost cosmopolitan feel, but now it seems like an ordinary small town centre.

"Anyway, what I was s-saying was that because I don't have all the female bits I will never be considered as fully female."

"Right."

"I will always legally, biologically, be male. For instance, if I was sent to prison, I'd go to a male prison, even if I'd been living as a woman for twenty years."

"God!"

"So you see, a simple courtesy like referring to me as 'she' might make all the difference."

"Yes, I do see. Sorry. But if I'm going to do that, then I'll have to stop calling you 'Richie'. The name doesn't quite go with a feminine you. Have you decided on a new name for your rebirth? Surely not Ruby?"

Richie smiles. "No, not Ruby. Ruby will always be a stage persona. I was thinking of Rachel."

"That sounds OK. Hello Rachel. Pleased to meet you." *Jack and Rachel* she thinks, and then puts the thought out of her head.

"Pleased to meet you too, Jack. Of course you wouldn't have the same problem, *Jack*."

"What?"

"Well, have you never wanted to change sex?"

"No!"

"Not even when you were small?"

"Actually, I used to think that I was going to grow a penis," Jack admits with a grin. "I was a bit annoyed when I didn't. But that was before I knew that women could be, well, could be free like men."

"I think that women are freer than men."

"What do you mean? Men have much more than women, more power, more opportunities. Boys in school…"

"Oh yes, boys in school. And in some countries women are still very oppressed. But I think in our society women have much more freedom to express themselves than men – they are emotionally free. The only emotion available to men is anger."

"Yes, you're right on that point," she concedes. "But I never had penis envy, not really. I prefer the flexibility of a removable version."

"Wish it was that fucking easy for me!" They laugh. "So, why do you do it?" Jack looks at Rachel, frowning as she doesn't follow the question. "I mean, dressing as a man. Is it a game for you?"

She is taken aback slightly. "I don't dress as a man. I mean, yes, I wear men's clothes but it's not the same. I do it because that's how I'm comfortable." Rachel raises an eyebrow and Jackie feels hot, continuing defensively, "Loads of women wear men's clothes, loads of heterosexual women. Women have been wearing trousers for years."

Rachel sips her coffee and smiles. "Precisely my p-point."

"What point?" She feels suspicious of Rachel now, like she is goading her to get angry and make a mistake.

Rachel waves a hand, and reaches for another Consulate. "What I'm always saying. Women dressing as men is not considered to be obscene, offensive, or absurd. If you want to be a drag king, then you'll need to go really over the fucking top – wear a suit or uniform and make sure you have a huge packet. Personally, I don't see why there should be a distinction between *men's* and *women's* clothes. We should wear what is practical or comfortable for our purpose."

"Umm, when is a femmy hanky-sized dress ever practical?" She opens her tobacco tin and inspects the small pack of Rizlas.

"Here, have one of mine. It depends what your purpose is. If your purpose is to seduce then it is exceedingly good at its job."

"So you're saying that women wear clothes like that for other people's benefit? That's one step away from saying they ask to be raped. Thanks." She cups her hands over the lighter as Rachel touches it to the end of the menthol cigarette.

"I said they were designed to seduce, to be attractive – didn't say who should be attracted to them. I think that women wear sexy clothes for themselves. That's why I do it, anyway."

"For themselves? You mean to make themselves feel sexy?"

"Yes. It makes sense, doesn't it? If you feel sexy yourself, then people are going to find you more attractive, don't you think?"

"Yes, I suppose so. Although personally, I'd feel silly

wearing all that get up, not sexy at all. But someone might see me in it and think that I look sexy." She laughs. "There's no accounting for taste."

"How do you feel when you're wearing your thing? What do you call it, by the way? I mean, have you given it a name?"

Jack looks down at the small foil ashtray, now full of their cigarette stubs, annoyed to feel a blush rising. She has noticed that the rest of the café has gradually become silent as if they are all waiting for her answer.

"Have you finished your coffee? Shall we go?" Rachel gulps down the last dregs and stands up. Jack looks around for a moment, unsure where to go now that most of the student haunts will be deserted. Then she brightens, remembering. "Want to see my new room, then?"

"I do feel very sexy when I'm wearing it," she admits as they walk. "But I only ever wear it when I'm having sex, so I think it's association." She stops walking suddenly, remembering Jude. "The first time I wore it I felt a bit silly."

"Do you wear it for yourself or for other people?" Rachel stops too and looks at her.

"Umm." Jack continues walking now as she thinks. "Other people I suppose, but *I* like it too."

"You never wear it when you're on your own?"

"No, why would I?"

"Just a thought."

Jack unlocks her door and leads the way in. She pulls out a chair and finds an ashtray on the floor, handing it to Rachel as they sit down on the edge of the bed.

Rachel looks around. "It looks fine to me. Very clean."

Jack shrugs. "Not got much to get dirty."

"Nothing like a Nazi attack to get rid of the shit from your life. How are you, by the way? Have you recovered?"

"Recovered from what? They didn't hurt *me*. If I'd been there, I know who would have come off worse."

"Oh yes, Jack the hero. No need to get defensive. Did they take anything important?" Rachel looks around the room expectantly.

"If you want to see it, just ask."

"Well, I'd be interested to see…"

She leans down and reaches under the bed for the box. She pauses. "Do you know, this is the first time I've shown it to anyone that I'm not going to shag." Rachel raises her eyebrows and Jack quickly opens the box without further comment.

She whistles when she sees the size of it. "Wow, that's a beauty."

"Yeah, that's the good thing about it being detachable, you see. I can be any size I want." She reaches under the harness and pulls out another two dildos. "It's not always a matter of the bigger the better. I've even got one of these." She drops the dildos and holds up a butt plug. "Never used it though, but you know, just in case."

Rachel looks impressed. "Did you use to work in a sex shop or something?"

Jackie laughs. "I've lived a long life for my nineteen years."

"So it seems. What's that?" Rachel points to the plastic wallet.

"Oh, nothing." Jack arranges them all back into the box and locks it again. "Coffee?" she says as she leans down to replace the box under the bed.

"Mmm, yeah," says Rachel thoughtfully. "So you're not going to put it on for me?"

"Maybe another time."

"Well, try wearing it by yourself sometimes. I mean, you've got to get used to walking around in it if you're going to wear it on stage."

"You really think I should wear it on stage?"

Rachel shrugs. "Don't see why not. Wear it under your jeans and then maybe get it out right at the end of the act. We'll work on that. You never said what you call it, surely you have a name for it, not just 'it'?"

"What do you mean, a name?"

"Well, most men have a name for their dicks, didn't you know?"

"No, what kind of name – like 'Tiger' or 'Love Muscle'?"

"Well the most common one is, for instance, if his name is John then it's Big John. Or 'hello, I'm Dave and this is Big Dave.'"

"Really?" Jackie laughs. "Not Little John and Little Dave."

"No, not little," Rachel laughs, "never little."

"So, what do you call yours?"

"The bane of my life," she laughs again. "Actually I did have a name for it once, when I was little."

"What was that?"

"Ruby."

"Ah," says Jack after a while.

"But actually, I didn't start calling myself Ruby until I heard Marc Almond's *Ruby Red*. Have you heard that song?"

"Think so. You know when you, er – after you've had the change – are you still going to be Ruby on the stage?"

"Yes. That'll always be a stage name. What do you think of Rachel? Really. I mean, not too biblical?"

"It's nice." *Jack and Rachel* she thinks again, *Rachel and Jack*, and blushes.

"Yes, it would be easier to keep the initial letter the same... what's wrong?"

"Nothing. Just names – I can't think of any really. I mean, I just call them 'the big one' or 'the medium blue one' or whatever."

"Well how about, 'hello I'm Jack and this is Big Jack'." Jackie laughs and can't answer. "It's meant to be funny – you know, the idea of drag is that it's a send-up of the opposite sex."

"But what about you? I mean, it's not really your opposite

sex, is it?"

"Ah, yes, now you've hit the nail on the fucking head. That's when it becomes more complex. And when I've had the change, maybe I'll be a drag king. It's a real gender fuck."

"So we're settled on Big Jack, then are we? I'll have to practise saying that without laughing."

"Yeah, practise it in front of a mirror. I can't believe you haven't done that already. Anyway, I'd better go and get myself sorted for tonight's performance."

"Did you find a co-tenant, by the way?"

"Yes, a mature student. Female. Psychology student. But you can't have everything."

"Indeed you can't; what's her name?"

"Melanie."

Jack thinks for a moment and then says, "Didn't know there were any Melanies in the class."

"No, she's a new first year. Come early to settle in. She looks like she could be quite intense."

"Tongues in the tuna or lonely for polony?"

"It's hard to tell with these feminist types darling, but she doesn't strike me as someone who hankers after pussy."

Jack lets the corners of her mouth droop. "Oh well. As you say, you can't have everything."

HARRIS MISTAKEN FOR MAN

Jackie Harris, the prison counsellor who killed a homeless man in North Valley, used to dress as a man herself, *Valley Gazette* can reveal today. She got kicks out of pretending to be male and seeing if anyone would notice. Sources reveal that she was taken to Birwood Hospital in 1990, aged twenty, after a motorcycle accident. During her stay she pretended to be a man until her true gender was discovered by nurses.

What kind of behaviour is this in a sane person? Why, we ask again, was this woman employed in a responsible position in the prison service? Every day more stories are being revealed about Harris and none of these stories show her in a good light.

Chapter Ten – 1990

"Hi, I'm Jack and this is Big Jack." She holds the bulge and thrusts her hips forward as she has seen men doing, the fag dangling from her mouth. Then she takes the fag out, runs her other hand through her hair and adjusts her stance. "Hi, I'm Jack and this is *Big* [thrust] Jack." She places the cigarette on the edge of the ashtray and reaches into her jeans to shift Big Jack over a tad. When she wears it, it feels how she imagines an erection would. But if she keeps it on for too long then it becomes uncomfortable. She doesn't know how anyone manages to wear one out to a club, and suspects that they never actually do in reality.

She looks back in the mirror and grins. Rachel is right: wearing it makes her feel confident, sort of cocky, and it changes the way she walks, the way she stands and everything. She's never really noticed before because she's always been tied up (so to speak) with the sexual situation, but it's true – in order to really know how she looks and feels, she needs to wear it on her own. She leers at herself. "Do you want to play with me?" she asks her reflection.

Slowly, she unzips the flies, imagining the roar of the crowd, and Big Jack pops out. She rings her fingers around it and strokes them up and down. Gently at first she enjoys how it looks, but then she starts to grip it tightly as she feels the base press against her clitoris and the familiar urgency takes over. She braces her hand against the wall and looks down at her feet

– she doesn't want to look in the mirror for this. She bites her lip and grunts, trying not to let any sound escape her as she pulls on the dildo, finally gaining her release with a shudder and sigh. She zips the flies back up and picks up the fag for a last drag.

***

"Well, what do you think?"

Rachel looks her up and down, smiling broadly. "Perfect."

She is wearing a brown pinstripe suit that she's picked up from a charity shop, with white shirt and grotesque purple tie, highly-polished black shoes and a trilby, under which she has slicked her hair back with Brylcreem. Above it all, she wears a long flasher mac style raincoat, which she opens to reveal the tightness of her trousers around the crotch area.

Rachel's eyes settle on the bulge. "Really, very good. Just need a bit of stubble and you'd p-pass in the street no problem."

Rachel steps back so that Jack can come in. She strolls through the doorway but freezes in the hall as she hears voices coming from the lounge. She looks at Rachel quizzically, hoping that she doesn't intend to parade her in front of anyone just yet. "It's OK," Rachel whispers, a hand on her shoulder. "Just Mel and some of her family; they helped her move in. Come to my room." Jack follows her up the stairs, wincing at the unexpected tightness on her hips as she ascends.

As Rachel opens the bedroom door, she looks amused to see Jack pausing at the top of the stairs to adjust Big Jack yet again. Jackie doesn't want to admit that she's already been watching men in public, staring at their crotches and comparing sizes with her own – it hasn't gone down too well. The music from *Madame Butterfly* emanates from the room. Rachel's eclectic taste in music amuses Jack. She would be equally likely to be playing Whigfield's *Saturday Night* or Handel's *Water Music*. Jack walks into the room, aware of Rachel watching her, and stands in the middle of it. "Well?"

"Well?" repeats Rachel.

"Well, do you want to see my act so far?"

"OK, go ahead." She settles herself on her bed and reaches for her fags.

"Oh, I need one of those. And can I borrow some eyeliner?" After she has painted on a moustache and some sideburns, she turns away and takes a deep breath, looking out of the window, and then turns back with a leer on her lips. "Hello, I'm Jack and this [grab crotch and thrust] is Big Jack. Do you come here often? Because I could make you come more often. Boom-boom! No, seriously. I'd like to get to know you – you know I respect the laydeeez. I was only saying to the wife the other day, 'I respect you I do, now get your head down and finish the job'. Yeah, 'cos that's how I like it…"

When she pauses to light the cigarette, she notices Rachel is sighing and wiping away tears. Surely a good sign? She lets the fag dangle from her lips and thrusts two thumbs into her belt as she goes on talking.

"What's the difference between a woman and a shit? You don't have to cuddle a shit for half-an-hour after you've laid it. What's the difference between a woman with PMT and a rottweiler? Lipstick. Ha ha ha, blah blah blah. Some more jokes here."

Jack stubs out her cigarette in the ashtray and puts her hand back over the bulge. "Want to see it? Come on I know you do. Anyone want to see it?"

Rachel calls out, "Yeah, yeah!"

Jack smirks and begins to unzip, then pauses suddenly and looks up. "Well, I'm shy!" Rachel frowns, as if unsure whether this is part of the act, and Jack winks at her. She turns her back and looks over her shoulder, legs apart and hips thrust forward. "Just having a waz!" She shakes it with an exaggerated shoulder movement and then pretends to zip up with a bend of the knees. "Aaaaahhh, that's better!" She pulls the coat around herself, covering up the still dangling dildo and turns back to the 'audience'. Then Jack opens the coat with a flourish and thrusts her hips forward again. "Ta-da!"

"Oh my word!" Rachel exclaims, in mock-horror, and they both fall about laughing.

"Well, that's the kind of thing that I thought I might do, anyway," she says, once they've recovered. "I'll have to work on the jokes a bit, but what do you think of the basics, you know, the actions?"

"I think they're great. You really do look like the worst kind of middle-aged man out on the pull."

"I could do a few costume changes, if you want it to be longer."

"No, short is good for now, just ten minutes is perfect, and maybe you could make it longer as you get into it. Maybe I could persuade you to sing if you did a duet with me?"

"Hmm, maybe."

"Fine, whatever." Rachel looks down at her still open flies. "So that's it then, is it?"

She looks at it herself and self-consciously stuffs it back into her trousers before standing to zip the flies up. "Um, it gets a bit uncomfortable if I wear it for long periods."

"I know the feeling darling; I've been wearing mine all my life and I've never been comfortable with it."

They stand awkwardly looking at each other for a moment and then Jack jumps as the front door bangs. "Oh, looks like my lovely flatmate has finally gone out." Rachel rolls her eyes.

"Well, I suppose I'd better go. When am I going to do this show?"

"Would you rather do your first to a packed or smaller audience?"

"Not sure? Smaller crowd?"

"Less nerve-wracking for sure, but you get more of a buzz

from a big cheer."

"Hmm, small crowd still I think."

"OK, next week then? Friday is cabaret night. Rehearse at home, work on the jokes and we'll have a dress rehearsal on Thursday."

"Well, I'll be off then." Rachel walks her down the stairs and opens the front door. It is then they notice Melanie is still home as she comes through from the lounge to the kitchen carrying a handful of mugs. She stops when she sees them.

"Hello?" she says, looking at Jack who holds her coat closed self-consciously. After a moment Melanie turns to Rachel and adds, "Well, aren't you going to introduce me?"

"Oh, this is um, Jack. Jack, this is Melanie, my new flatmate."

Jackie flashes Rachel a look and then holds out her hand to Melanie, saying gruffly, "Pleased to meet you."

"Pleased to meet you, too," she says, shaking Jackie's hand with mock-seriousness. "So," she smiles, looking from Jack to Rachel and then back to Jack again, "What are you studying, Jack?"

"Psychology."

"Ah. Another one of us."

"Not exactly," says Jack, trying to keep her mouth tense. "Well, I'd better go." It is only once she's outside and the door is closed that Jack remembers the eyeliner on her upper lip. Cursing, she wipes it off with her hand, thinking that Mel must have thought she was a prize prat.

***

"She thought you were a boy!" shrieks Rachel when Jack opens her door to her the following afternoon. Confused for a moment, she looks blankly at her friend. "I said, she thought you were a boy, Mel did – you realise what that means?"

"That she needs glasses?"

"No, fool! That she took you at face value. That you pass."

"But the eyeliner – I mean no-one could have thought that was real!"

"She didn't mention it, but she lives with me. She's already used to having strange people around."

"So… she thought I was a boy, but just a strange one?"

Rachel shrugs. "Well, let's see. After you left I said 'what did you think of Jack?' and she said, and I quote, 'he's lovely; isn't he shy?' and she had this simpering look on her face that older women get when they fancy young men but won't admit to it."

"She fancied me? As a man? She fancied me?"

"Honey, *every*one fancies you. That's why I want you in my act."

Again, it takes a while for this to sink in. It isn't so much that she's attracted to Mel – in fact she barely remembers what the woman looks like, dark hair and sort of matronly – but she isn't used to the concept of people fancying her. Not that she doesn't fancy herself or think that she's pretty cute. But for so long as a young person she was reviled and so she cannot imagine anyone would think of her as anything but repulsive.

After a moment, Rachel turns away. "Are you going out?"

"Well, I wasn't. But… do you fancy going out then?" she asks.

Rachel shrugs. "There isn't really much choice, but I fancy doing something. Want to come round mine and do some more rehearsing?"

"Want to come for a ride with me?" Rachel raises her eyebrows as Jack tosses her a helmet. "A bike ride, you idiot," she says, dragging on her leather trousers.

"Oh wow! Hey, I thought you'd never ask. I've never been on the back of a bike."

Jack looks dubious for a moment, almost wishing she hadn't offered. "Well, you have to be able to balance."

On their way down the hall stairs to the car park, Jack has the distinct feeling that Rachel is watching her, but when she looks around she's gazing out of the windows at the view. "Lovely place this is," Rachel comments.

"Yes, shame it's such a trek up the hill."

"So where will we go?"

"Oh, I usually do a circuit of the back roads towards Shrewsbury, sometimes go down to the Borders."

When they get to the car park, Jackie's red MZ TS125 is the only bike there. Rachel looks a little disappointed. "Well, it's not much to look at, I know, but it's cheap and it does the job. When I make my fortune I'll get a better bike of course but this one, it's a Hardly Davidson." Jack grins at her own pun then adjusts her stance and feels Rachel's weight balance on the back. It has been a while since she's had a pillion passenger. They are out of town before Jack shouts to Rachel, "So, what do you think?"

"Fabulous," she shouts back.

"You don't have to hold onto me, you know. There's a handle either side under the seat."

"That's OK, I feel safer like this," and Rachel snuggles deeper into her back, gripping her abdomen so tightly that she feels breathless.

They swing around curves in the road and over small bridges, through farm country and villages and back around onto the main bypass. Jackie goes a little faster than she should as she's enjoying showing off, but she stays safe. She stops by a village green and parks the bike. Rachel pulls off the helmet and flops down onto a nearby bench. "Phew, that was fantastic."

Jack sits next to her and leans back against the bench, helmet on her knee. "It's lovely on an evening like this. Not so good when it's pissing it down."

"No, well you wouldn't go out on it if it was, would you?"

"That depends, I mean sometimes you have to go – like if

you use it as transport for work."

"You got a proper job then?"

"No, but I'll probably have to next summer. Maybe I'll be a courier – you can earn good money doing that and then I'd be able to afford a better bike. Did you know they were stopping the dole for students?"

"Yes, I'd heard that. Well, I'll be graduating next year so I'll have to get a fucking job then."

"Do you get paid much for the cabaret?"

"No, not really. Keeps me in fags and above the breadline. If I did a different venue every night then I might be able to make a proper living from it, but then there's the travel and all – ah, the life of an entertainer."

"So what kind of job were you thinking of?"

"Well, once I've had the op I could just stay on the d-dole – it's only for the lead up to it that I have to be working."

"So when is it due?"

"Next summer. Just after the finals."

"Bloody hell!"

"What?"

"Well, talk about stress."

"Actually, the way I figure it, I'll be less stressed about the exams because I'll be that much closer to my real goal."

"And you'll have saved up enough by then?"

"I've already got enough saved for the operation itself. It's the recovery period that'll be the problem. I won't be able to work for a while."

"Ah, I hadn't thought of that."

"There are all sorts of other expenses too. For instance I'm having electrolysis."

"What?"

Rachel rubs the short hairs on her chin, "Taking it all off. It fucking hurts as well, no matter what they say about it being painless. Want to come with me? I'm going in tomorrow."

"Mmm, maybe." She doesn't like to say that she is squeamish in case Rachel thinks this is sissy. "So," she stands up. "Ready to go back?"

"Yeah, OK." Rachel walks over to the bike and strokes the saddle. "You know, I should be jealous of this bike."

"Why?" asks Jack.

"It gets ridden more often than I do." Jack laughs but is slightly uncomfortable. Again, Rachel has given her that frank stare and Jack is unsure how to deal with the feelings that arise. She climbs on the bike and indicates to Rachel to jump back on.

The wind is slightly chilled on the way back into town. When she parks up outside Rachel's house Jack is glad that she asks her if she wants to come in for a coffee. She begins to get off the bike and then pauses, remembering something. "Uh, will Mel be in?"

Rachel waves a hand. "She went off this morning. Visiting family for a couple of days, or something."

"Don't you think it's a bit strange that she's just moved in and then she's gone away again?"

Rachel shrugs. "Don't care. As long as she pays the rent."

Jack locks the helmets up with the bike and brings her pannier and gloves inside. Kicking her boots off and slinging her jacket down in the hall, she wanders through to the kitchen.

***

"No, don't take the leathers off, try the act with them on; I'd like to see how it looks."

"I paid a fiver for that disgusting suit! I'm going to use it; I'll never wear it anywhere else."

"Just for me," Rachel winks, "go on."

She groans. "Oh, ok." Jack unzips her leather jeans and lets them fall to her knees. She turns her back to arrange the dildo and harness, still finding it a bit odd to be donning it in front of Rachel, although she knows that they'll be sharing that pokey little 'dressing room' when it comes to the big night. When she turns back, Rachel has settled herself into the sofa and is surrounded by a cloud of aromatic smoke. "Hey! Is that what I think it is?" Jack makes a grab for the spliff and Rachel laughs, rolling away from her.

"You shouldn't – you're driving."

"I don't care, one puff won't harm anything."

"Oh, one pouf can do a lot of damage, darling." Rachel giggles childishly, but stands up and holds it to her mouth. As she draws on the end of it, Jack looks Rachel in the eye and realises that she seriously wants to kiss her. Shaking off this feeling, she steps back and falls into her act. She has to mime the flasher mac part but with everything else she is word perfect and feels great.

"Bravo, bravo," Rachel calls, standing up and clapping. She walks up to Jack, says, "Superb," and leans in to kiss her briefly on the lips. They look at one another for what seems like an eternity and then Rachel leans in again slowly and they kiss. It is such a surprise to Jack that her defences are down and she doesn't know how to react, only to kiss Rachel's soft lips and press her body close, feeling the weight of Big Jack between them. Rachel pulls away at last and says, "I've never fancied a woman."

"I've never fancied a man," Jack says, "or a transsexual," she adds quickly. "This is strange. Does this make you a fag hag, or me?"

"Very strange indeed."

"What are we going to do?"

"What would you like to do?"

"I don't know. I don't know how to, er… What do you do?"

Rachel laughs and steps back. "You mean, you don't know? Or are you just saying you've never done it before?"

"Well," she looks around the room, embarrassed. Then she decides to be direct. "I haven't had sex with a man and I don't intend to start. I would like to have sex with you; but you don't have a vagina."

"Yet." Rachel pauses. "No, I don't. But that hasn't stopped me being fucked before."

"You mean…"

"Do you have a problem with anal sex?"

"Only that I've never done it before."

"And I've never ridden on the back of a bike before. You were fabulous, by the way."

They stand and look at each other for a time.

"Well, we'd better do something about it before the moment is lost. I have condoms if that's what's worrying you?"

"I'm not worried. I'm just… nervous?"

***

"So this is going to be safe, right?"

"As safe as with a woman, darling. It's safer for you than me, anyway. Do you use condoms when you have sex with women?"

"No. Should I? I do wash it afterwards."

"Well, I don't know."

"Shall I go?" Jack looks around the bedroom, not sure how she got there.

"No, stay. It's ok; this will work if we stop thinking about it so much."

"I just… I'm finding it very difficult to stop thinking of you as a man."

Rachel looks pained but then a thought strikes her. "How about I wear my wig? Look, give me a moment and I can doll myself up." Jack steps back as Rachel opens drawers and lifts out feminine lingerie. She pulls out two wigs and smoothes the hair down. "The dark or the blonde?"

"Uh. I don't know. The dark? I quite like long hair and the blonde is short."

Obediently, Rachel puts on the dark wig and tidies herself up. She applies vivid makeup with a quick, practised hand and then turns back to Jackie. "Ta-da! Better?"

"Much," says Jack, smiling.

They kiss again. Jack pushes Rachel back onto the bed and Rachel lets her. Jack pauses for an instant and pulls back slightly. "Are you sure you're ok with this?" In answer, Rachel pulls her down onto the bed again.

The condom is slippery, and Rachel has to show Jack how to put it on. "There's an art to it, you know. You can make it sexy – it doesn't have to feel weird." Rachel bends her head over and smoothes the condom down using her lips, a hand up to her hair to stop it from falling over. Jack gasps and feels her breath coming faster. A flashback to a previous encounter in the back of a sex shop takes her by surprise. For a moment she is caught up in the memory, trying to see the face of the girl who gave her her first blowjob. But she had been high at the time and remembers very little of the deed, only the hangover the following morning and the surprise acquisition of a collection of sex toys.

Rachel brings Jack out of her reverie by rocking back on her heels and standing up. She undoes her jeans and steps out of them; she's wearing black satin women's underwear. Jack reaches out to touch the knickers but then hesitates. "My, it's quite erotic," says Rachel. "You're like a virgin." She catches Jack's hand and presses it to her lips.

"Well, technically I am a virgin, you know. I've never been penetrated." Jack stands up again and watches Rachel climb onto the bed, bending over on all fours.

"Is it ok for you to do it this way?" Rachel asks.

Jack feels the blood rush to her head and puts a hand on Rachel's back to steady herself. She thinks the first thing she should do is some foreplay rather than launching straight in. "Keep your pants on for a while, will you?" asks Jack. "I like them. And lie down flat, don't kneel up like that."

She feels rather silly as she stretches out on top of Rachel, but a bit of rubbing and whispering dirty words begins to get her going. Rachel also seems to be enjoying it. "You like that?" asks Jack. "Yes, I bet you do – you naughty little bitch." She pulls Rachel's head back by her ears and procures a startled cry. Then suddenly she is up and tearing at the satin knickers. Rachel also rears up so that she's in a kneeling position, half upright. Jack reaches round to grab her breasts and to her surprise finds a firm neat little pair. Of course, the hormones. She bites Rachel's shoulder and pushes her down again. "Ok, I'm going in."

"Be gentle."

It feels different. Odd. There's more resistance and it requires a different angle than she is used to. But in a way it feels better. On top of the taboo, the sense of perversity, there is a definite sense of more power – ultimate power over someone else. Breaking through the last boundary. She is gentle and begins slowly, just easing in and out, asking questions and checking responses. Then it begins to build up inside her and she feels less able to control the speed or the forcefulness.

Breathlessly, she asks, "Is this how you like it?"

Rachel's reply is almost a grunt. "Yes. Just like that."

Jack takes this as permission to lose control and pummels as hard and fast as she can. She comes like a train, dimly aware of Rachel screaming too. When it's over she flops onto Rachel's back, still inside.

After a second Rachel coughs. "Er, do you mind?"

"Oh! Oh, sorry." Jack had nearly fallen asleep. She leans back and simultaneously Rachel jumps forward, the dildo plopping out with a small thud onto the bed. Jack is first aware of the smell and then her hands pause over the dildo as she is about to take the condom off. She is totally disgusted and then immediately disgusted with herself for being disgusted. Rachel notices her hesitation and reaches for a tissue.

"It's OK, I'll sort it out." Rachel wraps the tissue around the condom and pulls it off expertly.

"I- I hadn't realised it would be..." Jack begins. Of course that's why Rachel had suggested they use a condom. Jackie had thought that the whole 'shit stabber' thing was a playground joke but logically there must be some truth in it.

"Just going to use the bathroom," says Rachel, dashing out with the tissue in hand.

Jack unbuckles her harness and collects her clothes. She looks around the bedroom properly for the first time. Pink fluff, teddy bears and hearts. It looks like the bedroom of a teenage girl. Jack wonders what kind of woman Richie will make; will he be the kind who's still in her teens even at thirty or forty?

Jackie sees Rachel's outline in the doorway as she walks back into the room and is startled by its lack of curvature. Then her eyes are drawn to his crotch area, where it hangs: his penis. While not exactly on the large side, it's still very much present. She feels a sick tightening of her stomach. She has shagged a man. Right, he had breasts; right, she had penetrated him. But he was still, in essence, a man. She'd had heterosexual sex. Hadn't she?

"Are you ok?" Rachel peers at her face.

"Yes!" she gasps. "Yes, just getting dressed." She struggles into her clothes.

"Well," says Rachel, not convinced. "I'll make us another coffee, shall I?" and she wanders off downstairs.

How can she be that casual? She has no idea how she's going to get out of this situation. Would it be cowardly to make a bolt for the door? Jackie creeps down the stairs and into the sitting room, gathering more of her things as she hears her clattering around and humming to herself. As she walks out of the room she hears the kettle whistle and the fridge opening. She has to leave now before she sees her or it'll be too late. The front door opens easily but she doesn't shut it properly, just pulls it back against her and backs down the front steps.

It wasn't the last time that I ran out on Rachel. It's difficult to explain how I manage to live with myself and still be such a chicken. Don't call me 'brave' for telling my story because I'm not. It's so patronising, you know that yourself, Jim. Although by now you might have worked out that I'm not an abuse survivor.

She runs, of course. The whole thing has disturbed her but she can't say exactly why and she doesn't want to face making bland excuses. Back at the bike, she unlocks her helmets and hooks the spare over her arm to carry it back. Kick starting the bike, she zooms out into the road without looking behind and receives an angry horn blowing from several swerving cars. She tries to breathe; she tries to be calm; images keep springing into her head; she counts one to ten as the traffic lights change and then speeds off as green light shimmers into the night.

Jack swears later that it was definitely a green light. She rides into the junction and out of nowhere a car swings around the bend. She only has time to register surprise before crunching sickeningly to the ground. She notices bizarre things: that the ground is not wet; that she has landed on the spare helmet; there is a wailing noise like a baby crying in the distance; her nose is running.

She spends maybe five minutes lying trapped under the bike while chaos erupts around her. People walk over the busy junction, annoyed motorists hoot their horns and a woman shouts, "Can't you see there's been an accident?" Someone stands over Jack's head; she sees heeled shoes and the bottoms of cerise leggings. Then they shift and someone's face comes close to hers. "Are you all right, love?" She starts to laugh at the question but it comes out as a croak and turns into a cry.

"I think I've broken everything," she manages to whisper and then hears the sirens getting closer.

"That'll be the ambulance," says the woman, standing up. She seems nervous and it occurs to Jackie that she might be the driver of the car that skidded close to her head. Jack cranes her neck to try to see above the bike to the car but can only make out the smashed headlamp, the bulb of which still shines brightly, unconcerned.

The siren is actually the police, but an ambulance arrives soon afterwards. Jack has to shout her name and address twice before the uniformed officer hears, and she overhears the woman giving her name as Clarice Morgan and her address in Small Heath. Jack's ears prick at the mention of Small Heath and, against the bright lights, she squints up at the woman's face, trying to discern her features or even her age, but all she can see is a halo of blonde frizzed hair. She thinks to herself, "That could be my birth mother."

It's amazing what pops into one's head at times like this; it's amazing what one remembers afterwards.

Later in the ambulance, they tell Jack that she's lucky she'd been holding the helmet in the crook of her arm, otherwise she could well have had a nasty break on the elbow. Lucky. Apparently she hasn't actually broken anything, but the searing pain in her sides every time she speaks or coughs or even breathes indicates bruised ribs. The fact that she's been unconscious, even for a short time, means a hospital stay. She's also sustained a twisted ankle and severe bruising to her shoulder.

Waiting in the casualty department is not a pleasant experience. She resents the bright lights and needles, the continual questions, pokes and prods and, most of all, the x-rays where she has to 'hold still, dear' in extremely uncomfortable positions. There is a moment's panic when a young police officer turns up to breathalyse her – "Just routine, love." She needn't have worried as there is not a drop of alcohol in her system. But for some bizarre reason she thinks they might detect that one inhalation of cannabis.

The kind PC tells her the bike is being held at the station for her, but he is unsure if it will be salvageable. She asks about the pannier and he says it's with the bike. Jack wonders if the police would search her stuff but doesn't want to pursue the matter.

Finally it is over and she is sent up to a ward in the early hours of the morning. The hospital bed is comfy and it's nice to be looked after. She is brought food and cups of tea the following day, for the most of which she sleeps a deep painkiller-enhanced sleep. She wakes occasionally when another patient shuffles past the bed. She is in a bay with five other women, most of whom are quite old, some of whom snore. Somewhere on the ward a patient screams, calling out, "Mam! Dad!" in a high-pitched voice that Jack can't identify as male or female.

She gets up to use the toilet and nearly falls over. Steadying herself on the metal end of the bed, she asks if she can borrow her neighbour's walking stick. The hospital floor is made up of dusky, pink tiles with white flecks, buffed to a shine. The doors are pale pink to match the floor or dark stained wood with metal panelling. On the toilet door is a small plate with 'Patients Toilets – Ladies' written on it. She returns the stick and goes back to bed, dreaming of Hillbank.

The nurses keep asking her if she'd like them to phone her parents and she keeps having to tell them that she doesn't have any. She is sure they don't believe her, that they think she's making this up because she doesn't want to see these non-existent parents. She manages to fend off their questions but eventually admits that there is someone who can bring her some clothes and that his name is Richie, but he doesn't have a phone.

She hobbles to the hospital payphone at the end of the ward and rings directory enquiries for the number of the club, then rings the club and leaves a message. Exhausted, she falls back into bed and sleeps, not dreaming this time. She is woken by the other patient's cries. Jackie doesn't hear what the patient says; she can only hear the nurse's answers. The nurse has a strident voice that carries through the bay and gets louder as the conversation continues. She turns over so that she doesn't have to look at the woman crying.

Richie doesn't visit that night and the doctor says she might be alright to go home soon, but that they are concerned about there being no-one at home to look after her. This puts her on the defensive immediately. "Why would there be? I'm an adult, I can look after myself." They ask her how she plans to get home. She hasn't actually thought about this and mentally counts the change in her pocket. She shrugs. "If I can't afford the bus then I'll walk. How far away is this hospital from Birwood anyway?"

The doctor looks exasperated. The sister speaks, "We can't let you go home without any clothes, anyway, can we?" She looks down at her hospital gown. They are right of course; her beloved leather trousers have been destroyed, against all her protests, by a long cut up one leg. She is due to sign on the following day; what will happen if she doesn't turn up? Jack realises with irritation that she does need other people after all. They seem to be treating her like a child or some kind of mental case, and she even overhears one of the nurses mentioning a call to social services. It feels like she hasn't been taken to a real hospital after all, but a social control prison camp.

Jack turns over on her side but then thinks she hears her name mentioned.

"Jack Harris? I was told he'd been brought in a few days ago; I've got some clothes…"

"Oh, Jackie – you mean Jacqueline Harris? Yes, she's over here in Bay Three, Women's Bay, second bed on the left." She hears footsteps but still doesn't turn around. Torn between gratefulness and mortification, she doesn't know how to react so closes her eyes and feigns sleep. After a few moments, she hears a sigh and the noises of a bag being put down and a coat pulled off. She rubs her eyes, yawns and turns over, acting surprised.

"Richard's idea of a joke, I suppose," Mel says with pursed lips. Jack is expecting her to turn around and go but her eyes are twinkling with humour. "More fool me; I should have known." She sits down and looks around at the other women on the ward, smiling and nodding to them until they stop staring and turn back to their crosswords or visitors. She also stares at the cluster of nurses giggling around the front of the bay until they disperse.

Jackie notices that Melanie has a very forceful stare and she feels a rush of gratefulness.

"He told me you thought I was a bloke. It wasn't my idea at all, you know. He wants me in the act; I'm not a – like him."

"I should hope so too; I don't know why anyone would want to be a man."

"So…" Jack flounders around for a subject and then remembers the clothes. "What clothes did you get me?"

"Just some things from the market, nothing special. All men's *of course*," she adds with a laugh. "Do you mind?"

Jack laughs too, and then winces and holds her side. "Not at all. Can I see?" She feels like a kid at Christmas, pulling trousers, socks, pants, t-shirts and jumpers out of the bag. There is even a pair of checked granddad slippers. Tears spring easily to her eyes and she sniffs, brushing them away. "Sorry. It's the drugs they've given me – I'm still not feeling right." She leans back into the pillow, suddenly weary of it all and lets the slippers fall from her hands.

"That's OK," says Mel, fussily tidying up the clothes. "I'll put them in your locker, shall I? Maybe you can have a shower after I've gone."

"Don't go!" Jack reaches out to her. "I don't really know why you're here, but don't go now."

Mel sits down again and holds her hand. "I won't," she murmurs, looking Jack in the eye. Then she reaches up and strokes Jack's hair. "Poor love, there really is no-one for you, is there?" And she does the most amazing thing and leans forward to kiss Jackie's lips.

"Richie said you were heterosexual." Maybe it's the medication. She feels herself slipping away again as if drunk. She certainly wouldn't have said that if she'd been sober. Mel's lips form a smile but Jack notices that it doesn't reach her eyes.

"Richie doesn't know anything about me."

Chapter Eleven

JACK

The dreams were getting worse. I hadn't spoken to Jimmie about them, but you would think that my lover must have been aware of the terrors that plagued my nights. Granted, we slept together less often than most couples, with Jimmie at the shelter. When we did find ourselves in the same bed, both of us were often too exhausted for more than a cursory 'goodnight'. But the chase, the panic, the trapped feeling, were so real to me that it was impossible to imagine how anyone close to me could miss it. But it seemed Jimmie was oblivious to my anguish, or worse, she didn't care.

The application form for the Women's Aid job had been sent on my insistence but Jimmie wasn't holding out much hope. She spent most of her spare time on college work or practising with the band, and I often found myself alone in the house even when she wasn't working. Jimmie was determined to get good grades on her counselling course and this involved a lot of time poring over textbooks in the college library.

The first course had been an evening class, but now she was on the diploma it was one afternoon per week and extra time on top of that doing voluntary hours at the local centre. She had tried to integrate her paid work at the shelter with the counselling hours, but the rules were strict on the course – it had to be done within specific agency conditions. So Jimmie was now counselling substance users in one agency and then putting them to bed with another. I could understand that she was preoccupied and that it was only necessary until the course was done, but I felt abandoned. I would have taken on extra work myself to counter the effect, but there wasn't much going and I didn't fancy a job stacking shelves. I contemplated approaching the local nursing agencies, doing health care work as I had done before, but found that equally depressing. Anyway, I swore back then that I'd never return to a residential home.

Most of the time when Jimmie was out I worked on the computer. I tried to write, had been trying to write my life-story for years, even though I had periods of self-doubt when I was sure no-one would want to read it, me not being a celebrity. I did a bit of music mixing, nothing special. I was trying to learn computer programming through some free online course. I imagined that someday I wouldn't be a counsellor any more. I felt like I was leading a double life as I was a completely different person inside my head to the person others saw. And of course there were the puzzles. That day I was back on the internet. I sat at the desk with bare feet and my sloppy joggers, and lied about who I was.

I had met Pie on several occasions and every time our conversation got to a deeper level.

BRITISHBEEF: I've told you more secrets than I've told my own therapist.

AmericanPie: maybe I should charge a rate?

BRITISHBEEF: lol. How about you? What's your big secret?

AmericanPie: well... i'm quite famous over here. In a cult kind of way. but no-one knows who I am.

BRITISHBEEF: oh yes? Go on. Sounds intriguing

AmericanPie: did you check out that website I patched to you?

BRITISHBEEF: a bit – no photos of you there

AmericanPie: no, there aren't any images of me anywhere on the net. I'm careful about that

BRITISHBEEF: why?

AmericanPie: just don't like judging by appearances. I'd rather be judged by my work, which is excellent.

BRITISHBEEF: modest.

AmericanPie: :) but of course. If you make your living by doing something other people can't, you have to be able to sell yourself.

BRITISHBEEF: so what *do* you do?

AmericanPie: I fix up websites.

BRITISHBEEF: that's not a particularly unique profession, is it?

AmericanPie: no, I mean I fix them up without their permission. I mean that I am a hired hacker, quite sought after which is why I am anonymous.

BRITISHBEEF: wow! Don't know whether to be impressed or appalled.

AmericanPie: be impressed, please. I do it for political reasons not profit although the money can be good.

BRITISHBEEF: my ideal job right now would be as a designer for a puzzle website.

AmericanPie: u don't like being a therapist?

BRITISHBEEF: let's just say it's beginning to get me down. I'm getting tired of other people's pain.

AmericanPie: ah, point taken. I'm also working on something of my own at the moment that may interest you.

BRITISHBEEF: oh yes?

AmericanPie: no-one likes a guy who beats up his wife, right?

BRITISHBEEF: true

AmericanPie: it happens all the time around this neighborhood, but the police aren't interested. Most of them are junkies anyway.

BRITISHBEEF: the police are junkies?

AmericanPie: no, fool! The neighbors. I've set up a webcam in a secret location watching this one apartment. The couple who live there fight most nights and sometimes he rapes her.

BRITISHBEEF: !? let me get this right: you are videoing this without their permission and broadcasting it live on the internet?

AmericanPie: cool isn't it?

BRITISHBEEF: do you have privacy laws in the states?

AmericanPie: yes, but since when was I bothered about any law? Besides, if the police won't do anything about this then someone has to take matters into their own hands.

BRITISHBEEF: but most people who watch that kind of thing would be doing so for the entertainment value, not because they're morally motivated, surely?

AmericanPie: I don't know what people's motivations are for visiting my sites, I only know that someday he's gonna get his just deserts. He don't know he's being watched by net geeks worldwide, and one of these days he'll be recognised on the street.

BRITISHBEEF: an interesting theory. I'd be more worried about him being exalted for a hero.

AmericanPie: he's no hero

BRITISHBEEF: so you say, but what do others think? What kind of feedback do you have?

AmericanPie: site hits are astronomical

BRITISHBEEF: what's the url?

AmericanPie: you can get links from my other sites. Patching it over now anyway.

BRITISHBEEF: got it. so how the hell r u 2day?

AmericanPie: not too good, not been well. what r u doing? Wearing anything nice 2day?

BRITISHBEEF: u haven't asked that 4 a while?

AmericanPie: just thought I'd lighten the mood

BRITISHBEEF: what about not judging by appearances??

AmericanPie: not judging at all, just want to imagine

BRITISHBEEF: ok, imagine this: leather jeans, lace up boots, ripped white shirt, red bra, hair spiked with glitter gel.

AmericanPie: wow, just for surfing the net?

BRITISHBEEF: i believe we should dress as we feel regardless of what we are doing

AmericanPie: you'd wear fishnets to go fishing?

BRITISHBEEF: if I felt the need to, but the only blood sport I indulge in is nazi baiting.

AmericanPie: a good sport for the well-rounded individual.

BRITISHBEEF: I like to think so.

AmericanPie: want to know what I'm wearing?

BRITISHBEEF: waiting with bated breath

AmericanPie: nothing

BRITISHBEEF: nothing?

AmericanPie: absolute zero

BRITISHBEEF: interesting. Cold?

AmericanPie: no, very warm in fact

BRITISHBEEF: lucky you

AmericanPie: want to know more?

BRITISHBEEF: you great big tease! Tell me, please

AmericanPie: it's so warm here, people walking down the street wearing underwear

BRITISHBEEF: you can see from your window?

AmericanPie: yes, can see the whole block.

BRITISHBEEF: what do you see? Are we getting back to privacy again?

AmericanPie: got cameras everywhere

BRITISHBEEF: don't know if I want to know this

AmericanPie: ha! Fooled you – I was joking.

BRITISHBEEF: fuck

AmericanPie: hahahahahahahaha

BRITISHBEEF: is any of it true?

AmericanPie: the website is true, check it out

BRITISHBEEF: I will. R u really naked?

AmericanPie: u will never know

BRITISHBEEF: u bastard

AmericanPie: u ever had sex blindfold?

BRITISHBEEF: ?

AmericanPie: not a subject jump, hear me out. Isn't not knowing part of the joy of discovery?

BRITISHBEEF: not knowing is being teased, I agree

AmericanPie: the whole thing is tease, isn't it?

BRITISHBEEF: the whole what?

AmericanPie: the net

BRITISHBEEF: interesting theory. do you have any boundaries at all?

AmericanPie: an interesting point. I have many physical boundaries, I cannot fly for example

BRITISHBEEF: why do you always go off on a tangent when we get to the meaty questions?

AmericanPie: now you sound like a therapist

BRITISHBEEF: I'll try not to.

AmericanPie: what are the meaty questions?

BRITISHBEEF: boundaries, I said

AmericanPie: boundaries like the white picket fence kind? Is that what you're interested in?

BRITISHBEEF: are you being deliberately obtuse?

AmericanPie: should I be paying you now?

BRITISHBEEF: ok, I can see you want me to drop it.

AmericanPie: we could talk about something else. What about your boundaries? This is obviously an issue for you.

BRITISHBEEF: yes it is as a matter of fact, i've got something going on here that's worrying me.

AmericanPie: now I'm intrigued

BRITISHBEEF: well there's this woman...

AmericanPie: always is.

BRITISHBEEF: she wants something from me that i can't give.

AmericanPie: why not?

BRITISHBEEF: I don't mix work with pleasure

AmericanPie: ah, she's a colleague?

BRITISHBEEF: sort of. thing is - when i think about her everything just goes haywire. I have to work with her and it's getting in the way. I can't think straight – I'm even dreaming about her now. And other people have started to notice.

AmericanPie: what's her name?

BRITISHBEEF: Lara, and yes, she is beautiful - stunningly so.

AmericanPie: hmmm, sounds like you need to get her out of your system

BRITISHBEEF: precisely. what would you suggest?

AmericanPie: well there's two ways you could do it – one: cut ties completely and never see her again. that would be difficult with her being in your workplace and you may still dream about her.

BRITISHBEEF: Two?

AmericanPie: fuck your rule and fuck her anyway.

BRITISHBEEF: i wish!

AmericanPie: really, what would be the problem?

BRITISHBEEF: it's not just my rule. besides which, I don't think my g/f would be very happy about that.

AmericanPie: your g/f?

BRITISHBEEF: yes, my girlfriend

AmericanPie: i know what g/f is - you never said you had a girlfriend?

BRITISHBEEF: didn't i? oh, well i do.

AmericanPie: and you're monogamous, i take it?

BRITISHBEEF: supposedly so, though the rate things are i may as well be celibate.

AmericanPie: so what about us?

BRITISHBEEF: us? are we in a relationship?

AmericanPie: you don't think so?

BRITISHBEEF: I hadn't really thought about it

BRITISHBEEF: Pie?

AmericanPie: ?

BRITISHBEEF: does net sex count then?

AmericanPie: catch you later.
BRITISHBEEF: Pie?
BRITISHBEEF: Pie?
BRITISHBEEF: ?

***

To: Pie,
From: Jack
Subject: I apologise

I'm sorry. My sincerest apologies for hurting your feelings. I was stupid: i realise of course that i can't just switch you on and off like a computer. I should have told you that I'm with someone but honestly it slipped my mind; it wasn't a deliberate plan to mislead you. I should tell you that my 'net' persona is very different to the real me. I'm not a punk for a start - just a normal-looking, respectable person. It's like a glass casing that surrounds me, reflecting to the outside world what they want to see, and to the inside world what I feel is the real me. but as it's glass - if i move it will break and cut me to shreds. it has been really liberating to talk with someone who can't see me and to describe myself as the person that i really am rather than as my outside appearance. maybe i've taken it too far.

You should know some things about me and maybe we could start again. maybe we could be friends? for much of my life I've escaped into a fantasy world to avoid thinking about real life. I'm trying to get over that now and make a life for myself in the real world. my partner is truly lovely and very supportive, but she can't give me the one thing that i feel i need. maybe no-one can, i don't know. maybe i don't really need it and I'm just using it as an excuse not to get close. how can such a screwed up person be a counsellor, you might think? well, it's like this: i can sort out other people's problems fine, i have an expansive brain and can learn all the theory and be empathic but i can't do this for myself and my own preoccupations.

Anyway.

Friends?

About your webcam site. I've looked at it and although nothing is happening at the moment, I've browsed the highlight clips pages so i see what you're getting at. I'd be interested in contributing to your forum once you've established it.

Please tell me first if I'm forgiven for the above misdemeanour.

:-, ?

I hovered the cursor over the 'send' button for a few seconds, and then made an exasperated noise and clicked 'delete' instead. Let Pie come to me.

Are you sure you want to delete? This will lose any unsaved data. Yes, no, cancel.

I wish it was so easy to delete the last few years of my life. Or maybe I should go further back, make a completely fresh start.

HARRIS THE ALCOHOLIC

Valley Gazette can reveal today that Jackie Harris, the prison counsellor who killed homeless Frank Little, had an alcohol problem while at Birwood University. Sally Hopper, 48, who was a student at the university at the same time as Harris, recalls how she would become aggressive when drunk. "We all had parties," says Sally, who now works as an accountant in the West Midlands. "But Jackie would always drink too much and then start a fight. We knew that she was a lesbian and she probably had a hard time with that, but it's no excuse. It doesn't surprise me that she's killed someone now. She was probably drunk when she did it."

Police sources reveal that Harris had not been drinking before the attack, but a search of the premises found containers of alcohol hidden in the house. This is a notorious habit of secret drinkers. Today, Jemima Albinelka, 35, Jackie's lover who is accusing victim Frank Little of raping her, was unavailable for comment.

Chapter Twelve – 1991

"Happy birthday toooo yooooo; happy birthday toooo yooooo; happy birthday dear Jaaaaaac-kieeeeee; happy birthday toooo yooooo. Go on then, blow out the candles."

Mel has made a cake. Jack blows out the candles with tears in her eyes. It takes several breaths. "*How* many candles?"

"There are actually twenty-one. You can count them if you like. I like to do things properly, you know that."

Jack can't remember the last time she's had a birthday cake with the right number of candles on. In fact, she can't remember the last time somebody has made a birthday cake for her. It might have been when she was thirteen. She shakes her head to rid it of the memory. This is by far the best birthday she could have wished for. One candle winks back on again and Jack stares in awe. Mel laughs.

"It's a relighting one. So you can have as many wishes as you want."

Jack blows it out and makes her wish: that this could last forever. And she blows it again and makes the same wish again. And again. Eventually Mel licks her fingers and squeezes them expertly over the wick. The candle fizzes and dies.

Life with Melanie is like a fresh start for Jack. For Mel it's simple: live together, love each other and everything else comes along. Jack admires this simplicity and believes in Mel, believes they can make it. For one thing, Mel is older and says she must therefore know best, and Jack, for once in love, accepts it without argument. It has lasted for a year just like this – bliss.

After Jackie had been discharged from the hospital, Mel became a semi-permanent fixture in her tiny residency room and brought along several mature student friends. Jack doesn't see Richie unless she visits Mel in the house they still share, when he is cool and aloof. She asks how the act is going and apologises for not being able to join it as planned due to the accident. But he doesn't apologise for not visiting her in hospital and doesn't ask her to join the act again.

It was Mel that took her to the police station to recover the bike; Mel that stood next to her when they handed over the pannier with a smirk; Mel that encouraged her to fix up the bike and sell it. To Mel she owes not only her life but now her ability to stay at university. Without her she would surely have dropped out and become depressed without work or purpose.

Mel organises finding a house for them – it makes sense to share and they could still have separate bedrooms. That way anyone would think they were two student housemates, which is exactly what they are. No-one needs to know what goes on behind closed doors. "It's not like we pry into their business, is it?" she says. Mel finds a small cottage in Bleakemore, a village a few miles from Birwood but on a regular bus route.

Sally, one of Mel's mature student friends, takes Jack aside one evening quite near the beginning of their relationship, when they are at a local pub. "I want you to promise," she says seriously, "that you're not going to hurt Melanie."

"What?" asks Jack. "Why would I hurt her?"

"She's a really lovely woman, and she's had a shit time in her life…"

"I know, she's told me."

"And I don't want you," she prods Jackie in the chest, "to give her any more shit than she's already had."

"I won't. I'm not like that."

"That's not what I've heard."

"What have you heard?" demands Jack, the colour rising to her cheeks.

But Sally won't spill the beans; she only says darkly, "I've warned you. And if I hear anything from Mel about you behaving badly, then, well... I've got my eye on you."

"Oh, like I'm scared," says Jack after she's gone. But she does feel slightly shaken. What can have been said about her? Richie had mentioned something similar – are there really rumours around about her?

"What are people saying about me?" she asks Mel when they are walking back to the hall together.

"What do you mean?"

Jack shrugs, reluctant to mention Sally's threats. "I've heard that there are rumours about me and what I'm like, and I just wondered if you'd heard any of them?"

"People obviously don't have anything better to do if they're talking about you, Jack. Don't worry about it – it's nothing to do with them anyway, is it?"

"Is *what*, though? I mean, if I knew what it was that's nothing to do with them then I'd feel a bit happier about ignoring it." But Mel won't be drawn.

***

There are so many plans, such a lot of things to think about. Now she's 'in a relationship', she has to consider another person and the responsibility of this sends her dizzy. She can't just decide to go out or stay in; she has to check with Mel first. She can't even decide what to watch on the TV without consultation. The effect is disturbing. At first she feels like a child again, but Mel isn't like a parent, especially as she sometimes demands sex at the most bizarre moments. Jack is happy to drop everything and oblige as this is what makes her the most happy and is why, after all, they are together. Once they have set up home together, it feels like playing house. A game. And an enjoyable one. There is much to do.

The first thing necessary is to tame the wild side of Jack. If she is to be tolerated in polite society, of which obviously she wants to be a part, then she will have to grow her hair a touch and tone down her more outlandish dress and behaviour. Of course, she can be as wild as she wants in the bedroom, but painting on a mustachio is simply childish.

Jackie practises speaking properly. It isn't just a matter of dialect, but tone. She has to give her voice a feminine but professional edge so she will be taken seriously when going for job interviews. At first it makes her laugh but she soon gets used to it and is able to slip into her 'telephone voice' during conversation. It's still an effort, though, and in moments of emotion or excitement, the Brummie accent leaps from her mouth.

Mel likes the house tidy and, as she doesn't have many possessions herself, most of the clutter belongs to Jack. Jackie does often wonder how Mel has managed to get to the age of thirty-two without accumulating boxes full of books and ornaments or even a full wardrobe of clothes, but she doesn't like to pry.

She soon finds out that the 'junk', as Mel puts it, is boxed away safely with Mel's parents. Jack hasn't considered this – she has presumed that someone Mel's age would have control of all of her oddments or would have lost them. She often forgets that other people have contact with their parents. Jackie's own special quilt lies at the bottom of her unused bed and Mel raises her eyebrows when she sees it but doesn't question its presence.

Eventually Jackie is no longer the untamed thing of her youth. She is sensible, grows her hair and colour co-ordinates her clothes. She has a handbag and carries tissues and breath mints. She is constantly vigilant for any small misbehaviour or appearance that might irritate Mel. They did have some pretty wild times during the first term of Jack's second year but, once she's thrown her lot in with Mel and there's no going back, there are more bites and every day it seems to get deeper.

***

During her third year, the expectations of Jack's lecturers accelerate: there are more essays; the course has become modular now and for each module there is at least one assignment; she has to attend more lectures and the tutorials are compulsory. Their small cottage is outside of town and they travel in for college so, even if there is only one lecture, Jack is out of the house for the whole day. She meets up with Mel for lunch and they talk over their lectures. Jack helps Mel with her coursework as she's done it all the previous year and they spend a lot of time in the library.

Because they are living out of town, they rarely go to Student Union events. Mel says they can't afford to go out much and when they do it should be to the local pub, like grown-ups. The Bleakemore Manor is a mostly brown establishment where Jack has to suffer men trying to pick Mel up. Jack sits with her half-pint of bitter while Mel drinks seven pints of lager and gets louder as the evening wears on. After the fourth pint, Jack tries to persuade Mel to come home. If she catches Mel before she's had five drinks, the sex is great.

"Just one more, Jackie. I've still got a fiver in my purse."

"We need to do some shopping tomorrow; there's loads of things we need: toilet roll, coffee..." says Jack, trying to keep the whine out of her voice. But Mel isn't listening because someone has offered to buy her a drink. If she'd listened, she would probably have corrected Jack's grammar.

Mel says she doesn't like male attention any more than Jack does, but she doesn't do anything to discourage it. As she won't allow Jack to behave in an obvious 'coupley' manner, the men who try it on with Mel either also try it on with Jack or look quizzically at her as if trying to work out why she's there. Sometimes Jack wonders the same.

Shopping has become the highlight of the week. Their budget is so low that Jack takes a calculator with her as she meanders around KwikSave. They live on packet soup and cheap white bread; one block of cheese per week which is gone after four days; dividing single-person portions into two and filling up with extra potatoes. They reuse floor-sweeping teabags and put water in the washing-up liquid. Jack is proud that she manages to feed the two of them on £10-a-week, sometimes less as this includes the cheap alcohol that Mel likes to buy.

There are two kinds of cheap alcohol: what Mel calls 'battery acid', a strong white cider at £1 for a litre bottle; and 'anti-freeze', white wine at £1 for 75cl. These are usually consumed on the day of shopping, or if Jack has managed to hide a couple of bottles she can use them to lure Mel away from the pub. Jack can't stand the taste of either although she makes pretence of sharing a drink with Mel, who hates to drink alone.

They often have parties and Jack invites her LGB group friends while Mel's co-students also turn up. Jack finds it difficult to think of them as Mel's 'friends' as she slags them off so much behind their backs. Mel also slags off Jack's friends, but to their faces and, gradually, one by one, Jack loses touch with them. Mel tells her they weren't worth it anyway. She says that they should only be friends with people who are useful to them, so if someone gives them a meal when they visit then that person is a worthy friend.

Weekends have changed. Jack is no longer able to stay in bed all day or mope around in her pyjamas. They go for bracing walks, visit Mel's cronies or do housework. At first it's just playing house but later it becomes real. Sundays are long and drawn out. Not since she was a child has Jack felt so unable to find something to do to relieve the boredom.

Jack immerses herself in studying but she also likes to read novels. She has discovered a lesbian detective writer, Fay McMullin, whose heroine Linda North is a journalist. The books are a few years old but have found their way into the local library among other Women's Press publications. Mel doesn't approve of 'lesbian books' and takes every opportunity to disrupt Jackie's reading pleasure when she sees the distinctive black and white stripe. "Why do we need a 'women's press'? If we have true equality, then all books would be published by any publisher. We wouldn't have to have this separatist nonsense." Jack finds she can't ignore her and go back to the book.

"Yes but, until there's true equality, we need to redress the balance and women need the opportunity to have their books published."

"But not if they're crap!" says Mel. "Formulaic rubbish like *lesbian detectives*. I mean, how many private detectives are lesbian in real life? It does the gay community a disservice if this is their voice, if this is what the general public see of them."

"Them? You mean 'us'. And anyway, there are formula novels in the mainstream. It's just escapism; it doesn't have to be real."

So when Jackie begins to write her own lesbian detective novel, *Manhunt*, she doesn't show it to Mel for approval.

***

One Sunday in the middle of the second term, Jack eyes her depressing pile of revision notes and decides to have a day off and do something she hasn't done in year - she takes out her sewing kit. Inside the box are scraps of fabric she's saved from various sources, each one significant for its own reasons. She unfolds the quilt and sits on her bed to look at it. There is the ragged piece of a t-shirt she was given by her first foster mother; here the blue blanket; there an airbrushed dragon design that she'd found at a jumble sale; here the top that Claire had given her, knowing it would become part of the quilt; a border down one side is the blue belt from Jack's karate years, the highest belt she achieved. The stitches for the first patches are large, childishly inexpert and worn, but the later patches are sewn with a neat hand and some of the pieces have dates embroidered on them.

Jack has always been proud that she doesn't use a sewing machine – doesn't even know how to use one – and making this by hand has made it more personal. Now it is time to add new patches. Jack takes out the new scraps and lays them in a row against the edge of the quilt. She rearranges them a few times until she's pleased with the mix of colours, patterns and textures. She then takes out her cotton reel tray and selects a colour. The familiar objects make it easy for her to slip into the ritualistic movements as she takes a needle from the tin and begins to thread it.

"What are you doing?"

"Ow!" Mel's voice and sudden intrusion have made Jack jump and stab herself. She sucks her finger and looks up sheepishly at her lover, speaking with her finger still in her mouth. "Oim thowin."

"Pardon?" Mel looks at the quilt with obvious curiosity and then back at Jackie who takes her finger out of her mouth.

"I'm sewing. More patches. On my quilt, look." Jack holds it up as if it's an explanation. She hopes that Mel won't laugh or dismiss this as a childish game; there aren't words available to tell how important it is to her.

Mel looks at the quilt, frowning as if she thinks it is a bit of a mess. Her mouth forms an 'oh' but she doesn't speak. "Does it need more patches?" Mel asks eventually.

Jack looks at the quilt again. This seems an odd question. Does it need more patches? Well, if there are more patches to put on it then the patches need to go on the quilt, but does the quilt itself need more patches? Does she need more life experience? She looks at Mel with a blank expression.

"I mean. How big do you want it to be?"

Then Jackie realises Mel is not seeing the quilt for what it is – a collection of memories. She's seeing the quilt at face value. Jack thinks about this metaphor for a moment. Here she is in a relationship, not planning to go anywhere else or do anything else; she has arrived. Should the quilt therefore stop growing? Should it stay this size and be done?

"You're right," she says, putting the needle carefully back in the tin. "It doesn't need to be any bigger." She folds the patches carefully away and tucks the sewing kit into the box.

"Of course I'm right," says Mel, half turning to leave the room. Jack folds the quilt, leaving it at the bottom of her bed and Mel waits for her before walking back through to the lounge.

After *Eastenders*, Jack comes out of the toilet and notices her bedroom door ajar. She goes to the doorway and sees Mel inspecting the quilt closely. Jack coughs and Mel turns around. She doesn't look ashamed to have been found snooping, or even defiant about it. She just looks back at Jack as if she were looking up from the kitchen table, as if she has every right to be there. She asks, "What are all these dates?"

"I – I put the date on when I add a patch. Sometimes."

"Why?"

"Just so that I remember it, really."

"Is this… is it some kind of diary or something?"

"Maybe. I suppose so, yes." Jack braces herself for Mel's sneer but instead she is surprised by a tinkling laugh.

"Oh that's so sweet! You know, you're really cute sometimes." Mel drops the quilt and moves over to Jack to kiss her. Jack resists at first, somewhat perturbed by the patronising tone that Mel has been using much more lately. But the kiss becomes heavy and Jack feels herself being pushed towards the bed. She brushes the quilt off the bed and onto the floor before Mel climbs on top of her.

Mel likes to be on top; this Jack worked out early on in their relationship. There are two things specifically that Mel likes: one is oral sex, and Jack has had enough practice at this to now be an expert, the other is to be fucked. But bizarrely (as far as Jack is concerned) Mel refuses to lie on her back for either. Standing, sitting, kneeling, crouching, but never on her back.

During their first year together, Mel would ask to be attended to, but now she nods her head or gives a hand signal and Jack trots over like a trained dog. At first she enjoyed it, but by now she often wonders whether she really needs to be there at all. As she lies quiet and still (Mel doesn't like her to move around too much or speak during sex), she imagines putting a shop dummy, dildo attached, in her place while the real Jack goes off to do more interesting things. Sometimes she gets sore and uncomfortable: the pressure against her pubic bone can bruise if it's prolonged. But most of the time it is just mildly unpleasant to lie there while Mel bumps and grinds, breathing heavily into her ear.

She lies obediently still and thinks of lists in her head: shopping lists, revision lists, 'to do' lists', lists of favourite things, lists of dinners to cook on a budget, lists of people she can still call a friend. At last Mel will have had her fill and then Jack can readjust the straps so she can come herself. Lately though she hasn't been bothering with that last minor detail. It was easier to do it to herself.

Mel lies heavily on her for a while and then rolls off and walks to the bathroom. Jack looks at the ceiling and then reaches down to the straps and flicks them off. She winces as she sits up and rubs the wheals at the top of her thighs. The strap safely stowed away in her tiny cupboard, she pulls on her pants.

Jack hears Mel clattering about in the kitchen and assumes she's making a cup of tea. She dresses quickly and goes downstairs. "Kettle's still warm," says Mel, not taking her eyes from the TV as she points the remote control. Jack goes on through to the kitchen to make herself a coffee. These little things are beginning to irritate. If Jackie made herself a drink without offering Mel one, then Mel would have a blue fit. She sighs. If you insist the other person does something for you then it would seem petty.

"What are you watching?" she asks when she goes back into the lounge, coffee in hand.

"Corrie," says Mel.

"Oh." Jack looks around for something to do. Mel doesn't like her to read in front of the TV as she says it is impossible to do two things at once. Jack argues that she doesn't want to watch TV anyway and is just sitting in the lounge for the company and warmth. She wonders whether she should go and get her sewing and then remembers that she isn't going to do that any more. She thinks about getting her writing and hiding it inside a large folder so that she can write while pretending to be studying. She stands up.

"What are you doing?" asks Mel.

"Nothing," says Jack, hovering.

"Well sit down then; you're disturbing me." Jack sits back in her seat. "Come here. Come and sit by me," Mel insists.

Seeing her in an armchair, Jack asks, "Where will I sit?"

"Here." Mel pats the bottom of the chair, next to her legs. Jackie is confused. "Here, sit on the floor." Mel pats the space again. "You can keep my feet warm."

Astounded, but unable to think of any reason why she shouldn't sit on the floor in the draught like a dog, and unwilling to give Mel reason to lose her temper, Jack hunkers down next to her lover's feet and leans back against the chair. Her eyes fix on the TV screen and her mind wanders into a fantasy involving a leather-clad motorcyclist who never removes her helmet.

HARRIS ABUSED ME

New sources reveal that Jackie Harris, who killed homeless Frank Little in North Valley, was an abusive partner. *Valley Gazette* reporter Viv Diggen has been contacted by Jackie's ex-lover, who does not wish to be named for fear of revenge from the killer.

"She used to beat me up when she came home from the pub," says the anonymous woman, who is now married and living in the Borders area. "We got together when we were at university. At first she was a real charmer but she soon turned nasty once we were living together. I wasn't really a lesbian in the first place, and she put me off women for the rest of my life."

See pages 23, 24, 25 & 26 for the full story, including photographs. The face of Jackie's ex-partner has been blurred to protect her anonymity.

Chapter Thirteen – 1993

Jackie drifts through her finals in a daze. She is more stressed by Mel's schedule than her own. Mel is fraught with worry that she won't pass the second-year exams and won't be allowed back for the third year. Jack is tempted to tell her that if she drank less and studied more then there wouldn't be a problem. Instead they revise together and Mel borrows Jack's revision notes from the previous year.

The exams are over, and the exam parties. Jack wakes up to the sudden realisation that she doesn't have a plan. All along she has known that Mel will have one more year of being a student than herself, but didn't think about what she would do for that year. She no longer has a grant and the student account is already stretched beyond its limits. After being offered a badly paid office junior role by the job centre, she decides it'd be better for her financially to sign-on the dole.

The parties continue over the summer and, as Jackie now has more income, they can afford more bottles of battery acid and anti-freeze. It doesn't occur to Jack to ask if she can buy some beer or good wine with her own money. For Mel, volume is more important than quality.

Jack doesn't like how Mel gets when drunk. First she is funny, the 'life and soul' character who makes everyone laugh with clever jokes and witty impersonations. Once the guests have gone – or while the last few are still around – she becomes maudlin, droning on about her shitty childhood, about how she was adopted and her real mother hated her and how she lived in a children's home for the early years of her life. The first time Jack heard these stories she was horrified, but lately is beginning to wish that Mel would just get over it.

Jack hasn't told Mel about her own childhood and when the news comes out about Hillbank being closed down she is careful not to follow the story too closely. Jack can't remember any abuse in Hillbank from the staff, only from the other girls. She is surprised to learn that even her own keyworker has been arrested. The witchhunt is on all over Britain in the early nineties and a fair number of homes, special schools and other residential places, are closed around the same time. Some charges are made but most of those accused are released without charge, out of a job and their lives ruined. It is important to Jack that she can believe both sides as, if the girls were telling the truth, their own lives are ruined as well. She has no-one to discuss this with and hopes fervently that she won't be called as a witness.

Sometimes Mel gets aggressive: she accuses Jack of hiding the alcohol or withholding money from her; sometimes she bangs the walls and doors, and sometimes she hits out, but only when no-one else is there. Then she gets sick. Sometimes she demands sex, either before or after she is sick. Jack never thinks to hit back. She blocks the punches easily, although she hasn't been to karate since living with Mel, hasn't even told Mel about it. Her trophies are packed away in a box under the bed.

The summer goes by in a haze, marked only by Jack's fortnightly trip into town to sign-on followed, three days later, by another trip to cash the giro. Usually she does the shopping on giro day. Mel stops bothering to give Jack the five pounds for her share of the food and Jack doesn't like to ask. She realises that she really must find a job when the gas bill arrives and they have no money to pay.

Jack fantasises about selling her novel and spends a lot of time in the computer lab typing away. She has abandoned

Detective Trent Tipper and is now on the third chapter of *Inside Out*. Jack has a chance to work on the novel when Mel goes 'home' for a weekend without her.

Mel gone, this is the first time she has been alone since moving in. She is left with a guilty feeling of freedom. She is not sure what to do with herself. Jack spends the Saturday morning after Mel has left strolling around the house before she decides to tidy her bedroom.

The time Jack met Melanie's parents she thought it was a joke; she couldn't believe that people like that existed. An elderly couple, they lived in a large estate house on the Borders in which a butler would not have been out of place. Only when Jack had hung up her coat and had a glass of sherry did she realise that they expected her to fill that gap. She had not done so much washing up or listened to such offensive Tory nonsense without being allowed to argue back since she'd lived with the Baptist Appletons of Bilgeworth. When they weren't spouting opinions on the jobless state scroungers whose campervans were parked on a nearby common, they were cooing over memories of Mel's old 'friend', who was 'such a nice girl; whatever happened to her, Melanie?' while simultaneously eyeing Jack with disdain.

Mel had warned her not to mention that she was adopted as she said this was a sensitive subject. But Jack had managed to find a moment with Mel's brother, John, and asked him if he were adopted too.

"Whatever do you mean?" came the belligerent reply. Thus Jack begins to suspect that Mel has invented the story of her traumatic childhood as a way of gaining sympathy. She finds this hilariously ironic but does not of course broach the issue with Mel herself.

Jack hates Mel's parents. And the feeling is mutual because they had thrown her out on the second day for daring to wear an unironed t-shirt. Or it might have been because she saw no reason to hide the fact she'd spent the night in Mel's bed, or maybe because of the 'fuck the world' slogan on her t-shirt. Who knows?

The second time she had visited, her hair was longer, her accent less broad and her clothes ironed. She had slept in the spare room with little argument. They openly congratulated Mel on a job well done but still expected Jack to behave like a servant and not a guest. Mel liked to visit her family regularly and Jack had accompanied her on every occasion since they got together. Each time they seemed less snooty and their Tory opinions were less offensive to her ears. Once she even found herself agreeing with them: the poor were indeed often responsible for their own plight.

On this occasion Mel has decided to visit without Jackie – she says there's a large family function and Jack would be bored. Less naïve after several years with Mel, Jack understands that she would be an embarrassment and Mel would be asked uncomfortable questions if Jack accompanied her. In any case, Jack prefers to stay where she is. She decides she will go to the Students' Union that evening. Mel phones after lunch.

"So, are you keeping yourself busy?"

"Yes. Cleaned the whole house already."

"Well, you can't have done it very well if it's only taken the morning."

"No, no. I started last night just after you left."

"Oh, right." Mel pauses.

"I was just reading."

"Look, I won't phone you tonight. I'll be too busy."

"That's alright."

"What are you going to do tonight?"

"Don't know. Haven't decided yet." Jack wonders why she is reluctant to tell Melanie that she'll be going out.

"Maybe have an early night? That would be a good idea."

"Maybe..."

"Well, see you tomorrow then."

"Yes, bye." Jack puts the phone down and looks around the house. She hasn't actually cleaned the rest of the house at all but now she's told Mel she has, it would be a good idea to do so. She sighs and gets the cream cleaner out from the undersink cupboard. After a couple of hours of intense scrubbing, Jack pulls off the Marigolds and gets her writing out. But she is too nervous to be creative and instead reads through some of what she has already written.

That night, Jack dresses in dark jeans and a white shirt. She grabs her scruffy old bike jacket from under the bed, where she has hidden it from Mel's past-disposal obsession. She is unable or unwilling to shake off her dyke dress code established years before and smirks to herself as she looks in the mirror. Mel would be apoplectic at the sight of Jack venturing out of the house looking so dykey. It is only unfortunate that her hair is too long to spike up.

She is ready far too early and jitters about the place not settling to anything. Oddly more nervous than the first time she went out clubbing as an underage teen, she wonders if the basement bar of the SU is still open or if it has been shut down as threatened. She has a bus timetable somewhere but can't find it, instead hoping there will be late buses tonight. There is always the possibility of walking the five miles or so out of town. It's a long, straight road from Birwood to Bleakemore.

Jack goes out and waits at the usual bus stop, noticing how different it looks in the semi-dark. Scary. She feels odd not to be smoking. Mel insisted she gave up when they moved in together and this is the first time in a few months that the absence of a cigarette in her hand has made itself present in her conscious thoughts. The bus turns up at last and Jack has plenty of opportunity to passively smoke.

In the bar, figures emerge through plumes of smoke. The

chatter rises and falls as Jack makes her way to the queue for drinks. "Beer, please," she says, smiling. Not cider; not cheap wine. Beer. She is not expecting to see many people she used to know, but wants to be in a place comforting and familiar. Looking over to the old LGB corner, she notices a group of students. Difficult to tell who they are at this distance, Jack decides to wander over.

As she approaches, a high-pitched squeal issues forth from one member of the group. "Oooh, lovely. Tastes like paradise!" Jack eyes the queen in the corner sipping pink fizz and nods to herself. The faces change but everything else remains the same. She looms over someone's shoulder, looking for a place to put her beer. The woman she is leaning over is nudged by the person sitting next to her. She turns her head to look at Jack.

"Hey! Jackie, isn't it? I remember you."

Jack twists her own head so that the woman's face is upright. At the same time Fiona turns bodily in the chair and faces her. She hasn't changed much: same shaved hair and checked shirts. In fact, it might even be the exact same checked shirt. "Oh, hi!" Jack says. "Didn't think I'd see anyone I recognised. Are you still here then? Did you take a year out?"

Bodies shuffle up on the bench and hands reach out to make space on the table for Jack's pint. She sits down as Fiona answers. "No, no. Graduated last year. I'm in a research job now. Hoping to sign-up for a PhD."

"What, in Sociology? Wasn't that what you were studying?"

"Yep. So what have you been doing with yourself? We thought you'd moved away."

"Oh, well. A few miles out of town but it seems like another country. Wow, research. You must have got a first."

"No, a two-one. That's why I'm not on the PhD yet. What did you get?"

"Two-one as well." Jack sips her beer. "I'm looking for a job now. Nothing much around."

"Why don't you try at the uni? Oh I'm sorry." Fiona goes on before Jack can answer, "I didn't introduce you." She points to the people around the table. "This is Harry," the queen with the pink drink.

"Bona to vada you."

"Likewise," says Jack.

"Jackie used to hang around with us a lot but then she got married."

"Hardly."

"Ah, Richie told us all about you and Mel. Love's young dream."

Jack looks around the table. "Is Richie still here?"

"No," says Fiona. "Moved away after the op. Don't know where he's living now. Sorry – *she*." Fiona grimaces as she says the last word and then laughs so Jack doesn't need to ask where she stands on gender reassignment.

"What degree did you do?" asks a quiet voice next to Jack. She looks round to see a young woman who wears the wide-eyed expression of a first-year baby-dyke.

"Psychology," says Jack. "What are you doing?"

"Psychology. Same," says the baby-dyke.

"There's a lot of it about," says Jack, smiling. She turns back to her drink, thinking that's it from this shy girl.

"Why don't you try care work?"

"What do you mean?"

"I worked in a care home before coming here. I'm Isobel by the way. Isobel with an 'O'."

"Oh. Hi Isobel with an 'O'." Jackie looks again at her, taking in the slim build, freshly cropped hair and tight t-shirt. "You don't look old enough to have worked before coming here."

Isobel blushes. "Just over the summer. I *am* eighteen if that makes any difference to you."

"Well, I should hope you are or you wouldn't be drinking that." Jack nods to the pint glass that looks oversized cradled in the girl's small hands.

"Don't tell me *you're* squeaky clean." Isobel smiles, looking sideways at Jack. "In fact," she puts a hand on Jackie's knee and lowers her voice, "you look quite dirty to me."

"Are you flirting with me, Isobel with an 'O'?" Jackie laughs to hide her embarrassment at the direct approach. She's sure she wasn't this intense as an eighteen-year-old. Can so much have changed in four years?

Fiona notices how close they are and butts in. "Hey, you be careful! She's a married woman, you know."

"I wish you wouldn't keep saying that," says Jack, but Isobel removes her hand and looks back at her drink. "Well, what were you saying about care work? You mean nursing?"

"Not really nursing. If you work in a residential home it's mainly feeding, washing and changing nappies."

"Children?" Jackie frowns, confused.

"No. Old people. There's plenty of homes on the Borders. It's like retirement city over there. If you need a job you'll find something. So long as you don't mind doing the dirty work."

"I don't know …"

"No," says Fiona. "Get some work at the university. Tutoring, or look for a research job. At least you'll be using your degree. No point in doing something that you could have done without it. Waste of three years."

Jackie shifts uncomfortably in her seat. The notion of approaching her old lecturers is not as frightening as the expectation of Melanie's reaction if she did get a job at the uni. Mel tends to be utterly scathing about Jack's intellect at the same time as relying on it to write her own essays. It's likely that if Jack worked as a researcher, tutor, or – heaven forbid! – applied for a PhD, Mel would quite possibly dump Jack. This thought hits Jackie sideways and she has to put down her beer for a minute.

"Are you ok?" asks Isobel. "You've gone pale."

"I'm fine," says Jack, picking up her beer again and taking a large gulp. Why doesn't she walk away? Mel says that she would never survive on her own. How would she support herself? She puts a hand on Isobel's knee. "I'm ok. So, where were we?"

The next day Jack wakes up tired but happy. Nothing had happened with Isobel, but the possibility that it could have done has cheered Jack up no end. She spends the morning remembering how they'd flirted and thinking about the smouldering look in the girl's eyes. Nice. Jackie promises herself that next time Mel goes away for the weekend, she'll have some money stashed away so that she can afford a few more beers.

Mel comes home in a bad mood. She slams the door and doesn't say hello, just goes straight to the bedroom to dump her bag. Jack finds she is feeling nervous. Whatever has upset Mel, whether it has anything to do with Jack or not, it's likely to be Jack that bears the brunt of her anger.

"What's this?" The shout comes from upstairs. Jack knows that Mel is waiting for her to go up. She stands at the bottom of the stairs.

"What's what?"

"This! In the washing basket." She still hasn't appeared at the top of the stairs and Jack considers waiting at the bottom, knowing this will infuriate Mel. She grits her teeth at the thought that Mel has dug around in the washing basket to find a reason for her rage.

"Washing?" asks Jack. Silence from upstairs. After a pause, she trudges up, shaking her head. When she reaches the top she turns to the bedroom. "Look, I don't know -" she begins but is interrupted as Mel flies out of the room at her, pinning Jackie against the banister.

"This!" she hisses, shoving a shirt in Jack's face. "Stinks of cigarettes. You've been smoking."

"No I haven't. I was – I went on the bus. You know what it's like."

Mel flings the shirt down on the landing and jabs her finger into Jack's chest. "I *know* you went out last night. I phoned."

"You said you weren't going to." Jack can't stop her voice from sounding whiney.

"Well I did! And you weren't here. Where were you? Who were you with?" With this last question, Mel pushes Jack on her shoulder.

For a fraction of a second she thinks she's not going to fall. She thinks she'll find her footing or gain a successful grip on the banister; Mel will reach out her hand and hold her steady; Mel will not let her fall. But she tumbles awkwardly, sliding down the stairs on her back, bumping on every step.

Jack lands on her head and momentarily blacks out. Later, after Jack has picked herself up and gone to Mel to apologise, she checks her bump in the bathroom mirror. She knows that the memory of Mel standing at the top of the stairs watching her fall will stay with her for the rest of her life.

"How's your head?" Mel asks and Jack turns to see her slouching in the doorway.

"Not too bad. I'll live." Jack walks out of the bathroom, past Mel.

"You should be more careful," says Mel. Jack turns around and looks at her but doesn't speak. Mel points to the shirt still on the floor. "You'd better get that to the laundrette, and while you're at it, I've got some clothes from the weekend." Mel goes to the bedroom to get her bag.

***

Once Jack begins as Care Assistant at Sunny Lees Residential Home, Mel's visits to her family become more regular, so that it is unusual for her to be around at all on a weekend, which suits Jack. She gets paid a higher rate for weekend work. Once she's been there for a few months, she volunteers for night duty during the week so she doesn't have to share a bed with Mel. Jack can't say that she enjoys the work – chatting to the old ladies on a sunny afternoon is pleasant enough, but if the management see her sitting down then she is in trouble. In the afternoons carers usually stand, lean against a chair, or wander around with a duster looking busy. The mornings are hell and bedtimes are just as bad, but there are long periods in-between where very little happens.

Night shifts are even duller. Most of the residents have already been put to bed by the day staff so it's just a matter of answering buzzers overnight and doing the 'turns'.

Sometimes Jack catnaps in a chair with the others; she usually brings in a novel but often can't focus on the words; sometimes she's restless. Lately she can be found wandering up and down the long corridors. Snores emanate from behind closed doors, along with intermittent screams. Some doors are left ajar when a resident is particularly unwell and some call out if they are aware of a carer walking past the room.

Her shoes are soft on the pink carpet. She avoids the dark, gritty stains that appear at sporadic intervals. She stops and leans against a handrail, counting the scratches and scuffmarks on the wall, or watching the pattern of a flickering light. She breathes deeply the aroma of strong industrial detergent, sharpened by the tang of urine. Comforted by the institutional feel of the place, she is cut off from the outside world. She stands by a window and watches patterns in rainfall.

Jack's favourite place is at the end of a long corridor where there are two empty rooms. The room on the north side she doesn't like, has a feeling that it may be haunted. The other is much pleasanter; it reminds her of one of her old foster homes. She sits in an old-fashioned easy chair, left behind by a resident long-gone and looks around at the dark wooden dresser, wardrobe and side table. A tree swipes its branches against the window occasionally and Jack gazes longingly at the bed. It's very tempting to curl up on there and fall asleep. She knows that if this happened she's likely to be in trouble, so she sighs and heaves herself out of the chair and back out into the corridor.

"Hello you, I wondered where you'd got to."

Jack is startled and stifles a shriek as she recognises Brenda, one of the senior carers who has recently bought into the business but still works shifts.

"Jumpy, aren't we?" Brenda tilts her head back and gives Jack a long, appraising look. "Been patrolling the passages, have we?"

"Yes," says Jack. "Can't settle tonight."

"Must be a full moon." Brenda smiles and Jack laughs, looking down. They walk back towards the residents' lounge together. "Fancy a coffee?" asks Brenda and Jack nods. They turn off the main corridor and into the kitchen. Brenda gets mugs out and continues to chat. "Listen, what are you doing over Christmas? Are you working?"

"Uh, I don't know." Jack shrugs. "I don't really know one day from the next at the moment. Haven't got any plans."

"I expect you'll be visiting family, will you?"

"No." Jack shrugs again. Brenda stops spooning coffee into the mugs and looks at her expectantly, but Jack gives no explanation so she continues,

"Well, we're having a barbeque on Boxing Day. Bit of a tradition. Wondered if you wanted to come over?"

"Oh." Dumbfounded by the casual invite, Jack is unsure how to respond. She doesn't want to say, 'I'll have to ask my other half', because it would be met with questions about the 'other half'. So far Jack has managed to evade any prying into her private life and she doesn't want to encourage interrogation now. She settles for, "Thanks, I'll think about it."

"I wanted to ask you, actually," says Brenda. "Do you mind

doing an extra shift this week? Only Sue is off sick again, and…"

"When?"

"Tomorrow?"

Jack shrugs. "Ok."

Brenda hands Jack her coffee and nods to the lounge. They walk back together in silence. "How's that agency going then, Bren?" asks one of the other carers when they sit down. Jack looks up, interested.

Brenda waves her hand breezily. "I've not got the paperwork sorted yet, but I'll let you know once I'm ready to take on any staff."

"What's this?" asks Jack.

Brenda opens her mouth but is interrupted by the other carer. "Bren's going to set up her own nursing agency. She reckons we can get paid a sight more if we go private. A lot of people want someone in their home these days – they don't like to send Granny to a place like this any more."

"Not a word around management, though," says Brenda. "I wouldn't want them thinking I'm going to poach any staff." The other carers snigger conspiratorially.

"Well, count me in," says Jack.

***

"What's this?" Mel asks, brandishing The Note in front of Jack's nose the minute she walks in from work.

"You've been through my stuff?" Jack makes a grab for it but Mel holds it behind her back.

"Why are you keeping a note from an old girlfriend?"

"I'm not! It's…"

"I can see that it's old, Jack. It's almost disintegrated, look." Mel waves The Note in front of Jack again, letting it flutter until it rips down the middle.

"Yes, it's old. But it's not from a girlfriend."

"I'm not stupid, Jack. You've kept it in a plastic wallet in the box with all the sex toys. And what does this mean anyway, 'look after my baby'? What's this crap?"

Jack now has tears in her eyes. "Please, just give it back."

"There is no place in this relationship for your past lovers," says Mel primly as she scrunches The Note and tosses it into the bin.

***

"What are we doing for Christmas?" Jack asks as she's cooking Mel's dinner later. Jack rarely eats at home when she's working but Mel still expects her to cook. She's dog-tired and can't believe she's about to turn around and work another shift after having so little sleep.

Mel looks up from the newspaper she's reading. "I don't know. My parents want me to go home, of course."

Jack grits her teeth. "Only, Brenda, one of the carers at Sunny Lees, is having a barbeque on Boxing Day and I've been invited."

"Oh? *Brenda*. One of the *carers*, is it?"

"You've no need to get jealous," Jack laughs. "She's old and ugly." The words are out before she can stop them and she holds her breath as she hears Mel deliberately fold the paper.

"How old?"

"I don't know. At least forty-five," Jack hedges. Mel will be forty in a few years' time. "And they're all straight as poles over there," she adds for good measure. "So can I go?"

Mel snorts and nods to the oven. "Is that nearly done?"

"Soon be ready," says Jack, putting the kettle on for gravy. "Then I have to get ready."

"You're working again tonight?" Mel raises her tone, irritably.

"I told you this morning when I came in. Brenda wants me to…"

"Does she?"

"Oh come on… I'm hardly going to go off with my manager."

"Your manager? I thought you said she was a carer?" Mel gets up from the table and looks suspiciously at Jack before walking up close to her. Jack backs up and Mel steps forward further, trapping her against the hob. "If ever you *did* go off with someone, I'd kill you."

"Let me go, Mel. I'm going to set fire to my cardie." Jack steps sideways out of Mel's reach and gets a plate out.

"I mean it," Mel continues. "If I think you're having an affair, I would kill you. Both of you."

Jack slams the plate down on the table, on top of Mel's paper. A slop of gravy spills over the side and lands on the smiling face of John Major. "When would I have time to have an affair?" she asks, but Mel has been distracted.

"Look at this!" she shrieks, picking up the paper and throwing it at Jack. "I hadn't read that yet. You're useless, you are. Completely useless. No-one would want you anyway."

Jack shrugs. "Well you did."

"I don't know why," says Mel. "Where's my knife and fork?"

Jack goes to the drawer and gets out some cutlery, slamming them down on the table next to Mel's plate. She is tempted to ask, 'do you want me to feed you as well?' but thinks better of it. "I'm going for a shower," she says, instead.

"What's this rubbish?" asks Mel when Jack returns, uniform-clad and rubbing her wet hair. Now it's much longer, it takes a while to dry.

"What?" Jack looks at the wad of paper in Mel's hand and recognises the university computer lab printouts. "What is it, an essay?" she asks.

Mel holds the paper in front of her and sneers as she reads it out in a sing-song voice.

Mel breaks in her rendition to clutch her sides, laughing uncontrollably. Jack tries to snatch the paper from her, but Mel holds her back. "What is this absolute balderdash? Do you really think you can write, Jackie? You'll have to do better than this load of bollocks. Nobody's going to publish this crap and no-one would want to read it."

"Give it back!" Jack yells, making another grab for the sheaf of paper. "You've no right to go through my stuff." She blinks back tears as Mel holds her precious book away from her.

"I was tidying up and it fell out, Jack," says Mel sweetly. "If you want to keep secrets from me then you should be more careful."

"Tidying up *inside* my old college notes?"

"Crap, that's what this is!" shouts Mel, avoiding Jack's accusation. She tries to tear the thick bundle of pages in half and when she can't do this, goes to the bin to dump them. Then she scrapes her plate over the top of them. "Not even worth keeping for toilet paper," she says with smug satisfaction as gravy blurs the words that have taken Jack months to create.

I still have it on disc, Jim. I'm not that stupid. But after this episode it was a long time before I could write again. And now maybe you'll understand why I didn't want to show anyone my book until it was finished.

Chapter Fourteen

JIM

"What are you going to wear to the interview?" Jack looked over at me. I had just got out of the shower. I stood in front of the wardrobe wearing nothing but a look of blind panic.

"I have no idea." I turned wild eyes on her. "I don't have any interview clothes."

"Well, wear a suit," she offered.

"Then I'll look too butch."

"Well, wear a dress then."

"Then I'll look too feminine."

"Well, look," she sighed, biting back obvious impatience. "It's two weeks away yet. We can go shopping at the weekend, get you a hair cut and a new folder for the presentation. We've got plenty of time. Only please, come to bed. It's nearly midnight."

Her attempt at soothing words had only stirred up more trouble. "A haircut?" My hand shot to my hair. "Do you think I need one?" She groaned, shook her head and pulled back the bedclothes. Looked at me with a pleading expression so I surrendered. I got into bed. I didn't relax. "The presentation! I'd forgotten about that. They want me to speak. About the effects of domestic abuse on children."

"Easy. You could do it now if you wanted."

"I know. But to stand up? In front of them all!"

"'Them all' are women just like us. A lot of Women's Aid workers get their jobs through experience not qualification.

They're not that threatening." I didn't ask where Jack got her inside knowledge of Women's Aid and I still don't know. Her past is, and has always been, a mystery to me.

"Not threatening? That's exactly what I'm worried about: experience. They'll all be like, major feminists. And activists. It'll be like speaking in front of my mother. All her lecturing friends."

This made her laugh. "Are you not a major feminist and activist, my dear? Who was it that fought for the right to have a lesbian and gay officer during her *first year* at uni?"

"Well." I was quiet for a while. She was right of course. "But what if they don't want a lesbian? What if they're fed up of all being labelled lesbians? They might want to recruit more heterosexual women?"

"Well, if they did discriminate then you'd take them to a tribunal, wouldn't you? Now *please* can we go to sleep? I have work tomorrow."

***

The date of the interview did actually come around quicker than we'd expected. I had found a nice feminine deep purple trouser suit. I was pleased with that. I wore it with a cream blouse. I spruced up my hair. Careful not to use hairspray in case they were an anti-adornment crowd. I polished my shoes. Scrubbed my face until it looked polished.

I'd had plenty of notice of the date, and it was Jack's birthday too. I'd booked three days off beforehand, so had had plenty of sleep. Jack had the day off too, although she doesn't always take the day off for her birthday. She doesn't seem to like to celebrate it much.

I knew my presentation by heart. So did Jack. I had a file full of notes nevertheless. My polished briefcase even contained some overhead projector transparencies. The time of my interview was 10.30am. At 8.30 I stood ready in the living room. I muttered snatches of my speech under my breath. Jack yawned over breakfast in her pyjamas.

"Aren't you having any breakfast?" she asked and I shook my head.

"Just a cup of tea." I held up my mug as evidence.

"Have something solid for God's sake!" she demanded. "You'll be starving later."

"I can't. You know I can't. I can barely swallow. It'd make me sick."

"Well, ok. But sit down, will you?"

I perched on the edge of the computer chair and fished a piece of paper out of my briefcase. I frowned at it for the hundredth time. "It looks like it's tucked away behind the town centre. They told me to look for a small notice. Next to the buzzer."

"What, they've got a buzzer? Not a secret knock?"

"Shut up. Stop taking the piss."

"Well, they're hardly going to announce their presence, are they? Being a women's refuge and all."

"It's not the refuge. You idiot. The interview is at their offices. Which are separate to the refuge itself."

"But even so, I would imagine they'd get a fair amount of flack from aggrieved ex-husbands if they picked a prominent spot."

"Yes. I suppose you're right."

She noticed me eyeing the toast on her plate hungrily. She pushed the last piece towards me. "Here. You didn't eat properly last night either."

"I'll get crumbs over my suit," I protested weakly.

She went into the kitchen and returned with a roll of kitchen towels. Wrapped it around me. As if I were an Egyptian mummy. "Another cup of tea while I'm standing?" I nodded through my laughter. She patted me on the kitchen roll clad shoulder. "That's my girl. You need building up, that's what you need."

***

"So in conclusion: The effects of domestic abuse on individual children will depend on the individual child. But there are a number of common factors. These include altered behavioural states. Such as withdrawal or aggression; inability to concentrate; fear and nervousness around particular adults or any adult; regression into behaviour immature for their age-group. And many other particular behavioural patterns denoting distress in children. Such as thumb-sucking and bed-wetting. If the children themselves are not being directly abused but are witnessing the abuse. Or the effects of abuse on one of their parents. Then those children may also suffer from this abuse and may be considered to have been, indirectly, abused themselves."

"Thank you, uh, Jemima," said a dark haired woman. She consulted her notes. I thought I remembered her name as Dianne. I hadn't been listening properly when the three women had introduced themselves.

"Call me Jim."

"Jim?" asked another of the Women's Aid women.

"Er, or Jimmie. Either is fine. But I'm not too keen on Jemima. Makes me think of Beatrix Potter." *Shut up. Shut up. You're waffling.* I sat down. Turned to lean my stick against the back of the chair.

Dianne was smiling kindly. The other two weren't scowling, which was something to be grateful for. "All right then," said Dianne. "Now that bit's over, we can get on to the next part of the interview. Would you like a drink of water and a little breather, or shall we press on?"

"Oh. Er. I don't mind. I'll just..." I reached for the glass in front of me. The sleeve of my new cream blouse rode up to reveal my bangles. I'd taken off the wristband and friendship bracelets. I was trying to be smart for the interview. I saw Dianne look at my wrist then look away. I picked up the water and downed it quickly. Hoped they weren't aware of my trembling hand.

"Right then," said the woman on Dianne's left. Cindy? She glanced at the empty glass. "The first question is: why is it important that a group like Women's Aid is run by women only and not mixed gender?"

"Oh. Well. I think that while a male worker might have a lot to give? In a caring and supportive position? The clients who come to Women's Aid may have had such traumatic experiences. At the hands of men. That they are not yet ready to establish trust relationships with men. However different those men are. To the men that…" I trailed off. I stared at the empty glass in front of me. I hate the disjointed way I speak. In this kind of situation I'm very conscious of it. It's as much of a disability as my limp. "And. Well. I think that politically? A women-only group. Makes a statement to society. In that we are sisters in arms. So to speak. But peacefully so. And that part of our role. Should be to raise awareness and er…"

"Yes, that's fine," cut in Dianne. "That's an excellent answer, thank you." She reached forward. She picked up a jug on her side of the desk. She poured some more water into my glass. She then leaned back again, smiling. I smiled at her gratefully and took a swig of water. This time I didn't drain the whole glass. I noticed the other two women making sharp pen movements. They scribbled notes on clipboards balanced on their laps. Dianne wasn't making notes. She was watching me.

"OK," said Dianne, "ready for the next question?" I nodded mutely. "What would you consider to be the definition of feminism?"

"Ah." I almost laughed. "It's a tricky one. Isn't it? Well. You could say that there are as many different definitions of a feminist? As there are feminists in the world. There are certainly so many categories of feminists: liberal feminism, feminist separatism, Marxist feminism, post-feminism." *Don't say lesbian feminist. Don't talk about the debate over women-identified pornography.* "To define feminism is almost as difficult as defining what makes women fundamentally different than men. But all feminists have one thing in common: the belief that women, due to their gender, suffer the effects of inequality; that they are defined by their gender as being inferior to men. And most feminists are campaigning for change. Some... some people don't like to be called feminists when they clearly are, and some people call themselves feminists when maybe, maybe... er – well I like to quote Rebecca West: 'people call me a feminist whenever I express sentiments that differentiate me from a doormat, or a prostitute.'"

I took a deep breath. I looked straight at Dianne. "Um. Well that's what I think." Dianne smiled back. She nodded over to the other women. I adjusted my stance to look at them.

There were nine questions all together. Of a similar ilk. I knew the answers. I hoped that I expressed myself well. It was very draining. I barely managed to stagger out of the office. My head was ringing much worse than an afternoon in college. I left with a promise: if I'd got the job I would know by six o'clock that evening. I'd receive a letter anyway within a few days. I passed the next poor soul on my way out. I noticed something with a sly but guilty glee - she was wearing make-up and an overpowering perfume.

I walked down the fire escape. Into the small alley at the back of the Women's Aid office. I realised that I felt a kind of exhausted elation. Akin to post-exam euphoria. My brain had taken a pounding. My throat was sore, even with all the water I'd swallowed. I was floating on air. A weight was off my shoulders. I walked back into town. I realised that I was desperate for a pee. I popped into a burger bar to use the toilet and bought a large carbonated drink. Full of sugar and caffeine, which at that moment I felt an odd craving for. Gulping this down, I remembered. I was supposed to meet Jackie for lunch. It was now after 11.30 by the town centre clock. Had I really been in that office for only an hour?

We had chosen an expensive sandwich bar for lunch. To celebrate if the interview had gone well. To commiserate if not. I sat and picked at my smoked ham and emmenthal cheese on focaccia. I sipped my elderflower pressé. I was unsure whether I should be celebrating or being commiserated with.

"Well, from what you say of the questions, I think you'll have done just fine."

"But I waffled terribly. What if there was someone better than me?"

"Do people better than you exist in the world?"

"Shut up. You know what I mean. What if they had another candidate lined up? A friend. Someone who'd been volunteering?"

"Ah well, that's something that can't be helped."

"That's what I mean. There's so much riding on this job. It could be –" I took Jack's hand over the table. Jackie looked around the café uncomfortably. "It could be what saves us."

"What do you mean, saves us?" Jack asked. She withdrew her hand. Inspected a red patch between her fingers, drank some latté.

"I *mean*," I insisted. "Saves our relationship. Come on. You've got to admit. We're hardly love's great dream. We just don't seem to be getting together much lately."

"No, well. Your night shifts." Jack waved her hand. She didn't look me in the eye.

"Precisely. This interview has been hanging over me. But if I got the job…"

"That's why I wanted you to apply in the first place. No more night shifts."

"And more money coming in."

"Well. When did they say you'd know?"

"They said they'd phone? Before six?"

"What are we going to do for the next five-and-a-half hours?"

***

Later in bed. I was reading my book. Jack dozed next to me. Her Fay McMullin was about to drop off the bed. I picked it up and read the back cover. It's not the kind of thing I like to read at all. But I know that Jack enjoys the twisted stuff. I looked over at the dim red light of the bedside clock radio. Three o'clock. Still another three hours. And I couldn't settle to anything. Couldn't read. Couldn't do college work. They might phone at any time. Before six. I extricated myself from the bed. Thinking I hadn't disturbed my lover. I dragged on my towelling dressing gown.

She stirred. "Mmmm, where you going?"

"Just going to watch some TV."

"Want me to come?"

"No. You stay there. If you want." I went downstairs. I put the TV and kettle on. I got my own mug down. I waited till I heard noises of movement from upstairs and took Jack's mug down from the shelf.

By five o'clock I was a nervous wreck. Jack didn't look much better. "Look, let's just go out. They've got your mobile number, haven't they?"

"Yes. But... Well. It's rude? To go out? When you're expecting a call?"

"Well, we were going to go out tonight anyway. What about the club? Come on, why don't we just go and get pissed?"

"I don't know…"

"If we plan to go out, we can get our clothes ready now and I'll make some dinner and it'll be six o'clock before you know it."

JACK

"We haven't been out. For a while." Jimmie said when I suggested a trip to the club after her interview.

"I wish we could afford to go for a meal."

"What'll you wear?"

"I might wear my leathers, I've been reminiscing lately on my misspent youth."

"Hmm. Your leathers. Nice!" Jimmie smacked me on the backside. "Sure you'll fit into them?"

"Cheeky monkey! Get back up those stairs now!"

We raced upstairs and spent half an hour pulling clothes out of the wardrobe. Jimmie had already hung up the purple suit and blouse and it stared down at us from the back of the wardrobe door. I lay my leather trousers on the bed and a clean white shirt, and turned to look at the suit critically. "Why don't you wear that?" I asked. "You looked damn sexy in it."

"Don't be an idiot!" she said. "I'm saving it. For my next official engagement."

"What?"

"Wedding. Funeral. You know. Maybe I'll need it for my next interview? After this lot have turned me down?" She was downcast again; I tried to brighten her up.

"Well *I'd* give you the job."

"Well, I know *you* would."

"And I'd shag you too, as soon as the interview was over."

"Well that wouldn't be very professional. Would it?"

"Whoever said I was professional?" I laughed, and then added quickly at the look on her face, "Joking! Only joking."

But she was staring at the alarm clock again: five-forty. I

sighed and squeezed around her to get out of the room. "I'll go and put the kettle on again, shall I?"

She was close to tears as she blew on her tea. "Of course. I haven't got the job. I don't know why I raised my hopes. Nobody in their right mind would take me on. I've got no experience of Women's Aid; I'm not properly qualified for anything; and I totally fucked up at the interview."

"No you didn't."

"Yes I did. You weren't there. I waffled. I got all mixed up. I was utter shite. I'm crap at talking usually. I can't do public speaking. At all."

"You're very articulate when you're talking about feminism and stuff. Haven't you noticed that?"

"No."

I hadn't put any dinner on yet and it looked like we wouldn't be going out tonight after all. It was five-to-six and they still hadn't rung. Jimmie had checked the telephone connection and picked up the handset a couple of times to listen to the dial tone. She had paced for a while and then forced herself to sit down. Now she sat next to me with her hands under her thighs, leaning forward intently. I picked my eczema nervously – her anxiety always rubbed off on me.

"Look, you *are* fabulous. You got the interview, didn't you? And even if you don't get the job –"

"So you think I haven't got the job?"

"I'm not saying that. I mean, whatever happens, you got the interview, which means that you'll get another if you apply. And maybe next time…"

JIM

The phone gave a chirp. Jack stopped speaking. Both of us stared at it. It sat mutely like an indignant dog. I put my cup down and stood up. I hovered over the phone. Then I reached for it. It rang again. I shrieked and jumped back. As if it had suddenly come to life. I looked at Jackie. My face was hot and cold. "Well answer it then!" said Jack. My stomach was flipping inside. I felt sick.

I picked up the phone gingerly. "H-hello?"

"Hello, Jemima? Er, Jim?"

"Yes?"

Jackie stood up. I looked at her like a frightened child. Not daring to smile. I had recognised Dianne's voice. That didn't mean it was good news.

"Hi, it's Dianne here from Women's Aid."

"Yes."

"Well, I'm sorry you had to wait but we had a hard time deciding…"

"Yes…"

"And I'm just ringing now to offer you the job."

"…"

"To offer you the job? If you're still interested."

"Ng-yes!"

"Oh good," Dianne's voice relaxed. "You were my first choice."

"Yes?"

"So, you'll be sent an official confirmation letter which you should have in a few days."

"Yes…"

"And we'll have to chase up your references."

"Yes, yes."

"And I presume you'll have to give notice with your current job?"

"Yes." I looked up at Jackie again. I saw her flapping her arms around wildly. She was miming 'what?'

"So… and hopefully I'll see you soon."

"Yes." I pursed my lips. Tried desperately not to laugh. "Yes. And thank you. Thank you Dianne."

"That's ok. Well, goodbye."

"Bye." I put the phone down and stared at it.

Jack was nearly bursting, "What? Oh for God's sake what?" she shouted. I looked up at her. I was unable to speak. Jack whispered, "Did you get the job?"

I'd just said 'yes' to Dianne. About twenty times. Now I couldn't force myself to say the same word to Jack. Instead I nodded. I flopped onto the sofa to stop myself from falling.

***

Later in the club. We saw some people we knew. Sandra and Bev had been to The Claires' a couple of times. Jackie remembered them as being friendly and bounded over to them. Like a proud parent at sports day. "Jimmie got a job! She went for the interview today and they phoned her tonight. She got the job. Isn't she fabulous!!!"

"Congratulations," drawled Sandra.

I stood to one side. I was embarrassed by Jack's enthusiasm. I tugged her sleeve. "Come on. Let's get a drink."

"Ok darling." Jack made her way through the crowd. She leant on the bar. I was impressed. Jackie always managed to get to the front of the queue at a bar. There were never objections. Jack returned. She had two bottles of beer and a grin. "Who was that barmaid?" I asked. I looked over at the woman she had been talking to.

"Oh, just someone I used to know," said Jack breezily. She followed my gaze.

"Slept with her?"

"Can't remember." Jack shrugged. "Why, jealous?"

I snorted as a retort. I noticed that the barmaid had watched Jack walk back.

"Anyway," Jack lifted up her bottle. She chinked it against mine. "Here's to us. And here's to you." Chink. "Getting that job. You fabulous woman."

I bowed my head. "It must have been a fluke. Maybe all the other candidates were crap."

Jack groaned. She sat back in her chair. Swigged her beer. Looked around the dancefloor. It was early yet. There weren't many in. "Want to dance?" she asked.

"Uh. Not yet." I felt mildly panicked. I held up my beer. "Another few of these maybe?"

"So what's this job then, Jimmie?" I half-jumped. I hadn't noticed Bev sidling up to me. As she sat down I looked around for Sandra. I couldn't see her.

"Oh, it's Women's Aid. Outreach Worker."

"Sounds interesting. Go on."

"Well. That's all I know really. About the job. But it's part-time. The pay is good. I won't actually be earning less than I'm on now. And I'm working full-time now. And it's local. Well. It's based locally. I'm not sure how big an area I'll have to cover."

"When do you start?"

"In about a month or so."

"Well, congratulations." Bev looked around. "Have you seen Sand?"

"No," said Jack. "Not since we saw her with you."

"Oh," Bev said. She looked down at her drink, a disgusting looking pink mixture. In a small glass. "She'll have done her disappearing act again then," she added unnecessarily.

I put a hand on Bev's. "You ok?"

"Not really," Bev sniffed. Then she smiled brightly. "But I don't want to burden you with my troubles."

I frowned concernedly. But Bev didn't explain further. "So there's a Women's Refuge in this town?"

"I think there's one in most of the larger towns?"

"Where is it?"

I laughed. "I don't know. And anyway it would be a secret location. I wouldn't be able to tell you."

"Oh," she looked at the table blankly. Jackie sat up. As if noticing her for the first time.

"Do you need somewhere to go?" she asked. Bev was startled.

"No! No, I'm fine. Really." Bev looked wildly around the club for a moment. She spotted Sandra in a far corner. She escaped without any further comment.

Jack followed her with her eyes. Then rested them on Sandra. I was taken aback to see the vicious expression on Jack's face. I raised my eyebrows when she turned back to me. "What?" asked Jackie.

"Have you got something against Sandra?"

"No. Only that it's obvious what's going on."

"Well. Enlighten me."

"Don't be surprised if Bev comes knocking on the refuge door one day when you're at work."

"She won't know where to come. I've said it's a secret –"

"She'll find out. It doesn't take much."

"What do you mean?"

"Well, taxi drivers for example."

I opened and closed my mouth a couple of times before I spoke. "And what makes you assume that she's being abused?"

Jack shrugged. "I know the signs. Seen them often enough."

"But by a female partner?"

"It's not that uncommon." I looked over at the couple again. They appeared to be rowing. "Women can be equally as nasty as men. We interpret behaviour between two women as arguing or a fair fight when that same behaviour between a heterosexual couple would be abuse. Look at them." As Jackie spoke, Sandra slapped Bev across the cheek. Then she stormed off. Bev started to cry. A few people in the crowd around them looked on curiously, then looked away.

"Oh, yes," Jack laughed cynically. "Welcome to the world of an abuse counsellor."

"What do you mean?"

"I mean you can never get away from it. Once you are aware, you see it everywhere. You see parents hitting their children, people kicking their dogs, people exerting power over each other in relationships, within families, in the workplace, on the street. It's the way the world works: power and its manipulation."

"How come you never talked about this before?"

Jack shrugged, "You never asked."

"Is that really how you see the world? As one big power struggle?"

"Don't you?" I shook my head. I looked at my beer. She continued, "No. I know you don't. Even though you more than anyone have every right to. But you know, you are the first person I've been in a relationship with who didn't try to dominate me or expect me to dominate them. We are equal, I mean truly equal. It takes a bit of getting used to. Even after five years." She finished off the beer in her bottle. One long gulp. She looked over at the bar again. "Want me to get another? It'll have to be a pint of cheap stuff this time or it'll be the last one."

"Whatever," I said. I was suddenly very weary.

"Love…" Jack leaned over. She put her hand on my knee.

"It's ok." I smiled through my haze of tiredness. "I feel like I'm finally relaxing now."

"Good," said Jack. "So do I."

"What do you mean?"

"Well I'm glad you got the job for one thing. And…"

"What?"

"I didn't want to tell you before in case you got worried. But I had a very difficult client recently."

"How do you mean: 'difficult'?"

"Just a bit scary. She had a crush on me and it developed into a kind of obsession."

"Oh."

"But she's gone now. She's been released so I won't have to

work with her again. And I'm glad about that, I can tell you!"

"Good. Why didn't you tell me before? I don't need protecting. I work with difficult clients too. We could have talked things over."

"I know. But there's the confidentiality issue…"

"I had noticed you were down lately. I hadn't realised it was that bad."

"Well. It wasn't really *that* bad. I mean I only feel the relief now that it's over. You know how it is…"

"Maybe if I hadn't been so engrossed about this interview? I'd have noticed… Well. Hopefully now things can be different."

"Yes."

"Where's that beer then?"

"Coming right up."

Chapter Fifteen

JACK

"How was it?" I asked even before Jimmie had managed to get in through the front door.

"Well. As first days go, it wasn't so bad. I still haven't been to the refuge yet. I spent the whole day in the office? Going through the policies and procedures." She groaned and rolled her eyes. "But they're not a bad lot. Most of the workers seemed more nervous than me. Dianne says that they were very impressed with my background."

"Oh does she? Well, what did I tell you?"

"I know. I know. I just don't think of myself as particularly impressive. I mean. I may as well have grown up on Greenham bloody Common. It's normal for me to be aware of feminist issues."

"Well, it's not a bad time to be coming home, anyway," I said, glancing at the clock. "We've got the whole night ahead of us. What do you fancy doing?"

Jimmie yawned. "To be honest. I'd like an early night? I'm dead beat. I've been sitting around in a stuffy office all day. I hope I can get some outreach soon. Or I'll die of boredom like a caged animal."

"Cup of tea?"

"Hmm. Yeah. They plied me with coffee. Does no-one drink tea these days? In offices?"

I thought of Annette and her percolator setup and smiled. "So what's all that then?" I nodded to the sheaf of papers, folders and assorted files that Jimmie was digging out of her bag.

"Policies and procedures. They have an on-call rota. You know? It said on the application details. They run a twenty-four-hour on-call system. Well. There's only five of them. Which means it's a commitment. Once or twice a week. But you get paid extra for it," she added to my dubious look.

"I should hope so. I'm glad you didn't take up Babs' offer then."

"Huh. I'd rather just cut off from that place altogether. It'd be too much to be working in Women's Aid during the day. Then doing shifts at the shelter at night."

"Here." I passed her a steaming mug and Jimmie gratefully accepted. "So. Only five workers? Are they recruiting?" I wasn't interested in a job, but in whether Jimmie would have support. I always worried about the safety issue. And as it turned out I was right, wasn't I?

***

To: Pie,
From: Jack
Subject: r u there?

just a quick email. wondering if you're still around. the website looks busy, still haven't noticed a forum tho'. Are you tied up with other things? How's business? Please get back to me. I'll try emailing your other addresses too.

Jack :-)

JIM
"So that's the downstairs. Do you want to see the rooms upstairs?"

"Well. I could. If it's no trouble," I said. What I wanted to do was slump into the very comfy looking sofa in the communal lounge.

Dianne smiled sympathetically. "Come on, let's get ourselves a cup of tea first. Meet the women properly. No point going upstairs just yet, I don't think Donna's up yet anyway." Dianne looked at her watch. She frowned.

"Donna?"

"One of the women. Stacey's mother. Why aren't you in school?" I looked round to see who Dianne was speaking to. I noticed that a slight girl with long brown hair was leaning in the kitchen doorway. She was watching us.

"Mam said I didn't have to go today."

"Oh did she?" said Dianne. "Well, I'll have to speak to your mother, Stacey. This is the fourth time you've missed school since you've been here. What is it this time?"

"Bad toe." The girl held out her foot as evidence.

Dianne rolled her eyes. "Where are your brothers and sister?"

Stacey nodded in the direction of the playroom. Right on cue, a scream and cry issued from that room.

"Just..." Dianne waved her hands at me, "...just one second." She dashed off. I looked back at Stacey and smiled. Stacey folded her arms. She leant back against the doorpost. Looked suspiciously at me.

"How old are you?" I ventured.

"Eleven."

"Oh." I looked in the direction of the playroom. I heard children's piping voices complaining. Dianne's patient voice talking slowly and soothingly. I glanced back at Stacey.

"So. Where do you go to school?"

"I don't."

"Oh, Dianne said..."

"Yeah, well – I've been to so many different schools I don't remember anymore."

"Oh."

"It's shit anyway." Stacey slouched into the kitchen. She

filled the kettle. "Are you having a cup of tea or what? I've got to get one for my mam."

"Right. Ok. Yes please." I sat at the enormous table, looked around the large kitchen. It had yellow walls. White tiles. The toaster, kettle and microwave all dark green. Argos special. I turned to the door. Three children trooped through. Dianne followed.

"Stacey, have they had breakfast yet?" Stacey shrugged. Dianne sighed and opened a cupboard. "Is there any cereal?"

"Mam hasn't been shopping yet," said Stacey. She emptied the last few slices of a bag of bread onto a plate. She plugged the toaster in.

I was trying hard to control my expression. I didn't want to meet Dianne's eye. Instead I focused on the children. A petite girl in a fairy dressing-up costume was trying to crawl onto my lap. I put a hand under her and hoisted her up. I felt the weight of a full nappy underneath the tutu. "Hello. Who are you?"

"Vat's Shabina," said a small boy through a mouthful of fingers.

"Sabrina," said Stacey. "Come here, I'll get you a cup of milk."

Sabrina smiled at me and slid off my lap. I turned to the boys. "And what are your names?"

"I'm Tyler, and that's Tosh," said a boy of around six. He pointed to his brother with his thumb. "Who are you?"

"I'm Jim."

Tyler snorted. "Jim's a man's name."

"Yes. It is," I said patiently. "It can also be a woman's name. And it's my name. Do you go to school here?"

"*I'm* not going to school if she's not." He pointed to Stacey. Again with his thumb. Stacey put a cup of tea in front of me without a word. She walked back over to the kitchen surfaces. Began buttering toast. *If it weren't for her size,* I thought, *she could be their mother.*

"Oh, you get a lot of that here," said Dianne back in the office kitchen. "You get used to it." She shrugged. "Doesn't make it any less painful to see I suppose. A young girl being robbed of her childhood, and you know that as soon as she turns sixteen she'll be pregnant - just to get away. It's the only thing she knows." In answer to my look she held up her hand and said, "I know, I know – it's a generalisation and some of them don't, but you see it over and over again. You know, I've been working here for nearly ten years and I've seen women come in with their daughters her age and then go back to their violent partners. In and out, back and forth. And then there's a few years' gap, and then lo and behold there's the daughter coming into the refuge as an adult, escaping a violent partner herself."

"But you're not saying that it's their fault?" The kettle switch popped off.

"Not at all. I'm saying it's the only thing they know. It's a cycle that can't be broken, no matter how much you try."

"But we are trying to break the cycle." We walked through to the office carrying our mugs.

"Yes. We are. And hopefully boys like young Tyler there will learn that not all women are to be used and downtrodden." She sighed. She looked at her files. "But I don't hold out much hope."

"Maybe you need a break," I suggested. I pulled my chair over so we could sit together at her desk.

"Yes. Maybe I do. Trouble is, when I go home it's no break. I've got three kids myself."

"Oh." I never know what to do when women tell me about their kids. Am I meant to seem interested? Ask to see photos and the like? I so wanted a child myself. Without a hope in hell of getting one. When people moan about their kids I think how lucky they are.

"Anyway. Enough about me; what about you? How are you settling in?"

"Fine? I'm sleeping better. Now I'm not working in the night shelter." I laughed. Dianne joined in.

"So, do you think you'd like to take on a client soon?"

"Great. Get my teeth into it, you know."

"Is it very different to the night shelter?"

"Well. There are differences. But there were nearly always problems, too. I mean drunkenness and violence."

"Oh, we get our fair share of that here. We have an evictions procedure. Did you have to do many evictions at the shelter? How did you feel?"

"A bit scared. But there were always two of us. The most difficult one was when this guy? I'd been getting on really well with him. Suddenly blew up one day. Out of the blue totally. He was a really nice guy. I'd developed a good professional relationship with him. My co-worker Pete always said you should never completely trust a client. One minute he's fine and the next, bam."

"So what happened?"

"I think he'd had a bad day or something. He was in a bad mood. He picked a fight with one of the other residents. I tried to calm him down and... Well. He went for me. I was so surprised. I almost didn't duck. Luckily though I got out of the way. Pete intervened. We called the police. Got him out of there. I'll never forget the look on his face: pure hatred." The thought of Frank's face then. Still gives me the shudders now. Actually I was in a terrible state afterwards. Couldn't speak for ages. Pete was going to call Babs. He said I shouldn't be on duty.

We were quiet for a while. I reached for my tea. My bangle chinked against the cup. Dianne looked. I had noticed her looking at it a few times but she never made a comment. If you know what to look for it's easy to see. Bangles and bracelets don't hide the pain.

"Scars of a misspent youth," I quipped. It's what I usually say if anyone asks.

"Looks like you had a tough time," she said. I sipped my camomile tea.

"So this client…?"

"Yes. Donna Little."

"Donna?"

"I know, she's in the refuge at the moment, but we're hoping to rehouse her soon. And she'll need a worker straight away. She needs a lot of support."

"You're telling me!"

"Well, you'll meet her in person this afternoon when we go back. She's usually up by lunchtime. And I need to have a word with her about the kids' schooling. This just isn't good enough."

"So. You think I should start working with her? Before she leaves the refuge?"

"Yes. It won't be like that every time, but, you know, we're flexible. Are you happy with that?"

"Yes. Sure. It makes sense to me. I suppose we can't expect her to welcome someone into her new home? If she doesn't already know them."

"Precisely, and you can help her choose her home and some furniture and whatever. Are you interested in that kind of thing? I mean, it may sound tedious but you're actually there for emotional support. We're not expecting you to take over and do it all for her – it's about enabling her to do it herself."

"Right. And what about the kids?"

"Exactly. Even if the older two are in school, she'll still have the younger two in tow – you can understand how it might be difficult for her to get herself together."

"Yes," I said. I frowned.

"She *can* cope. Those kids are being neglected, yes, but not to such an extent that would mean social services' intervention yet."

"But is that a judgement we can make? Surely the social should know?"

"The SS *do* know. She's got a social worker. She left her husband in the first place because they threatened to take her baby off her. Sabrina was on the 'at risk' register. And Donna was eight months pregnant when she left him. But in the last two years he's been following her round the country. She'll tell you herself, it's a very sad story. Still, she has her good days – today is not one of them."

"But the kids. Not having breakfast. Not going to school."

"The other women chip in and help out and it's lucky for the younger ones that they've got Stacey. But then you've got to ask yourself what went on before they came here."

"What do you mean?"

"Sometimes we get women who cope when they have to, and then they get to the refuge and it's a safe place for them to fall apart. They know the kids are ok, they're no longer in fear for their life and it just hits them. That's what happened to me." Dianne fiddled with her pen for a second. She was supposed to be writing a report. She hadn't actually written anything since our conversation began.

"To you? You were in the refuge?"

"Not this one. But, yes. A lot of Women's Aid workers have been there themselves. Once I'd got my life together I started to volunteer. My kids were only small when I ran; it was hell."

"But when you got to the refuge?" I prompted.

"I had a lot of support. And I'm glad of it too, or I may not have survived. The most difficult thing is persuading the women not to go back to the relationship. I mean, it's to be a woman's own decision. If she wants to go back then there's nothing you can do to stop her."

"I can't understand how anyone would go back."

Dianne looked at me pityingly. "No. If you haven't been there yourself, then you wouldn't."

"I don't mean…" I began defensively. What does she know about me? What I've been through.

"Don't worry about it." Dianne was staring at the blank report form. She still held her pen over it.

"I'm sorry."

Dianne laughed. "Don't be. I'm OK. I really must finish this paperwork."

"You were going to tell me about Donna's move? When's it going to be?"

"Oh, there's no definite date. She's applied to the housing association and she's waiting for them to allocate her a house."

"She's at the top of the waiting list, though?"

"Yes. But it still takes time. Look, why don't you phone the refuge. You can go after lunch. You know you shouldn't go there on our own, don't you? Unless it's an emergency. If Jo's there then you can go over and meet Donna yourself. You remember the way?"

I nodded. I moved over to another desk to phone the refuge. Dialled the number pasted on the wall. Jo answered herself. She said in hushed tones that Donna was downstairs in the lounge. "I'll be right over," I said. I replaced the receiver.

I got a small Tupperware container out of my bag. Dianne strained to look over at my desk. "Are you on Atkins?"

"What?" She nodded to the piece of cheese in the tub. "Oh. No. I just don't eat that much."

The walk between the office and the refuge was a surprisingly short one. The refuge was tucked away in a side street with a lot of other Edwardian-style houses. I had noticed that it was three storeys high. I still hadn't seen the upstairs. I presumed that it was simply a rabbit warren of bedrooms and bathrooms. Not very interesting. I was surprised then, at the air of mystery Jo assumed. She wanted to show me the empty rooms.

"We can't go into the occupied ones of course," said Jo.

"Of course."

"But we've got three vacant at the moment, so I'll show

you those."

"Ok." I looked around. I really wanted to meet Donna before she decided to go back to bed.

We laboured up the stairs. It had a red carpet. Jo panted as she heaved herself first to a landing halfway between floors. She waved towards a closed door. "Bathroom," she said breathlessly. Then continued climbing. "First floor, Donna's room," I glanced curiously at the door. Dark stained wood. A number 'one' dangled by a screw. A children's drawing blutacked on. Jo was already along the corridor. "These rooms are all occupied. We usually fill up this floor first, but there's a single room at the end here if you want to see?" Jo opened a door. She stood expectantly aside as I politely looked in. I wasn't sure what I was supposed to look at.

"Hmm. Yes. Nice." I looked around the small, bare single room. An uncovered duvet was folded on the bed. Pillows placed on top.

"We make the beds up when we know a woman's due in, otherwise the kids mess them up. Ok, next floor is the room I want to show you."

"Why?"

"You'll see." I followed her. My curiosity was now raised. We arrived on a smaller landing. Three rooms led from it. "This is the converted attic," said Jo. I noticed that it was warmer and stuffier than the other floors. "This one is occupied," She indicated a room on her left as she walked past. "This one is empty, and *this* one…" The last door along this corridor was ajar. Jo walked through it. I followed her. "What do you think?" she said. She turned round and beamed.

For a moment I wondered if the woman were quite sane. This room looked exactly the same as every other room in the place. It was slightly bigger and seemed to be L-shaped rather than square. But even so, that was nothing to drag yourself up three flights of stairs to see. "Er. What am I supposed to be looking at?"

Jo made a frustrated gesture. She drew back the curtains. I noticed first the bars on the windows. I saw what the light had illuminated. I stepped back quickly. I looked at the soles of my shoes: they were clean. Then I looked again at the large brown stain. On the already dark carpet it looked like freshly spilled blood. A lot of freshly spilled blood. "Is that what I think it is? Blood?"

Now I was sure that this woman was completely batty. I started to back out of the room. Jo came towards me.

"Right! Tell that to the management committee."

"Pardon?"

"They won't fork out for a new carpet because they say that this one is perfectly fine. But I'm asking you: would you want to stay in this room with a huge bloodstain?"

"Well. No. But. Is that what it is then?"

"No. That's just it. We don't know what it is." Her low voice dropped even lower. It was barely a whisper. "It just appeared one morning. And there's a story behind that." Jo paused dramatically. She looked at me with raised eyebrows. I knew the woman was waiting. She wanted me to beg to be told the story. I cocked my head to one side expectantly. I refuse to play those games. Jo frowned at this lack of participation in the drama. She continued, "A woman killed herself. Slashed her wrists and…"

"Hang on. So a woman slashes her wrists in this room. Then a huge bloodstain mysteriously appears."

"No, you're not listening," said Jo irritably. "A woman who had been in the refuge, in *this room*, went back to her husband and then two days later killed herself. And *then* the stain appeared."

"Right. And it's not blood."

"No."

"Well. What is it then?" I knelt down and put my fingers to the stain. Then sniffed them. Ignoring Jo's sharp intake of breath, I licked them. There was a metallic tang to it. But it wasn't blood. Maybe rust. I looked at my fingers. Then looked up at the ceiling. To see if there were a crack or a leak.

"Well anyway," Jo was saying as she bustled out of the room. "The women refuse to sleep in here; they'd rather double up. They say it's haunted."

"Ah. And I'm sure that you reassure them that it's not," I said, smiling.

***

Donna leant back in her seat as Jo and I entered the room. She stubbed her cigarette out purposefully. Left it in the ashtray that balanced precariously on the arm of the chair. "So you're Jim then."

"Yes," I said. I was slightly perturbed.

Donna laughed a throaty laugh. Then coughed. Stacey looked around at her. Then back at the TV. "Don't worry, they haven't said anything bad about you. Just that there was a new worker. And you're for me, are you?"

"Well. I'll be working with you? If that's OK?"

"Fine." Donna waved a hand. She rested it on the gold packet next to the ashtray. Her other hand went to her hair. She made an attempt to sweep back some split ends. Tidied them into the loose clips that held the rest of the hair up. She had the kind of hair that looked as if it had been dyed to death. *Suicide blonde*, I thought.

"I'll be in the kitchen if anyone needs me," said Jo.

I smiled at her and she left. I sat down tentatively on the sofa. Next to the sleeping Sabrina. I noticed that Donna didn't smile at Jo. She waited ostentatiously for her to leave before turning to me. "That woman is a *nutter*."

I swallowed. I tried hard not to nod in agreement. Donna laughed again. Then picked up the packet and opened it.

"Smoke?" She picked two cigarettes out of the packet. Proffered one to me. I shook my head. Donna put one in her mouth. Leant right back into the chair to light her fag. She pulled long and hard on the fag. As if she hadn't smoked in days. Then coughed again. "So you want to hear my story, or what?"

"Well. If…"

"I was married when I was eighteen, pregnant with this one at nineteen…" *She's younger than me* I thought with a shock. "She was premature because he kicked me. Should have left him there and then." I noticed Stacey roll her eyes. The girl turned the volume up on the TV. Donna frowned at her daughter. "Stace, go and see what your brothers're doing, will you?" Stacey steadfastly ignored her. "Stace!"

"Oh *Mum*!" Stacey indicated the TV with an indignant wave of her hand.

"It's a repeat for fuck's sake. You saw it yesterday."

Stacey got up. She stomped off without another word. I opened my mouth and closed it again. I'd never heard a parent swear so casually in front of a child before.

Donna took another few drags of her fag before continuing. "His mother was very helpful, you know, with the baby. But quite controlling – typical mother-in-law really. Anyway, he promised that he'd never do it again; like, he even went for counselling with me and everything. Stacey was a lovely baby. But he wanted a son and wouldn't leave me alone until I gave him one. Before Stace I was meant to go to college, was going to be a nurse you know. And even when she was a baby I was still set on it, got a place, got her a place in the crèche. Then Tyler – oh, Tyler was his pride and joy. Spoilt him rotten, he did. That's why he's a cocky little bastard now. We had a few years where it was going ok. He was working, we had money, the kids were well looked after…" she trailed off and stared at the TV for a moment. Then tapped the ash from the end of her cigarette.

Took another long drag.

"He could be very charming, you know. He was quite intellectual and well brought up. All my friends were jealous. He is seven years older than me, and when we met he had a job and his own car… He's a sales rep. Anyway, so Stacey was in school, Tyler was in nursery, I was in college doing a course for the nursing. And then I fell with Toshie, totally out of the blue – I don't even remember him being conceived, must have been drunk. He started accusing me of sleeping with other men, which – when did I have time for that? And anyway Tosh looks like Tyler, so… But Ty is the spit of his father – he's really gorgeous, already has the girls swooning over him wherever we go. I managed to finish the access course just before Tosh was born and then couldn't get on the nursing course because of arrangements for the kids. But what I started doing was working as an auxiliary, you know – care assistant. And his mother would look after the kids while I was there."

She stubbed out the cigarette. Picked up the packet again. Changed her mind and put it down. She continued, "I wanted a bit of money for myself; he gave me money for the housekeeping but nothing for myself so that's why I did it. But then he stopped giving me money, he said that now I was earning I should pay my own way. I wouldn't have minded but he expected me to pay all the bills and for food and everything, and he kept all his wages to himself. It was stupid – I'd gone to work to get more money and ended up with less. And whenever I asked him for money for anything he made this great big deal out of it, how I was working and should be able to pay for stuff and how I was obviously useless and incapable of looking after myself, *and* a bad mother. He started phoning me up at work and waiting for me at the end of shifts, with the kids in the car, you know *ten* o'clock at night! I thought they were going to sack me because of the way he was. He would phone up and have a go at the ward sister if I couldn't come to the phone. The funny thing is, we never argued about money before I started working. Not at all. He just paid for everything, no question. I gave up the job in the end, hoping we could go back to that but no, he wouldn't let it go how I'd failed and how pathetic and useless I was. And then I believed him, and I started *being* pathetic and useless. Then it got worse. There comes a point when you just, you need someone to tell you that you're ok. You know?"

"Yes." I nodded. I felt totally inadequate. Donna sniffed. She dug out another cigarette. She looked over at Sabrina and smiled.

"My little girl. My baby, all mine. He never saw her." She gritted her teeth. "He never got his – claws – into her." She smoked pensively for a while. I shifted in my seat. "So. I was pregnant with her, and I didn't tell him. I wasn't going to let him use that against me. He knew I wanted to leave him and he'd told me that he'd kill himself and the kids if I ever did. I think he knew that I wouldn't have cared if he'd killed me. He'd already put me in hospital a couple of times and if it wasn't for the kids I swear I'd have committed suicide long before. When he got into a rage it was like he was looking straight through you, like you weren't there at all. And he used to say afterwards, 'I was angry, you just got in the way'. I always forgave him – I knew he was under pressure with work, all the targets they had to meet with the sales and that. But the last time he broke my ribs and in the hospital they told me I was lucky I hadn't miscarried – they said it in front of him so then he knew. He was livid, but he couldn't do anything about it then. His mother had the kids. I arranged it all from the hospital. I discharged myself while he was at work, before he expected me to leave, went straight over to her house to pick them up and straight on to the refuge. Not here, this was in Yorkshire, that's where I'm from. And Frank." She tapped her ash in the ashtray. I felt my mind go *click*.

"Frank? That's his name?"

"Yeah, Francis. So then you'd think that would be it, wouldn't you? I'd done it; I'd left him. But no, Frank doesn't give up that easily. He's pursued me across the country; I've moved five times in the last two years and he's found me every time."

I felt myself going hot and cold. Frank's wife. Of whom I'd heard so many negative things from the man himself. Donna didn't notice my expression and concluded her story.

"You know, when we first met I thought it was romantic – the fact that he followed me round persistently until I agreed to go out with him. It sounds kind of creepy, doesn't it – like a stalker – but it wasn't like that at the time. He was just persistent, that was his nature. Now it feels like there's nothing I can do, there's nowhere I can go but he'll find me. Every time I get myself settled, the kids in school, a couple of times I've even had a job. The first time it happened was about two months after I'd left him. I was out of the refuge and I'd got childcare sorted. I was working in the hospital and someone called me for a personal call – they got shitty with you for taking personal calls – saying it was my husband. I said no, they must have the wrong person, but I took the call. And it was him. I was in such a state of shock I couldn't speak. He said, 'Oh, I've found you then.' Just like that! As if it were a game. I can't imagine what he'd done, phoned every single hospital and care home in Yorkshire asking for Donna Little? So then I put the phone down on him, but it was too late – he already knew where I worked which meant he'd be there at the end of the shift. I rushed off saying I had a family emergency and went straight to get the kids out of school and left that day. Another time he was waiting outside the school gates but I saw him before he saw me. I went into the school and got the kids and got out a back way. But the problem is, Tyler wants to see him, he really does, and he's starting to clock on now to what's going on. He knows that when we move it's because I'm running from Frank and he's always a little shit for weeks. In a way I'm glad I don't have any family myself because I know the bastard would be on at them the whole time as to my whereabouts." She tapped her ash again.

"I don't always go to a refuge, though. Sometimes I've got friends and whatever, who can help me, but every time I move I have to make a whole load of friends again and I know that sooner or later he'll come along and wreck it all. I don't have a life, you see, I'm just on the run. You might think, why doesn't she stand her ground? Why doesn't she stand up to him? But it's not possible with him. He said he'd kill them and I believe him. I've got an injunction out against him but it doesn't do any good. You haven't seen him when he's angry…"

"No," I lied.

"The last time he found me it was six weeks ago. That's when I came into the refuge. I was out in town, luckily didn't have the kids with me, and suddenly there he was standing in front of me. It's the first time since leaving we've actually come face-to-face. He's all charming and nice and saying 'why don't we go for a coffee', so I say I'm in a hurry, got to get the shopping home. He says, 'later then, and bring the kids'. He's got that edge to his voice but I know he won't do anything in public. I know it's Ty he wants to see. I agreed to meet him because he wouldn't have let me go if I hadn't. And then, well, I came straight here. And the rest I suppose you know."

"Well. All I know is that you've been here six weeks." And, yes. It was six weeks ago that Frank had been evicted from the shelter.

"Yes." Donna stubbed out her cigarette. She looked in the packet at the last one. At this moment the boys came careering in. Tosh leapt onto the sofa. Sabrina woke and wailed in shock. Stacey ran in after them. Donna tutted.

"Sorry," said Stacey.

"That's ok," I said. "Have you been playing pirates?" I asked

Tyler. He was painted with a curly mustachio and wore a paper eye-patch.

"Yeah, an I'm gonna cut you up!" he shouted. He rammed his cardboard sword at me.

"Tyler!" snapped Donna. "Don't do that to the lady or she won't want to come back."

"That's. OK," I said. Trying to breathe normally.

"Why do you talk funny?" asked Tosh.

"It's just. The way I talk."

"Tosh..." Donna began.

"It's OK. Really. Children are. Refreshingly direct."

Tyler sniggered. He made a strangled sound in the back of his throat. "It's just. Uh-uh. The way I talk."

I left soon afterwards. My mind was in a whirl. The memories of Frank came to the surface. Frank talking politics. Talking about literature and art. All he'd said about how he loved his kids. About his bitch of an ex-wife. She wouldn't let him have contact with them. And how I'd sympathised. I had thought the woman must be a hard cow. Not to even let him see them. All this was now distorted.

Chapter Sixteen

JACK

Jim, you didn't tell me about Frank and Donna. Maybe if you had, then the whole murder thing wouldn't have happened. Or maybe it still would have: we never know what would have been, only what has been. So don't think that I'm blaming you. In any way.

I noticed that Jimmie was preoccupied but put it down to her new job. And I was preoccupied myself. I hadn't been able to contact Pie and had stopped trying. I still went on the chat networks and bulletin boards regularly, though not having the evenings to myself meant that I couldn't do this as often as I had previously. But Jimmie still went to band rehearsals and gigs. We were just getting used to having evenings together when Jim had an invite from Dianne to go to dinner, "…and bring Jack."

JIM

I had, of course, mentioned Jack. I said very little about her. Dianne showed obvious curiosity. "Where does Jack work?" "Do you two have any kids?" When she invited us for dinner: "What kind of things does Jack like to eat?"

The way that Dianne carefully avoided the pronoun. Made me smile. I decided eventually to put her out of her misery. "She's a counsellor; she works in the women's prison. You know Newpark? And she's also a musician like me. And a writer. She eats most things. She's not vegetarian or anything. Not fussy at all. But I am. I'm not veggie. But I don't eat much meat. Fish is ok. And you know that I don't eat very large portions. Don't you?"

"Ah," said Dianne. "Well, see you tonight then."

"Ok. I hope we can find the place."

"Just get to the Bull's Head and phone me from there if you need any more directions."

***

"Tonight?" squeaked Jack. I had told her as soon as I got in from work.

"Why? You're not doing anything? Are you?"

Jack looked distractedly around the room. At the computer. Back at me. She smiled. "No. No, only a surprise. We haven't had a dinner invite for a while." She took the E45 cream out of her briefcase. Rubbed some on her hands pensively.

I plonked down my own briefcase. I flopped on the sofa. I noticed that Jack was still wearing her work suit. "You only just got in yourself? You know. You're right. When was the last time we got invited to dinner? Or had anyone over here? They were an unsociable lot at the shelter."

"Unsociable hours they worked. Funny how you don't notice something like that until afterwards."

"You don't mind? That I said yes? Should I have phoned to check?"

"No, that's ok."

"So how was your day?"

"Not bad. So, apart from Dianne inviting us to dinner – and thank God I'm finally going to meet this woman that you keep going on about and I've been wondering if you're going to have an affair with her – how was your day?"

"What? An affair with Dianne! I should cocoa. She's heterosexual."

"How do you know?"

"Well. She's never shown any interest? In me anyway. And she's got kids."

Jack shrugged. "Doesn't rule her out as a lesbian."

"No," I said slowly. "But she's hardly my type."

"What *is* your type?" Jack looked at me square on. I looked back incredulously. I laughed. Wondered if Jack was joking.

"Tall. Dark and handsome." She frowned. I elaborated: "You. You nutter!"

"Really? I mean, really?"

"What's wrong with you lately? Do you think I don't love you?"

"The thought had crossed my mind. I mean, joking aside. I wondered whether you do still love me or whether you're only staying around out of habit."

"What? What brought this on?"

Jack shrugged again. She looked into her lap.

"Jack." My hand reached up to Jackie's cheek. I stroked her hair away from her face. I leaned forward. Then I inched myself towards her on the sofa. I tilted her chin up. I looked her earnestly in the eye. "I love you." I kissed her softly. On the side of the mouth. "I'll always love you." I kissed her again. On the other side. "Don't ever think that I don't." I kissed her full on the lips. Beginning gently, becoming more passionate. I held Jack by the back of her head. Tangled my fingers in her wiry hair. Jack responded. She cupped her hands over the back of my head and shoulders. Pulled me closer. Pushed her own body forward.

Then I drew back. I had so much to do that evening. I didn't want to be messed up. "There. Now that's sorted. Let's get changed. Ready for tonight." I stood up from the sofa. I saw Jack slump back in her seat as I went upstairs.

JACK

"Glad you found it ok, and you must be Jack – I've heard all about you of course. Come in, never mind the mess. Josh! Get back upstairs, you're supposed to be in your pyjamas. Just ignore him, he always shows off to visitors. This is my youngest daughter, Kim, and this is Mandy, my eldest. Not much between them as you can see, they're actually both ten at the moment but it's Mand's birthday next week so… anyway, come in, come in! Sit down, can I get you a drink?"

We edged through the hallway strewn with toys including a doll's house and a small bike. I noticed that Dianne seemed nervous as she ushered us through, but once the girls had gone into the lounge and Dianne into the kitchen I turned to Jimmie and raised my eyebrows. Jimmie rolled her eyes and followed Dianne through.

I watched for a minute from the hallway as they pottered around the kitchen making cups of tea. The silent interactions between them spoke of an intimacy that usually would take more than a couple of weeks to establish itself.

They came back with the drinks and I managed to get a proper look at Dianne. The woman had long dark hair, pale skin and dark eyes, was almost as tall as me and had a square jaw that seemed to be set in a determined expression.

"What was that you said about her not being your type?" I muttered as Dianne began to order the children back up to bed. Jimmie elbowed me and I was quiet. I never planned to be a jealous lover.

"You are supposed to be in your rooms. We have visitors." Kim gave Jimmie and me a cursory once-over and then sauntered out. Mandy stayed. "Mand…" Dianne began, warningly. The girl sighed deeply and flounced off.

"Teenagers seem to be getting younger all the time," commented Jimmie.

"Don't they just," said Dianne. "So. Jack. Jim tells me you're a counsellor."

"Yes."

"That's an interesting job. And in the prison?"

"Yes."

"Jackie doesn't talk much. About work," cut in Jimmie, looking daggers at me. "You might be able to get her to talk about her music."

"Ah, music. Of course," said Dianne. "What instrument do you play?"

"I mix."

Dianne's mouth was just forming an 'oh' when a wail came from upstairs and she backed out of the room apologetically.

"You might at least make the effort," hissed Jimmie when Dianne was out of earshot.

"What? I'm answering her questions."

"Well. It's obvious that you don't like her."

"Is it?" I asked innocently. "Did I say I didn't like her?"

"You don't have to. It's the way you look at her. Maybe it was a mistake coming here tonight."

"Oh, I don't know, love. We'll get a free dinner and you can see at first-hand why we shouldn't have children."

"Is that what you find so offensive about her? That she's got children?"

"I don't find her offensive. She's too boring to be offensive."

"You know. For a counsellor. You make judgements about people pretty fast."

"Hey. Who says I have to be a counsellor twenty-four-seven?"

Dianne was back in the room before Jimmie could answer and breezed through, picking up toys and books and muttering apologies for the state of the place. When she was done tidying up, she turned to us and said, "Want to come through to the back room? Dinner won't be long and we can talk while I cook."

I tried to make more of an effort for Jimmie's sake, but soon found myself bored again and stared out of the window while she and Dianne talked about work colleagues. The food was good and I consoled myself in not having a completely wasted evening. Dianne turned out to be a good cook. I noticed that Jimmie ate more for Dianne than she would for me. This irritated me slightly. Halfway through desert, Josh came downstairs and crawled onto his mother's lap, insisting he get a lick of the spoon. Dianne eventually gave in to his demands and dug out some chocolate from the cupboard.

He sat on his booster chair with a smug expression and proceeded to smear the chocolate over the lower part of his face, making it look like he had a beard. Josh's pyjamas where bright white in contrast to his brown skin, with tiny pictures of cars and buses on them. His hair fell in long ringlets, brown tinged with blonde, which shook when he laughed and his soft brown eyes glittered with mischief.

"He's going to be a real charmer. When he grows up," said Jimmie. "Look at his dimples!"

"He's my little angel," said Dianne, her fingers in his curly hair, "but he can be a devil when he wants to be." When he was finished, he got down from his seat and held up his chocolatey hands. Dianne got a cloth to wipe them with. "Now go – back – to – bed!" she said and tapped him jokily on his pyjama'd bottom, making him squeal with delight and turn to her with a 'chase me' expression. She growled at him and he scurried away like a little monkey, leaping up the stairs on hands and knees.

Jimmie and I both laughed at his antics and at the obviously loving relationship between mother and son. When we had finished laughing, we turned back to the chocolate mousse and there was an awkward silence. "Hmm, so have you two ever considered having kids?" Dianne asked, her mouth half-full of mousse.

"Well, I could hardly get her pregnant by accident, could I?"

"No," said Jimmie, ignoring my comment. "Well. I'd like to one day. But Jack doesn't like kids."

"I do like kids," I said defensively, aware of Dianne's incredulous expression. "I just couldn't eat a whole one."

"Ha ha. No. Really. We're both too busy at the moment. You know. Work. College. And everything. And they do, kind of take over your life? Don't they?"

"Yes, I suppose they do. But I would never be without mine. Anyway, there's time for you yet."

"Yes. There's time."

I didn't make any more comment on the subject and all that could be heard was the clinking of spoons against glass bowls as the mousse went down. I wasn't sure if Jimmie was likely to confide in Dianne the reason why she couldn't have her own child. Why she wouldn't even go for artificial insemination. I wondered if Jimmie had said anything at all about her past. She surely hadn't told them that she'd had a child when she was sixteen, or Dianne wouldn't have raised the subject of children.

Jim usually spares interrogators the details and is vague about the origin of her disabilities. She doesn't want to embarrass nosy people. Another non-comment to join the silence of Things Left Unsaid. If she has to explain what happened then she slips into robotic speech, mechanically listing all the particulars. As we ate I imagined the possible reaction at her interview.

"What experience do you have of domestic abuse?"

"I was abducted when I was thirteen and raped repeatedly for the next three years. I was kept prisoner in a cellar. I was beaten to within an inch of my life. My legs were broken. My hip was dislocated. I was half-strangled. My best friend was killed. My baby was taken from me. I now not only have a disability, a speech impairment and an eating disorder. I also have a problem with penetration and can't let anyone near my vagina."

"I'm sorry, it has to be domestic *abuse. Next!"*

It was soon time to go as everyone had to be up for work in the morning.

"It was lovely meeting you, Jack."

"Same here, nice meeting you."

"See you. Tomorrow," said Jimmie.

"Bye, then…" Dianne waited at the door to watch us drive off in the car.

We smiled and waved. As Dianne's house grew smaller in the distance, Jimmie said, "Well. I don't think she'll be inviting us back."

"Why not?"

"Don't you realise? How rude you are to people?"

I paused for a while before answering. "Well, to tell the truth, I don't really want to be invited back anyway. But if you get another invite, you go without me; she's your friend after all."

JIM

"I'm worried. About Donna's husband? Finding out I'm working with her?"

"You think he might?" said Dianne.

"Well. If he follows her home. She says he's done that before. Then he may see me with her. Or with the kids."

"Do you think he would recognise you? How long ago was he at the shelter?"

"Not that long ago. I think. Maybe three months now. But he was there for a while. We knew each other fairly well. I think he would recognise me. If he saw me on the street."

"I suppose the best thing would be to be careful in public places."

"But part of my job. Is to take the kids out. Like to the cinema. Isn't it?"

"Yes." Dianne shrugged. "Would you rather not work with Donna? Shall I find you another client?"

"No. She wouldn't get support from elsewhere. Would she? If I wasn't working with her?"

"No. Well, social services, but…"

"I'm fine. I'll work with her. I only wanted. To tell you about Frank. In case there was a conflict?"

"Oh, what's her new place like? I meant to ask you before."

"Lovely. It's four-bedroomed, as you know. And they are nice sized rooms. You know how some of these places can be really pokey? Like two rooms made out of one? Well. There's a big lounge. The kitchen is like an extension. But then there's only a small garden. Then a downstairs toilet as well as the bathroom upstairs. Stacey has her own room. The boys share. Sabrina is still sleeping in with Donna. Donna's sorting out the small room for her."

"Decorating?"

"All done up. Before she moved in. Not bad really. A bit bland I think. Donna's got curtains and pictures. Things to put up. It's amazing really. She opened up this one suitcase. And it was all there. Like an instant home. Drapes. Hangings. Some ornaments." I noticed Dianne's dark look.

"I meant to ask you something actually?" she said after a pause. "I wondered if Jackie would mind coming round to have a word Josh?"

"*Jackie*? Why on earth? Why would you want that?"

"*I* don't know any black people, you see. Josh's father… well, he was a quick fling – I never even knew his surname. He was a lovely man, don't get me wrong. Very special to me and now I've got a little reminder of him, haven't I? But Joshi's starting to notice now. He's at that age, and he's noticing other people's skin tones and comparing them to his own, kids in nursery are making comments. And soon enough he'll notice the way people look at me and his sisters as if he doesn't belong to us. I'm not very well up on black identity, and I just thought…"

"I'm not sure? Jack's not the best person to ask. She doesn't like drawing attention to her mixed race. She's got some books. But they're all adult really. She wouldn't know what to say. To a child." I caught myself thinking that Claire-O would be a better role model. Then immediately felt guilty for the betrayal of Jack.

"I don't know what to say to Josh when he asks questions."

"Tell him the truth." I shrugged. "If you make it as simple as possible. So that he'll understand. Then it'll be easier later on. When he's old enough to understand more. Kids soak up a lot. I'm sure you know that from your older two. How are they with it?"

Dianne smiled wryly. "They were a bit confused when he was a baby, although he was quite white when he was born. They never met his father but I'd told them that there was a good chance the baby would look different to us. We've lived in some fairly cosmopolitan areas and so I think they just took it in their stride. They have a rudimentary understanding of genetics; they understand the basics of why children look like their parents."

"Don't worry about it then. At least if you're open with him? I think if you sat him down and tried to talk it through. At this age anyway. That might cause more harm than good."

"Right. Good point."

***

"There's the bills paid. Can you post them? On your way to tomorrow?"

"Yes. Sure. That's amazing; *you're* amazing." Jack leaned over to kiss me on her way through to the kitchen.

"What? It's only the bills."

"Well, I think it's the first time we've ever got them all paid on time. And it's all down to you with your fabulous new job."

I snorted. "Hardly fabulous, darling."

"Compared to the night shelter, it's the Ritz; isn't that what you said?"

"Yes." I laughed. "But now I'm doing the outreach work? I don't spend much time in the refuge."

"But to get *paid* to go bowling and to the cinema, I mean, dream job or what?"

"We hardly watch the kind of films that *I* enjoy! And you know how much I hate burger bars. Why is it that the most famous organic eco-warrior in town. Ends up taking kids to the cow-killing rainforest destroyers. For a light snack. Before moving on to watch a sickeningly commercial film in a multinational conglomerate cinema complex?"

"Because it's their choice? Talking of which, what would you like for tea?"

"Cheese on toast?"

"Do you want fries with that?" Jackie ducked as a pile of sealed envelopes flew at her head. "Only joking, darling. I was going to ask you, how are they with you having a Thursday off for college?"

"They're fine. No problem. I'm just fitting my hours around having one day off. Now I'm on thirty hours a week."

"And you weren't too tired last night when you came back from college either. So that can only be a good thing. Hey! Is it Friday? We're going to the Two Claires' tonight."

"Friday? Oh God. It's been months since I left the shelter. And I still can't remember what day it is."

"How is the job anyway? You don't really talk much about it – apart from to tell me where you've taken the kids. I know you can't tell me their names or any details, but what are the women like? What are your other workers like? Is Dianne a fair representation of the others?"

"Well. They're all different. Really." I leaned back against the fridge door. I looked at the sink contemplatively. "Jo's a drama queen. If ever I saw one. Cindy is an ardent feminist. Quite frightening really. I'd hate to be a man around her. Liz keeps herself to herself. I still haven't met Janice yet. She's been off sick."

"But you've been there two months! She can't have been off for the whole time?"

"Everyone is overworked. When one gives into the strain and goes off sick. It puts more pressure on the others."

"Oh well, at least you don't have to think about it now till Monday."

"I do. I'm on call tonight. Remember?"

"Shit, yeah. That means you can't drink tonight then?"

"Yup. Though to tell the truth. I'm really tired."

"Oh, don't say you don't want to come out! We haven't been out for ages."

"You've changed your tune!"

"I'm getting used to it even though I can't stand certain people. Don't worry: I'll be good. I'll keep my mouth shut and won't make any trouble."

"Well. Maybe for a short while? But I'll have to bring the mobile."

JACK

I finished my toast quickly but as usual Jimmie just picked the off melted cheese and left the base. It was beginning to annoy me that she asks for cheese on toast and then only eats the cheese. Why don't I just do her melted cheese and save the damn bread? As she was pushing crumbs around on her plate, I remembered that she hadn't answered my previous question. "So what are the women like? Are they anything like the night shelter lot?"

"I can't really group them." She started speaking as she was picking at crumbs on her plate and I let her continue because I was fascinated. Sometimes I liked hearing her speak; it made me feel proud that she's come all this way. Before we met she hardly ever said a word to anyone. "Like, you can't say what all women prisoners are like? They're all different? They have one thing in common: that they've left their abusive partner. But even in that.

They react in different ways. Some are frightened; some angry; some know the system and are quite manipulative; others have never had any kind of social support. They are bemused by everything. The clients are mostly grateful. Although you get a few who treat the place like a hotel. And the workers like servants. But no. In general? They aren't like the night shelter lot. I think what's different. Is that it feels like their home. They make it a home. They club together with a kind of community spirit. Homeless people in general are more disparate than that. They hang around together. They sometimes have a sense of pride in themselves as a group. But they don't have the mutual support that women, especially women with children, develop in the refuge."

"I'm interested because I see that mutual support with the women in prison. They don't have kids – or at least not with them – but they still behave in a communal way sometimes. Not all do – like you say, they are all individuals, some know the system and some don't. I'm not comparing the refuge to a prison at all, but I'm interested in institutions. I wondered how much the refuge is an institution."

She thought about this. "It doesn't. Look like one. It doesn't have the institutional décor. It looks like a home. But I think. It probably is. In the sense that hospitals, schools, government offices are institutions. Yes. There is an incestuous air to it? It has its own system? Everything revolves around that. New people get sucked in. Yes. I would say that it's an institution."

"But would you have said that the night shelter is?"

"No," she said slowly. And then more determinedly: "No. I wouldn't. Do you know? I've never thought of it like that. I wonder why."

"Why would you say that the night shelter isn't an institution?"

She sucked her lip for a while. Then said uncertainly: "The members aren't *invested* in it?"

"Exactly!" I slapped the table making Jimmie jump. "My point exactly."

"Your point?"

"My point about institutions. If an institution is to work, then the members must be invested in it – whether they are there voluntarily or not. In a hospital, patients go there to be cured and staff to work – everyone is invested and everyone is there voluntarily, well, 'of their own volition'. So then you get prisons – the staff are there to work and the prisoners don't want to be there, but on a certain level, they do."

"They do? Want to be in prison?"

"On a certain level. Because they are invested in it. It's part of their self-image, a part of who they are – they have become institutionalised."

"Ah. I see."

"It's like the opposite of you, Jim. You've fought against the disability label; you're so fiercely independent that you'll never get stuck in a 'sick' role."

She was quiet for a while and then, "Do you think you're becoming institutionalised? In your job?"

"No," I said a little too quickly. "Why would I think that?"

"No reason. Only that you were talking about it. I wondered why you were interested."

"I'm interested in anything that makes people tick."

I picked distractedly at my eczema while I read my book. Something landed in my lap and I looked to find my E45 cream there. "Thanks," I said to Jimmie and rubbed some in.

JIM

The Claires' was busy. As usual. For once Jack was pleased. She knew that we were going to stay. For as long as we could. And leave together. The car was parked outside. So I could drive home. She wouldn't have to wait for the bus. She could have a few drinks too because I'd promised to drive. The Claires had organised a trip. To *The Vagina Monologues*. A whole crowd of people were talking about it.

"I can honestly say that I haven't laughed so much at a play," Claire-T was saying. "Especially the bit when the woman has all these orgasms on stage."

"Yes, she really looked like she was coming, didn't she?"

"So how is your vagina today? Is your vagina thirsty?"

"*My* vagina is desperate for a gin and tonic," said Claire-O. "Would your vagina like a G and T, Jackie?"

Jack pulled a face. She followed Claire into the kitchen. "My vagina. Isn't drinking tonight," I said. Joined in with the joke. "I'm on call; I have to drive home."

"Ah, that's a shame. Why didn't you come with us? We had such a laugh."

I turned my lips down. Imitating Jackie's disgust. Said in a deep Brummie accent, "Why would I want to see a play about vaginas?" Then added in my own voice, "Well. Not really. We've been skint lately. And tired out. Maybe next time."

"You know Jim," said Claire-T. "There was a time when you'd come along on your own – never mind what the girlfriend said."

I smiled but didn't say anything. That's not quite true. Jack reappeared. With a glass of sparkling water for me. "Thanks," I said. I turned away from the group – I wanted to sit with Jackie. Claire-T watched us for a second. Then returned to her conversation.

"Of course, you can reclaim the word 'cunt' as much as you want, Tilley," said Jack loudly. "But it'll still be used as an insult and it'll still be seen as offensive. Just like 'dyke'."

Claire-T winced. She looked as if she could hit Jackie. Claire-O put her hand on her lover's shoulder. She spoke with a laugh in her voice. "Don't be so defeatist. That's the point of the play, or one of them anyway: to force people to say a word that is usually hidden."

"You may as well say that there's no point in being a feminist because the world ain't gonna change," said Lisa. She stood next to Claire-T. Lisa looks like a seventies throwback. Overweight, shaved hair, dungarees. She is public school. The fake accent really grates.

"Another one?" asked Claire-O. She nodded towards the kitchen. Jack got up to follow her. She stopped in front of Lisa.

"Are you really telling me that the next time someone shouts 'fat lesbian cunt' at you in the street, you're going to thank them for the compliment? Or are you just going to run away and cry like they expect you to?"

"What would you do?" asked Lisa. She squared her shoulders.

"Actually, someone did shout that at me only the other day, didn't they?" She turned towards me for support. I duly nodded. "Little wanking penis," I said. I laughed. "It was fantastic! You should have seen. The look on his face. Mind you. He was all of, oh, ten-years-old?"

"He's thirteen – I know the family," said Jack.

"Oh great. So we're going to get an irate father banging on the door now. As well as the neighbour." Jack shrugged. She followed Claire-O into the kitchen.

JACK

"What's up, sister?" asked Claire when I appeared in the doorway.

"What do you mean?"

"Well, something's up. You two – not exactly the vagina dialogue at the moment, are you?"

I smiled despite myself. "No. We're not 'getting it together' as Jimmie puts it. Not…"

"Not fucking."

"Ouch. Fucking – it sounds like a nasty habit."

"*Claire of the Moon*."

"Got it in one." Claire handed me the gin bottle and I helped myself.

"My lover's favourite film, funnily enough. I thought Jimmie had stopped working nights."

"Oh yes. She's stopped working nights. But she hasn't stopped being The Ice Queen." I sighed. "Well, you know – we never really fucked in the first place. But now she will hardly let me near her. The only conclusion I can come to is that she just doesn't fancy me anymore. I mean, she says she loves me…"

"Lesbian bed death."

"Please God, no."

"Happens to the best of us." She shrugged and I was about to ask about her and Tilley but she continued. "It's a known phenomenon. When the sex life between two women fizzles out, what can you do? Didn't that happen with you and Mel?"

"Ye-es, but that was different."

"And you haven't had any other long-term lesbian relationships?"

"Well, there was Rachel…"

Claire snorted, "You can hardly call *that* a normal lesbian relationship."

I concurred. We both sipped our drinks silently for a moment. "So what is the cure for 'lesbian bed death' then? Oh great and wondrous expert of the multiple decade relationship." I made a mock bow.

"It's simple really. You just have to remember each other. What happens is that you get all domesticated and into a routine and the sex gets put to one side, kind of like cleaning behind the microwave. You can live without it and there are always more important things to do." I was just thinking, *I can't live without it,* when Claire continued. "Sex between women is as raw as it gets: wild, passionate, intimate…"

"Stop it, you're making me jealous."

"Well anyway, when the sex is good, it's amazing and goes on forever –"

"I know, I know!"

"– but then… but then LBD – lesbian bed death."

"Yes," I said miserably and took another swig of gin. "So, Doctor Claire, what can I do?"

"Romance her; woo her like you did when you were first together. Take it slowly, tease her, make her want you. You really need some lessons in seduction, Jack, 'cos you're like hands in the pants, what's the problem?"

"Not any more, I'm not!"

"Well, think of some way of spicing it up – you know, pretend you're strangers who've only just met, do a bit of role playing. She'll love it."

"How do you know she'll love it? She's not really the type for role play."

"Then buy her a toy: give her a buzz."

"Jimmie would kill me if I bought her a vibrator! You don't know her very well, do you?"

"So go sexy underwear then, God I don't know! Use your imagination. Come on, they'll notice we're missing." She walked out, leaving me staring out of the window into the dark garden. Dart crept in through the cat flap and then froze half inside the kitchen, staring at me suspiciously.

I looked around at her and smiled, "Here puss, lovely pussy," I said, reaching out my hand to the cat who backed out and scurried off into the night. I straightened up again. "The story of my life," I said as I poured myself another gin.

When Claire-O went back into the lounge, her lover was sitting next to Jimmie in the seat that had been previously occupied by yours truly. "She is *the* most miserable git I've ever met. You really could do better, you know." I stood in the doorway and didn't go in because I wanted to hear Jimmie's reply.

"We've made a life together. I'm not going to just dump that. Because we're going through a difficult patch," she said and then looked up startled to see Claire-O standing next to her.

"Come on, you cunt," said Claire-O, laughing, "get your yoni over there and start socialising instead of hiding in the corner."

Jimmie doesn't like meeting new people. They think she

doesn't notice the exchanged glances when she speaks but she does. Claire-O is gentle but firm with Jim and with the others too. She won't let anyone laugh at her openly. I sipped my gin, still standing in the doorway and watched Jimmie reluctantly reach for her stick and follow Claire-O across the room. Then I looked back at Tilley, who was also watching Jim. I thought to myself, *I wonder if my friend knows that her lover fancies mine?* She must have felt the hairs on the back of her neck singeing, because she turned and looked straight at me. Her first reaction, I saw, was surprise that I was there. But she recovered quite quickly and scowled at me. I smiled at her and raised my glass. *Hands off, bitch.*

JIM

Later. In the car. On the way home. I looked over at Jack. She was almost asleep. In the passenger seat. "Good night? Tonight?"

"Yeah," said Jack. She didn't open her eyes. "Not bad."

"How is your vagina?" I asked.

"Hungry," said Jack. She opened one eye. Looked at me.

"Fancy a takeaway?"

"Fancy you."

"Ah. I'm really tired…"

"Yeah. I know, so am I," she said. She closed her eyes again.

When we got home. The Women's Aid phone rang. I got caught up in a phonecall. From the police. They were trying to find a woman. Who'd been reported missing. "No. The name. Doesn't ring a bell," I said. I tried to get out of my coat with one hand. "Well. I'll make a note. If she does contact us…"

"I'm going upstairs," said Jack. I nodded. By the time I got to bed. Jack was already snoring.

JACK

To: Pie,
From: Jack

Subject: ?
It's getting cold over here.

***

"How're things?" asked Gail when I saw her in the library on the Monday morning after the visit to The Claires'.

"Fine. And you?" I wondered how Gail would react if I asked, 'how is your vagina?' I stifled a smile.

"Good. Couldn't be better." I noticed that Gail did have a spring in her step.

"New love in your life?"

"Mmmm!" Gail's eyebrows shot up. "Can you tell?" she hissed melodramatically.

"Just a bit," I laughed. "Anyone I know?"

"No. No-one from the prison staff. Someone I met on a re-enactment."

"A what?" I asked, frowning.

"A battle re-enactment. I'm part of an historical society. We dress up in Seventeenth Century gear and re-enact battles. Something to do at a weekend. It's good fun, you should try it."

"Er…"

"Hang on, I've got some photos here, just had them developed." She dug into her bag and, to my dismay, pulled out several large envelopes. Luckily she only had time to show two of them before the women prisoners began to troop in for their writing group. I made excuses and left, but not before I had seen Gail dressed as a wench standing next to a bearded man who would be nondescript if it weren't for the high boots, breeches, waistcoat and long sword. I contemplated how little one really knows about people as I made my way over to Mr. G's office.

"Ah, Jackie, our resident counsellor. I was just wondering if I'd have to come and find you."

"Hello, sir. Anything the matter?" I looked at my watch, sure that we'd agreed on ten-thirty.

"No, no. I just wanted to check you were alright."

"Oh."

"I mean, after that fiasco with er…"

"Larissa Thomas?"

"Yes. That's the one. How *are* you?" he said with an attempt at sincerity.

"I'm fine."

"Any problems with any of the other inmates?"

"No. None at all."

"And she… and you… how do you feel now she's been released?"

"I feel fine. I wish I could have helped her more, I mean. But as it turned out I think it was best all round."

"Yes. Quite. Well, I wanted to look at your timetable. At the moment you're in three days…?"

"Yes."

"…a week, and you have a total of ten…?"

"Yes."

"…clients. Ah." He looked at some papers in front of him and seemed to have forgotten I was there. My mind was racing: I couldn't afford to drop any hours and if my workload was increased then it might be too much for me. At the moment I was managing, but with more clients I might get burnout. I picked at my eczema while I waited for him to notice me again. Unable to stand the suspense any longer, I coughed and he looked up startled. "Good. Good. So, what were you saying?"

"My workload. You wanted to look at my timetable."

"Oh yes. Good." He leaned forward, frowning in a falsely concerned manner and spoke quietly. "We may have a conflict. With the room. There are, ah," he waved his hand distractedly, "complications. I'm going to find you somewhere else. Will that be ok?" I nodded, wondering who would want to use the tiny cupboard I'd been allocated and what possible other place could be available for use. "You see, this whole – ah – Larissa Thomas business has highlighted the issue of the room; I'm sure you understand."

"Oh," light had dawned in my mind and I let out an involuntary gasp, feeling my cheeks begin to colour. He wanted me somewhere more public. "So, where…"

"The problem is that the room you could use is also used for classes, so we may have to do a bit of juggling. And you may need to change your days. Would this be an issue for you?"

"To change my days? No – not really, I can't see that being a problem. As long as I can arrange things with my clients…"

"Oh, they'll be told." He made a dismissive gesture. The clients' own personal timetables were not particularly high on his priorities. "How do you feel about working weekends?"

"Oh. Er…"

"It may not be necessary, but…"

"No. Weekends are fine. But preferably not evenings, if possible."

"Right. Right. I'll get a timetable to you, then. Ok?"

"Ok," he said with a chuckle. "Lovely. Great. Right, well I must get on." I took this to mean that I'd been dismissed.

***

"Weekends?" wailed Jimmie when I told her.

"He said it might not come to that, but what can I do, love? If I refuse then I might have to drop some of my clients, which means a drop in hours."

"Well. I suppose. It can't be helped. But we'd only just got our weekends back. Since I've left the shelter."

"But we haven't really, have we, seeing as how you're on call almost every weekend anyway."

"You said you didn't mind!"

"I don't. It's just, well… it's not like we go away anywhere or

301

do stuff at weekends at the moment."

"Would you like to? What kind of things would we do?"

I thought about the historical re-enactment society and wondered how Jimmie would look as a wench, or even in high boots and a waistcoat, but didn't mention it. "Well, it's been a while since The Girls had a gig. Maybe we could organise something, like we used to – a festival or something?"

"That takes a *lot* of work. I'm not sure I've got the energy. I don't know whether Liv. Or the others would…"

"Oh, when are you lot ever going to get your act together? What did they think of those mixes I did, when was it, last year?"

"About four months ago. And they loved them. But we just don't have the money. To cut another CD."

"I could do it for you – we'd just need another computer."

"Good God."

"It's nearly Christmas…"

"You are just. A complete nutter."

"A complete and utter what?" I asked, grinning.

"Don't deliberately. Misunderstand me." She threw the magazine onto the sofa and pointed a finger at me, her other hand on her hip, but her expression was mirthful.

"Oooh, I love it when you get mistress-full. Tell me off again, go on!"

"You," Jimmie came closer, wagging her finger menacingly.

"Me?"

She stepped closer again and our lips were about to touch when the mobile phone in the corner chirped, like a child waking up just as the parents are about to have sex. "Ignore it," I pleaded.

"I can't." Jimmie reached for it. "It may be a woman in distress." She pressed the button. "Hello? Women's Aid?" and listened for a moment before going into the kitchen, so I knew that it was a confidential call and might last a long time.

"I'm a woman in distress," I said to the empty room.

HARRIS THE HEARTBREAKER

New sources reveal Jacqueline Harris, the notorious 'counsellor who killed' as a woman who has had a string of lesbian lovers.

Fiona Jarvis, 45, a lecturer in Sociology at Birwood University in the West Midlands, where Harris studied Psychology, remembers Jack as a predatory lesbian. "She made a habit of seducing young female students. Even after she'd graduated she was always drinking in the Students' Union bar, on the prowl. I knew one girl who was completely devastated when Jack slept with her for one night and then didn't see her again. We heard Jackie got married but we didn't believe that."

For more on the Jackie Harris story, turn to the centre spread on pages 23 & 24.

Chapter Seventeen – 1994

Jack glances at the computer clock. It's four-thirty. She must have been writing for two hours solid since coming in from her early shift. She hits 'save' and gets up from the desk. She stretches, her back cracking as a grinding noise emanates from the reconditioned computer. Blinking, she looks around her room trying, and failing, to focus on objects further than thirty centimetres away. The bedsit is so small; paper litters the floor, a mattress with tangled bedding leans against the wall and her crash-helmet sits in the centre.

Jack pours herself a pint glass of water from the bottle she keeps next to the bed and drinks it down in one. She flexes her fingers as she realises they are rigid with cold. The computer eventually finishes saving the file and Jack closes down the program. She struggles with the button on the floppy drive until the disk springs out and she stows it in a box with the others. This computer cost her £300 – two weeks' wages. It's worth it: she no longer writes longhand except in her notebook when on long shifts or notes in the margins of a printout.

She had never thought that she would be happy to be alone. After Mel had left, her life descended into chaos. She thought she would never pick herself up again. She couldn't afford to keep on the house and had to find a room quickly. As it had been Mel's choice to live in Bleakmore, it made sense to return to Birwood town. Surrounded by boxes she didn't have the energy to unpack. Days off were spent in bed. She lay there berating herself for not being the one to end it. It was Mel who told

Jackie that she was leaving but it was already a *fait accompli*.

The timing had been perfect. Mel had just graduated. Jackie's labour on Mel's behalf led to her gaining a two-two. Mel could not forgive her for failing to generate a two-one: the magic number. She blamed the project – which Jackie had written for her – for not getting a 'good' degree. On top of this, Jack had been at work during most of the exams and had left Mel to travel to them alone. Mel said that Jack had let her down. It is only now that Jack realises Mel was probably having an affair for several months before completing her degree. Her new lover, Fabio, is a civil servant and owns a house quite near to Mel's parents. A man. And they intend to get married. That explains all those visits 'home'. Cynically, Jack now sees herself as part of Mel's great scheme to get through university. Jack realises that, like Mel's other friends, she was disposable and therefore ignored when no longer needed.

Mel made no bones about why she had decided to sleep with someone else: Jackie had become boring and no longer satisfied her. All the hard work Jack had put in to becoming conventionally correct: acting and sounding 'just right' to be acceptable for Mel – was all wasted. It turned out that Mel had wanted a caged tiger, a dancing bear, not a lap dog or tame pussy.

Jack had been working extra hours at Sunny Lees, as much to avoid Mel as to subsidise her increasing financial demands. When the bombshell hit, Jack continued to work the extra shifts and fell into bed exhausted and alone. It was Brenda that had noticed. Brenda had lifted Jack out of her spiralling depression when she realised that she was planning to spend her twenty-fourth birthday alone. BBJ Nursing Agency is going from strength to strength, and Jack has been there as a Home Carer from the beginning. Earning three times as much per hour as she had at Sunny Lees, she can afford to work less. Brenda usually gives Jack the peachy clients and it was even Brenda that had found the bedsit for her.

Somehow Mel discovers Jack's change of circumstances and locates Jack's bedsit. She tries to wheedle her way back into Jack's life just when she is getting her confidence back. Her offer was non-negotiable: Mel will continue to live with Fabio while visiting Jackie for sex. The attraction has suddenly returned since Jack has become unavailable. Very politely, as she is still wary of the woman's temper, Jack informs Mel that she has been recruited by The Jesus Army and is now celibate.

This is not a complete lie: The Jesus Army *has* tried to convert Jackie and she considered the offer for all of three seconds. Sex is something that comes and goes and she considers herself a 'serial celibate'. Although Jack is still perfectly able to pleasure another woman, she is disturbed to find that she can no longer let herself come. She is trapped yet again in the evil cycle of trying too hard which beset her as a teen; her only release is in masturbation. She has been so screwed over by Mel that she wonders whether she will ever trust another woman again. Currently, she gets her romance vicariously via her writing.

She is four chapters into *Ellenweorc's Challenge*, and hopes that she will get further on this book than the others. She still hasn't managed to produce anything longer than ten-thousand words before another book intrudes and she is off again on a tangent. She wonders if she will ever finish anything, or if the epitaph on her grave will be 'Jack: of new beginnings'.

As she is working a late shift tomorrow – a new client for the agency that might become regular – Jack decides to go out tonight. She laughs as she realises that she is still wearing her uniform, ID badge and all, as the minute she arrives home she habitually turns the computer on. Now she strips down to her boxers – the luxury of not living with Mel – and grabs her grubby towelling robe, soap bag and towel before heading for the communal bathroom.

Ten minutes later she is back and shivering.

Turning the heater on to minimum, Jack begins to dress. The usual routine is dark jeans and a white shirt, but as it's a cold November day and promises to be a cold November evening, Jack slips on a white t-shirt under the shirt. She flips the radio switch as she considers what to eat before going out.

Jack hums along as she sifts through her kitchen box. Most of the food she eats is tinned or dried due to the ubiquitous unidentified food thief, scourge of the communal kitchen. She even keeps dried milk rather than risk leaving anything in the fridge, which would quite probably offer a salmonella garnish anyway. Far from depressing Jack at the lack of available facilities in this three-storey block, she is still grateful for the freedom from Mel it affords. And at least she's on the ground floor, not in the mouldy basement. Opting for a packet of savoury rice and tin of beans, Jack makes her way to the kitchen to hunt for some clean crockery.

The thought amuses her that she looks and acts more like a student now than while doing her degree and living with Mel. Except for her first year, of course, which she still remembers with fondness, being the last time she felt wild and free.

After her food, which is unexciting but fills a space, Jack piles the dishes into the already full sink and cleans her teeth. By six she is ready to go out although it feels later since she's been awake for over twelve hours, but she's determined that tonight, for a change, she will have a late night. Eleven o'clock at least.

She tidies up the room a bit thinking, as she does so, that it's always a good idea to have a tidy room waiting when you come home from a night out - you never know who you might bring back with you.

Jack is currently reading a Fay McMullin book she picked up in Birwood Library. After reading a couple of chapters, Jack picks up her keys and leaves the house. Two minutes later she's back again, cursing, to turn off the heater and pick up her wallet.

It is a short walk to the Students' Union now that she lives in town and she prefers to stroll on a dry evening. On the way out, Jack can't help but saunter down the side of the house to glory over her latest acquisition. Still present, the 500cc MotoGuzzi teases her by showing a hint of sparkling chrome exhaust pipe from under the skirt of tarpaulin she wears. Jack pats Betty's saddle appreciatively. She is beginning to feel back to her old self again. The new leather jacket does nothing to diminish this.

***

"Hey Jack, haven't seen you here in a while," Fiona calls as Jackie approaches the bar. Jack turns and smiles, then gestures that she'll get herself a drink. Returning with a pint, she squeezes in between Fiona and the queen whose name she has momentarily forgotten ("Harry darling, don't worry I don't expect a dyke to remember my name.") and realises she's interrupted a discussion about a woman in America who killed her sons and then made up a story about a black man stealing her car with them inside.

"I mean the thing that gets me is, like, not just that she made the story up, but that she was *believed* immediately," says one earnest student.

"Yeah, criminalising black people. I mean, if she had said it was a white guy, what then?"

"What do you think, Jack?" asks Fiona, turning to her just as she's about to take a swig of beer.

"Uh," she coughs. "I'm not sure. On the one hand, yes it's a stereotype in that if someone were to imagine what a carjacker looked like then they might think of a black man." Nods all around. "But on the other hand, there *is* a high crime rate among the black community, especially young black men." She is uncomfortable discussing race issues when all the faces at the table are white. If they are aware she is mixed race, like Fiona, then she feels patronised. She'd rather just stick to superficial subjects, like music. "Anyone heard k.d.'s new album?"

A few people shake their heads and the earnest students continue their conversation without her. Through the smoky haze, she is not sure whether she knows any of them. Jack glances around to see if there's anyone she recognises other than Fiona and Harry. Fiona notices her looking. "If you're looking for Isobel..."

"I wasn't," says Jack, nonchalantly sipping her beer.

"She'll be in later. Working on a tough essay. If she'd known you were coming then maybe she'd have brought it with her."

"Where does she live? I *could* go round and give her a hand." It's a genuine offer and Jack only realises the double meaning once she's spoken.

Fiona shrieks. "I'm sure you could give her a hand."

"And something else besides, from what I've heard," interjects Harry.

"What have you heard?" demands Jack, a little too harshly. Harry is taken aback.

"Nothing, darling. Nothing at all. No need to get your boxers in a twist."

"Well," Jack rounds her shoulders, unconsciously lowering her heckles and takes a gulp of beer. Fiona and Harry exchange glances.

"So how's the new job, Jack?" Fiona asks. She always asks, still hinting that Jackie should do something more academic, more 'worthwhile'.

"It's fine. It's good. I get to go lots of places, meet new people. To be honest there's so much work that lately I've been turning down shifts. And it's not all shit-shovelling, you know. Some of these people have got quite complex medical problems and social care needs. I'm not just a glorified home help."

"No, I'm sure you're not." Fiona is about to say more but

Harry nudges Jack.

"Here she is, talk of the devil." Jackie looks up to see Isobel walking through the basement bar with a pained look. She hasn't noticed Jack, who stands and walks over to her, ignoring the catcalls from the corner.

Isobel hears the commotion and turns, frowning. Her expression clears when she sees Jack and she smiles, her eyes crinkling in a genuine welcome. "Hi," says Isobel, unwinding a long, stripy scarf and exuding sexiness with the cold air she has brought in with her. "Love the jacket." She reaches out and touches the zip, sending a shiver through Jack. Isobel's cheeks are slightly flushed from the cold and her blonde hair, no longer gelled to spikes, flops down over her face. Jack has the urge to kiss her there and then.

"Hi," says Jack, uncharacteristically shy. "Uh – can I get you a drink?" Students don't do 'rounds' or at least Jack doesn't, otherwise that would be the first and last drink of the evening.

Isobel's grin gets wider and she thrusts her hands into her deep coat pockets. "That would be nice; I could do with one." Jack turns to the bar and Isobel follows.

"I hear you've been hard at work. Second year's a bit more strenuous than the first, isn't it?"

"Yes," Isobel smiles ruefully. "This essay is on perception and I haven't the first clue. I mean I can draw a diagram of the eye and that's about it."

"Oh, but there's so much in that topic! I mean, you can go into eyewitness testimony, stereotypes, reaction times... what's the title? Maybe we can thrash it out together."

Jack orders another pint for herself and a Southern Comfort for Isobel, who it seems has expensive tastes when she's not buying. They ensconce themselves at a table away from the corner group, who respond rowdily and receive hand gestures in reply from both women. They spend the next three hours discussing the essay topic, the wider subject of Psychology, the lecturers' lecturing styles and finally the lecturers' sex-lives, always a popular focus of student conversation. Isobel tells Jack that she's still in halls – quite rare for a second year but she had managed to get a place. She fills Jack in on the gossip about Alicia, the Assistant Warden, who is apparently having a thing with Warden Wilson's teenage son. All the while Jack is explaining about how the signals our eyes receive are transmitted and interpreted by the brain, she's receiving plenty of signals from Isobel's body. By the end of the evening all she can think about are Isobel's pert breasts and tight muscled thighs.

Jack drains her third pint and looks at her watch. "God! Is that the time?"

"Yes," Isobel giggles. "Didn't you notice when they called last orders a couple of minutes ago? I thought you were just being stingey."

Jack is miffed. "Just for that I won't offer to buy you a takeaway on our way back to your room."

"How very presumptuous of you!" But Isobel is laughing and dragging her coat on. She gestures to her own empty glass. "Come on, I've got a whole bottle of this stuff under my bed."

"I wish you'd told me that earlier," Jack grumbles as she reaches for her leather. "Could have saved me a few quid."

"See!" Isobel laughs. "You *are* stingey; I was right."

"Oi!" Jack grabs Isobel's lapels and pulls her close. "I'm generous where it counts," she says and pulls her closer still into a standing kiss that lasts long enough to silence the bar. When they draw apart again, Jack looks around at the faces of the other students and bows. She receives a round of applause, wolf whistles and shouts of 'encore' from the corner, and she waves at Fiona as she drags a flustered Isobel out of the fire exit and onto the street.

"You didn't have to do that in there," says Isobel as they walk up the hill path to the hall of residence. "I mean, so obviously."

"Best way to come out, darling. Get yourself snogged by a butch dyke in the middle of the Students' Union. More than the Women's Officer could ever hope for."

"Well, if you've *seen* this year's Women's Officer then it is more than she could..." Isobel collapses into giggles and Jack wonders if she's had one Southern Comfort too many.

"Are you going to make it up the hill?" Jack asks, sneaking an arm around her in pretence of support.

"Oh yeah, sure. Don't worry about *me*." Isobel runs on ahead and Jack strides to keep up with her. She looks back at the SU and realises that this path is not very well lit. No-one's following them as it's still within drinking-up time, but she nevertheless feels slightly nervous. How can it be that five years ago this walk didn't bother her at all? In fact several times she had fallen asleep under that very bush on the way back to hall. The invulnerability of youth, she now thinks, feeling all of her quarter-of-a-century age.

"Come on." Jack catches Isobel's elbow and walks her up the steps to the gate. "I used to live here, you know, in my first year."

"Did you? What was it like back then?"

"Ha! Back then? It wasn't that long ago, cheeky." Jack smacks Isobel on the rump, making her squeal and run for the entrance. She swipes her card and pushes the door as a buzzer sounds. "Well, this is new anyway. We just had a keycode and a miserable-looking porter in the..." Isobel laughs as she follows Jack's gaze to the porters' lodge.

"As you can see," she says sweetly, "we still have the porter."

"Oops," says Jack, belatedly whispering and they both giggle.

"Come on, I'm on the second floor."

"Oh my God." Jack sniffs the air as they walk along the corridor. "The smell takes me right back."

Isobel wrinkles her pretty nose. "Always smells like boiled

cabbage to me. Here's my room." She produces a key and opens the door. Isobel flicks the light switch and Jack stares around, aghast. Isobel shrugs apologetically. "I try to be untidy because I know it's the studenty thing to do, but I can't help it. I'm neat by nature." She takes off her coat and hangs it in the wardrobe.

"You never cease to amaze me," says Jack, laughing. "My room wasn't this immaculate, even on the day I moved in!" Jackie puts her arms around Isobel, who reaches up and grabs her jacket collar.

"Fiona reckons I'm anally retentive."

Jack pulls back slightly. "Fiona? Fiona's been here?" In Jack's mind that can only mean one thing.

Isobel groans. "She came *once* for a *coffee*. What, you don't think I'd sleep with her, do you?" She looks at Jack defiantly. "And anyway, what if I had? What's it to you?"

Jack relents. "You're right. It isn't anything to do with me; it's just she's so much older than you. Eugh, it's a gross thought." She wonders as she says it whether this is what other people had thought about her and Melanie.

"Actually she did try coming on to me, but I told her in no uncertain terms where to get off." Isobel breaks the embrace and slinks over to the bed, sitting on the eiderdown and reaching for the promised bottle.

"Ah, that explains a lot," says Jack.

"Like what?" Isobel straightens up, Southern Comfort in hand. "I haven't any glasses, by the way, so we'll have to swig from the bottle."

Jack moves to sit on the bed next to Isobel. "Like how she's always trying to wind me up about you. Should have known she was jealous."

"Hmm, you're much nicer than her, anyway." Isobel takes a long glug of Southern Comfort and then offers the bottle to Jack, wiping her mouth with the back of her hand.

Jack holds up her palm. "Actually, no. Can't stand the taste –

it's far too sweet for me."

Isobel screws the top back on the bottle and places it uncertainly on the bedside table. "I hope that's not going to stop you from tasting me?"

"I shouldn't think so," says Jack and she leans in to kiss Isobel again, this time lingering particularly around the edges of her mouth and allowing her hands to wander over the girl's upper body. When she pulls back, Isobel is out of breath. Jack knows that the next thing she has to say will be hard and might mean she has to leave.

She catches Isobel's hand and looks solemnly at her. "Isobel, I need to tell you something."

"Oh, shit," says the girl, reaching again for the bottle. "You're a man."

"No, I –"

"You've got AIDS?" Isobel's eyes widen in horror.

"No!" says Jack, laughing. "I – I just wanted to tell you that I'm not looking for a relationship right now. I mean, I like you, but I don't want anything serious."

"Oh." Isobel's disappointment is palpable. Whether she's disappointed because she had genuinely expected a relationship, or whether it's because Jack isn't an HIV positive transsexual, she will never know. Isobel shrugs and smiles pleasantly. "Well, we'll just have to make tonight really special, then, won't we?" she says.

And it is. For the rest of her life, Jackie will remember sweet, sweet Isobel with an 'O my God!' Soft honey skin, tender lips and vanilla tastes. A few hours of stroking fingertips and lightly teasing kisses, coupled with the occasional swig of Southern Comfort to which Jack eventually succumbs. She's glad the demands made of her are not too energetic and that Isobel doesn't expect Jack to orgasm. But she knows that she would soon get tired of it. At 1.30am, Jack rubs her face and props herself up on an elbow looking down at Isobel's trouble-free expression. "Mmmm," Isobel snuggles into her. "I'm going to have one mother of a hangover tomorrow."

Jack laughs. "I'm sure you'll still be as pretty as a picture." She strokes the hair out of Isobel's eyes, marvelling at how young and fresh she looks.

"Don't you believe it!" says Isobel. "I'm a dragon in the morning."

"Well, I'm not planning on sticking around to see that," says Jack, laughing more light-heartedly than she feels. "I'd better go now, before I change into a pumpkin." *Or a rat.*

Isobel groans, but she doesn't try to stop her. Jack sits on the side of the bed to put on her boots and then picks up her jacket from the floor. She turns to Isobel, who is watching her silently. "I'll see you around." Jack plants a kiss on Isobel's cheek and straightens the mat on her way out. She walks home whistling, the sticky syrupy taste of Southern Comfort and Isobel still on her lips.

***

JACK

It seems harsh, looking back. Love them and leave them; break their hearts and deceive them. Something that might have been the beginning of a beautiful friendship I chose not to continue. Perhaps in an alternative universe, an alternative Jack and Isobel are snuggled up together on their Laura Ashley sofa. They are watching repeats of *The L Word* on Living TV; a cat named Navratta is asleep on the mat in front of the fire. They celebrate their ten-year anniversary with a couple of glasses of Southern Comfort, bottle conveniently placed on a neatly polished coffee table. The sickly savour now flowing through Jack's veins rendering her incapable of inspiration. I shiver at the thought. I'd rather have murder and mayhem any day, thank you very much. Perhaps that's just me.

If I'd turned a different corner; if I'd turned down the client the next day; if I'd decided to pay a surprise visit to Isobel in the morning. Bringing carnations and croissants and ignoring her dragon-breath; propositioning her with a life of two instead of one. If I'd trusted. Perhaps it would have been different. But I'm not sure. The longer I live, the more I believe in fate. Things are meant to be.

***

Jack groans and rolls over to look at the clock on the floor next to her. Her body wakes up at 6am regardless of her shift pattern, but on a day like today she has the pleasure of turning over and falling asleep again for another three hours while the rest of the world heaves itself out of bed and into the rat race. Perhaps this is why she likes to work shifts.

She dreams of soft touches, legs and abdomens, honey skin and sticky lips. She wakes on the brink of an orgasm. Caressing her quilt, she puts her fingers to her mouth and smells Isobel. She moves her legs and can feel that she's wet. Luxuriating in the warmth of the blankets, Jack turns onto her back and lets her hands do what they naturally do. The one person who can be relied on to give Jack pleasure with no strings attached.

Several cups of coffee and a burger later, Jack is riding Betty through the November drizzle on her way to her shift. The handwritten directions are sellotaped to the fuel tank and she swipes blotches of rain from the paper to see the words and makeshift map. Luckily she's in the habit of leaving early, when it's a new client, to allow time for getting lost.

Jack pulls the bike up in front of a nondescript terrace and rips away the soggy paper that's falling from the petrol tank. She draws off her gauntlets and holds them in her lap, sitting back in the saddle so that she can unzip her waterproof overalls. She takes her notebook out of the inside jacket pocket and checks the client address. It doesn't do to go knocking on the next-door neighbour's house.

However, the client doesn't seem inclined to worry what the neighbours think since he's hung a *Terrance Higgins Trust* banner in the front window. Jack reads the client's details again. Byron is thirty-years-old and he's dying. She sighs and returns the notebook to her pocket.

A mature woman answers the door and walks away without a word; Jack recognises the uniform as that of a rival agency. She steps over the threshold and puts her panniers just inside the front door, looking around the hall for somewhere to hang her waterproofs. The early shift carer appears again from the front room pulling on her coat and carrying a bag. She looks at Jack and then starts to check the contents of her bag. Classical music trickles through the door behind her.

"Er…" Jack says.

"He's got a visitor," says the woman in a loud, disdainful voice. "He's been playing that crap all day. He usually sleeps in the afternoon, but I don't know if he will today. He's been incontinent of faeces twice," she continues in an equally loud tone that the neighbours can probably hear, let alone Byron and his visitor. "You know he's got hepatitis, don't you?" she says and then proceeds in a stage whisper: "You know he's *got AIDS*?"

"I'll just say 'hi'," says Jack. "He's in here, is he?" She pushes through to the half-open lounge door and knocks.

"Come in," calls a hoarse voice.

She puts her head round the side of the door and her eyes search for the client. A large hospital bed dominates the centre of the room, complete with cot sides and air mattress. A white sheet hangs on the sidewall displaying various graffitied quotes, poems and messages. At the centre, in six-inch high burgundy letters, is the legend: *Life is a terminal illness*. Apart from these two items, everything else in the lounge is as you might expect in anyone's front room. You might miss Byron if you weren't expecting him to be there, as he's thin and small as a child, propped up on a mountain of pillows. Wispy hair protrudes from under a pale blue fleece hat that might actually be a baby's. Incongruously large spectacles balance on a beak of a nose, behind which Byron's eyes are bright with spirit.

"Hello," says Jack in her professional voice. "My name's Jackie and I'll be your carer for this afternoon." She smiles; Byron has understood the humour and is chuckling in a wheezy kind of way.

"That's great," he says. "Make yourself at home. Coffee, tea, it's all in the kitchen."

"I'll just get out of my bike gear," says Jack. "Can I get you anything?" Byron waves a hand and she backs out again.

She looks around the hall, the other carer has gone but Jack can hear movements upstairs. Perhaps the visitor. She places her helmet on the floor next to the panniers that contain a tub of food and her Fay McMullin's, and steps out of her waterproof all-in-one. Emerging miraculously pristine in her uniform, she has metamorphosed from biker to carer in one swift movement. She hangs the waterproof on the banister and Jack wanders to the back of the house to put the kettle on.

As it's boiling, she hears a toilet flush and creaking floorboards above her. Curious, Jack lingers in the kitchen doorway as someone clumps down the stairs. She is rewarded with the sight of a very feminine woman straightening her skirt, hoisting a handbag on her shoulder and flicking her long auburn fringe from her well-made-up face. "Well, I'm off then," the woman calls and Jack hears Byron begin to respond before launching into a fit of coughing.

She strides in, business-like, past the flapping visitor and leans him forward, rubbing his back. "Are you ok now?" she asks, once he's stopped coughing. He nods and she hands him a feeder-cup from a side-table. "This yours?" He nods again and takes it in both hands. As he's drinking, Jack looks at the visitor to smile reassuringly but her smile is thrown off kilter as she thinks the face is familiar.

Her attention snaps back to the client as Byron passes her the cup. "Thanks," he says. "This is Rachel, she's from Buddies."

"Oh," says Jack, and looks back at Rachel.

"Yes," says Rachel. "Jack and I have met. We go way back."

***

JACK

You must know by now, Jim, or you will soon enough. It won't be long before there's a blazing headline 'HARRIS HAS AIDS' or whatever. But you have to believe me that I've only just taken the test. I didn't want to do it. I've seen people die like this and I didn't want to face the fact that I might go the same way. Of course, it's very different now, so the doctor here tells me; the various medications work much better than back then. There have been a lot of breakthroughs. Now we have people living with AIDS instead of dying from it. But it amounts to the same thing at the end of it all. We're all going to die. No-one is immortal.

I expect you'll have had the test yourself by now anyway; it's routine after a rape. But I don't think you and I ever did anything that endangered you. Don't hate me for not telling you. If I'd put you at risk I would have told you. You might have wondered why I didn't want to touch you when my eczema flared up.

***

"So it *was* your bike?" says Rachel as Jack enters the coffee shop the following day and shakes rain from her jacket.

"Yeah," she says, hanging the damp leather over the seat of a chair. "I bit the bullet and got another one. You never forget," she winks. "It's like riding a dyke."

"Now *that's* an experience I shall never forget, darling." Rachel purses her lips and Jack laughs.

"Wow, it's changed a bit in here, hasn't it?" She looks around the café. Formally a greasy spoon, it now sells cappuccinos and lattés from a machine behind the counter. The square tables and cheap wooden seating have been exchanged for unbalanced round tables and spindly wrought iron chairs.

"Yes," Rachel laughs. "Gone upmarket."

"Well, I think I might splash out on a mocha-chocca." Jack rummages in her leather trouser pocket for some change and approaches the bar. She's disappointed, however, with the overpriced synthetic frothy garbage that the machine produces, and glares at the chair before settling down next to Rachel. "Is this thing safe, do you think?" she grumbles.

"Nice to see you're still a cheerful old soul," says Rachel.

"Less of the old," says Jack, spooning froth into her mouth.

"I suppose I should be grateful you turned up."

"On the contrary, I've been looking for you. Fiona reckoned you'd moved away."

"Yes well, I did, for the operation." Rachel stirs her cappuccino and watches the swirls. "Then I moved back again. You know that lot – if you don't drink at the SU then you don't exist."

Jack laughs, remembering how Fiona had thought that she'd moved away when she was only living a few miles out of Birwood. "So you're working for Buddies?"

Rachel corrects her: "Volunteering."

"Is Byron a friend?"

Rachel shrugs. "He wants me to speak at his funeral. We were discussing making a video. A lot of people are doing that these days."

"Yes," says Jack. "I'd heard it was popular in America. Are

you well?"

Rachel looks at Jack and then back at her coffee. "I'm quite positive these days."

"Positive as in...?"

"Yes." Rachel pauses before she answers the unspoken question in Jack's eyes. "Two years ago. You should be safe, but take the test if you want. You can do it anonymously now."

Jack feels uncomfortable and fishes around for a subject. "Do you still do the cabaret?"

"Occasionally." Rachel looks up from her coffee, a twinkle in her eye. "I'm still looking for a partner."

Jack gives Rachel a sideways glance. "I'll think about it."

"Oh yes, of course you're respectable now. I like your uniform, by the way."

"Shut up. I like your hair. Is it real?"

"Touché." Rachel swings her fringe back self-consciously but doesn't answer the question. Soon they are laughing and exchanging pleasant insults; Jack feels as if she's fallen into a time warp where five years haven't happened. "So what else are you doing, apart from wiping dear old Byron's bottom?" Rachel asks after a while.

"You mean, am I seeing anyone?"

Rachel shrugs.

"Nothing serious. Nothing to write home about. I've got a room in town. It's not too bad."

Rachel grimaces. "I can imagine, sweetie. Bedsit hell."

"Well, it's big enough for me to sleep and write. That's all I need at the moment."

"Are you writing?" Rachel raises an eyebrow. She gets out a packet of Consulate and offers one to Jack.

"I've always written, thought you knew that," says Jack defensively, shaking her head at the cigarette and then relenting and taking one. "Though I'm not sure how well it's going."

"Got writers' block?"

Jack laughs. "No. More like the opposite. I've got writers' diarrhoea and I'm just recovering from a terrible bout of adjectivitis."

Rachel sucks her teeth. "Sounds fucking agonizing."

"Yes. For the readers, I'm sure."

"So what are you writing?"

"Drivel," says Jack. "Absolute tosh. All froth and no substance. A bit like this mocha-mucka. Promises to be something it's not." Jack stirs the now cold suds in her cup while Rachel lights up a menthol and declines to reject Jack's assertion that she can't write. Jack takes the lighter from Rachel and lights her own cigarette, drawing deeply on it. "Good God!" she exclaims.

"What?"

"I'm getting a head rush."

"Dear boy," says Rachel. "It's been so long for you. Like I said: you got respectable."

Jack blows smoke out of the corner of her mouth and eyes Rachel, as much for the 'boy' as for the 'respectable' jibe. She decides to ignore it, however. "These things'll kill you, you know."

Rachel waves her cigarette dismissively. "We're all going to die. No-one's immortal. Tell me about your writing."

"I started with a detective novel, then I tried sci-fi and now I'm doing fantasy-erotica."

"Why stick to a genre?" says Rachel. "You've always been a gender-bender, why not be a genre-bender?" Jack laughs but Rachel insists, "I mean it. Why not write an erotic space detective *with* fairies?"

"Probably because it won't sell. At least if I stick to an obvious genre there's a market for it."

"Ah, now the rub," says Rachel. "But who are you writing for? For yourself or for someone else?"

"I know. I know." Jack sighs.

"What about writing your autobiography?" Rachel suggests.

Jack snorts. "Is that with the fairy? Oh, come on, who'd want to read that?"

"You never know. You don't seem the type to have had a dull life. And at least it'd be real: from the heart. I'll be the fairy if you like."

"I don't know. Most of my life has been a fantasy novel anyway."

Rachel sucks hard on her cigarette as if it has done something to annoy her. "This whole thing about lesbian detectives, lesbian sci-fi - why don't lesbians write some real literature? I mean, why set your standards so low?"

Jack feels her heckles rising. "Who are you to pontificate on what lesbians write or read? Are you a lesbian?" Rachel raises an eyebrow, never able to take an insult without a wry smile.

"Ok, ok. Point taken." Rachel nods and stubs out her cigarette in the crystal ashtray. "So how about it? The autobiography?"

"I would be sued left, right and centre."

"Not if you fictionalised it. Changed a few names, wrote in third person, that kind of thing. You don't think dearest Radclyffe made up all that depressing tripe, do you? And I'm sure yours would at least be humorous in places, darling. You won't be throwing yourself off any bridges at the end, will you?"

"I'll think about it."

"You'll think about throwing yourself off a bridge?"

"No. About the autobiography. It would be a lot of work."

"But imagine releasing the demons, sweetie. You'd save thousands on therapy." Jack smiles and Rachel continues, "Well, while you're thinking about that, *and* thinking about joining me on stage," Rachel pauses and smiles, "Here's something else for you to think about."

"What?" Jack looks at her cautiously.

"Let's get married."

"*What?*" Jack shrieks and several heads turn so that she leans over the table and hisses. "Are you completely off your rocker?"

"Don't be so quick to refuse me darling. It'll be a blast. A real queer wedding. Think about it – I've got life assurance. And it'll give you something to write about at least."

***

JACK

And, as they say, reader, I married him. Or her. Whatever. But don't think I did it for the money, because I didn't. And as it turned out I didn't see a penny because of some loophole in the policy. So not only was I lumbered with a huge credit card bill from our exuberant lifestyle, but I had to pay for the funeral.

I'm not going to tell you about how pretty her vulva was - I'm sure you won't want to know, Jim. All I'll say is, just try to imagine a perfect rose, straight from the factory production line and without a hint of a blemish.

Rachel is the only person I know for absolute certain who will not be unearthed by Vivienne Diggendirt of the *Valley Gazette*. That's unless reporters now have a pass to the afterlife.

Chapter Eighteen

JIM

Dianne stared at the newspaper. Her hands shook. Her face was white. Jo looked over her shoulder at the page. "Oh, they're lovely! They're your daughters, aren't they?" I was irritated by her tone. She obviously hadn't noticed Dianne's anguish.

"Can I see it?" I asked. I moved around the desk to get a look at the hidden page. Staring out at me with smiling faces, Dianne's two daughters. *Budding artists Mandy and Kim Chapman prepare for Christmas with classmates at North Valley Primary.* "Oh," I said. In a different tone to Jo. "They didn't tell you. Did they?" Dianne mutely shook her head. "Well. They *do* look lovely. And maybe… maybe he won't see it?"

Dianne blinked a couple of times. "No, maybe he won't. Maybe no-one from his family or circle of friends will see it. It's a big maybe but…" she sighed. She dropped the paper. "I know, I can't keep running forever. I knew this would happen one day. I mean, Kim wants to go to stage school for heaven's sake – she has plans to be a pop idol – and I can't stand in her way, can I?" She looked beseechingly at me. "What else can I do? If I stop them from being themselves, being normal children, then he's still abusing us now, even after all this time."

I put a hand on Dianne's shoulder. I could find no words of comfort. Instead, I picked up the discarded paper. I turned to the front page to see if there was a mention of the circulation. It was quite wide. I didn't comment, folded it up. Put it on the corner of the desk.

"There's nothing I can do about it now. I should have a word with the school." She reached for the phone. Then changed her mind. "No, maybe a personal visit would be best. I need to tell them not to let the girls be photographed if possible, and not to hand them over to their father if he turns up." She shook her head. "I used to do that regularly. Every time they had a new teacher. But it's been so long…"

I realised now that Dianne was talking to herself. She was not even aware of my presence. I looked around the office. Jo had wandered off. I felt another twang of irritation at the woman. "Shall I get you a cup of tea?" I asked. She looked up. Startled.

"Oh, yes. Thank you."

I picked up the paper and went into the small office kitchen. While the kettle was boiling, I perused the main story. A grainy photograph of a girl of about eleven covered slightly less than half of the front page. It looked like a blown-up holiday snapshot. I knew by instinct this girl had either been killed or abducted. Not exactly the kind of thing that I wanted to show to Dianne as a distraction. My eyes flicked to the headline. STILL MISSING. FLEUR DAY 3. My heart sank. I read the caption underneath the photograph: *Pretty Fleur Baker in a family photo taken last week, just days before she went missing on Saturday.*

The kettle hissed. I put down the paper. I made tea. There's always someone missing, someone's body being found, something like this. And it's nearly always young women. When's it going to change? I carried the tea through to the office. I settled down at my own desk. To read the rest of the story.

Police still have no leads as to the whereabouts of Fleur Baker (12) from Valley area, who went missing on a trip to the fair with friends. "We are keeping an open mind," said Superintendent Williams yesterday. "We are looking at all options."

"My daughter would not have run away," said Mrs Mary Baker (39). "She knows not to go with strangers and she's a sensible girl." Fleur's mother raised the alarm at ten o'clock on

Saturday night when the girl did not come home. Her friends say they left her at nine to walk the remaining few hundred yards home.

"She was having a new mobile phone for Christmas," said a tearful Mrs Baker yesterday. "Her old one was broken. If only I'd given it to her before she went out that night."

The appeal is on. If anyone has seen this girl or anything unusual happen in the last few days, they should contact the police immediately.

I folded the paper again and sipped my tea thoughtfully. I looked over at Dianne. She seemed absorbed in her work. Then I looked at the clock. I had a visit arranged with Donna that afternoon. If I was quick I could probably pop into the refuge on the way out. To see how the women were. Mondays were always crisis days.

***

"That's disgusting."

"That's just awful."

"How can they put things like this on during the day? Isn't there such a thing as a watershed anymore?"

"I mean, look at the size of her tits – it's unnatural."

But you're watching it. Aren't you? I thought. I stood in the corner of the refuge lounge. There were two new residents I hadn't yet met. Along with two that had been there a while. Gemma and Lucy. And a baby asleep in a buggy. Gemma looked around. She saw me standing there silently. She picked up the remote control. Flicked channels until she got to the news. She shot a warning glance at Lucy who was about to object. "Don't turn it off on my account," I said.

"Oh, we weren't watching it," said Lucy. "Only keeping the telly on low so that Pixie'll sleep."

"Pixie? Is that the baby's name?" I asked.

"Yeah, this is Holly, she came in last night. Hol – this is Jim, one of the workers."

"Hi," said a slight girl. Long mousy hair. She was sitting next to the buggy. She put her hand possessively on the buggy's handle. "Actually, my name's Holiday, but everyone calls me Holly." I could hardly see her face underneath a long fringe. But what I could see was badly bruised. I felt slightly sickened. The girl couldn't be much older than seventeen. This was Stacey in five years' time. I was reminded of Dianne's comments. I wondered if I would ever get used to this.

"Is this the national news?" I asked. The now familiar face of Fleur Baker appeared on the screen. "Do you mind? If I turn it up a bit?"

Holly shrugged. Lucy, who was nearest, leaned over. She muttered, "Remote volume's broken." We watched the news footage. It didn't seem that there was anything new happening. Just that it had now become a national story. Due to the length of time the girl had been missing. An appeal number scrolled along the bottom of the screen. A reporter stood in front of a row of terraced houses.

"Hey, I know that street," said Gemma. "My uncle lives there. That's over Westway, isn't it?"

"I know the family," came an older woman's voice from the corner of the room. I looked towards her and smiled warmly; another resident I hadn't yet met but knew by name – Doreen. "Went to school with her father, I did. Malcolm Baker, we used to call him Milky Malcolm; look there he is now. His wife's called Mary." I looked back at the TV. I saw the girl's parents sitting down at a desk. They were surrounded by microphones and flinching under flashing lights. They looked red-eyed and tired. They seemed resolute as they prepared for the press conference. An all too familiar sight in recent years. "Aye, Milky – lost his hair a bit but apart from that he looks just the same." We went quiet as the couple prepared to speak. Holding hands and clutching paper notes. They took turns to speak directly into the camera. Mary first.

"We don't know why you went away, Fleur, but please whatever happens remember that we love you. If-if you're in trouble then we can sort it out. Just come home and we will do everything we can to make things better. You're still our little girl and we will always love you no matter what. Fleur, it's been nearly three days now without you. We miss you and we know you must miss us. P-please come home, or get in touch just to say you're safe, just... please..." Mary bows her head into a handkerchief. Malcolm puts his arm around her. Bending his head into her face. Whispering. Cameras flash. Then he straightens. He wipes under his eye with a finger. Cameras flash again. He blinks. He smoothes his piece of paper out. Then coughs and begins to speak.

"If anyone knows anything about our little girl, if anyone has seen Fleur or knows of her whereabouts then please contact the police. She is still only a child and we miss her. If you have got Fleur, then please let her go. Please. She is our little girl and we want her back. Thank you."

Lights flash again as the couple turn away. Several policemen and women surround them. Leading them away from the cameras. The image on the screen switches abruptly to the reporter standing in the Westway street.

A shudder ran through the women in the refuge lounge like a Mexican wave. Several reached for their cigarettes. Holly's grip on the pushchair had tightened. Lucy leaned forward to turn the volume down again. "Well," said Gemma. "Do you think it's likely she'll come back?"

"She's dead already," said Holly, with a finality that shocked me. "No chance for her."

"Why so sure?" asked Lucy.

"If they're not back within twenty-four hours and there aren't any clues then you can guarantee it's abduction and murder." The women were silent for a moment. Then Holly added: "My grandfather is a police officer."

Doreen blew out smoke before speaking, "My husband was in the force; where does your granddad work?"

"Special Branch." Gemma and Lucy exchanged looks but didn't comment.

"Well. Anyway," I said. "Let's look on the bright side. At least they haven't found a body."

***

"Breaking news coming in from South Valley area: the body of a young girl has been found in wasteland just outside the village of Stranglehold near Westway. A local man was out walking his dog when he spotted something suspicious and alerted police. As yet we have nothing definite regarding the identification of the body but police are not ruling out the possibility that it might be that of twelve-year-old Fleur Baker who went missing last Saturday from Westway town."

I groaned, put down my cup of tea.

"What?" asked Jack. She looked up from the computer.

"That girl. Fleur that went missing. They've found a body."

"What girl?"

"She's been missing a week, Jack. It's been on the news; in the papers; there's posters all over town. You can't tell me that you haven't seen anything about it?"

"Nope." Jackie shrugged. She jolted halfway through her shrug as the phone rang. She was standing right next to it. She always waited for it to ring at least twice. "Hello? Hello?"

"Who is it?" I asked. Jack shook her head.

"Hello-oh," sang Jack.

"If it's my mum..." but Jack held up her hand. I stopped talking.

"Is anyone there?" asked Jack, and to me: "I think I can hear something." Then a long tone sounded to indicate that the line had been cut off. Jack put the receiver back down. "Must have been a wrong number."

JACK
YOUR INSTANT MESSAGING SERVICE REPORT
To: CrackerJack
From: AmericanPie
Subject: where I am at
Sorry about the delay in getting back to you, babe. I've been offline for a time. So, what's up with you? How's the g/f? how's the job, how's the life? Blah blah.
I've been up to my nipples in it as usual. What's been going on with you? Been blue?

To: Pie
From: Jack
Subject: the way the cookie crumbles
Dead girl on the horizon, local. Nothing to do with me but it's everywhere I look. Less stress at work for a time and then more stress again (oh don't ask). Getting some strange phone calls – had two so far. Just the silent type but worrying, might be an ex-client. g/f has new job so life different but then the same as ever too. Getting a new computer for Christmas!! What are you up to your nips in? some interesting images in my head.

To: CrackerJack
From: AmericanPie
Subject: keep them in your head
Usually up to the nips in dirty laundry and takeaway cartons. Lately I've been working on a heavy site, top secret. Not much going on with the wife beater; he's laid off lately. Thought about your forum idea and may do it soon, but so busy lately with other things. What's with the dead girl?

To: Pie
From: Jack
Subject: body parts

Your tits, my tits, everything gets on my tits. The girl was assaulted, murdered, left in the woods. Usual story. Police have no leads, la la la. I need some distraction. I wish a celebrity would be caught with cocaine and a whore so that we can have something different on the news; it's depressing. I'm not being heartless: it gets me down that this goes on all the time. I don't think there's any actual change in the numbers of murders or rapes, it's the reporting that is changing. The world is not a happy place. But has it ever been?

To: CrackerJack
From: AmericanPie
Subject: never promised you a rose garden

What do you want?

To: Pie
From: Jack
Subject: I beg your pardon

A desert island? An ivory tower? For Christmas to be over and done with so I can just get on with my life. I really hate Christmas so much. Don't you just hate it when you see people who aren't even Christian (respect to all) going absolutely crazy from 1st December onwards? Christmas is far too materialistic; I groan every time someone says 'but it's Christmas' as an excuse for idiotic behaviour; I hate those flashing lights and red-nosed reindeers; I really want to rip the head off the next jolly santa I see. I'm launching a campaign to keep Christmas celebrations till 24th December. And another thing – why is it that when you're desperate for cash, like when you're a student or something, you can't get any credit or overdraft. And then just when you're settled and sorted financially, the credit card companies are falling over themselves to entice you to get into debt with them. Rage rage rage.

To: CrackerJack
From: AmericanPie
Subject: the world debt
The world owes us something, don't you think? Give credit where credit is due. Let's all go and live on planet lesbos. mwahaha

To: Pie
From: Jack
Subject: planet lesbos
Do you require a visa?

To: CrackerJack
From: AmericanPie
Subject: re: planet lesbos
Cheeky monkey. You can't get it out of me that way. Men have nipples too, you know.

To: Pie
From: Jack
Subject: bribery?
How can I get it out of you?

To: CrackerJack
From: AmericanPie
Subject: morf
Why is this so important to you?

To: Pie
From: Jack
Subject: re: morf

Why do you think it isn't important?

To: CrackerJack
From: AmericanPie
Subject: I don't think it isn't important. It is as important as hell. Labels are put on us and we are pigeonholed. We become who we are told that we are; we become our labels. This applies to race, gender, sexuality, intelligence... all categories and labelling systems. You are female therefore this is how you will think, this is how you will behave, this is how people will react to you, this is what you want, this is where you are in the world, this is your status, this is your life. There is no spoon, Neo. There is no label. Deny it and be free.

To: Pie
From: Jack
Subject: Rage More
I agree with the ethos, but in a world organised along the lines of categories of people, it's difficult to deny. I am not stuck in a role. I have my own system of fighting expectations.
INSTANT MESSAGING SERVICE REPORT ENDS

JIM
Riiiiiing.
I looked at the phone.
Riiiiiiiiiiiiiing.
I looked up the stairs. Jackie was digging Christmas decorations out of the spare room. It didn't sound like it was going well. Thuds and grumbles drifted down to me.
Riiiiiiiiiiiiiing.
I looked at the phone again. I considered not answering. Then gave in and grabbed the receiver. "Hello?" I said. A little too sharply. It could be someone important, after all. "Hello? Who is this?" I asked in a hiss. "Will you please stop ringing!" I slammed

down the phone. There was a groan and a loud thud from upstairs. I went to help.

"Stop that fucking racket!" The familiar muffled bangs and shouts from next door halted me. I crept up the last few steps.

"You ok?" I asked. I put my head through the doorway. I put my hand over my mouth. To stop myself from laughing at the sight. Jack was sprawled on the floor. Underneath a pile of decorations. They had fallen out of the box. She'd been trying to pull it down from the top of a cupboard.

"I know. I look like a bloody Christmas tree. Ha bloody ha. Here, help me up, will you?"

I reached out my hand. I was too weak with laughter to be of much use. Jackie had to lean on the spare bed to drag herself to her feet. Disentangling the lights and tinsel from her body, brushing off baubles. "Oh, come on. You've got to admit it's funny," I said.

JACK

"Bah humbug," I said, pushing the decorations ungraciously back into their box. "There's just this box and that one. Can't find the tree. Do you remember what we did with it last year?"

"Threw it out. The base bust? Remember?"

I groaned, knowing this would mean a trip to Christmas Shopping Hell. "Who was that on the phone?" I asked, trying to sound nonchalant.

"Oh. Just one of the women. From work," Jimmie said as she reached for the nearest box. "Downstairs with this lot then?" I nodded and grabbed the other box, hefting it up to breast height. "Careful on the stairs, little Hitler is on the warpath."

"I know. I heard."

"Hey, what's this?" Jimmie asked, pointing to the corner of the spare room.

"What?" I tried to look over the top of my box but couldn't see. Jimmie pulled at some netting that poked out of one of my other boxes. "Oh no, don't touch that stuff," I said. "It's not important."

"I thought it might be the fairy. You know, for the tree." She opened the box and lifted out the dress. Then said, "Oh."

"Well it's obviously not, is it?" I said, putting down my Christmas box and taking it from her. I carefully folded it and placed it back in place in the box.

"It's your wedding dress, isn't it?"

I shrugged.

"I never realised you'd been that thin."

I shrugged again and went to pick up my Christmas box.

"Why don't you ever talk about it?" she said.

"I just don't want to, that's all." I looked at her over the top of the box I carried. "Shall I take these down, love? You shouldn't strain yourself."

"I am perfectly capable," she said huffily. I always know how to get her to change the subject.

JIM

"Hello?" I called. I walked into the main part of the house. "Hello?" I can understand why they think it's haunted. A big house like that, it's no wonder they get the creeps. I walked around the downstairs area. The lounge was empty. TV on as usual but the volume down low. No-one in the playroom. I thought I could hear some movement above. I was about to go upstairs. A cry from the kitchen startled me.

"Hello, you," I said to Pixie as I entered the kitchen. I looked around for her mother. The baby gurgled at me. Blew raspberries and then mouthed for her dummy. It was attached to the front of her babygrow with a safety-pin and a grubby green ribbon. I popped it in her mouth. She sucked placidly and looked at me.

I sat at the kitchen table. Pixie rocked herself in the baby-carrier. I held onto the side of it. Worried that it might fall from the table where it had been left. "Holly," I called. "Pixie's awake." I would have gone to look for her. But I was afraid of leaving the baby alone.

Instead I struck up a one-sided conversation with Pixie. "You're a lovely little girl, aren't you?" She blinked. "So pretty." I smoothed her hair down. It was fine and blonde. She farted. After ten minutes, Holly was still not forthcoming. I had said all the baby-talk things that people say to babies. Now I was talking to Pixie inside my head. The things you don't say out loud.

How could she leave you alone? If you were mine, I'd never put you at risk. I've heard the way she talks about you. How she was too late for an abortion. I know you don't understand the words. But she must surely realise that you pick up the sentiment. She doesn't deserve you. You should be with someone who wants you. Someone who cares…

I have begun to appreciate what turns a woman into a baby-snatcher. Not that I would ever do anything like that myself. Never. But when you see a neglected child. It makes you think. I have to tell myself: I'm doing the best I can. You can't save everyone. And anyway, the majority of the women at the refuge were not like this.

Presently Holly wandered into the kitchen. She was towelling her hair. "Oh," she said when she saw me. She picked up the baby-carrier and walked out again.

JACK

"Hello?" Silence. "Hello-oh. You know, this is getting a bit daft. You're going to have a huge phone bill and you still haven't told me who you are." Silence. "We're not going to get anywhere like this, are we? For a start, is it actually me you want?" Silence. "I can give you the Samaritans number if you'd rather." Silence. "Oh well, suit yourself. But do you mind if I just carry on eating my lunch while you, uh, don't talk?" I chewed on my ham and mustard sandwich for a moment, cradling the phone between my shoulder and ear. "Would you like me to put you on hold? I've got some cool music you could listen to. Do you like jazz?"

Click. "No?" I took another bite as I heard the tone kick in. "Arsehole," I said ungraciously and continued to eat.

A couple of times I thought that Jimmie had answered a silent call, but each time she said it had been someone else. The only one that had happened with Jimmie around was the first one, which I had assumed was a wrong number. But now they were happening several times a day and I was getting worried that one day she would pick up. There was no guarantee that it was Lara, of course. It could be anybody. But who else would be so relentless?

JIM

'A local man and woman have been arrested in connection with the Fleur Baker murder case. They have not yet been named. We will have more on this and other news throughout the day. Stay tuned to Valley Radio...'

I flicked the button on the car radio. I pulled over in front of Donna Little's house. A lone tricycle lay on its side in the front garden; the curtains were closed; no movement came from within.

I paused for a moment. Taking stock. The calls could have been coming from Frank. I remembered that time in the shelter. He'd been hanging around the workers' desk and the address book had been out. But if it was Frank, then that might mean he knew I was working with Donna which also might mean he knew where Donna lived. Or that it was only a matter of time before he found out. Should I warn her? Would that scare her unnecessarily? I still wasn't certain that the silent caller was Frank. But who else could it be? I should really tell Dianne. But Dianne was already in a state of nervous exhaustion since her own scare. And that had been two or three weeks ago. Was Dianne worrying unnecessarily?

I sighed. Rubbed my face. I moulded a smile out of sagging jaws. What would I give for the simplicity of working in a bookshop? I got out of the car, looked around the estate, leant on the open door. At 10am the place was a ghost town. An emaciated greyhound trotted past on the other side of the road. He eyed me suspiciously, stopping to sniff at a discarded Barbie doll. Then cocked his leg to urinate against a rotting fence. I slammed the car door and locked it.

I carried my folder. I picked my way down concrete steps. Carefully avoided a circuit of small racing cars that were taking an extended pit stop on the path. At the front door I had the urge to turn and run. I could report back that I'd knocked and had received no answer. That often happened on visits to my clients. Even the scheduled ones. Then, as I was standing there, I heard a familiar siren wail from inside. I knew that Sabrina, at least, was awake. I leaned against the wall at the side of the door. I waited until the shouting had died down before I knocked. After a minute, Donna answered.

"Hi," I began cheerfully.

"Oh, it's you." Donna walked away from the door but left it open. I took this as an invite to step inside. I wiped my feet on a square of carpet in the hallway. I wrinkled my nose as I shut the door behind me.

"I've brought the Action Plan," I said. I held up my folder. Donna looked at the folder and said nothing. Sabrina ran through from the kitchen. She was naked from the waist down. The child clutched a packet of custard creams. She was trying to open it with her teeth. Her long, uncombed hair gave her the look of a werewolf.

"Where did you get those? Give! Give here now!" Donna held out her hand for the biscuits. Sabrina tried to run in the opposite direction but her mother was too fast. She grabbed the girl with one hand. Wrenched the packet out of her grasp. Then landed a slap on Sabrina's bare bottom.

"Shall I make a cup of tea?" I asked. I stepped over Sabrina. She was now sprawled on her back. Rolling over the cold hall tiles. Screaming lustily. I walked into a scene of devastation in the kitchen. Then turned back to Donna. "Uh-" I was about to ask another question. My words died as Sabrina's tantrum hit level six on the Richter scale. The child kicked chubby legs in the air, rolled her head from side to side, screamed rhythmically. I began to worry that she might induce a seizure. Or was already having one. Donna ignored her daughter. She inspected the damage done to the packet of biscuits. She opened them and tutted at the mess.

"One biscuit. Ok? One." She held out a custard cream by its crumbling corner. Sabrina immediately stopped crying. She sat up and sniffed.

"Eh," said the little girl. She reached up for the biscuit. "Eh." She made a grab at it as Donna held it out. Then stuffed it whole into her mouth using the flat of her hand. She sat there crunching for a few seconds. Then stood up and scratched her crotch. "Eh," she held her hand up for another biscuit. Crumbs and saliva dripped from her mouth as she spoke. "Eh, eh!" Donna walked past her calmly into the kitchen. She put the open packet on a high shelf. Two biscuits fell forwards out of the packet.

"There aren't any clean mugs. And I've only got coffee."

"That's ok. Look. I'll do some washing up. If you like?"

Donna shrugged. "If you want to."

"Eh! Eh eh eh." Sabrina jumped up and down in the hallway. Then she started running on the spot. In her rage she toppled backwards. She was once again in the legs-in-the-air pose. She exposed herself towards the kitchen. I noticed a brown tidemark around her buttocks. I turned back hastily to the kitchen sink. Began to run the taps.

Twenty minutes later. The kitchen was as sparkling as it was ever going to be. The packet of custard creams was half-empty. Donna and I were sitting in the lounge. Sabrina happily scribbled on the back of my folder with a drying felt pen.

"So. This Action Plan," I began. I looked at the papers on my lap.

"I saw him today."

"You saw…?"

"Frank. I saw him in town. He didn't see me; I ducked into Kwicksave. But he's here. I knew I should have moved completely out of the area." She took a fag out of the ubiquitous packet. "I really like this house as well." She looked around the lounge. I followed her gaze.

She'd been here a month. The place was trashed. I remembered the new bunk beds being delivered; I had organised the second hand sofa; I bought the curtains and helped to hang them. The beds were now broken. I could feel a stab in my back that suggested the sofa was on its way out.

"Eh!" My attention was caught by Sabrina tossing a pen over her shoulder. "Eh, eh, eh!" Sabrina stabbed at the folder with a new pen. Its nib broke. She grabbed another. Then changed her mind. Then she expressed her frustration by falling backwards and launching into another tantrum. Donna calmly continued to smoke.

"Got her father's temper, that one," she said.

"What are you going to do?"

"I don't know. Sit tight I suppose; he doesn't know that I haven't moved away. Maybe he'll think I've gone and go off looking for me."

"A double bluff?"

"Something like that. At least till after Christmas, I've got to get my decos up."

"The kids'll like that. So," I shuffled my papers meaningfully, "point one. Getting them to go to school regularly."

"Yep." Donna looked around the room. "You see them here?"

I laughed. "No. So they're in school?"

"Took them myself. Dropped them off on the way to take Tosh to nursery."

"So. How's it going? With the nursery?" I ticked off points one and two.

"Not so good. But we're sticking it out."

"When you say 'not so good'…?"

"Well it's alright so long as I'm there with him. But then as soon as I have to leave, he does a limpet on my leg and won't let go. When they manage to pull him off, he's screaming the place down. Always been sensitive."

"Well. That does happen. Separation anxiety."

"Hmm, well it's making *me* anxious. And he's wetting the bed every night now."

"How long has he been going? A week?"

"Just a week, yes."

"Give it a bit longer then. He's still in mornings only?"

"Yep. I pick him up at midday." Donna looked at her wrist. It was naked. She looked instead at a white plastic kitchen clock that was balanced on the windowsill.

"What happened to your watch?"

"Sabrina happened to it."

"Ah." We both looked down at Sabrina. She was lying motionless on the floor, having screamed herself out. "That brings us to point three. Sabrina. I've made an appointment for her? To see a child psychologist. I –"

"No." Donna made a cutting motion with the flat of her hand. "No, I'm not taking her to a shrink. She's just a normal toddler. Just a bit more out of control than most. I'm handling it."

"Donna…"

"I mean it. No."

I sighed. "Fair enough." It'll be picked it up when she goes to school anyway, God help them. "But generally everything's been going ok? I mean apart from seeing Frank in town?"

"Fine. Stacey wants to know when you're taking them bowling again."

Chapter Nineteen

JACK

They come round to the house to look for the girl. She's not here I tell them; I haven't seen her, don't know what you're talking about. They're not listening. But I don't know, I don't even know her – only heard her name on the news. Didn't they find the body? Haven't they arrested the killer? What are they doing? Digging under the floorboards, pulling the boards up, made a great big hole. I'll fall in that, I say. No, you won't they say; you won't be here. We're taking you now, taking you down to the station. But why? What are you talking about? Then I see her, see the body rotting, worms and maggots and she stinks. All under my floorboards! I didn't know! Mum! Tell them! Tell them it wasn't me! Please, please, you've got to stop them. No, young lady, we know all about you. I run. I get away and run. But my legs don't work and then I fall in the hole and I can't get out. I fall into the body and it breaks and covers me. I'm covered with stinking flesh; it's getting in my mouth and in my eyes. I can't open my eyes. I can't breathe. I can't...

"Jack! Jackie. It's all right. It's ok. Calm down."

"It wasn't me! Don't let them take me!"

"It's ok. It was just a dream. Come on. Come on love." Jimmie put her arms around me as my body shook with long wracking sobs.

"It was horrible. Horrible."

"It's ok. It's over. Just a dream." After a while I calmed down and let go of Jim. "Can you talk about it?"

"It was… what time is it?" I looked over my shoulder at the red LED display of the radio alarm clock. 1am. I rubbed my face. "Nothing. I can't remember," I said, not looking at Jimmie.

"You said. 'It wasn't you'."

"I don't know. Something, I was being chased or something."

"You usually are."

"What do you mean?" I asked, a little too sharply.

"You seem to be having these nightmares? A lot lately. And you're always running."

So she *had* noticed. "Yes."

"Are you going to see that counsellor? The one that Annette recommended?"

I regretted telling Jimmie that my supervisor had told me to find myself a personal therapist to counteract the stress I'd been under. "Maybe. I – don't want to talk about it right now. Let's just get some sleep." I turned over and shrugged my shoulders up to ward off any more hugs from Jimmie. Staring at the clock I knew that this was going to be another long sleepless night.

JIM

"That is appalling."

"They should bring back the death penalty."

"I can't believe that a woman would do that."

"What's going on?" I asked. I took a seat with the self-appointed jury in the refuge lounge. I looked at the TV. Recognised the footage of the local field. Where Fleur Baker had been found.

"That woman enticed the poor girl into the house. If it had been a man she wouldn't have gone inside."

"So, who's saying this? This is what the police have found out?"

"They say she procured the girl for him, that he told her to get a girl and she went and did it."

"Have they got a confession?" I asked.

"No, both of them deny it. But, you know, she was there in the house and they've got DNA and everything. Anyway, it was in the paper."

"Right."

"She must have known about it! It's a tiny house; she must have known what was going on and she didn't tell the police, even afterwards. I say she's just as guilty as he is."

"It's disgusting. You don't expect that kind of thing from a woman."

"Maybe she was scared of him?" I offered. "They say he's a violent man. Maybe he threatened her? Maybe he told her he'd kill her? If she didn't back him up."

There was an uneasy pause. Then Holly spoke quietly, "I'd still have told the police. It's not right, doing that to a little girl." The other women assented loudly.

"Yeah, too right. I'd have got out. If my ex ever did anything like that I'd have left him right then."

"They're on remand now, it says. Look – there he is." A picture had appeared on screen. A police van pulling up into a jeering crowd. A figure huddled under a grey blanket. Surrounded by uniforms. "That bastard. I hope he gets life."

"And her. She should get life too. The trial's going to be after Christmas they say."

"Looks like she's already been found guilty," I said. I wandered off to see what the children were doing.

***

"What gets me," I said later to Dianne, "is that they think it a more heinous crime. For a woman to be involved than for a man. I mean. It's not like she was the one that assaulted the girl? I'm not condoning what she did at all; you know, covering up for him. But it's like it's expected of men to perform violent sexual acts. It's just an extension of their manliness. But for a woman to…" my sentence tailed off. I realised that Dianne wasn't listening. "So how are things? With you?" I eventually said.

"Ok, I suppose."

"Everything all right? With the kids?"

"Yes. No sign of their father after all. Maybe I was just overreacting. But I'm still picking them up from school myself instead of letting them walk home alone. A lot of the other mothers are as well; this murder's got everyone nervous."

"Hmm. Although statistically a kid is more likely to get killed in a road accident. On their way home due to the build up of traffic. Due to all the cars of parents who are picking their kids up."

"All right, smart alec. If it were your kids, you'd want what's best for them too, and hang everyone else."

I shrugged. "Possibly."

"How's things going with Donna?"

Now I groaned. "Don't ask."

"I'm asking."

"Well. The house is a shit pit. I'm not being judgemental. My house is hardly pristine. But there are levels of dirt. I think a health inspector would have apoplexy. If they saw Donna's kitchen."

"Stacey's going to school then."

"Yes. How? Ah. You mean it was Stacey that did the cleaning?"

"It's getting the balance between what's good for everyone all round. Are there any rats? Are the kids getting food poisoning? You think I'm being extreme – you should see some of the places I've been in."

"I know what you're saying. It's better for Stacey to go to school? Than for the house to be clean?"

"What do you think? Maybe one day Donna will think of doing some cleaning herself."

"It looks like it's got so bad that she just can't face it. And now she's talking about moving again. Since she saw Frank. She says she'll sit tight till after Christmas. But I don't know."

"He hasn't approached her yet, has he? I've been working on this injunction, and now with the new law…"

"He hasn't approached her. No. I wonder whether he's going to try a new tactic. If he just followed her round? Made sure she saw him? That would be intimidating enough."

"We'll just have to wait and see."

"Yes. Oh. I meant to tell you. Donna has refused to take Sabrina to a child psych. I don't know if I can do anything more? To persuade her?"

"Leave it then. You don't want to harm your relationship with her. Maybe bring it up again after Christmas if it's still the same."

"You don't think I should inform social services?"

"Not just yet. And anyway, if the social worker's worth her salt she'll have noticed herself."

I shrugged. "It could be just uber-toddler behaviour. You know. Donna says that anyway."

"Yes, there were a couple of incidents when she was in the refuge. Of course, it doesn't help that the other mothers were so anti-Donna because of everything else; they could have exaggerated what happened."

"But once a child has a label…"

"Exactly. And if the whole family has a label then what chance does the child have?"

"About Frank…"

"Yes?"

"I think. I mean. I've been getting nuisance calls? At home."

"From Frank? But how…?"

"I don't know if they're from him. They're silent calls. It

could be anyone. But they've been going on for a week or so. I don't know anyone else who I've pissed off that much."

"How would he get your number? Aren't you ex-directory?"

"No. The number's in Jack's name. But there was a time in the shelter. Where he might have seen my number written down. My home number is quite easy to remember. It's similar to a local taxi number."

"And these silent calls couldn't be wrong numbers?"

"Not as many as three a day. Not silent like that. When it's a wrong number. People usually say something."

"Have you thought that it might be directed at Jackie?"

"No. I hadn't thought of that. But it's mostly me that answers them? She hasn't mentioned anything."

"Have you mentioned it to her?"

"No. I didn't want to worry her."

"What do you say? When they call I mean."

"Well. I wait to hear if they're going to say anything. When they don't I tell them to stop ringing. Then I put the phone down."

"Try saying something funny. Catch them off their guard."

"What do you mean?"

"If you say something that surprises them, then they might laugh or make a noise and then at least you'd be able to tell whether it was male or female, and you might recognise the voice."

"Well. I'm not usually in the mood to say something funny. What kind of thing could I say?"

Dianne shrugged. "I don't know – ask if they want to order a taxi?"

JACK

"So how's the re-enacting going?" I asked Gail when I saw her piling up books in the library.

"Oh." I had caught Gail off guard and a book fell from the

top of the pile. "We don't do battles in the winter. There's a banquet in February and then the season starts again in March."

I picked up the book and handed it to Gail. "Bronte? I read a lot of classics when I used to work nights in a residential home. But I never got around to Bronte. Any good?"

"Yes, you should try it. Very passionate."

"I never have the time to read properly these days. Mostly magazines or stuff on the internet. Maybe I will one day."

"So how are things with you? Settling in to your new hours?"

"Hmm. Not sure yet, I'll keep you posted."

"You seem stressed still."

"Not work this time. I'm getting nuisance calls at home."

"Oh! That's awful. What do they say? Are they sexual ones?" I was amused to notice that Gail was excited by the prospect.

"No. They don't say anything at all. Just silence. It's annoying because, you know, you leave whatever you're doing to pick up the phone. I've been thinking about unplugging it but then what if someone was trying to get in touch? I worry about Jim answering the phone when I'm not there."

"Jim?"

"My partner."

"Oh, I thought…"

"What?"

"Nothing."

"No, what?"

"Only… it's silly really, but I had it in my head that you were with a woman."

I gave her a blank look for a moment, enjoying letting her suffer, before smiling and saying, "Yes, I am. Jim's short for Jemima. She has the same problem with calling me Jack."

"Ah," Gail didn't hide the relief on her face. "I didn't want to insult you."

"Why would I be insulted?"

Gail laughed and then coughed into her hand, clearly

embarrassed. "So do you know who the calls are coming from?"

"I thought maybe Larissa."

"Larissa Thomas? But how would she get your number?"

I shrugged. "I'm in the phonebook."

"Oh. Well, you know the easy answer would be to change your phone number. Have you informed the police?"

"You think I should?"

"It is a crime after all."

"Hmm, but if it was Lara and I set the police onto her, then who knows what she'll do? She might end up back in here."

"I see your point."

"Best just to wait for her to get bored."

"But you're worried that Jim will answer?"

"Yes. She gets worked up about things like that. But as far as I know she hasn't had one yet. She hasn't told me anyway."

"It hasn't happened when you're together?"

"We're not together that much lately, with my new hours and her new job. When she's not on call she's doing a practice with The Girls. She plays in a band," I explained to Gail's confused reaction. "We sleep together and that's about it. Funny really, because we thought now she's working days we'd have more time together but we've got less. I suppose that's the way it goes."

"But at least she's not tired all the time. You told me before your partner worked nights. So where's she working now?"

"Women's Aid."

"Oh," Gail raised her eyebrows but made no other comment.

JIM

I walked home through the town. Jack had the car once a week. I had managed to arrange for that one day to be in the office with no client visits. Sometimes I popped over to the refuge. But I was glad of the time in the office. To catch up on the plethora of paperwork now expected of social care workers. It had annoyed me at first that Jackie's boss had suddenly decided to shift her hours. With no warning or reason. He had given her a 9am slot. That made using the bus impossible. I had told Jack that she ought to complain about it. But Jackie had said that she preferred it this way. It meant she only had to do two days per week. If you didn't count supervision. And even though one of these was a Saturday. I was starting to think that we ought to sit down together. Really talk about our separate lives. But when was there time?

As I mused, I noticed the splendid array of lights in the town. They really made me feel Christmassy. Whatever Jack said about it. It was dark already. Not yet 5pm. I felt bitterly cold. I could see my breath as mist. Late shoppers with that dogged I-am-going-to-be-happy look that only comes at Christmas. Bumped into me without apology every second step. And yet I felt a swelling of my heart at the thought that Christmas was barely a week away. I was resolute to make it good. Living with Ebenezer didn't make it easy. But I felt that I had enough Christmas spirit for the two of us. The only thing that was getting me down was those phone calls. But I reminded myself of Dianne's advice. I had made a plan. I practised in my head: *do you want to order a taxi?*

The crowds thinned as I left the town centre. I headed for the bus stop. At least it wasn't raining. Too cold to rain. The hairs on the back of my neck prickled. I had the sudden feeling that someone was watching me. I turned abruptly. All I could see behind me were dark silhouettes of people. Milling around in the shopping centre. I shrugged my coat up around my bare ears. But couldn't shrug off the feeling that someone was looking at me. Or following me. I reached the bus stop just as a number seventy-two pulled in. Without thinking I scrambled on.

"How much is it? Just to the top of the hill?" I leaned on my stick, breathless.

"Forty pence, love."

"Forty! Oh well. Here." I pulled off my glove and produced some silver from my jeans pocket. Much tutting and sighing went on behind me. I realised that I'd jumped the queue. And I was being slow to take a ticket. An odious crime in the world of public transport. Even for someone with a disability. "Sorry. Sorry," I muttered. I shuffled over to an empty seat. Stood for a moment looking out of the window before sitting. I could see nothing suspicious. Maybe I had imagined it. I was thrown into the seat as the bus lurched forward. Then lurched again to a halt. I watched the people walking past. With their red noses and their mist for breath. I was glad of the warm ride. The heavy traffic meant that I was no quicker on the bus. I may as well have walked. But this way I felt slightly safer.

JACK

"Hello love, cup of tea? How was your day?"

"Brrr. It's freeze-your-tits-off-weather out there. Not bad. New woman in the refuge. Some kids? Don't know if she'll stay? But the kids are nice. How about you?"

"Oh, so so. You know. Traffic really bad on the way home, I've only just got back myself."

The familiar chugging noise of the computer as it warmed up caused Jimmie to look at the desk. It wouldn't be long before we had a new one, then I wouldn't have to wait so long for it to start. "Honestly. That thing. You'd think you had to crank it up with a handle? Like an old gramophone?" she said.

"Oh, you haven't noticed my slaves in the backyard on their bicycles? Hang on a minute, I'll just go out and whip them, then it'll go faster." I went into the kitchen and made whipping motions at the back door, making Jimmie laugh. Then I turned to the already boiling kettle and got some mugs from our broken wooden mug tree. Jimmie was still laughing when the phone rang.

Both of us froze. I looked at Jimmie and she looked at me and I could tell by her expression that she thought the same thing as me – she knows. "I'll get it," I said, unfreezing and making a dash. But Jimmie was standing just next to the phone.

"Hello?" We looked at each other, both holding our breath. Then Jimmie broke eye contact and put on her best telephone voice. "Would you like to order a taxi?"

JIM

"Wha-?" I held my hand up to silence Jack. I thought I heard a similar noise on the other end of the line. Then the long tone as the line went dead. I put the phone down. I gritted my teeth in frustration. If Jack hadn't spoken I might have heard what the silent caller had said.

I let out my breath. I looked back at Jack. "You knew? About the calls?"

"You knew."

"Why didn't you tell me?"

"Why didn't *you* tell *me*?"

Both of us were angry for a moment. Then we both burst out laughing. "You idiot!" I said. "I was so worried? That you'd answer them? And you knew all along."

"Same here!" said Jack. "Why were you worried I'd answer them? You know I can deal with silent calls."

"Because. Well. Because I thought it was my problem? I thought it was one of my ex-clients."

"Well, that's funny. I thought it was one of my ex-clients."

I laughed. "God. We're a pair of berks. Well. Who did you think it was?"

Jack hesitated. "No-one really. You know, I just thought it was someone I'd pissed off at some point in my counselling career. It could be anyone really."

"Yeah," I said. "Me too."

"So what made you ask if they want a taxi?"

"Just something Dianne said. She said it would get a reaction from them."

"And did it?"

"Well. It might have done. If you hadn't –" My sentence was cut short. By the phone ringing again. Perhaps the caller had checked the number and dialled again. Jack answered it this time.

"Hello?" Silence. She nodded at me. Then turned away trying to keep her face straight. "Do you want a ta-hahaha-xi? Oh God, I can't do it without laughing!" She held the receiver away from her face. Both of us burst into hysterical laughter. When Jack had recovered she put the receiver back to her ear. She held it out to me. I heard the tone. Our silent caller had obviously not been impressed by our hilarity. And didn't call again.

JACK

YOUR INSTANT MESSAGING SERVICE REPORT

To: Pie

From: Jack

Subject: Christmas?

So it's the 24th and now I'm actually starting to feel festive. How 'bout you? I'll be glad when it's over, mind you. What I'm really not looking forward to are the 'review of the year' programmes that we get on every single channel (still only have five of them and lucky the gf even allows a tv in the house). The news is depressing, the soaps are boring, I wasn't interested in who was shagging who in the world of celebrity the first time around and now I'll be forced to sit through it all again on fast forward. Maybe that's how I could watch my life – fast forward through all the crap and keep the special moments to make a ten-minute review programme.

To: CrackerJack
From: AmericanPie
Subject: you got ten minutes?
Wow, your life must have been full of special moments to get ten whole minutes' worth. I might have to reduce mine to a two-minute animation. Blink and you'll miss the eighties.

To: Pie
From: Jack
Subject: the eighties
No, the eighties weren't that good to me, either. And have you noticed the clothes are coming back. Pleeeeeze! They really were atrocious the first time around – those knitted mohair monstrosities with slash necks and the cerise pink stripes. Yuk! I walked past a trendy clothes shop the other day and thought I'd fallen through a time warp. If I ever see someone in a ra-ra skirt then I'll be fourteen again and reaching for the razor blades.

To: CrackerJack
From: AmericanPie
Subject: didn't realise you were so fashion conscious
My dear. you would never be forced to wear a ra-ra monstrosity if you lived in my palace. What happened to your silent caller?

To: Pie
From: Jack
Subject: silence
Silent Caller finally gave up calling and now there is just silence.

To: CrackerJack
From: AmericanPie
Subject: re: silence

The silence of screams unheard is the sound of one hand clapping. For something to be spoken there needs to be a listener, or the speaker is just making noises.

To: Pie
From: Jack
Subject: *shudder*
Tell me about your palace.

To: CrackerJack
From: AmericanPie
Subject: where do I begin?
It's hardly Buckingham or even Beckingham (ah yes, I've seen those glossy mags all the way over here). My palace is more of a construction of the mind. Just as iron bars do not a prison make, so marble staircases do not a palace make. My palace is whatever I want it to be, and it can be in your dreams too, if you let it.

To: Pie
From: Jack
Subject: iron bars
My dreams of late are filled with iron bars so this might not be the best comparison to entice me.

To: CrackerJack
From: AmericanPie
Subject: entice you, moi?
Sorry to hear about your dreams. It's obvious to me that you are trapped in this eighties-ridden world. Perhaps you could let Dr America sort you out? Come lie on my couch and I'll massage your groin- eh brain.

To: Pie
From: Jack
Subject: not today thank you
What do you take me for? Do you take me at all?

To: CrackerJack
From: AmericanPie
Subject: humblest apologies
Deepest, sincerest, apologies for the perceived sexual harassment. It didn't cross my mind at all. Not a bit. I was only thinking about my palace and what you might find there.

INSTANT MESSAGING SERVICE REPORT ENDS

Chapter Twenty

"Hi Jackie. What would you like to talk about today?"

"I have an intimacy issue."

"Yes? Go on."

"The people who I should be intimate with, I'm not; and then I'm connecting with other people in intimate ways that are maybe inappropriate."

"Inappropriate people or inappropriate ways?"

"Both I'd say. For instance you – I feel an intimate connection with you after only two sessions of counselling. Would you say that was inappropriate?"

"I'm not so sure about that. It often happens…"

"I know it *happens*. What I'm saying is that I feel sexual."

"You are confusing intimacy with sexual feeling?"

"There's a difference? Of course there is – I'm being rhetorical, ironical, whatever. Yes. I think all my life I've confused intimacy with sexual feeling."

"Why do you think this is?"

"Because I never felt intimate with anyone until I began to feel sexual. I think sadly it happens a lot. A person is distant from their parents and carers. Lacks intimacy as a child, doesn't make friends easily at school, becomes an adolescent and the first intimate feelings come hand in hand with sexual development."

"A person?"

"Ok. Me. I. I felt distant from my carers and lacked intimacy."

"And now you find yourself in intimate situations that you feel should not happen."

"I feel."

"You feel…?"

"You said that I *feel* they shouldn't happen. You are equating thoughts and feelings. I *think* that they shouldn't happen – but I feel… I don't know what I feel."

"Give me an example of an inappropriate intimate situation for you."

"Well, there was my client. Larissa. The reason that Annette told me to get a personal counsellor and the reason I'm here."

"Tell me about Larissa – I know you've told me already what happened but tell me how you felt at the time and how you feel now."

"I told you; I don't know how I feel."

"Try. Humour me."

"At the time I felt – I was flattered that she was coming on to me; it doesn't happen that often these days. I was scared because I knew it was a dangerous situation – I mean it could have cost me my job. I was excited, nervous, I had heightened sexual feelings and felt like a teenager on a first date. Afterwards I felt like a fool. I thought she'd made a fool of me and I felt foolish. I was embarrassed at the way I'd reacted; I was ashamed. But in a way I was still excited. I was frustrated, very frustrated."

"For someone who doesn't know how she feels, you seem to be doing a good job. How about now? How do you feel now?"

"Now this minute?"

"Yes."

"Like I've relieved myself of a burden. But still a bit ashamed."

"You've no need to feel shame. You reacted as many people would have, given the circumstances. Shame is not a useful emotion."

"No it isn't. But it stopped me from taking it any further."

"How would you have taken it further?"

"What do you mean?"

"What would you have done if you hadn't stopped yourself?"

"Well – I would have… it would have… become sexual."

"It was already sexual, from what you say."

"I mean that I would have had sex with her."

"There in the counselling room?"

"Probably. There wasn't anywhere else."

"That was what made it exciting for you? The fact that it was illicit?"

"Not necessarily. I don't see what you're getting at. Lesbianism is always illicit. For me it is, anyway."

"Would you have been attracted to this woman otherwise?"

"Yes. Yes I think so."

"If you'd met her elsewhere. And you were single with no ties, so there were no taboos to break?"

"She is a beautiful woman. Breathtaking."

"Describe her to me."

"Blonde. Long blonde hair, very smooth and silky. Blue eyes, deep rather than pale. Honey skin, unblemished. Rich lips; a rich voice. A good figure, waist, hips, breasts like… well. What can I say? She's stunning. It's not surprising she's a whore really. She makes a lot of money from it. But look – I'm getting turned on now, just describing her. Imagine what kind of state I'm in up close. I should be feeling like this about my partner. My partner is blonde, blue-eyed, gorgeous figure, beautiful – everyone says so. But she leaves me cold most of the time. She freezes me. I call her The Ice Queen, though not to her face of course."

"Is it that you are attracted to people who are unavailable? Your client is unavailable to you but your partner is available and so -"

"I wouldn't say that she is available actually. My partner I mean. Most of the time we could just be roommates."

"Ah."

"What do you mean, 'ah'? I hate it when counsellors do that as if they have stumbled on the crux of the problem."

"Well, you have said yourself that you are frustrated. You are sexually frustrated and now this is spilling out into your work. Wouldn't you agree?"

"So you're suggesting that I should shag more often and that will cure me?"

"I wouldn't be so simplistic as –"

"Can I bring Jim here and you can tell her that? Maybe if she thought she was helping me then she'd actually let me fuck her."

"There is no need to be antagonistic about this. If I've hit a raw nerve I apologise. That is what this is about after all."

"I'm sorry. I shouldn't have shouted. You're right – I'm frustrated. About everything, not just sexually. My hands are a barometer of my stress levels. Look at them: covered in eczema. And you're right too about the unavailability thing. Taboos have always excited me. I was married to a transsexual, you know – almost went that way myself... Most people are surprised when I tell them that but you didn't bat an eyelid. Aren't you the least bit surprised?"

"It's my job not to be shocked by anything I hear, isn't it?"

"I don't mean shocked. I said 'surprised' – meaning that it was not unexpected."

"Going by what you've said already about your life, I don't think I could predict anything and therefore nothing would be unexpected."

"Hmm. The usual non-committal counsellor's answer. Do you find it difficult to counsel me because I'm a counsellor myself?"

"No client is easy. Everyone has their own reasons to be difficult."

"So I am difficult?"

"Do you think that you're difficult?"

"Why do you always answer a question with a question?"

"Why do *you* avoid answering *me*?"

"About being difficult? Ha – I've always been difficult. I was a difficult child, apparently – I don't remember being difficult myself, I just remember everyone around me being difficult. But I suppose it amounts to the same thing when you're a child."

"Do you like to think of yourself as difficult?"

"Well, I wouldn't like to think that I'm easy!"

"…"

"What? It was a joke."

"You are proud of being a difficult person to get on with?"

"No. Not really. Sometimes I wish that I was easier to get on with. But if that was at the expense of my personality then I wouldn't want to. I mean, I wouldn't turn myself into an airhead just so that I could make friends, because what the hell kind of friends would they be anyway? I don't make superficial friendships – for me they are deep or they are nothing."

"What about acquaintances?"

"Acquaintances?"

"People you work with, partners of close friends, friends of your partner… and suchlike."

"People that I don't choose to be friends with don't really get much out of me."

"What makes you choose someone?"

"Intelligence helps. Do I sound like a snob? I'm sorry, I meant that I don't have much time for idiots."

"You should speak your mind; it doesn't matter to me what you sound like. I'm just trying to get a picture of what your relationships are like. How many close friends would you say that you have?"

"Including my partner?"

"No."

"One. Oh – two, if you count people I've never met."

"I don't understand. You're counting someone you've never met as a close friend?"

"I've met this person over the internet and we've become close but I've not seen or met, er – her."

"So, not counting this internet person, you have one friend. And this is…?"

"Claire. I knew her when I was thirteen and then we met again as adults and we've been friends since. Her girlfriend doesn't like me but I don't care."

"And what are your intimacy issues surrounding Claire?"

"I – how did you know I had any?"

"But you have, haven't you?"

"I suppose I still carry a torch for her since we first met. She was my first love, but we never – we were just friends then."

"Describe her to me."

"She's a black woman. She wears dreadlocks, short now but they used to be longer. She has a regal air about her, in the way she carries herself, tall like an African queen. A deep voice, a beautiful smile and a warm, welcoming embrace."

"You like queens."

"*What?*"

"Sorry, I mean that you like to describe people as queens. Your partner is an ice queen and your friend is an African queen."

"I never… I never really thought of that. I do see women as queens. I suppose I can put people on a pedestal sometimes."

"Mm-hmm. So to sum up, you have a partner with whom you are not in love; a best friend with whom you are in love; an ex-client with whom you are in love or possibly lust; and an anonymous person you met over the internet with whom you are… also in love?"

"With Pie? In love with Pie?"

"And no other friends."

"I'm in love with Pie? Maybe I am. I don't know. Is it possible to be in love with someone you've not met?"

"You tell me. I was only asking the question. You hadn't told me anything about… Pie?"

"American Pie; it's the username sh-she, he uses. I don't know whether Pie is male or female, you see. It makes it very difficult to talk or even think about a person when you are using a language with no gender-neutral pronoun. I can't really refer to Pie as 'it'. I don't know about in *love*; I think in *love* is maybe putting it a bit strong. We flirt. We get very philosophical at times. But in love? I don't know."

"What attracts you to a person over the internet?"

"Everything that attracts me to a person personally, except looks. It's a real meeting of minds, you know? It could be that Pie is only a teenager or is an old wrinkly person, or disfigured or physically unattractive. It's funny because I've been accused of superficiality and only being attracted to people by their appearance. It's not like that with Pie. I mean, we've described ourselves to each other but… well for instance I've told Pie that I'm a punk. You only see what they want to present to you and they only see what you present to them. And this seems safe, doesn't it? It could be safe if it were just kept superficial and a lot of my internet connections are. But if you *really* connect with someone, it can get much deeper much quicker than a physical meeting, because you don't have all the social barriers."

"Social barriers?"

"Eye contact, facial expression, tone of voice… you know."

"It's interesting that you refer to these as 'barriers' where they are generally termed as non-verbal communication."

"Yes. Well of course they *are* non-verbal communication, but I also see them as social barriers because they are what people use as defences against interaction. Especially for someone who doesn't get the rules and is frightened of making mistakes."

"Defences against interaction. Is all social interaction attack and defence for you? Are you the person who doesn't get the rules?"

"I've never got the rules. Since I was a child I can always remember being awkward in social situations. I'd either be too brash or too surly; too open or too closed. I just can't make the balance. I don't *do* social occasions."

"How many Christmas cards did you get?"

"One that was just to me, from Annette. But a lot for Jim and me together."

"How would you feel if your partner threw a surprise birthday party for you?"

"Fucking hell! I'd run and hide! Mind you, would there be any guests?"

"Maybe you'd be surprised. Maybe a lot of people count you as their friend even though you don't count them as yours. How would you feel if you found out that a lot of people thought of you as their friend?"

"Surprised. Very surprised."

"You are doing yourself a great disservice with this low self-esteem."

"I don't have low self-esteem. I think I'm fabulous – but I'm realistic enough to know that not everyone else does."

"Interesting. You're full of ambiguities."

"Thank you."

"And the fact that you took that as a compliment says a lot about you."

"Yes it does."

"What would you like to do for the next half-an-hour?"

"I'm not sure. Shall I just recap what we've said?"

"Go ahead, if that would help."

"Well, you say that I'm in love with all of my friends but not my girlfriend. I said I had intimacy issues and you tell me that

I'm equating intimacy with sex. A couple of times I've mentioned my childhood – which I try not to talk or even think about most of the time. And now you're saying I have low self-esteem and I'm ambiguous. That about sums it up."

"Yes. And now we have a half-hour left of the session. Would you like to talk more about your childhood?"

"Not really. Nothing much to say."

"Tell me about your mother."

"Which one?"

"You have more than one?"

"I was fostered. I have a biological mother somewhere. I don't even know when my real birth date is, just an estimate. All I have is a string of foster mothers too long for me to remember them all."

"I see."

"What do you see?"

"I see the groundwork for someone with intimacy issues."

"Oh, do you? And where do you get that from? I haven't told you anything about them yet."

"It's not so much what you've said as the tone you say it in. You didn't get close to your foster mothers? Are there any that you stayed in contact with?"

"There was one long-term foster family. I stayed from the age of five till eleven. They talked about adopting me but didn't. We didn't stay in contact."

"Any reason?"

"She didn't want me."

"Why do you think she didn't want you?"

"She thought I was evil. Something happened – I did something when I was eleven and she just freaked out."

"What did you do?"

"I don't want to talk about it."

"Ok. In your own time. But you realise that we must talk about these things if we are to exorcise the ghosts of the past."

"Yes yes. I just don't want to think about it at the moment."

"So after this thing that you did… she rejected you?"

"Yes. She called the police and I was taken into care then."

"It was illegal?"

"Not – yes, I suppose it was. If it had been successful then it would have been very illegal."

"You are ashamed of what you tried to do, or are you ashamed that you failed?"

"No! Don't try to goad me into talking about it."

"Your life before this thing, before you were eleven. Tell me about that."

"Good. It was good. I did well in school. I didn't really have any problems at all. It was idyllic in many ways. I used to run around barefoot, climb trees and chase rabbits. Quite *Cider with Rosie*, in fact. You know the book? I did used to have times when I felt frustrated as a child – like I was stuck. I didn't want to be a girl because I wanted the freedom that boys had. But I think that was more to do with the fact that I'd been given freedom as a small child and then this had been curtailed as I got older. So it wasn't until I was nine or ten that I started getting bouts of depression. Before then I was fine."

"What do you remember of your mother at this time? The long-term foster mother."

"She was clean. Always cleaning the house and tidying up."

"Did she work?"

"She did a lot of charity stuff and was always on the go – but if you mean work to earn money then no. My foster father had a good job and they didn't have any other children. So we were quite well off comparatively."

"What was your relationship with your foster-father like?"

"I don't remember many times with him as he was always at work. I did look up to him and I used to help him fix bikes and things. But he didn't have much time for me once I was older. They divorced when I was nine or ten."

"Nine or ten? You don't remember?"

"I seem to remember that it took a long time. My memory blurs around the late-Seventies."

"What were things like in school when you were nine or ten?"

"I used to get into fights. I got tall very quickly and I got picked on because of that and because of being clever."

"You got into trouble because of these fights?"

"Yes. It was always me that got the blame even when other people would pick the fight."

"Why do you think that was?"

"Because I used to win."

"Do you always win a fight?"

"Physical fights? I don't really have physical fights anymore. I manage my temper very well these days."

"What happens when you lose your temper now?"

"I don't. I told you – I manage it."

"You seem to be an angry person, Jackie."

"What do you mean?"

"You've been on the brink of losing your temper for most of this session."

"No I haven't."

"Let's look at a definition here. How would you define losing your temper?"

"When someone loses control and says things they don't mean. When they do things that they would regret or do things that hurt other people."

"Ok. Control is an interesting issue. But that is only a part of anger, is it not? It's ok to feel anger, Jackie. It's ok to feel…"

"By anger, do you mean righteous indignation? I mean, there are times that I'm angry at the state of the world."

"It can mean that. But surely you must get angry in your personal life at times. Do you argue with your partner?"

"No."

"What happens if you feel angry with your partner, what do you do?"

"Nothing. I just feel angry for a while and then it goes away."

"Do you discuss issues with your partner?"

"Not really. We discuss the world, but we don't discuss our relationship."

"You are distant, then, from your partner."

"I suppose so."

"And you were distant from your parents?"

"Yes. No – I was close, very close to my foster-mother before…"

"Before?"

"Before she discarded me."

"This is how you see it? That you were discarded?"

"Yes. Abandoned. First by my biological mother and then by a succession of foster-mothers. I have always known that there is only one person in the world that I can rely on: myself. Only me."

"That is sad."

"Not really. Truthful. Realistic. At the end of the day it's the same for everyone. But they are conning themselves."

"This is how you see relationships?"

"Possibly. I haven't been given any reason to see otherwise. I was an unwanted child, always."

"Somebody wanted you – they fostered you so they must have wanted you. If you look at it from the other side…"

"They didn't want *me*. They wanted a child, yes. But then when *I* began to be me, they didn't want *me* anymore."

"What is you being you?"

"Ha! Everything that they didn't want from a child. They wanted a sweet little girl who was going to dress up in ribbons and be polite and play with dolls and grow up to be a respectful, demure young lady who would help out around the house and look after them in their old age. And they got me."

"You said earlier that you were given freedom...?"

"Yes. I was. I demanded freedom."

"So maybe they did allow you to be you for a time."

"There are two sides to everything aren't there? On the one hand, yes, I was spoilt – I was allowed to do what I wanted and given every opportunity to learn new things. My father I think, secretly wanted a boy and he liked me being curious about manly things like carpentry and plumbing. But then when it was time to show off for the family, when it was anything special, my foster mother put her foot down and insisted I wore a dress and was prettied up. She liked to think of herself as a feminist, my mother. She voted for Margaret Thatcher because she said that was the feminist thing to do. And she was proud of me being a tomboy to an extent – but only to an extent. When I got too boyish she would freak out. Like the times I used to go without a top."

"Without a top?"

"Yes. It was hot. All the boys and men were walking around bare-chested, in jeans or shorts but nothing on top. I was nine. I didn't have any tits, why should I cover up when I looked just like them?"

"Indeed."

"I hate those stupid bikinis you get for girls, with the top designed just to cover up nipples. What's the point? I had been going without a top for every summer previous to that one. Sometimes there'd be looks or mutterings but no-one really bothered because I looked so much like a boy anyway. Then suddenly when I was nine she started freaking out about it."

"And you say that you had no breasts?"

"No."

"Not even ones that were just developing?"

"No. Not at all."

"What else happened when you were nine? You mentioned that your parents were divorcing around then."

"Nothing really. I was in the same school."

"I'm trying to think of something like that would explain her sudden protectiveness."

"I've thought about something…"

"Go on."

"It affected me a lot but I don't know how much it influenced her. I suppose it must have done. There was a murder. The winter before I was nine someone was abducted and murdered and it was all over the news. She was local, but I didn't know her – she was in a year above me in school. All the mums started to walk their children to and from school again. I never associated that with her reaction to me baring my non-existent breasts. But I do remember her sudden protectiveness. I remember that particular murder because we were all so horrified that it could happen. The child was offered a lift home. And I think he was a neighbour or a friend of the family. All I could think about for years was that they must have driven past our house. She lived nearer to the village than I did, and she was dumped further out. So logically I knew that at the time they drove past my house, she would have been panicking. I read about it in the paper. I started reading then about other murders, got a book on true crimes from the library. I was having nightmares and my mum took the book away. That was the first murder that I was really aware of and it was another thing that made me want to not be a girl."

"Because it had been a girl victim?"

"Because girls are targeted for abuse. Because it's not safe to be a girl."

"Many boys are also abused."

"Yes. I know that now. But as a child that was never talked about. Rape and abuse of women was talked about. It was the whole 'stranger danger' thing. And girls just weren't safe walking on their own after dark."

"You wanted to be a boy to be safe?"

"Yes. No. Not just that, but that was part of it."

"For what other reasons did you want to be a boy?"

"For the freedom. The unrestrictive clothing, the freedom of expression, because they got bigger portions and better deals, because they weren't expected to do housework or be particularly academic."

"And yet you say you were proud of your intellect."

"Yes. But as a child the pressure is on, isn't it?"

"Did you feel pressure to succeed?"

"All the time. And she just wouldn't give me praise. She'd criticise if I got something wrong, but if it was right then she'd just nod as if that's how she expected it to be."

"This *thing* that you failed in when you were eleven…?"

"It wasn't like that. It wasn't an academic thing or a test. It was an attempt to…"

"To what?"

"I suppose to perform an operation."

"On yourself?"

"No. On someone else."

"And…"

"I told you I don't want to talk about it. It's over. It's in the past and I'm sorry about it. I paid my price and now I want to get on with my life. I wish it would stop coming back. It was twenty-four years ago after all – over two-thirds of my life."

"In what way does it come back?"

"In my dreams. Sometimes I'm dreaming about it or dreaming that I'm there again."

"Where?"

"Back there where I was then. In that state of mind I mean, not in a physical place."

"Could you tell me what happens in your dream? Is it always the same dream?"

"No, not the same. They are different dreams, the usual kind of thing in a dream with odd connections but nothing freaky, and then something happens which makes me *know*. You know how that is, in a dream when you just know something? When you're happily going about your business and then someone turns to you and says something or just looks at you in a certain way and then you know they're after you."

"After you?"

"They're out to get you. And they're going to get you – they're relentless and the only option is to run because you can't stand up to them."

"Who are 'they'?"

"I never see them. I see their messengers."

"In your dream."

"Yes. Of course this is a dream. I know that this is a dream not reality; you asked me to describe it to you."

"I'm sorry. Go on."

"People come for me. It's like – I don't know – when I hear people describe alien abduction encounters it reminds me of these dreams. They come for me, and it's usually because they've found out that I've done something bad and they want to take me away. Except I haven't done anything or I can't remember doing it and I'm trying to plead my case but they won't listen. Sometimes there is someone there – my mother or Jim or someone from my past and they're either gloating or ignoring me. I plead for help but I get ignored. There is nothing I can do, no way I can stand up to them. Then I wake up, usually when they're just about to drag me off. By that time I'm fighting with the bedclothes and I assume this is what wakes me up."

"How long have you been having these dreams?"

"On and off since I was a teenager. I didn't have them for years in my twenties and thought they'd gone, but they came back a while ago and they've got worse lately."

"Are you reading true crime books now?"

"No, not really. I mean, I've always read thrillers and detective novels. There's been a murder locally, which is what got me thinking about this. But these nightmares started up before that."

"Do you think they are related to stress?"

"I don't know. Possibly."

"Do you know who these people are? Are they always the same people?"

"Just nameless, faceless enemies."

"Men?"

"Yes. Always men."

"Hmm."

"So come on! You're the Freudian, can't you tell me what they mean?"

"As you know, there is more to Freud than interpreting dreams."

"But it's hardly wish fulfilment is it?"

"Perhaps it is a re-enactment of the events that took place when your foster mother phoned the police when you were eleven? But if you don't tell me the details then I won't be able to compare them."

"I realise that much. I just want to know if having the dreams means that it is likely to happen again."

"I am a psychologist not a psychic."

"I know that. I just wondered... oh, it doesn't matter."

"There's something else you want to tell me?"

"..."

"Jackie?"

"The hour is up now anyway."

"Yes it is."

"Will you send me a copy of the recording?"

"Yes, if you'd like one."

"Have a good New Year."

"Thank you."

HARRIS THE 'DRAG KING' AND DRUGGIE HUBBY

MORE SHOCKING REVELATIONS about Jacqueline Harris, the counsellor who battered a homeless man to death in a Valley town earlier this year. Ten years ago, she was performing as a MAN on stage under the name 'Cracker Jack' with her husband, transsexual Rachel X. Rachel was born Richard Jones and had a sex-change operation in 1993. They married in 1995. Frederika Stoner, 30, who used to travel with them, witnessed 'Rachel' shooting up HEROIN backstage several times and says that both of them were highly promiscuous with members of their audiences.

Ms Stoner, who now works in a record shop, tells of the times that she had to help Harris carry Rachel back to their van. "They would both drink a lot in the bar, because they got the drink for free when they were performing. Sometimes they would ask me to get drugs for them, but I wouldn't touch it myself. They carried on working even when Rachel was ill but they couldn't do it forever. We all knew that. We had good times and tried to live each day as if it were the last."

Rachel died in 1997 of an AIDS-related illness and Jacqueline moved to the Valley where she was living in January this year when she killed homeless Frank Little. "After Rachel died, there was a bit of fuss about whether she'd had an overdose but nothing was ever proved. Jack moved away very quickly afterwards."

See our full-colour supplement for photographs of the infamous wedding of 'Jack and Rachel'. Did you attend this 'wedding'? Do you have photos or a story to tell? See inside for details of how to contact us.

Chapter Twenty-One – 1996

Hi, I'm Jack and this is [hip thrust] *Big Jack* (cheers). *Want to meet my wife?* [produce blow-up doll] (boos) *Oh, come on, girls, it's not that bad. Want to know the secret of a good marriage? Women: keep your mouth open and men: keep your mouth shut* (cheers and boos). *Go on darling, back in your box* [sling blow-up doll into corner] (boos). *Yeah, yeah, she's glad of it. She likes a bit of rough. And I throw her me credit card once in a while so she can buy a new pair of shoes* (hisses). *But let's not talk about me, let's talk about you.* [cue Jack's music] *You've got beautiful eyes* [hip circles] *I wanna see your eyes go wide with surprise, baby. I wanna taste your lips, oooh, you know you want it.* [hip thrusts. Jack sings Queen's Fat Bottomed Girls] *Come on, give it to me! How bad could it be?* [music fades] *But I know what you're really here for. You want to see my real wife, don't you?* [cue Ruby's music] (cheers) *Well, wait for it, wait for it. Here she is… let's hear a big round of applause for… Ruuuuby Riiiich!* [Ruby enters stage right, Jack steps to left] (cheers, hoots, wolf whistles etc.) *All right Freddy, mine's a pint* [Jack exits and Ruby sings].

Even after a full year of performing on stage, Jack still trembles with excitement as she steps down and takes her pint from Freddy, their roadie. It will take her all night to chill out. She knows she's only there as a warm-up act for Rachel but she likes the fact that the billing gives them equal weight: *Ruby Rich and Cracker Jack*. She's only on stage for five minutes but varies the songs and the banter. Last time here she sang The Kinks' *Lola*. She would like to try a slow romantic one, maybe John Lennon's *Woman*, but Rachel wants her to stay upbeat and not get too serious.

Sitting in the bar, while Ruby struts her stuff, gives Jack a chance to eye up the girls. She's surprised at how many women come to see a drag act. Jack drinks the first beer far too quickly and belches as she calls Freddy to bring her a second. She's pleased that the drag king outfit lends her freedom to belch, fart and behave as badly as she likes, yet still receive admiring glances. One of the admirers she knows is Freddy, who is secretly in love with both Rachel and Jack. Poor Freddy, trying her best with her shaved hair and Doc Martens. Neither of them is interested.

Rachel has never expected Jack to be monogamous, although she prefers not to know about any infidelity, even though they rarely have sex these days. Certainly nothing has come close to that first time, all those years ago. Jack just can't get her head round all that dental dam rubbish and Rachel is too prudent to offer the forbidden pleasure of unsafe sex. Rachel is getting tired a lot lately, keeping an eye on her T-count and mixing the medications with various not-so-legal concoctions. She needs to keep her strength up for the shows, although she's quite handy for a blowjob if all else fails.

Jack is still working as a carer for the agency. Sometimes she does hospital shifts, but she dictates her own days of work as she wants to avoid gig times. Rachel gigs for the thrill, not the money, and the Social would take back anything she earned anyway. They mostly manage to break even, what with travelling all over the Midlands and paying Freddy's paltry wages. But Jack can't live on the disability like Rachel does and she prefers to have some independent earnings.

While Rachel is on stage, Freddy flaps about in the bar ferrying drinks to Jack and generally being an irritating twenty-year-old. Was Jack ever that annoying? She doesn't think so. Jackie has her eye on a pretty little tart who's sitting on her own at a table near the front. Short denim skirt and red, fake leather jacket, lipstick and little round glasses. She's noticed Jack watching her and looked over a few times, smiling over her stemmed glass. Just as Jack is getting up to saunter over, Freddy bustles self-importantly into view and waves a cellophane-wrap in front of her. "I could only get a 'teenth. D'you think it'll be enough?"

"Yes, I'm sure it will. But keep it in your pocket, will you?" growls Jack. "And get me another drink. It looks like white wine."

"You want wine?" Freddy sneers.

"Not for me, you idiot." Jack pushes past her and pastes a smile on her face before approaching the wine-drinking girl at the front table. "This seat taken?" she asks when the girl glances up. She sits down without waiting for an answer and shifts uncomfortably, remembering she's still wearing her 'friend'. "My name's Jack and, er, well I'm sure you know the rest. How do you like the show?" Jack has a shufti at the stage and can see Ruby's knife-high heels frighteningly close. But Rachel hasn't noticed her yet; she's still crooning to the crowd, her true lover.

The girl offers her name, which immediately exits Jack's brain, and mumbles something about having been stood up by her mates. "Well you look like you're having a good time, anyway, mates or no," says Jack, now grinning because she can see Freddy tiptoeing over with a wineglass in one hand and a pint of bitter in the other. "Atta-girl Freds. Nice one. Now you go and make sure our Rach has a mellow half-hour in the interval. That's right, off you go." She is tempted to pat Freddy's bottom, just to see the reaction from both the girl and Fred herself, but refrains. Sometimes playing the man can get you a slap, even if the moustache is only eyeliner.

Jack smiles through gritted teeth as Freddy slops the drinks down on the table and trudges off, just as the closing bars of Ruby's last song flow over the audience and the patter of applause turns to louder claps, stamps and cheers. The girl watches Freddy go and then looks back at Jack, who shrugs, a wry smile on her lips. "Honestly, you can't get the staff."

She knows that Freddy and Rachel will be spliffing it together in the dressing room and that later on Rachel will be too tired and Freddy too stoned for any fun at all. Jack has tried dope several times since the bike accident but throws whiteys and gets sick from it. She blames a Pavlovian association with the crash, but suspects that she's actually growing up. She is the one to stay sober and drive home while Freddy snores in the back and Rachel jabbers melodramatically in the passenger seat ("I mean, did you *see* the curtain in that place? Shocking, darling. Absolutely shocking."). Tonight they are doing their monthly stint at Birwood's local gay club, so she's taking advantage of the free beer and freedom to drink it. They will quite probably stagger home together singing k.d.'s *Sexuality*. How bad could it be, indeed?

"Haven't seen you here before," Jack says to the girl and then laughs at her own cheesy chat-up line. She leans back in her seat and says in her Cracker Jack voice: "Do you come here often?"

The girl giggles. "Not that often, but I've seen you before."

"Have you now?" says Jack. "Well that surprises me because I'm sure I'd have noticed a gorgeous babe like you. You must have been sitting at the back last time. Hiding your light under a bushel."

The girl simpers and takes a sip of her wine. Soon they are leaning forward over the table, laughing together, knees touching. Jack gets an eyeful of cleavage, deliberately shown, and her hand goes to the girl's leg. Jack likes a skirt; it makes everything so available. The sheer silkiness of the stocking tantalises Jack's fingertips and she is obliged travel further up to check that they are indeed stockings. Both Jack and the girl gasp as her fingers touch bare flesh and she skims around the tips of the stockings, not venturing further yet. The girl's legs open slightly of their own accord. "So are you what people call a 'lipstick lesbian'?"

"I might be." The girl's breath is hot and her voice low. "Although I hate that phrase."

"I've always wondered," says Jack, her fingers walking to the inside of the thigh, feeling the legs part just slightly more. "Where do you put your lipstick?" She lingers on the 'lips', and as she says it her hand jumps from the relative safety of the stocking-top straight to the unprotected lips. The girl tries to close her legs but is too late. Jack draws her finger down in a line, pressing through the material and feeling first a hard bump and then a softly yielding wet area.

The girl lets out an involuntary "Oh" before clamping her fingers around Jack's wrist and yanking her hand away. At this point it could go either way. Jack has tried this trick before and has received slaps or kisses in equal proportions. Once a slap *and* a kiss: that was an interesting evening. The girl pushes Jack's hand back down to her knee but not completely away, and holds it there. She gives Jack a sideways glance. "What are you like," she says but it doesn't seem to be a question. She laughs and downs half a glass of wine.

Jack drinks some of her beer and points to the wine glass. "Are you up for another, or are you up for... something else?" The build-up music for Ruby's next stint is playing and Jack knows that she doesn't have much time to lose. At this point, the dressing room is vacant and Rachel is not yet on the stage. It doesn't do to let Rachel see her leave with someone – the histrionics are more than any rival could deal with. She stands up, still holding the girl's hand. "Come on," she says and begins to walk towards the staff exit.

With barely any protest, the girl grabs her handbag and follows Jack out of the bar, through a back corridor. Muffled cheers filter through the door behind them and Ruby begins to sing. As they reach the dressing room, Freddy appears from the other direction. She looks as if she'd wanted to go in there but Jack signals with her eyes that she's to fuck off back to the bar. The girl turns away, embarrassed at the sight of Freddy there – perhaps she imagines that Jack and Fred are an item. Perish the thought! Jack pulls the girl close and puts her arm around her shoulder. She kisses her on the neck and then looks back at Freddy, who is bull-headedly still standing there. "Can't you see I'm busy?" asks Jack. Fred skulks away.

Jack opens the door and turns around to pull the girl in. She seems reluctant and Jack asks, "Are you shy now?"

"No," she says, "but what about…?" she looks back in the direction of the bar.

"Oh, don't worry about her. She'll get over it; doesn't get much." They laugh and the girl allows herself to be drawn into the small room. Jack closes the door and then leans her back against it. The smell of sweat and cigarettes is stifling in the small airless room. The girl is staring at the gaudy lights, large mirror and tiny dresser, unable to hide her disdain.

"Sorry darling, did you expect something better?"

"No. I…"

Jack sits down in the shabby office chair and swivels it around to face her. It creaks comically when it moves. "You should have seen some of the places we've worked. At least this is a proper room and not a toilet."

The girl smiles nervously and her eyes take in the items on the surface in front of her. A large ashtray filled with roaches and a bit of old cellophane, surrounded by discarded lipsticks and mascara. A box of tissues to the side and a vodka bottle in the corner. Jack picks up a glass and wipes the lipstick mark with a tissue. "Fancy a drink? My dear old wife won't mind."

At the mention of the word 'wife', the girl blanches and Jack hurries to reassure her. "It's a marriage of convenience, you know," she says, pouring a generous helping of Rachel's favourite Blue Label and handing the glass over. The girl sips tentatively and Jack reaches out to put her hands on the skirt again. "Come on," she murmurs, "come and sit on my lap." She pulls her forward by the hips and is met with little resistance. The girl puts the glass back down and giggles, but stays standing. Jack puts both hands underneath the skirt and slides them up, lifting it to the hips. She is pleased with the effect this has of showing the stocking tops and a lacy suspender belt. "Mmm," says Jack, "you really were sent from heaven just for me, weren't you?"

Jack is very aware of the bunched up dildo inside her suit trousers and pushes up against it. She listens for a moment to the thud-thud of music from Ruby's act, then takes a large gulp of vodka and looks up at the girl. "Give us a kiss, then," she murmurs. Sliding her hands around the girl's hips to her buttocks, she draws her closer still. The girl bends forward to touch lips, taking off her spectacles and placing them next to the glass on the dresser. Jack takes one hand from her backside and cups the back of her head. The girl's hands slip inside the suit jacket and downwards. "Can I touch it?" she asks.

"Of course, you can," she says and leans back again to unzip. It springs out, upright and ever-ready, and the girl gasps and giggles. "What do you think, up close?"

She is covering her mouth with her hand and trying to tear her eyes away from the prominent dildo. "I've never seen one in real life," she admits.

"You should get out more," says Jack, laughing. She takes another swig of vodka and hands the girl the glass again, entirely comfortable with having the dildo on show. It isn't *actually* a part of her anatomy after all. "Well?" Jack asks once the glass is drained. "Think you can handle it?"

In answer, the girl kicks off her heels and pulls off her knickers in one swift, practised movement. Then she places her hands carefully on Jack's shoulders and puts one knee either side of her on the chair. *That's what I like to see: Sluts R US.* They kiss again, more deeply, and the girl begins to rub up and down against the dildo, keeping it on the outside. Jack feels the pressure mounting and senses the shudders that travel through the girl's body. She pulls back slightly to speak, "Do you need lube?"

"I could, if you've got some," she says and stands again. "It's just so big."

"Bet you say that to all the boys," says Jack, winking as she reaches into her inside pocket. She pulls out a couple of sachets of the free stuff that she picks up in these bars. It's a very handy bonus of working in gay clubs. She tears the tops away and expertly squeezes a glob of lubricant from each sachet onto the tip, watching it roll slowly down the side. Jack catches the drip and wipes her hand around the whole thing, the silicon glistens and darkens to a different shade of blue. With her dry hand, she pulls the skirt again and reaches up to wipe the lube where it's needed, perhaps a tad too roughly.

That little shocked 'oh' gets her blood racing and she can't help but let her fingers do the talking. Just skimming around the edge and it works well. When the girl speaks it is in a guttural tone: "Oh, fucking hell," as if she didn't want it. She straddles Jack again and this time she sits right on it. The eyes go up and the mouth widens into a silent groan, then she starts to move. Riding together on the chair, Jack grabs the fake leather jacket lapels. She pulls them down and thrusts her hips, trying to get as deep as possible as this girl obviously likes it. Jack knows she won't come like this – the dildo is at completely the wrong angle and its base skims past her clit frustratingly – but the girl enjoys it and it only takes a few minutes for her to come, so why not let her? Meanwhile, Jack is quite happy to nuzzle into that cleavage. She licks the beads of sweat that dribble between her breasts.

They are slumped in the chair now, which groans as Jack twirls it to and fro with her feet. Big Jack is still inside the girl and the movement of the chair sets her off again. Surprise evident on her face, she experiences a short sharp orgasm *right* inside the aftershock of the previous one. Her head is buried into Jack's shoulder while she recovers and a long, low laugh rumbles into Jack's neck. "It's been a while since I've done anything like this," the girl admits in a breathless whisper.

Jack pats her on the back. "It's not over yet, darling. Come on, stand up." She hesitantly eases herself off Jack's lap, a twinge of pain causing her to grimace, and stands uncertainly in front of the mirror.

"Oh God, look at my hair," she says, straightening her top.

"Don't worry about that now," says Jack, also standing. As she leaves the chair, it drifts backwards and hits the wall behind, swinging to one side with a whimper.

Hooking her foot under the chair leg to bring it back, Jack pulls the girl around and leans her up against the dresser to kiss her. With practised ease, Jack slips her hand between the girl's legs and lifts one thigh. She props the girl's foot on the chair and kneels down in front of her. "Oh no!" says the girl.

"No?" says Jack, looking up.

"I can't," says the girl, grabbing the back of Jack's head.

"You mean you really can't, or you shouldn't?"

The grip on her hair tightens and Jack feels her face being pushed forward. So much for 'no'. So warm and soft, so salty and sweet, so seductive. Heidi was wrong when she said it's impossible to get a tongue inside. It's not easy to get right inside, but gliding around the edge is a cinch. But now Jack doesn't want her to come. She wants to tease. So it's a flickety flick, lickety lick and standing up again. This time the chair spins away and stays there.

"What?" The girl is confused as Jack wordlessly directs her to turn around and lean her forwards against the dresser. She soon catches the drift, however, when Jack moves to stand behind her and lifts up the skirt, exposing her bare buttocks. The girl pushes the clutter from the surface in front of her to one side and braces herself against the dresser.

"That's right," says Jack. "Push hard against it." She strokes the girl's thighs and watches her legs part, relishing the sight. It isn't often you see suspenders with no pants outside of porno mags and Jack wants to have some good memories to look back on. She holds Big Jack and directs it to the spot, just keeping it pressed against the opening of the vagina for a moment. The girl pushes back but Jack holds her down. "Easy tiger," she says, laughing, then, "Are you ready?"

"Yes, I'm fucking ready," comes the frustrated reply. Jack pushes forward and lets it enter slowly, in one long easy movement. "Ooooh," the girl groans and puts her face on the dresser. Jack pulls back again till only the tip is inside and waits a beat. As expected, the girl's head turns to look at her.

"Beg," says Jack. "Say please."

The girl leans up on her elbows and looks at Jack's reflection in the mirror. "Please," she says. "Pretty fucking please."

"Now, now," says Jack, laughing. "Patience is a virtue." Then she thrusts forward at full force, grabbing the girl's tits and pulling her up so that she is forced to watch herself. She takes a moment to check the girl's face to be sure this is what she wants before losing herself in the long steady strokes. The first time you're gentle; the second time you catch them unawares; the third time you can be as rough as you like. And now Jack is pleasing herself, not caring when or whether the girl comes. Only thinking about her own imminent orgasm. As it happens, they both reach it together, their screams ringing out wildly in the tiny room.

The moment over, Jack withdraws and the girl slumps forward again over the dresser. Jack reaches for the vodka bottle then pauses, trying to work out what's missing. "Shit!" she says, hurriedly stuffing Big Jack back into her trousers. "The music's stopped. We'd better get out of here."

"What…?" The girl looks at Jack with bleary-eyed post-orgasmic bewilderment.

"Get your stuff," Jack hisses, picking up the ashtray from the floor and attempting to return the roaches to it. "You really don't want to be here when Rachel turns up."

"Rachel…?" says the girl, grasping the sense of urgency and stuffing her feet into her shoes.

"Ruby – she'll be on her way back." Jack grabs the knickers from the floor and hands them to the girl, who slips them into her handbag. She gives her a quick peck on the cheek and then pushes her out of the door. "Go out the fire exit." The girl reaches back and seizes her specs before teetering along the corridor, one foot not properly in its shoe.

As she's disappearing around the corner, Freddy materializes from the other direction, a smug look on her face, while Rachel storms behind her. Freddy comes to a halt in front of Jack and folds her arms with a 'now you're for it' expression. Jack advances fully out of the dressing room and stands aside while Rachel elbows past.

"Hello love," says Jack to Rachel, trying for joviality. "You're back early."

"Thank you for ruining my show!" screams Rachel and slams the door in her face.

Jack turns to the grinning Freddy, who is clearly enjoying this show more than the one on the stage. "Well?" she says, "I'm sure you're dying to tell me what's going on."

"There was a problem with the music," Freddy says, leering. "We heard you screaming. We heard you both." Jack recoils for a moment at the thought of a whole club audience – her local club! – hearing her orgasm. Then she smirks, realising that this can only improve her status as a drag king. But of course, if Ruby has stormed off stage early and refuses to continue with the act then it won't go down well with the management. There is stomping and shouting from the front of the club and Jack can hear shouts of 'Crac-ker, Crac-ker'. It won't be long before someone comes looking for a performer.

Before she can decide what to do, the dressing-room door swings open again and a red-eyed Rachel stands glaring at Jack. In response, she opens her arms wide and gives a half-smile, her head to one side in what she hopes is a placating gesture. "I never said I was perfect."

Rachel refuses to speak to Jack but instead turns to Freddy in outrage. "It's not so much that she brings the little slappers back here for sex, although that's bad enough." She pulls her hand from behind her back to reveal that she's holding the bottle of Blue Label. "She's even giving them my vodka now!"

"Rachel, Rachel," says Jack. "You know I don't drink the stuff."

"There is *lipstick* on this glass!" Rachel shrieks, pointing at the glass on the dresser.

"Honey, *you* wear lipstick," says Jack reasonably.

"THAT'S NOT MY FUCKING SHADE!!!" Rachel slams the door so hard that the whole wall wobbles. Jack rolls her eyes and sighs. Within minutes she is back in front of the audience, to hoots and catcalls much louder than when she was on stage previously.

"Sorry about that, my darlings. It's a bit Angie and Den back there as I think you can imagine. Now, where were we?" She takes a tin of Café Crème from her jacket pocket and pops one of the cigarillos in her mouth. "Tell you what, remind me in my next life never to marry a fucking drama queen."

***

While Rachel is still in bed, Jack phones the agency. "Have you got anything for tonight?" she asks.

"Thought you didn't want to work tonight?" says Ash, the girl that Brenda has hired to staff the office.

"No, I didn't. But I do now." It would be prudent to avoid Rachel for a while. And besides which, Jack needs the money since she's bought a couple of bottles of Blue Label, which isn't cheap, to compensate for the single glass she'd drunk. At the moment she's barely able to make the interest payments on the credit card and has no hope of paying off the balance - at least, until Rachel dies and she can get the insurance money, but she doesn't want to think about that.

"Got a hospital night shift Valley way," says Ash.

"Valley! That's a good hundred miles or more each way."

"You get the mileage, remember. You've got transport?"

"Yes," says Jack, eyeing her crash helmet. "I've got transport." She calculates that she'll have to leave at seven for a nine-thirty start and will be home around nine the next morning. Depending on how heavy the traffic is. "Ok, you're on. I'll take the shift." Ash gives her the details and she jots them down. North Valley General Hospital.

Jack puts down the phone and goes into the kitchen. She flips her bacon and checks the coffeepot to see if it's ready. She prepares her food for the night, opening and closing the cupboards in the kitchen a few times. Rachel's hangover does not feature too highly on her list of priorities.

When Rachel gets up, Jack announces that she's working tonight so needs to have a sleep in the afternoon.

"Tonight?" says Rachel. "What about the gig?"

"I'm sure you can manage without me," says Jack. "Look love, Ash was desperate to fill this shift – she can't get anyone else to agree to it because it's so far away. I need to keep her sweet, you know? I need the job." Jack is no longer surprised at how quickly she can lie. It now comes as second nature.

Rachel flops dramatically onto the sofa, pulling her silk dressing gown tightly around her thin frame and reaches for the remote control. "Whatever," she says, pouting. "Maybe I'll get Fred to do your act."

Jack snorts. "Yeah, right."

***

"Hi, I'm Jackie Harris. I'm from the agency; are you expecting me?" Jack stands shivering next to the nurses' station; the ride over was a long one. She has locked her helmet onto the bike and stashed the waterproofs into the panniers, but she still draws a stare from the tired-looking staff nurse at the desk. It is probably her bloodshot eyes, caused by the wind in her face, or maybe the boots. "Is there anywhere I can change?" It's early yet and she feels like she's earned the right for a pre-shift cup of tea.

"Qualified?" asks the nurse, whose name-badge reveals her to be Geraldine.

"No, I'm an auxiliary." Jack's heart sinks. This might mean no cup of tea. "Sorry, health care assistant. I keep forgetting the job title has changed."

"Locker room and toilet's over there," Geraldine points with a pen. "But don't expect to find a spare locker. Sister's in early. You'll have to check with her; she'll have your name written in the book." She looks down again, back at her notes and Jack takes this as a dismissal.

She goes to the locker room, which is really a toilet with a set of grey lockers and coat rack just outside the cubicle. The heavy fug of cigarette smoke hangs in the air. Jack swings the rucksack from her back, tugs off her boots and gets her work shoes out. She finds a locker with a broken door and puts her boots and bag inside. There is nothing valuable in it, anyway, only food and her latest Fay McMullin's.

Jack has a pee and clips on her ID badge. She inspects the red patches on her hands. They have started to appear in the last week or so and Jack hair-tailed it to the GP, thinking that she'd caught scabies from one of her clients. The doctor had reassured her, suggesting it might be eczema, and asked Jack whether she might be allergic to anything. Jack is perturbed to find that it is a common condition among people who constantly wash their hands. She draws a tube of recently bought E45 cream from her pocket and squirts some into her palm.

"Erm, where *is* Sister?" says Jack. Geraldine doesn't look up from her paperwork but lifts the pen and jabs it over her shoulder impatiently. Jack looks in the direction the pen is pointing and sees a door marked 'Sister's Office'. "Ah, thanks," she says, and Geraldine shakes her head.

The door is ajar so Jack pushes it slightly. She sees the back of a tall black woman in a navy uniform, who is leaning over a filing cabinet trying to dig out a large set of notes. Jack notices the woman's shapely legs and behind, but straightens her face as Sister turns towards the desk.

"Hi, I'm Jackie. I'm from the agency," Jack begins. "I know I'm early, but…"

"Ah, hello. Yes, Jackie…" Sister doesn't look up but drops the heavy notes on the desk and then runs her finger along a line in an open diary. "Jackie Harris," she says and then looks up at Jack.

"Yes. Jackie Harris."

"Jack…" says Sister and takes a step closer. "Jack Harris from Bilgeworth in Warwickshire? You don't remember me, do you?" Sister stands there with her head to one side and a smile creeping across her lips.

Confused, Jack looks at her name badge and then her eyes go wide with shock. "Claire! Claire O'Malley!! I thought I'd never see you again."

"My God, girl. You've grown."

Jack shrugs. "Yeah, well sideways a bit. And look at you, *Sister*. You've done well for yourself."

"Are you living round here?"

"No, I live in Birwood. In the West Mids, you know."

Claire sucks her teeth. "Ooh, that's a hell of a way to travel for an agency shift."

"Don't I know it," says Jack. "I mostly do domestic, around the Birmingham area."

Claire shakes her head. "It's going to the dogs, what with all this NHS Trust rubbish. Talking about patients as if they were customers. I don't know how much longer I'll stick this job."

"You live here?"

"Yeah, just down the road. I trained here and now I work here."

"Wow. You settled down then."

Claire smiles but doesn't venture any more information. "Well, I'm a bit busy at the moment but let's get a cup of tea before the others crowd in the office. Maybe later on we can have a good chinwag. Catch up."

"Lead the way to the kitchen," says Jack, grinning widely.

The ward is a busy medical ward and it isn't until 1am, once Claire has finished the drugs round and Jack has done most of the observations, that the chance of another cup of tea comes along. Jack is guarded when talking to Claire and she senses that Claire is also unwilling to reveal too much of her own private life.

"So you're in Birwood, then?" asks Claire.

"Yeah, that's where I went to uni."

"Oh, you've been to university?" asks one of the staff nurses, looking at Jack and obviously reappraising her.

"Yes," she says through gritted teeth. "Studied Psychology."

"So," says the other staff nurse. "Why are you an auxiliary? Didn't you want to use your degree?"

"You don't think I'm using my degree in this job?" says Jack, and the staff nurse blushes. Jack notices Claire smiling into her mug.

"I only meant, well, *I* haven't got a degree. If you've got a degree then you're more qualified than me."

Jack shrugs. She refrains to point out that she's probably being paid more than the staff nurse too, for this agency shift. After a moment's silence, Claire catches Jack's eye and they both smile conspiratorially. "So, Claire, how's your little sis?" The two staff nurses exchange glances – no-one calls a Sister by her first name.

"She's fine. Very happy. She's married, got a little girl and another one on the way. Lives in South Warwickshire. She visits sometimes."

"That's nice," says Jack. "Must be nice to be an aunty. How about you, did you have the hoards of kids you always wanted?"

"No," says Claire, a faraway look in her eye for a moment. "You got any kids?"

"No, no," Jack says. "I'm married though." It's always a good line with the health care assistants who like to chat while bedbathing or toileting patients, but it doesn't wash with Claire.

Her brow wrinkles. "It's funny, that," she says. "Somehow I never thought you'd marry." Claire's head goes to one side and Jack smiles at the unasked question in her eyes.

"No. Well, you'd be surprised," she says, raising her eyebrow. "How about you? Are you with someone?"

"Yes," says Claire. She hesitates a moment, looking at the two staff nurses. "Listen, I'll give you my phone number and maybe if you're ever down here again we can meet up?"

HARRIS PREVIOUSLY INVESTIGATED
FOR MURDER

NEW REPORTS IN TODAY suggest that Jacqueline Harris, currently on remand for killing Frank Little in North Valley earlier this year, KILLED HER HUSBAND transsexual Rachel X. In September 1997, the West Midlands Police Force investigated the death of Rachel, who it is now believed died of a drugs overdose and not AIDS as was previously reported. Jackie was accused at the time of killing her husband for life assurance money. The investigation was not conclusive and she was never charged.

However, a source very close to Jackie in North Valley has now contacted *Valley Gazette* reporter Viv Diggen to give the true story. Once Rachel was dead, heartless Harris moved from Birwood in the West Midlands to the Valley, where she was living when she killed homeless Frank Little, 37. Our anonymous source has also given a detailed description of Harris's lifestyle in the Valley in recent years.

See inside for more on this story and other breaking news.

Look at that, Jim. I actually made the front fucking page. I don't know who this anonymous bitch is, but I've got my suspicions.

Chapter Twenty-Two

"Hello?"

"Hi, is that Claire?"

"Which one?"

"Which...? Claire O'Malley?"

"I'll get her for you now."

A pause, during which Jack looks at the receiver.

"Hello?"

"Hello, Claire? It's Jack. What on earth was that about? Which one what?"

"Hi Jack. That was my partner. She's called Claire as well."

"Oh my God!"

"Yep."

"Oh my God!"

"Ha ha, yes Jack. I'm a dyke."

"Oh. My. God!"

"Jack, are you going to say something different?"

"You know, it's just so ironic. After all these years it turns out that I'm married and you're a fucking dyke."

"Is that a problem for you?"

"No, no. Not at all. And if you ever meet my wife you'll see just how much of a problem it isn't."

And so begins a beautiful friendship. Jack and Claire, erstwhile childhood sweethearts, meet up in later life and both live with jealous women.

They write to each other, giving potted histories of all that's gone on in the thirteen years or so since they were thrown together in the Bilgeworth foster home. It turns out Claire had gone back to live with her family for a while and then left as soon as she could to train as a nurse. She had met the other Claire at a gay club during her second year as a student and they'd been together since. She doesn't seem to be at all screwed up; in fact she's the most stable, well-adjusted person Jack knows. The only negative point she can see about Claire O'Malley's life is that she wants children and her partner doesn't. But Claire has even adjusted to this, insisting that she's satisfied to be an aunty, albeit from a long distance. She tells Jack that she's planning to get a couple of rescue kittens; these might fulfil the mothering instinct.

Jack is so happy to have a friend outside the suffocating Birwood scene. She knows that when the shit goes down – as it inevitably will – she has an escape route. The Valley is quite a rural area, at least compared to the West Midlands, and lends the tantalising possibility of a new beginning in relative anonymity.

1997 comes around and Jack is busy with gigs all over New Year so can't respond to the invitation to The Claires' party. She is sorry to have missed it because, from what Claire has told her, it's the highlight of the North Valley lesbian scene's year. She does, however, promise that she'll visit one day in January.

***

When Jack plans her first visit to The Claires, she tells Rachel that she's working a late shift. She even packs her uniform and some food so as not to arouse suspicion. Rachel is becoming more and more highly strung and has hissy fits at the slightest thing. She is so thin that Jack worries one day she'll snap in half. And lately she is consuming more medication than food.

It is lunchtime when Jack is ready to go and Rachel has just risen. "Shall I make you some smoked salmon and scrambled eggs?" says Jack.

"No," replies Rachel, reaching for her cigarettes.

"Have one of these nutrition drinks then, Rach. Come on, you need some protein."

"They taste like cack," says Rachel. "They are really revolting. The only people who drink those things are people who don't have a choice and are hooked up to some machine in a hospital."

"Rachel, *you'll* be hooked up to a machine soon enough if you don't get some meat on your bones."

"I will *not* go into hospital!" shrieks Rachel, resurrecting an age-old argument. "I will die when and where I choose. It's my death and I will decide."

Jackie sighs and opens the fridge. Strawberries, smoked salmon, double cream, eggs, butter, steak. What will Rachel eat? It's breaking Jack's bank balance as well as her heart. She goes back into their small lounge to find Rachel wrapped in her dressing gown and concentrating on an American talk-show. *I seduced my wife's best-friend's daughter.*

"Look, hon, try something new, will you?" Rachel takes a long drag of her cigarette and blows the smoke out, studiously ignoring Jack. "If you don't fancy eating, how about a milkshake? I'll make you a strawberry milkshake, what do you say?" Rachel shrugs and continues to watch the drama unfold on the screen.

Jack goes back into the kitchen and digs out the blender. She puts in half a banana, two strawberries and half a pot of cream. She checks to see that Rachel isn't looking and then adds a half-carton of nutrition drink, strawberry flavour. Fingers crossed she won't notice. Jack whizzes it all up and then pulls out a cocktail glass. The frothy pink stuff looks just fine, with a *piece de résistance* tinselled straw. She is certain that Rachel will drink something that has a pretence of alcohol.

"How about this then?" says Jack, returning to the lounge and holding up the glass triumphantly. Rachel is mesmerised by a black couple on the TV screen who are fighting. Eventually they are pulled apart by security guards while the audience cheers and boos. Jack stands there holding the drink and also watching.

"Hmm, what?" Rachel says, noticing Jack there.

"Drink," says Jack, offering the cocktail glass.

"Oh thanks, sweetie," says Rachel, as if Jack had made a vodka and cranberry juice. She stubs out her cigarette and takes the glass. Still watching the TV, Rachel has a long pull from the straw, then sighs loudly and puts it on the table next to the ashtray.

Jack is pleased that Rachel has actually consumed something, but at the same time slightly perturbed at how easy it was. She shrugs and gets her coat.

"Right, I'm off to work then, love. Back late tonight, ok?"

"Ok," says Rachel and Jack pecks her on the cheek before leaving.

The ride down from Birwood to North Valley begins as a pleasant one. It's a crisp, sunny day, rare for January. But it soon turns bitter and the approach to the M5 brings a torrent of icy rain. By the time Jack has taken the Valley exit, this rain has turned to hail and is rattling on her helmet and petrol tank.

"Oh, fucking hell!" is Claire's reaction when Jack appears on the doorstep, still wearing her helmet. "You idiot! Why didn't you come on the *train*?" Jack shrugs stiffly and allows herself to be pulled inside the house. "Let's get you out of those wet things and warmed up or you'll catch your death."

Jack tugs off her leather gauntlets and fumbles ineffectually with her helmet strap. Her fingers have petrified and are as much use as a bunch of bananas. Claire laughs at her attempts and undoes the straps for her. She lifts the helmet off and Jack shakes her head, blinking in the light. Claire progresses to the zip of Jack's waterproof all-in-one and helps her step out of this, then laughs again to see that Jack is wearing leather trousers and jacket underneath. "You're like a babushka – how far does it go down?"

Jack steps back and unzips the jacket herself. "I'm wearing thermals," she says. "But I'm sure you wouldn't want to see them."

"Your teeth are chattering!" Claire exclaims. "Look, why don't you have a bath and I'll bring you a hot cup of tea. Have you got anything to change into?"

"Well," says Jack uncertainly, "I brought my uniform. Told Rachel I was working," she adds to Claire's look of confusion.

"Is it that bad?" Claire asks, concerned.

"It can be." Jack shrugs. "Where's your bathroom?"

"Top of the stairs and straight in front of you. I'll come up too and get you a towel. Do you want to borrow a sweatshirt to wear with your uniform trousers?"

"Oh, I don't know," says Jack, beginning to thaw out at last as she's walking up the stairs. "I thought you quite liked me in uniform."

"Cheeky," says Claire, laughing.

In the bath, Jack lies back and lets her legs soak. Claire knocks on the door and Jack sits up abruptly, clutching her chest, thinking that she might come in. Water slops over the side of the bath and saturates The Claires' dolphin mat. "Tea's just outside, ok?" Claire calls and Jack calls a relieved "thanks" back.

Once she is dried and dressed, Jack wanders downstairs and on her way she looks at the pictures in the stairwell. A mixture of posters of cats and photos of The Two Claires. Jack stops to look at her friend's partner, who she thinks reminds her of a white mouse. "You've got a lovely home," she comments.

"Thanks," says Claire. "It's really all Claire's doing, you know. She's the one with the sense of style. She's a hairdresser, you know."

"Oh," says Jack, totally unable to picture this. "I can't get used to this Two Claires thing. It's like you're schizophrenic or something when you talk about Claire. What's her surname?"

"Tilley," says Claire.

"Well then, that's what I'll call her."

"Oh, she'll love you!" Claire laughs.

They chat about life, work and pets. Jack meets the two new kittens, Sheba and Dart. She catches a brief glimpse of Dart on her way to the toilet, but Sheba is not shy. "She's beautiful," says Jack.

"Thanks," says Claire, as if the compliment were directed to herself.

"Are you going to have them sprayed?"

"*Spayed* you mean!" Claire laughs. "Yes of course."

"How do you know they don't want children?" Claire looks at her sideways and doesn't answer. "I can't have a cat," says Jack. "Or any pet really."

"Oh, why's that?" Claire asks. "Terms of your tenancy?"

"No, no. Rachel is... allergic." She is reluctant to reveal Rachel's low immunity, knowing that Claire is astute enough to guess at her HIV status. Jack doesn't want the pity.

Claire talks a lot about the hospital. Jack asks about the likelihood of any more shifts going on Claire's ward and whether she could request her by name at the agency.

"Perhaps," says Claire, smiling. "Although it would be good if you could invest in a car. Not that I don't *adore* your purple bike."

"I'm not sure I can afford a car," says Jack. "The thing with a bike is that you can keep it ticking over but a car – it's all a mystery to me. Like women." She laughs.

"So what else are you doing at the moment, then? The care work is hardly intellectually stimulating, is it?"

"Well, no. But I'm writing a lot lately." Jack sips her tea.

"Oh yes. What are you writing?"

"Well, I don't really talk about it," Jack begins.

"A novel? Poetry?"

"A novel. Though I don't show it to anyone…"

"You don't have to show me - just tell me what it's about. Come on, I'm interested. As you can see, I'm a big reader myself." Claire spans her arm around the room to take in several sets of bookshelves, one that seems to be devoted to nursing textbooks and another with a large proportion of the black and white striped spines indicating *The Women's Press*. The other shelves are a combination of fiction and non-fiction. Jack had spotted them on the way in and itched to organise them into subject order.

"Yes. So I see. Well, promise you won't take the piss then."

"I solemnly swear." Claire holds up her hand in a parody of the Girl Guide salute.

Jack takes a deep breath. "It's about this writer, who's writing a book about a hack journalist who…"

"Hang on, hang on," says Claire. "Let me get this right. You're writing a book about a writer who's writing a book about a writer?"

"You said you wouldn't laugh."

"I'm not laughing," says Claire, covering her mouth with her hand. "I'm not laughing, honestly. I think it's brilliant that you're writing. But don't you think that storyline's going to get a bit… confusing?"

Jack shrugs. "It's already confusing. But Rachel thinks I should be writing something literary. I'd love to write a lesbian detective novel, you know, like Fay McMullin. I started one…"

"Oh, not Fay McFormat! Beating away at the same tired old routines."

"Well, she's found something that sells and she's stuck to it. At least she's making a living."

"You *do* know she's sold out, don't you?"

"What do you mean she's sold out?"

"She doesn't have any gay characters any more!"

"She does, in this one I'm reading now the victim is gay."

"Precisely. The only gay characters in her books are victims, criminals or cameo roles."

"Claire, they're *detective* stories. The only *characters* in the book are victims, criminals or cameo roles."

"Haven't you seen her latest book? The detective is a *man*. All right, so she still includes the occasional token dyke. But look, she's switched to a male detective in order to sell the book to a wider market."

"Does that make her a sell-out? I still like to read them anyway."

"We're not allowed to have a positive image in the media. I mean, look, everyone saying how brilliant it is that there's been a lesbian kiss in a soap opera. Fandabby-bloody-dozie and about time too. Then we find out that she's really screwed up and she kills her abusive father and buries him under the patio! How many lesbians do you know who've done that?"

"How do *you* know they haven't?"

"Well I know I haven't for sure. What I mean is that it's all very well saying we should be more visible but we're always going to be seen as deviant. We'll always be portrayed as having problems."

"But some of us do have problems, Claire. Not all of us live in a perfect world. Do we have to go around being all jolly and happy and nice to each other and pretending shit doesn't happen just so hetties can't point the finger at us and call us deviant?"

"But we should portray all aspects of lesbian culture, positive and negative," says Claire, taking a gulp of her tea.

"What, like a lesbian soap opera? Have you seen *Go Fish*?"

"Yes, but that's American. And it'll be out of date soon if it isn't already. I'm talking about British lesbian culture."

"But that would be impossible, to have them all in the same book. There are more types of dykes than there are Barbie dolls. I mean there's butch dyke, femme dyke, city dyke, the only dyke in the village, baby, sporty, scary…"

"Sounds like we should start a pop group," Claire laughs and Jack joins in.

They are sitting in the lounge with a second cup of tea, Sheba firmly ensconced on Jack's lap, when Claire Tilley arrives home. Claire-O leaps up from the sofa to hug her and then introduces her to Jack. "Hello," says Tilley and then looks at Jack's SuperDyke top. "Did you get that at Pride? I've got one just like it upstairs."

"Erm..." says Jack and looks at Claire-O, who laughs.

"That *is* yours, love. Hoped you wouldn't mind. Jack turned up drenched and didn't have anything to wear."

Tilley frowns slightly but says she doesn't mind one bit, so long as she gets it back before Jack leaves.

Claire-O cooks sausages and mash for dinner, with lots of gravy. "You remembered my favourite dinner," she says to Claire smiling. She notices that Tilley is eating a different kind of sausage. "Oh, are you vegetarian?"

"Yes," is the short answer.

When they've eaten, Claire-O clears away the dishes. Jack offers to help but Claire won't hear of it. Once she's gone, Jack tries to fill the awkward silence that has arisen between herself and her friend's partner.

"So, Tilley, I'm told you're a hairdresser?"

Tilley ignores the question and launches into an interrogation of her own. "You and Claire were friends when you were kids?"

"Yes, we were," says Jack. She's unsure of how much Claire-O has told Tilley of her background and doesn't want to mention the foster home.

"*Just* friends?" Tilley insists.

"Yes," says Jack, "just friends."

"So you won't be expecting to resume any romantic involvement, then."

"I..."

"I just want to make it quite clear that she's off-limits, Ok?

She's in a relationship."

"Absolutely," says Jack. "Really, I'm just happy to be friends with her again after not seeing her for so long. I'm married myself, you know, Tilley."

Tilley sneers. "Yeah, I heard about that."

"You don't agree with marriage? If gay marriage was finally made law, you and Claire wouldn't…?"

"I don't agree with mimicking heterosexuals. I don't agree with pretending to be something you're not."

"Ah," says Jack, light dawning. "You're trans-phobic."

Tilley opens her mouth to object but Claire-O re-enters the room so she shuts it again, satisfying herself with a scowl. "Here's the coffee," says Claire-O cheerfully. "Hope you two are getting on ok."

***

Jack waits until spring before she visits The Claires again, or takes on any shifts at the hospital. She's working almost full-time now as they are no longer doing any gigs. Rachel's illness has progressed to the extent that she barely leaves the house. Freddy visits but doesn't stay long. She is back on benefits but has been scouting out the local record shop for a part-time job. She seems to have more money than one would expect for someone on the dole. Jack comes home early one day to find Freddy on her way out with a mobile phone.

"Good grief," says Jack, eyeing the contraption. "I thought only pop stars and drug dealers had mobile phones."

Freddy looks at Rachel, who laughs. "Well they're coming down in price now," she says defensively and shrugs. She leaves quite quickly and Jack turns to Rachel.

"What's going on with her?" she asks.

Rachel sighs. "Who knows, darling. Who knows."

"What on earth are you wearing *that* for?" Jack asks,

suddenly noticing that Rachel is wearing her wedding dress.

"I just tried it on, sweetie. Freds suggested we sell it, you know, make a bit of cash. I'm hardly going to wear it again, am I? Look at it, it's like a sack on me." She pulls at the material with a disgusted expression. "Besides which, it's *sooo* 1995, sweetie, I mean, who would buy it?"

"You can't sell it!" says Jack, outraged.

"Whyever not?" Rachel raises her eyebrows. "Don't tell me, you want to keep it for your second wife?"

"No, I…"

"I absolutely *refuse* to allow you to cut it up and add it to that quilt of yours!"

Jack pleads. "I just want something to remember you by. It's not going to be easy for me, you know, once you're… gone."

"Honey, you make it sound like I'm going on holiday. Once I'm dead, darling, once I'm dead."

"Don't sell the dress," Jack whispers, holding back tears. "Just, don't let Freddy get her hands on it."

"Darling, if I didn't know you any better I'd swear you were a fem. You want to wear it yourself, don't you?" Jack shudders and Rachel laughs, holding up her hand. "All right, if it'll keep you happy. I'll bequeath you my dress in my will. Here, help me get out of it now, this netting is irritating."

Jack carefully folds the dress and takes it upstairs. She goes to the small cupboard at Rachel's side of the bed. Opening the door to cram the dress inside, Jack feels the stab of something sharp on the back of her hand. She pulls her hand out and stares in horror at the hypodermic needle sticking upright from her hand. "Fuck!" she hisses. "Holy shit." It's a few moments before she can jolt herself into action and pull the thing out. A few drops of blood fall onto the hem of the dress and she slams the cupboard door.

Jack makes a bolt for the bathroom and stands with her hand under the tap for so long that Rachel calls up the stairs. "It's ok,"

Jack shouts back, tensely. "I'm fine. Just got a splinter." She doesn't want to ask about the needle, confronting Rachel is never a pleasant experience. Now Jack knows definitively about the drugs. Up until now it has been a case of ask no questions and tell no lies. She has wondered if something like this might happen, one day. The risk of living with someone with HIV. She thinks *I might as well have fucked her after all*. But you never know, clean it up, put on a plaster and hey, you might be lucky.

Over the summer Jack spends all her waking hours working as a carer. When at home, she is tending to Rachel, who now spends her days and nights downstairs, her bed placed in the corner of the lounge. Then she goes to work and cares for someone else's dying relative. She feels guilty for going to work but they need the money and she takes on a few more shifts in The Valley as these pay well. The debts are really pressing and the only hope of reprieve is Rachel's life assurance money. Jack feels guilty for thinking about that

The smell of death pervades the house. It is entrenched in the clothes she wears and the food she eats. It is everywhere. She doesn't want to come home and then she feels guilty for that too. Every day she thinks about running out on Rachel. Leaving her to it. But she can't. She's made a commitment and she's sticking by it. This is possibly the only commitment she will fulfil in her whole life.

Jack promises Claire-O that she will visit but then keeps on cancelling. The only time they see each other is on the occasional shift they work together, which is hardly conducive to conversation. Claire has noticed that Jack looks drained and tells her to take it easy. Claire is very caught up in working towards becoming a nurse lecturer so she doesn't notice her friend letting her down, or doesn't ask why. Jack has not told her that Rachel is dying. But eventually she feels she's going to crack. Something has to give. She phones Claire.

"Hello?"

"Claire, I need to talk."

"Who is it?"

"It's Jack. I…"

"I'll get her for you." *Damn*, thinks Jack. *Damn damn. Will I ever get used to this?*

"Hi Jack, what's up?"

"Claire…" Jack begins and then can't say any more. She had thought she'd be able to keep it together for long enough to at least tell her.

"What is it, Jack? Are you ok? You sound like you're crying."

"No, I'm fine," says Jack, sniffing. "Really. I just have to talk to someone. Rachel's… Rachel's…"

"Rachel's what, Jack? Has she left you? The bitch!"

"No, she's… she's dying, Claire."

"What?"

"I didn't want to tell you. She's HIV-positive and now she's really near the end and I don't have anyone around. I don't have anyone, Claire."

"Oh my God, Jack. I'm sorry."

"It's ok. I just. I don't know how much longer I can do this. All on my own."

"You're not alone, Jack. I wish I could… if I could take some time off… We're under investigation now with this missing diamorphine and I've got my interview next week…"

"No. I know. I don't want to lay a heavy on you, Claire. It's good just to hear your voice. I needed to talk to someone."

"Jack, what are the local services over there? Surely there must be something, a voluntary agency; why don't you contact them?"

"I did, but Rachel has pissed them all off. Won't have them in the house now. She's so melodramatic Claire, honestly."

"Jack…"

"I need to know that I can come to you. When it's over. I need a change of direction. I have to get out of this hell-hole. Do something entirely different."

"You know you're always welcome here, Jack. We've got a spare room and…" Jack hears Tilley's exclamation in the background.

"No, I didn't mean that. I don't want to cause any problems for you. I just meant that I might ask you to find me a flat or something. I've been thinking about going back to college. I need to know there's a future for me because all I've got at the moment is death and decay."

"Oh Jack… I'll do anything I can. You know that. If you want to go to college, the one locally does a good counselling course."

"Counselling?"

"A change of direction, like you said. And you studied Psychology, didn't you? They're crying out for counsellors."

"I'll think about it."

"Well, whenever you need to talk, just phone."

"Thanks."

"And when you need a good party to blow away the cobwebs, you know where to come."

"Ha! Thanks. Really, thanks Claire."

After the phone call, Jack goes back into the lounge. She pauses at the door and Rachel tears her eyes away from the TV screen to look at her. "What?"

"Nothing," says Jack, then, "What are you watching?"

"Darling Diana." Rachel breathes heavily between each sentence. "The Queen of Hearts. Her life is so tragic, sweetie, so tragic."

"They're not still on about that interview, are they?" Jack snorts and walks away into the kitchen.

Rachel coughs and reaches for her drink. "Here, turn it off will you and stick Puccini on."

As Jack gets the *Madame Butterfly* CD, Rachel coughs again. "Light me up a fag, will you?"

"These things'll kill you, you know," says Jack.

Rachel raises an eyebrow. "Not if you kill me first," she says quietly.

Jack looks away. "Don't say that." She lights the menthol and takes a drag herself before passing it over.

"Thought you'd given up," Rachel comments.

"I have," says Jack.

"If you knew you were going to die, what music would you want to die to?"

"What kind of a question is that?"

"I think it would be Queen for you."

"Do you? I'd never really thought but it would most likely be *Bat Out Of Hell*. Plus I would choose to die quickly, on my bike."

Rachel pushes herself up on her elbow and gazes intently at Jack. "You shouldn't be here," she says.

"What?" says Jack, taken aback.

"You should be out getting a life." Rachel points with her cigarette. "Or holed up somewhere writing that fucking autobiography that you keep saying you're going to fucking write."

"Rach…"

"I'm a burden, Jack. And I don't want to be. Neither do I want to spend my dwindling days in some fucking hospice. You've got to help me out of it. Look, if I could do it myself, then I would."

"Rachel, you don't *know* what you're asking."

"Yes I fucking do. And if you weren't such a coward you'd help me."

Jack doesn't answer and Rachel smokes for a few moments in silence. When she speaks again her tone has changed. "Write it, Jack. Write the bloody thing. And make sure I'm in it. I want to be the love of your life, not some tragic dying queen."

Jack laughs, in spite of the tears in her eyes. "What makes

you think that you'll be the star of my autobiography?" Rachel shakes her head and doesn't answer. "Can I get you something to eat?" says Jack.

Rachel holds her hand palm-forward like a traffic policeman, "Talk to the hand, sweetie. Talk to the fucking hand."

Jack snorts. "You've been watching too many fucking American talk shows."

***

Jack arrives home from shopping just as Freddy is leaving. Freds now has a key and pops in and out whenever she feels like it, day or night. Jack nods to her and Freddy nods back, a strange look on her face. Jack bustles in to put the shopping away. More nutrition drinks that she knows Rachel will refuse to drink but Jack refuses to stop buying them. She goes into the lounge. *Madame Butterfly* is playing softly in the background. Rachel is resting so she tries to sneak past but is startled as Rachel's arm shoots out.

"I was waiting for you."

"Oh? I wasn't long."

Rachel breathes heavily. "Lie me down, will you. Take some of these fucking pillows away and let the bed go down."

"You're supposed to be up, you know. Your chest…"

"I just want to lie fucking down for once." Rachel is on the brink of tears. "I just want to lie down normally, like a normal person and go to sleep."

"Ok, ok," says Jack, and lets the bed down. She takes a couple of pillows away and organises the others under Rachel's head. Rachel's wig slips slightly and Jack straightens it. Jack notices a small Tupperware box tucked under Rachel's elbow but doesn't comment. "All right now?" she asks.

"Yes," Rachel breathes. Then she sniffs. "You're working this afternoon?"

"Yes," says Jack.

"Come and say goodbye to me, won't you, before you go. Even if I'm asleep, come and give me a kiss goodbye."

"I always do," says Jack.

"Don't forget."

"I won't."

"Don't forget me, Jack."

"I won't."

Jack goes for a shower and changes into her uniform. She lies on her bed reading the second John Collins mystery. When it is nearly time to go, she creeps downstairs and into the lounge. Rachel is asleep on her side, a deeply peaceful expression on her face. Jack goes to the bed and leans over to kiss her.

I should have known: Madame Butterfly. She's cast me as the callous Captain Pinkerton.

When she straightens up, Jack notices the open Tupperware box and the works inside. She sees the recent injection mark in Rachel's arm and the old tracklines that she has always meticulously ignored. Jack takes the syringe and carefully puts it in her uniform pocket. It will be disposed of in a sharps bin in Birwood Geriatric Unit this afternoon. "Goodbye Rachel," she says. "*A Voi Pero Giurerei Fede Costante* and I hope my accent is good enough for you, darling." It is 30th August 1997. When Jack gets home that night, Rachel is dead.

Jack doesn't take on any more shifts. She stays at home and waits for everyone to come and go. Soon enough, the police arrive.

"Where were you when he, er… she died?" the plodding young officer asks.

"Birwood Geriatric Unit."

"Do you work there?"

"Sometimes. I do agency work. I go everywhere."

"Was anyone else in the house?"

"No."

"Does anyone else have a key to the house?"

"A few people. People come and go here. Rachel has a lot of friends. Had."

"Would you be surprised to know that your husband died of a heroine overdose?"

"My wife. No, I don't think I would be. I knew that she used it."

"Do you use heroine?"

"No, I don't."

"Did you give her the drug?"

"No."

"Do you know who did?"

"No."

"Oh, come on, Mrs…Mrs. Harris. Surely you have some idea."

"I have no idea at all."

"We have reason to believe that you have worked at North Valley General Hospital."

"Well, you would be believing correctly."

"Are you aware that there is currently an investigation going on about some missing diamorphine?"

"Yes, I am."

"Did you know that diamorphine is in fact heroine?"

"Yes, I did. What are you getting at?"

"Did you steal the diamorphine and give it to your… to Rachel?"

"No, I did not."

"Did Rachel ever… ask you to help her die?"

"Yes, she did. Several times."

"And you agreed to do this?"

"No I didn't. I don't believe in euthanasia."

"Murder is murder, Mrs. Harris. Euthanasia is a pretty word for an ugly act." The other officer pats him on the arm and he coughs and continues. "Are you aware that Rachel had a life assurance policy?"

"Yes, I am."

"Are you aware that you are the sole beneficiary of this policy?"

"Yes, I am."

"And so you have a motive for killing her."

"For killing someone who's going to die anyway? I suppose in your eyes, yes I do."

"We know that you're in debt, Mrs. Harris."

"Do you? Oh, well done for that insightful piece of investigation, officer. Now if you'll excuse me I've got a funeral to arrange."

"We won't take up any more of your time. Just to warn you, though. Don't be spending too much on that funeral. You do know that if someone commits suicide then their life assurance is invalid, don't you?"

***

Jack must leave the house, although she doesn't want to. She knows that when she returns, things will feel different. There is already an empty space in the lounge, the other furniture still pushed back to make way for the bed that is no longer there. She will have to throw away the nutrition drinks from the fridge. The friends no longer visit; odd to think that they only came around for Rachel.

There is the funeral; it has mostly been arranged with Rachel before her death. There are a few things to organise that can be done over the phone. Some of the friends have plans to speak. Jack has a letter from Rachel to read out.

It is a beautifully sunny day. So hot. The kind that Rachel used to like to spend outside in a deck chair with a large tumbler of vodka and tonic. "Fucking gorgeous darling," she would say, lighting up the ubiquitous menthol and pushing her sunglasses up her nose, "Fucking gorgeous." Jack doesn't think she can cope with being assailed at every step by things that remind her of Rachel.

She goes into a newsagents' on the way back from the funeral home to buy some milk. The first thing she sees is the row of cigarettes. She turns away and then sees Blue Label vodka. Her eyes are stinging with tears and she's desperately trying not to cry. She looks around the shop to see other people weeping. She can't understand what's going on. Jack gets her milk and then picks up a newspaper. The headline screams FUNERAL at her and she blinks twice, thinking she's seeing things. Has Rachel's death made the front cover?

"What's this?" says Jack at the counter, skimming the by-line. "Who... Diana?"

"Where've *you* been these last few days, love?" asks the tired-looking assistant. "On the moon or something? Haven't you heard? Princess Diana is dead."

Chapter Twenty-Three

JACK

"Well I've had three sessions so far and it doesn't really seem to be getting anywhere. So far she's suggested that I am in love with everyone I know."

"Oh?" Annette turned away slightly from the desk and looked at the coffee pot in the corner.

"So, I don't know how useful it is really. Maybe I should fight these demons on my own."

"You know yourself that we always recommend sticking out the course. It was six sessions, wasn't it?"

"Yes."

"So you're halfway through. It's always worse before it gets better."

"But it's not worse as such. It just seems to not be going anywhere."

"Are you not opening up?"

"Maybe not..."

"Hmm, it won't be any use if you don't open up. It'll be a waste of time. I got you to the top of the waiting list – you'd have had to wait six months for her otherwise; she's good."

"Yes. She's very..."

"Yes?"

"Determined to get to the root."

"Try to go there next time with a more open mind. Try to just talk without thinking about the consequences."

"How do you know what I'm thinking about?"

Annette smiled, "I have been in your situation myself. That's how I know."

"Oh."

"I know more about you than you think, Jack."

My heart lurched, "What?" But Annette didn't answer. Instead she stood up to pour coffee for us.

"Did you find the Christmas break restful?"

"Not really. I had a week off, but there was a lot going on at home. Family visits and stuff. I actually find it more restful to get back into the routine of work. Jim's mum can really *talk*."

"Have you thought any more about taking some time out properly? Just until you've got over the Larissa Thomas incident."

"You think I haven't got over it yet?"

"Have you?"

"I don't know. I thought I already had before but you said that I hadn't."

"What do you usually do to release tension?"

"I write."

"You write?"

"Yes, I write it out of my system. I keep a dream diary for instance. And I'm writing my autobiography."

"Oh," Annette raised her eyebrows. "That's interesting."

"Apparently not. It keeps getting rejected."

"Am I in it?"

I laughed. "It's funny, that's what people usually ask, but I wouldn't have expected you to ask it."

"I wouldn't be insulted if I were in it or if I were not, just curious as to how you see me."

I looked at Annette who seemed to be waiting for an answer. "Um. This is why I don't usually tell people what I'm writing."

"Ah. Well anyway. So how long have you been a writer?"

"Since I could hold a pencil I suppose. I lived in a fantasy world for most of my childhood."

"Mm-hmm. Is this something you should talk to the therapist about?"

"Maybe. I've told her about my dreams."

"When are you seeing her again?"

"Next week, same time."

"Well, I think if you told her about your writing, maybe take some along, then you'd get further. What do you think?"

"Ok." I looked at my watch and made to stand up. "Sorry I have to rush. I really have to go." I stood up and went for the door.

"Jack…"

"Yes?" I turned, my hand on the doorknob.

Annette paused with an unreadable expression on her face. I looked again at my watch and back at Annette, who eventually said, "Nothing," and looked down. I left the office, skipped down two flights of stairs and sprinted to the bus stop two hundred yards away.

JIM

I arrived at the Women's Aid office earlier than usual. I was hoping to get some paperwork done before a client visit at ten. I let myself in through the outer door. It was always locked. Then put the keys back in my pocket. I shook snow off my boots before stumping up the stairs. I blew on my hands; it was freezing cold. Usually the heating would be on. Only Mondays were this cold after the weekend. But it was Tuesday. It was after nine. Someone was usually in by now. That should have been the first clue. I was still surprised. I banged my head on the door as I tried to push my way through to the main office. Muttering swearwords, I fumbled again with my keys. I unlocked the door. Immediately upon entry I dropped my bags and my stick. I reached for the heating switch. There was something wrong with the timer – as with the toilet light, as with one of the printers.

I looked through to the room where my and Dianne's desks were. I saw the light flashing on Dianne's answerphone as usual.

Her phone was the main office phone and took all the out-of-hours office calls. I diverted into the kitchen. I switched the kettle on. Warmed my hands on the back of the fridge. When the kettle started to boil I transferred my hands there. Once I had a cup of tea I would be able to face whatever messages were there.

But where was Dianne? It wasn't like her to be late. I began to worry that she was going to call in sick. What would we do with another member of staff down? We'd had to close the refuge over Christmas. That was a difficult decision to make but a relief in the end. We'd only had one resident, Holly. She'd decided to leave for the week. To stay with her mother. Now it was open again. And filling up. When it was all new women it tended to be very busy. Everyone needed workers' time. I sighed and sat down at Dianne's desk. My finger hovered over the flashing 'play' button.

But what if they were personal messages? Should I wait for Dianne to come before I listened? Should I ring Dianne? I stood up and squinted at the noticeboard on the opposite wall. I lifted up sheaves of papers. I eventually found the list of workers' home numbers. I dialled the number written up on the list. It rang for a minute as I stared out of the window at the snow. I put the receiver down again when there was no answer. There was no other way. I'd have to listen to the messages.

The tinny voice of the computerised telephone sounded loud in the quiet office.

'*Message* ONE. *Message received* today at SEVEN thirty am. Hello, it's Dianne," my heart sank. Dianne's voice was that of someone with a severely blocked nose. "Something… something's happened and I won't be able to come in today. I'm sorry. Could people rearrange my clients for me? I'm not sure how long I'll be off but I'll try to keep you informed. Bye. *BEEP. Message TWO. Message received* today at EIGHT o-three am…"

"What, what?" I quickly pressed buttons on the machine. Tried to skip back. To listen to Dianne's message again.

"Message deleted. *Message THREE. Message received…*"

"No! No, I didn't want to delete it, you stupid machine." I pressed the skip button a few times.

"*End of messages.* You have *NO new messages. BEEP.*"

"Nooooo!!" I thumped the desk in frustration. Tried to count to ten. Got as far as five. Then pressed the 'play' button again. I wished I was more technical. Where was Jackie when I needed her?

"You have *NO new messages,*" the answer phone repeated. "*BEEP.*"

I put my head on the desk. Something had happened to Dianne. Now I wouldn't be able to find out what. It wasn't the kind of thing you'd say if you were ill. *Something's happened.* It must have been an accident or… I hardly liked to think of the thing it could be. I tried to ring her again. Again there was no answer.

I thumped the desk in frustration. Then rubbed my sore hand. What was I going to do? My mind raced. I'd have to cancel Dianne's client appointments first. I dragged the new, pristine desk diary from her drawer. Turned to the second week of January.

"Tuesday, Tuesday," I muttered. I turned the pages. "Ah. Hmm, nothing in the morning. Good. Afternoon…" My finger ran down the side column of the day while I looked. Dianne only had one appointment that day. With a woman in the refuge; that would be easy to rearrange. Just a matter of phoning down there at lunchtime. I looked at the clock. I'd have to rearrange my own appointment as well. If I was going to be on office cover this morning.

Whoever was on call might phone any minute. To say they'd transferred the phone over. So someone needed to… of course! Dianne was on call last night! I picked up the office phone. I dialled the emergency number. It was engaged. I thought for a moment. Then went over to the phone on my own desk. Dialled again. The rings sounded through the receiver before they began on Dianne's phone. I put the receiver down. Dianne's phone stopped ringing. I banged my own desk this time. Why was there never any communication in this place? Why did I never know what was going on? Obviously the phone had already been transferred over to the office at some point this morning. Now I would have to deal with emergencies. As well as the usual office calls.

I suddenly felt cold. I'd just deleted four messages. Three of which I hadn't even heard. What if they were emergencies? What if they were women in desperate need? I groaned. I put my head in my hands. I felt like crying. This was just too much responsibility. I wanted to go home and crawl under Jack's security blanket. Forget about everything. The door banged downstairs. I straightened up. I waited as I heard the footsteps on the stairs. It was either Chloe or Jo. By the heavy breathing I could hear, I deduced the latter.

I had three seconds in which to decide: come clean or pretend I didn't know anything. It was no contest really. I've always been a crap liar. I moved around the side of the desk to face Jo. The woman heaved herself, her overfilled briefcase and several carrier bags inside. Jo took one look at my face. "What?" she said.

I pointed at the answer phone. Jo looked. "I can't – do you know how to retrieve deleted messages?"

"Why? What's happened?" Jo put down her bags. She moved over to Dianne's desk. She sank gratefully into Dianne's chair. Tugged at the scarf around her neck. Jo gave the 'play' button a finger punch. We heard the same bland, uncaring response as previously. Jo looked up grimly. I nearly burst into tears. Then Jo smiled. "Go and put the kettle on, be a love," she said gently. "It'll be ok. This has happened before. Two sugars, remember!" she called after me.

I came back with Jo's tea and a fresh one for myself. The

woman was poring over a dog-eared instruction booklet. Concentrating hard, Jo looked first at the phone, then the book, then at the phone again. She pressed the hash key twice. She keyed in a code and received a beep. "As long as there haven't been any other messages since you deleted it...?" she looked up at me. I shook my head dumbly. Jo pressed two more buttons and, "There." She sat back. She pressed the 'play' button confidently.

"You have *FOUR* saved messages. *Message ONE. Message received* today at SEVEN thirty am. Hello, it's Dianne..."

"Oh, thank God for that!" I shrieked. I flung my arms out. I was ready to launch myself at my co-worker. Give her a massive hug. I managed to stop myself in time. I saw by the look on Jo's face that it wouldn't be appropriate.

We listened through the next three messages in silence. I was relieved to find that none were emergencies. There was one from Chloe to say she was going straight to the house; one from the police asking after a woman who had already left for another refuge; and one from Jo herself. "Just diverting the emergency number back to the office."

I frowned at Jo. "You were on call? Last night?"

"Yeah," said Jo. She hauled herself out of the chair. Fished around in her briefcase. "Ah, it's in my coat," she said. She stood up. Removed the office mobile phone from her coat pocket. "Dianne phoned me at six last night and asked if I'd do it – said she'd swap with me for Saturday. Luckily it was a quiet night – I've been on three times already this week and it's only Tuesday."

"What did Dianne say?"

"Still, some Women's Aid groups take turns in being on for a whole week at a time. Then you have one week on and five off or whatever."

I gritted my teeth. "Did Dianne say what her problem was?"

Jo shrugged her coat off. She made a non-committal facial gesture. She turned her back on me. Hung the coat and scarf on the dilapidated coat stand that only Jo used. I was ready to thump the desk again when Jo spoke, "Oh yeah, she said something about her kids being late home from school or something. Didn't sound very important to me, but..." Jo broke off in surprise. I pushed past her. Grabbed my stick. Ran out of the office.

JACK
YOUR INSTANT MESSAGING SERVICE REPORT
To: Pie
From: Jack
Subject: what do you know?
Well, what do you know?

To: CrackerJack
From: AmericanPie
Subject: re: what do you know?

Sharks' teeth point inwards. They are designed to hold onto their prey and give maximum injury. They are also aligned in rows and keep replenishing. What do you know?

To: Pie
From: Jack
Subject: shark bait
Women are three times more likely to be diagnosed with a mental illness than men. New research demonstrates that in mental health a single woman is statistically more healthy than a married woman and the inverse is true for men. This proves what we have known for a long time: the institute of marriage is good for men and bad for women.

To: CrackerJack
From: AmericanPie
Subject: love and marriage...
...go together like a horse and carriage. Marriage is an institution;

is it a mental institution? Have you been married? I have not.

To: Pie
From: Jack
Subject: marriage
Yes.

To: CrackerJack
From: AmericanPie
Subject: re: marriage
Woah, long answer. LOL. Nothing interesting to say about that?

To: Pie
From: Jack
Subject: re: marriage
Possibly plenty of interesting things to say, depends what you want to know. My husband was my wife. We were on stage together. In fact, it's funny that you call me Cracker because that was my stage name. The wedding was more of a statement of our queerness than a statement of love. It made the papers.

To: CrackerJack
From: AmericanPie
Subject: celebrity status
So you *are* a celeb! Tell me more, I'm intrigued. Either of you a TS?

To: Pie
From: Jack
Subject: TS
Yes. Rachel (my husband/wife) was TS (M2F). I am and have always been a woman and a lesbian. I've never been bisexual, but this did fuck up my identity for a while. I have always been attracted to sexually ambiguous people. How

about you?

To: CrackerJack
From: AmericanPie
Subject: sexually ambiguous
Of course. Sexually ambiguous people make the world go around. We are products of evolution; forget the X-men, we are the Sex-Men. Gay sex is nature's contraceptive and if we are ever going to have an answer to the global population problem then it should be made compulsory. Put it on your national curriculum!

To: Pie
From: Jack
Subject: Sex-Men
Cool. 8-) I can just see the lessons now. As for depopulating the world with gay sex, isn't that what HIV is doing?

To: CrackerJack
From: AmericanPie
Subject: gay sex
How non-PC of you! It is not gay sex that is spreading HIV but unprotected sex of any persuasion. Surely you British have grasped that concept???

To: Pie
From: Jack
Subject: politically cunterect
Now you know I don't do PC. And yes, I do understand that it's unprotected sex, but anal is a high risk activity is it not? Correct me if I'm wrong. AIDS is really quite controllable now, if you live in a rich country and have access to the drugs. It was too late for Rachel. It's a shame because she would have loved you! I wondered when I first 'met' you if you were her, come back to haunt me.

To: CrackerJack
From: AmericanPie
Subject: high risk
It is indeed a high risk activity, with or without a condom. Is this a sensitive area for you (excuse the pun)? My mind is now on overdrive as I'm thinking about the kind of things a lesbian and a M2FTS would get up to.

To: Pie
From: Jack
Subject: sensitive areas
Well as areas go, it's about the most sensitive I've got. And if your mind is boggling then that is your own damn fault! Go give your brain a wash.

To: CrackerJack
From: AmericanPie
Subject: brainwash
Already tried that. It didn't work, just dirtied the rag.

To: Pie
From: Jack
Subject: eeewwwww
I don't want to even begin to think about that.
INSTANT MESSAGING SERVICE REPORT ENDS

JIM
"Dianne! Dianne, it's Jim!" I called through the letterbox. I banged on the door. There was no answer. I stood on the doorstep for a while. Looked around helplessly. I thought I saw a curtain twitch in the next-door window. Decided I'd better leave. Didn't want to make a scene. Make things difficult for Dianne. Maybe I was overreacting.

Then the door to the adjoining house opened. A voice called,

"She's not there, love."

"Well. I realised that," I muttered. But looked politely over at the old woman standing in her own doorway. "Do you know where she is?" I called.

The woman shook her head slowly. "Went out early this morning. I couldn't tell you where."

"Well. Thanks anyway," I turned to go. The woman's next words froze me to the spot.

"Probably still out looking for them."

I turned around slowly. Walked towards the woman. She inched her slippered feet out onto the cold doorstep. Stood beaming at me, waiting for me to get close.

"Out. Looking for them?" I asked quietly.

"Yes. She was out half the night looking for the girls. Had the little one here meself. Took him to nursery this morning, poor mite. He knowed somethink was wrong, I could tell. He was all subdued, like."

"What. Happened. To. The girls?"

The woman shrugged. She put her head to one side. Looked me up and down. "Who knows? Just dint come home from school, did they? Here, are you one of them social workers Di works with?"

"Social...? No." I thought for a moment while the old woman looked at me. Then an idea clicked into place. "Do you know what school the girls go to?"

The woman pointed vaguely. "Yeah, North Valley Primary, just up the road, turn left and you'll see the school crossing sign. Lollypop lady, I am," she added proudly.

"Right. Good. Thanks," I waved my hand at the woman. I ran back to the car. I dug in my pocket for the keys.

"Quicker to walk!" the woman called. I turned around and held up my stick. "Still," she said, "there's nowhere to park by the school."

I looked back at her. "Right."

I walked up the street as fast as I could. I turned to look again at the house before walking left. The woman was still watching. She had taken a few steps onto the path. She gestured to me to turn left. Then gave the thumbs up sign. I waved again and turned. In the distance I saw railings. Zig-zag yellow lines on the road. I presumed this indicated the school's position. I walked towards them. I thought about the old lady as a lollypop lady. Dianne had said that this village is twenty years or so behind the times. That's why she loved it here.

I arrived at the locked school gate and hesitated. I leaned against the fence-post and rested my hip. I wasn't sure what I planned to do. Obviously I couldn't stroll in there unannounced. Ask after another woman's children. When I had done something similar for clients, I had always telephoned the school first. This was hardly the same situation. I realised I was dithering I had no real idea of how I could help. I just wanted to see Dianne. I squinted into the deserted yard. Imagined the crowd of children out playing. How vulnerable they are, I thought. Yet is it fair to keep them caged up for their own protection? A hand on my arm made me jump and gasp. I turned around to see Dianne standing next to me. A puzzled look in her bloodshot eyes.

"What are you doing here?" Dianne asked. Her voice was shaky.

"I... I thought..."

But Dianne simply dissolved into tears. I put my arms around her.

JACK

A knock on the door made me jump up from the computer. "Coming!" I called, and pulled my towelling dressing gown closer around my shoulders. I fiddled with the chain attached to the front door and dropped it again. The metal was so cold that it hurt my fingers just to touch it.

"Hang on a minute!" I called again, and heard an angry thud

from next door.

"Just the postman, love!" came an impatient voice from outside. I gave up on the chain and yanked the door open. "Couldn't fit it through the letterbox," said the young postman loudly. "Did I get you up?"

"No. I haven't gone to bed yet," I growled, squinting in the stark winter sunlight at the familiar large brown envelope in his hand. "Thank you," I said and snatched the envelope from him while he stood open-mouthed. I turned from the door and let it slam, then immediately regretted it. I sighed and walked through to the back room, tossing the envelope onto the sofa on my way back to the computer. I'd completely lost the thread now of what I'd been writing. At least I heard the neighbour having a go at the postman and not at me. I sat tense, waiting for the argument to be over and then heard the door slam once, twice, three times before I let out my breath.

We really had to move from here. We had discussed it and Jimmie had put her foot down about it. She said that it would be unfair on the next tenants to move out because the guy next door would know then he'd won. But surely it came to a point when you had to move anyway? Did we really have to live here for the rest of our lives just so that he wouldn't think he'd won? If we stayed here when we wanted to move then he was ruling our lives just as much as if we'd moved out when we wanted to stay. It was like the old argument about rebelling – if you change your behaviour because you are rebelling against your parents or society, then you are being controlled by other people's opinions just as much as if you change your behaviour in order to conform.

But Jimmie didn't see it like this. She refused to follow my convoluted logic. Besides which, we still didn't have the money for a deposit.

I took a deep breath and released it, looking at the envelope on the sofa. I heard a single slam of next door's front door and braced myself for the knock on my own door. It didn't come. He had gone out. Now I could begin to relax. I picked up the envelope and looked at my own name written in my own writing, and sighed again. I would have to read it, of course, see what excuse they had this time for rejecting my work. But it was disheartening. Coping with rejection is not what you might call a strong point for me. I tossed the envelope back onto the sofa and stood up to go and put the kettle on.

JIM

"I was late. For the first time ever!" Dianne sobbed into a tissue. I offered the box that was on the stacking tables next to her settee. "It was a month ago their picture was in the paper and nothing bad had happened. Not a thing. I can't believe it."

"What did the school say?" I asked. I felt totally helpless.

"He turned up early and said they had an appointment at the dentist."

"And they let the kids go with him? Usually a school…"

"She said she asked Mandy if he was her father and Mandy said yes."

"But? Didn't you…?"

"It was a supply teacher. I can't blame her. She feels terrible about it."

"But – but surely…?" I blustered.

"Mandy would just about remember him and of course she'd recognise him from photos. She wouldn't think to say, 'but we haven't seen him for eight years', not when he's standing there grinning with a big bag of Christmas presents. She was probably excited to see him."

"Christmas presents? Didn't the teacher think that was a bit odd?"

"Yes, she did, that's why she mentioned it. But the girls wanted to go with him and she didn't see why they shouldn't. That kind of thing doesn't happen around here, she said."

"Well obviously it *does*."

"There's only so much you can do to protect children though, isn't there?"

"Aren't you angry with the school?" I asked, incredulously.

"Yes. But I'm more angry with myself. And with him, the bastard. Why did he do this to me?"

"Have you called the police?"

"Oh yes. And they've got a photo and they're putting a watch on the airports and whatever. But they say there isn't much they can do because he's their father. Unless he was on the child protection bloody register or something. I'll have to go through a solicitor and that could take... weeks!" She broke down again and leaned on my shoulder.

After a while I stirred. Dianne sat up, sniffing. "Sorry." She blew her nose. "Oh look, you're all wet."

"That's ok. Don't worry about that. Have you made an appointment with a solicitor?"

"Not yet."

I reached for the phone. "Well. That's one thing I can do for you. Do you want to use the one we usually use?"

"Yes. I may as well – she's the best for this kind of thing after all, isn't she? Oh, God. I can't believe it's happened to me, after all the times I've discussed this with clients." Dianne's shoulders shook. No tears came this time. *She's cried herself out for now*, I thought as I dialled.

JACK

Dear Jackie,

Thank you for the submission of your novel.

Unfortunately we don't feel that it is suitable for our list. We have a large number of submissions every week and can only take on a few new authors per year. Good luck with finding a publisher.

Yours sincerely,

Scrawl

I gripped the letter in my fist so that the paper creased and then laid it flat on the table and smoothed the edges down. I stuck it on the spike to join the other rejections. Some were standard photocopied letters like this one with the names filled in by hand, and others were handwritten or typed with personal messages – but all were rejections. Some of the letters I knew by heart and phrases came back to me at odd moments of self-doubt. *Main character not convincing; far-fetched plot; not original enough.* I ask myself, how can it be far-fetched and at the same time not original? I'm the main character – am I not a convincing person?

YOUR INSTANT MESSAGING SERVICE REPORT
To: Pie
From: Jack
Subject: another rejection
Feeling crap. Cheer me up.

To: CrackerJack
From: AmericanPie
Subject: who rejected you this time?
Suggestions for cheering up:
watch old cartoons and see how many non-PC references there are
eat lots of luxury ice-cream
forward porno junk mail to most hated people
play mindless shooting game.

To: Pie
From: Jack
Subject: publisher rejecting my book
Some great ideas there, thanks. Think I may go for the ice cream as the others look like a lot of effort. I'm well miffed. You know, if I was an airhead teenage manufactured celebrity, I would have no problem in selling my uninteresting, uneventful autobiography which would be hack-written anyway. They know

they're gonna make a mint from someone who's already famous.

To: CrackerJack
From: AmericanPie
Subject: miffed? sounds like a sexual position
So screw a celebrity or become one. You could do a stunt or join one of those reality shows. Next thing you know you'll be on Oprah and the book will be selling millions. Will you show me a copy?

To: Pie
From: Jack
Subject: not that easy
I'm too old to be a reality TV celebrity or pop wannabe. You can't be older than 20 for that, should be malleable, willing to subvert your personality to become something you're not and easy to manipulate. That just aint me.

To: CrackerJack
From: AmericanPie
Subject: don't be defeatist
The ones who make it are usually smarter than that. It's called 'reinventing yourself' darling. I cannot imagine you would ever be easy to manipulate even at 20. what is the book about?

To: Pie
From: Jack
Subject: reinventing myself
Something I've done all my life. Every time I turn around a corner I'm a different person. It's got to the point where I can't remember which one is the real me any more. Everyone has a time in their past they can look back on and realise they were manipulated. I'm no different. I'm trying to sell my autobiography but they're not interested because they think that

the public wouldn't want to read about someone who they don't already want to read about, if you see what I mean.

To: CrackerJack
From: AmericanPie
Subject: create the need first
I see. So what you need to do is to pull a stunt and become a 'name' and then you will generate the interest. Of course, you should only do this once you have finished your autobiog so that you can just add the last chapter while your name is still floating about in the collective subconscious. If you believe a certain Mr A Warhol then you have all of fifteen minutes in which to achieve this feat of elegance.

To: Pie
From: Jack
Subject: where does it end?
There is the crux of the question regarding autobiog – I mean, it's easy to begin at the beginning (for some, I'm not sure about me) but until you get to the end then you don't know it is the end, do you?

To: CrackerJack
From: AmericanPie
Subject: tomorrow and tomorrow and tomorrow
Now there's a philosophical question for me.

To: Pie
From: Jack
Subject: endings
Where will it all end?

To: CrackerJack
From: AmericanPie

Subject: re: endings
Speaking of which, I have to go.
   INSTANT MESSAGING SERVICE REPORT ENDS

JIM

I limped purposefully into Dianne's kitchen. "Right. The first thing we need to do is make you a cup of tea. You look like you haven't slept all night."

"I haven't." Dianne hovered in the hall. Between lounge and dining room. She watched me in the kitchen.

"When will you need to pick Josh up?"

"Oh God!" Dianne quickly looked at her watch. Then sighed with relief. "It's only eleven; I thought it was later. I pick him up at twelve and bring him home for lunch then he goes round to Mrs-Next-Door so I can go back to work. Do you think it's best if he sticks to his routine?" I was aware that Dianne went home at lunchtime. I hadn't realised how pressured this must make her days. She came back into the lounge while the kettle boiled.

"Why doesn't Mrs... she pick him up herself?"

"I don't like to impose. Besides which I miss Joshi and she does pick him up if I absolutely have to be in work all day."

"So. Do you think she'd pick him up today? If you asked her?"

"Yes. Probably. Why?"

"Because I really think you need to get some sleep. Or you won't be fit to be anyone's mother. You heard me agree to the appointment tomorrow morning? That's the earliest she could do. Is that ok?"

"Yes, that's fine. I don't feel like sleep, Jim. I feel too jittery."

"Do you have any idea where they might be? We could go and look. If you want."

"I don't know. I've already looked everywhere obvious. He doesn't have family in this area as far as I know. Heaven knows how he got that paper. I'll have the tea now that you've started making it and then we'll get Josh. Don't you have to go back to work?"

"Well. I haven't got a client this afternoon. I was planning to go to the refuge. I suppose I'd better phone Jo and Chloe. Explain to them." Dianne's face set in a grim expression. "I don't have to tell them about your kids. If you'd rather not? I can make something up."

"No. You tell them. They'll find out soon enough anyway. Haven't you got stuff to do? You shouldn't be hanging around with me – honestly I'm ok."

"No really. I want to." I didn't want to tell Dianne that I'd rather be with her at the moment than alone. I'd rather feel that I was doing something useful. I could block out the memories. My growing feeling of unease. I didn't want to say that I suspected someone was following me around. I didn't want to face the implications of what this might mean.

Instead I focused on Dianne's problem. I told myself that this was different. Their father abducted them. Not some stranger. Different motivations. They wouldn't be at risk. At least, not as much.

JACK
Where will it all end, indeed? When will I find true love? When will I will I be famous? I can't answer. What is life all about in the end? Is it really love and be loved? Kill or be killed? At the end of the day, do we know? When we have shuffled off this mortal coil, will we ever find out?

Chapter Twenty-Four

JACK

"Here's the thing: my lover is a person who is drawn to people who need her. I needed her; she was drawn to me. Do I still need her? I don't know, but she has obviously decided that there are more worthy causes. The refuge. This Dianne. And I'm like, hello? Here I am, remember me? I feel like an abandoned child." I looked miserably into my mug of coffee. Claire had recently got one of those posh machines that make you think you're sitting in Starbucks. "I wanted her to get this Women's Aid job so that we could be together more. Now I'm beginning to regret it."

I looked up and caught Claire pursing her lips as if trying not to say something.

"What?" But I knew what. I'd said it again: the abandoned child thing. I was getting a bit too old to be pulling that one. I distracted myself by looking around the room. "Haven't been here during the day for ages. It looks different somehow."

"Yes. The sun makes all the difference." Claire stood up and went to the window. "How sunny it is today; you wouldn't think it was the dead of winter. Good old British weather."

"Ha. Yeah, good old British."

"I never understood why you don't like the sun, Jack," said Claire. "Are you a vampire or something?"

"It could be all the night shifts. But mainly, I think, it's because it reminds me of Rachel." I left it at that and she didn't expect me to elaborate further. I very rarely mention Rachel these days.

Claire turned again towards me, her back to the window. The sun framed her hair, giving her an angelic halo and making her face seem darker than it was. It hurt my eyes to look directly at her. "What is it that you need?" she said.

"What do you mean?"

"You say that you're a needy person, that you need Jimmie. But do you know what it is that you *actually* need?" Claire paused while I thought about it. She walked away from the window towards the sofa. "Because I don't think that you really do. And until you know what you need then you've no way of getting it. You might even have it already, but you don't know because you don't even know what you want."

I laughed bitterly. "Trust me to be surrounded by shrinks. What happened to tea and sympathy?"

Claire came and sat next to me on the sofa and patted my arm. "There, there. So tell me about Dianne. What does she look like?"

I shrugged. "Nothing really. Nondescript. Kind of dark hair and a bit tall, not what you'd call a beauty."

"You think she's a dyke?"

"No. I don't think so."

"So not a threat in that way, then?"

"No. Not in that way. And I don't think that's what Jim wants. I mean, she's not a very sexual person. She's not demonstrative but very intense. With someone like Dianne she could get intimate without the sex. And of course there's the fact that she wants kids. That's one thing that Dianne can provide and I can't." I put my mug on the small table in front of me and leaned back, sighing and rubbing my eyes. "I don't know. I shouldn't be complaining, at least she isn't working nights now."

"Nights can do strange things to you," said Claire, and I

turned to look at her. "It can take you ages to recover. I should know."

"I'm sorry I keep talking about myself. I should be asking how you are. How was the New Year do?"

"Fine. Surprised you didn't come."

"Couldn't face it really. All that lot, you know."

"I know what you mean. It gets Claire down too."

"Really? I mean, I wouldn't have thought that Tilley... She seems such a..."

"There's a lot you don't know about her. I know you don't like her."

"Oh, I wouldn't say that..."

Claire held her hand up to stop my protestations. "Don't pretend. It's ok. But you should know, she hates all the social crap as much as you do. She deals with it in a different way."

"Well, she comes across to me as if she loves it all."

"Yes, and so did you, remember? You used to adore being the centre of attention, I seem to recall." A smile twitched in the corner of Claire's mouth as if she were recalling a particular incident.

"Oh well..." I began.

"It wouldn't have worked, you know."

"What wouldn't?" The sudden change of subject had caught me off guard.

"You and me. We're too similar."

"You... I – I never..."

"We're better off just being friends." She nodded with finality, although it seemed by her tone that she was saying this to reassure herself more than tell me.

"But I didn't..."

"Anyway I'd better get changed for work." Claire patted my knee and then leaned on it for support as she rose from the sofa.

"Work? Surely you're not giving lectures over the Christmas break?"

"No you daft ape. I'm doing agency. I have to keep my registration going so I do shifts in the holidays. I wouldn't do it if the pay wasn't good. This Agenda For Change rubbish – the NHS is going to the dogs, I'm telling you."

I smiled. That's been Claire's line for at least the last eight years but I know she'll never give it up.

"Remind me when I'm looking for a suitcase to borrow the bags under your eyes."

"Thanks a lot!" Claire looked at her watch. "Now get lost or I'll be late."

I slipped into my coat and lingered by the front door. "Can't I hang around just to see you in uniform?"

"Piss off!" Claire laughed despite her harsh words and pushed me out onto the cold path. "And get some sleep," she shouted after my retreating back. "You look like death."

"Great," I muttered, as I stuffed my hands into my pockets and my chin into the top of my coat.

JIM

I had finally managed to persuade Dianne to have a nap. After we'd picked Josh up from the nursery. He'd protested at being left with the lollypop lady next door. I produced an emergency packet of chocolate stars from my workbag. Now I was driving back to the office. I hoped that no-one had noticed my absence. One of the benefits of being an outreach worker: you can do your own errands on the way to calls. If you aren't in the office for any reason. Then the others just assume you're out with someone. The downside is the isolated feeling the outreach worker has.

The roads were icy. The sun sparkled. It gave every metal object a glittery edge. I squinted and pulled down the sunshade. I wished I'd brought my sunglasses with me. I twisted knobs on the dashboard. Tried to coax the heater into life. I wiped my gloved hand on the misted windscreen. It was impossible to clear the vapour, but I endured. Not far to the supermarket car park. Then a short walk through town to the office.

The car turned off the main road. The sun suddenly screamed into my face. I felt rather than saw a shape streak across the road. In front of the car. I slammed my feet down on the brake and clutch. I gripped the steering wheel. Braced myself for the inevitable skid. Thankfully it didn't come. I put the car into neutral and sat forward, breathing more mist onto the window. I wiped it again. I looked around for whatever it was that had made me stop. Nothing. Breathing heavily, I put the car back into gear. I slowly pulled off. I nervously checked my surroundings. Soon I was in the car park. Locking up the car. I felt the hairs on the back of my neck prickle again. I looked over my shoulder. It was stupid, I told myself. Stupid. All this talk of kidnappings and stalkers had got me unnecessarily nervous. I gripped my stick and walked determinedly on.

I got back to the office. The others had just returned from an extended pub lunch break. "Sorry," said Jo unapologetically. "We would have phoned you but thought you were with a client."

"No worries," I said. I hate going out for lunch in those places where you get huge portions and suspicious looks if you don't eat. "How's the refuge?"

"Quiet," said Chloe. "Amazingly."

"Good. Because Dianne's probably going to be off for a while."

"Oh no," Jo groaned. She flopped dramatically into her reinforced chair.

"Don't worry. I can fill in. I've only got Donna since Sarah moved. I haven't taken any new clients on yet. Probably need to get to know the women in there now. They'll be mine soon enough."

"Yeah, good plan," said Chloe. "Always good to be flexible in this place."

I looked at the phone on my desk, frowning. Something… something I should have remembered… "Oh shit!"

"What?" Jo half-rose from her seat to look at my desk as if a slimy thing had suddenly crawled out of a drawer.

"Nothing. I just have to ring Donna." I didn't want to say, *I was meant to see Donna this morning.* They might ask me where I'd been.

I knew Donna's mobile number by heart. I liked to have the scrap of paper in front of me. Just to be sure. I punched in what felt like twenty digits. Waited for the ring tone. I sat down at my desk, looked over at Chloe and Jo. They were in animated conversation about a heavily corrected rota.

"He-lo?" came Donna's cautious voice over the crackle of static. She must be outside.

"Hi Donna it's Jim. I –"

"Oh Jim! I'm sorry! I know I was meant to be there this morning but…" Donna launched into a string of familiar excuses. I exhaled with relief. I wouldn't have to admit to having forgotten the appointment myself.

"That's ok. That's ok," I soothed. "Look. It's got really busy in the refuge this week. So can we make it sometime next week? Wednesday ok for you?"

"Yeah. Yeah, Wednesday's fine." Donna breathed a ragged sigh. It was audible even over the static. She waited.

"You ok?" I said. I was conscious now of Donna's routine.

"No. Oh, you know, just the usual shit."

"Yeah. I know. Kids back in school this week?"

"Yes, thank God. Don't know how I managed, I really don't. Tosh broke his Christmas present on Boxing Day. Stacey didn't have the right trainers so now won't wear them. Sabrina ate too much and was sick." She sighed again dramatically.

"Have you seen Frank again?" I realised that I was cutting into Donna's customary grumble. But I felt a sense of urgency about this point.

"No," Donna replied slowly. "Why?"

"I just wondered. You know. With you saying before Christmas? That you'd seen him and it was worrying you?"

"No. I haven't seen him since that time."

"You know when you said, when you told me how he used to stalk you?"

"Yes."

"How did it feel?"

"What do you mean?"

"I mean. Would you see him? Or did you just know that he was there?"

"Oh. I dunno." She seemed to have been caught off-guard with this question. She paused as if thinking. "Shuttup Sabby a minute, Mummy's talking."

"Sorry. Have I got you at a bad time?"

"No, I'm just getting home now. Hang on a minute." I heard a lot of scuffling over the phone. Sabrina's voice whining. Then the door slam. The background noise recede. "Here, take it in there – and leave that! Oh Christ, no! Sab*rina* no." I winced as I heard a slap and a scream. Then Donna came back to the phone. "Erm. I *did* see him, I think. A couple of times." I began to relax. "But most of the time, no. It was like I just felt him there, felt him watching me. It was weird; I couldn't really describe it." The creeping sensation came back. I opened my mouth to speak. I couldn't think of what to say. "Why do you ask, anyway? This was years ago."

"*Was* it years ago? You haven't felt it since?"

"Well I dunno. Maybe he *has* followed me and I just didn't know it."

"I think you'd know it. Wouldn't you?"

"Yeah. I think I would."

"Ok. Well…" I heard Sabrina nagging again in the background. "I'd better let you get on. I'll see you next week."

"Yeah, ok. See you then."

I rang off. I stared at my desk for a moment. Then became aware of the other two workers in the office. And the on-call rota.

JACK
YOUR INSTANT MESSAGING SERVICE REPORT
To: CrackerJack
From: AmericanPie
Subject: r u online?
Sorry I had to go earlier. Had a client waiting in another chatroom. My carefully considered answer to your question is that it will never end. Life goes on in cycles but there comes a point when we as individuals must decide that 'enough is enough' and let the next generation take over the shackles of repetition disguised as innovation.

To: Pie
From: Jack
Subject: those shackles
How philosophical are you today? I like that phrase, 'repetition disguised as innovation' because that's what it is, I agree. 'There is nothing new under the sun' is how I would normally put it. It's like the seven basic stories idea. So that even if you're writing an autobiog which must surely be unique, in the way that it is written it still adheres to the three-act-play or the quest or whatever.

To: CrackerJack
From: AmericanPie
Subject: seven stories
Aristotle, was it? It amazes me that those seven stories are still doing the rounds. And if you take out the ones where the boy doesn't get the girl at the end then you're only left with one or two to choose from. And yet Hollywood is still happening.

To: Pie
From: Jack
Subject: boy getting girl
I have yet to see a film where the boy doesn't get the girl. And that's even in the lesbian ones I've watched. There's always a boy in there somewhere.

To: CrackerJack
From: AmericanPie
Subject: always a boy
Once a boy always a boy?

To: Pie
From: Jack
Subject: re: always a boy
Too true, blue.
   INSTANT MESSAGING SERVICE REPORT ENDS

JIM
"They say she'll get life."

"What kind of a life, though? They've already attacked her in there."

"I read they want to scar her; it's what they do with paedos."

Different residents; same sentiments, I thought as I walked into the lounge. "Which prison is she in?" I asked. I had given up trying to explain to people that the woman herself wasn't a paedophile. Only the man who'd done the act.

"Newpark, of course." The women turned to look at me. As if I'd just returned from an all-inclusive holiday on Jupiter. "She's on remand but then when she's sent down they might transfer her to Holloway. That's were they all go, the pervs."

"Right."

"Like Myra Hindley, isn't it? And she was a lesbo too."

I had a sick feeling in my stomach. I didn't want to know any more. I didn't want to listen to their opinions. Which one of these women could say that they had not protected their man at some point; had not made excuses for him or allowed him liberties with their bodies or the bodies of their children; had not convinced themselves of his innocence contrary to all of the evidence that pointed to his guilt? And yet here they were sitting in judgement. On the actions of another woman probably similar to themselves in experience. Who was forced to take it that bit further. And who got caught up in it when he got caught. According to them, she was the evil one – not him. How skewed can a person's perspective be?

"It said in the paper…" I walked out before I heard the rest of the sentence. I didn't want to hear another pronouncement of 'ultimate truth'.

JACK

Jimmie arrived home to find the lights off and the house cold. She must have thought that I'd gone out as she bustled through to the back room, dropping her bags and stick on the sofa and going straight to the toilet. Cold weather always makes her want to pee. As she came back into the kitchen, she noticed me in a bundle of blankets under her bags. "Oh Babe!" Jimmie cooed and I stirred.

"Hmm?"

"Sorry to wake you, love. I'm on call again tonight, Jack. Sorry. We're another member of staff down since Dianne's kids…" she broke off then restarted. "God I haven't told you? About her ex-husband or anything? Has it really only been one day?"

"Mmm, what? Dianne's kids what? Are they sick?" I couldn't follow her; it's difficult enough generally with her awkward way of speaking but she was talking so fast.

Jimmie flicked the switch on the kettle and walked into the lounge. She hesitated, as if she was unable to think of where to begin. When she finally came out with it, I realised why: "They've been abducted."

"*What*?" I stood, letting the blankets fall and revealing myself still to be wearing pyjamas.

"By their *father*. They'll be ok. We hope. It's just that Dianne doesn't know where they are. It's quite distressing for her. As you can imagine..."

"But how... why...?" I picked the blankets up and rearranged them around myself as I sat back down on the sofa. "How?"

"He turned up early. To pick them up from school. Simple as that."

I snorted. "And the school handed them over, I suppose."

"Oh. Well," said Jimmie, her own indignation already exhausted. "There's always someone to blame. We often forget to blame the actual perpetrator."

"So what's Dianne doing?"

"Tearing her hair out. She's been everywhere she can think of already. She's seeing a solicitor tomorrow. I told her, *now it's the waiting game*. Same as I tell my clients. The house is a state. Even more so than usual. It's odd that she's –"

I interrupted: "Hang on. Have you been over there today?"

Jimmie spun around, teabag balanced precariously on a spoon and her hand underneath to catch drips. "Oh. Well," she began as she turned back to the bin, "I rushed over. As soon as I heard. Wanted to see if she needed me. She's my friend after all." She brought the mugs into the lounge and sipped from one as she offered the other to me.

"Of course."

"So." Jimmie looked around the lounge and then back at me. "You've been writing today, then. Did you get much done last night?"

"A bit. I got this." I pulled the creased brown envelope out from underneath me and held it up for her to see.

"Oh," Jimmie took it and held it on her lap. "I'm sorry." She leaned over and held my hand. She always manages to grip a sore bit of eczema. "You'll get there someday. Soon."

"Yeah, I know." I pulled my hand out from her grip and took the envelope back. What is it that I'm not giving them? Maybe I should change the title again? *Breaking Out... Breaking Through*? In a flash of inspiration I grabbed a pen from the desk and pulled the title page out of the envelope. I scribbled *Breaking Thru* on the front and crossed out the typed title. Then I got up and went into the front room to put the manuscript on the settee there. I knew it would be safe. Well, safer than under my arse anyway.

"So about Dianne..." I began as I returned to the room.

"Oh. I hope you don't *mind*. I offered to look after Josh? On Saturday? If she still needs me to." She noticed my shocked expression. "I thought I could take him to the park or something. If the weather's ok."

"Uh..."

"Well. You're working anyway. So I didn't think you'd mind?"

"I – well, I don't mind. I just..."

"What?" I took Jimmie's hand back and now it was her turn to pull away. "*What?*"

"Be careful not to get in too deep, love. That's all. People can take advantage..."

Jimmie snorted and stood up to switch on the TV. "I think it's a bit late for that warning."

I opened my mouth to answer but she had turned up the volume. I picked up my book. Jimmie suddenly distracted me by pointing to the TV screen, which showed the familiar photographs of a killer and his accomplice.

"*...for the brutal killing of Fleur Baker. Fleur's body was discovered three weeks ago in fields just outside the tiny village of Stranglehold...*"

Jimmie said, "As if we didn't already know. It bugs me. You know? Whenever they've got anything to say about this story. They always do the whole gruesome lot. And you see the same video footage. The same photos of the parents. The suspected killers. And you…" Jimmie looked around at me to check I was listening, as I wasn't responding as usual.

"Yeah, yeah. I know what you mean," I said, shaking myself into action. "They dig out the photo that shows them in the worst light, with a sneer or mad eyes, or whatever, and show that photo again and again so that it's there in the collective subconscious: the smile of a killer or the eyes of a killer. You know, they might be quite normal looking usually. It reminds me of a story I read by Angela Carter about Lizzie Border."

"Lizzie who?"

"Lizzie… you know, American woman, hundred years or so ago, killed her parents." Jimmie was shaking her head. "They made up a rhyme, er: *Lizzie Border took and axe and gave her father forty whacks*."

"Oh yeah. I vaguely remember that."

"*And when she saw what she had done she gave her mother forty one*."

"She could probably get off for it now. Claim abuse."

"She probably *was* abused. So many people were, back then. Didn't talk about it. The silence of victims perpetuates abuse. But some survivors are silenced."

"So what was the story?"

"Hmm?"

"You said there was a story? By Angela Carter?"

"Yes, I can't remember much about the story apart from the mention of a photo of her with mad eyes. She said that everyone has had at least one with a wild expression – where they look like a murderer – but only those who become murderers will ever have this photo tracked down and exhibited - as if it were evidence of the crime. Something like that." I followed

Jimmie's gaze and looked back at the screen to see the photographs of the man who was to be tried for the murder of Fleur Baker and the woman who was to be tried as his accomplice. "I used to practise mad expressions in photos."

She turned abruptly back to me. "What, because of that story?"

"No. This was years ago. It was the punk thing to do."

"Oh. I forgot you'd been a punk." It's the one thing that I've told her about my past, and even on that I haven't told the whole truth.

"Well, I never forget that you were a hippy." I poked Jimmie in the ribs and she spun round laughing to grab my hands. "But that might be because you still are."

"Gerroff!" shouted Jimmie and we struggled for a moment before the TV caught our attention again. "With all this lead up. You'd think the trial was over now."

"I'm not really following it. The whole thing makes me sick, and what makes me more sick is the way the media make a meal out of it and the public lap it all up."

"I know. It's like Christians and lions. Throw on another one? Just to keep the Romans distracted. While their civilisation is falling down around their ears."

"Politics? God, no, we don't want to hear about that – that's boring! Give us the *real* news. Let's hear more gory details about what that sick pervert did to the poor little girl before he killed her and how did he kill her, and what did he do with the body, did he chop it up, did he eat her flesh, how did he dispose of her and the clothes, and what was she wearing, what colour underwear…?"

"Ok. Ok." Jimmie patted my arm and I became aware that I had been ranting.

"Sorry. Sorry, it's just – see, this is why I don't watch it. I get so angry."

"I know."

"I mean, thousands of children starve to death every day. People are being killed by harsh regimes. Child soldiers are killing other child soldiers. Genocide, mass rape, deliberate infection with HIV... and the news that gets the most coverage is one child killed in Britain. One white child."

"Jack..."

"I know, I'm not saying it isn't a tragedy. I'm not saying the perpetrator shouldn't be brought to justice. But the level of reportage is not based on the number of people affected, but because the public want to know. They think they've got a right to know 'the truth'." I held up my hand dramatically. "The truth is out there."

"There's a lot of truth out there. They're not interested in most of it."

"That's it. That's exactly it." I looked at my empty envelope that had now fallen to the floor. "A lot of truth," I said quietly.

Jim sipped her tea. She glanced again at the news, which had switched to the next story. Tanks rolled across the screen.

"Have you met her?"

"Who, Angela Carter?"

"No. That woman? Whatsername. The one who's being tried. She's in Newpark. Or so I heard from the refuge women today."

I arranged my face into a closed expression. "You know I can't talk about my clients."

"I only asked if you'd met her," she said defensively. "I wasn't asking you to repeat anything she might have said to you."

"Well I haven't. I've got a waiting list already and they tend to only give me the ones who're in for a while, not those on remand."

"Oh."

We sat together for a while drinking our tea in silence. Both of us always have so much to say and neither knows where to begin.

***

It's too late, now, to talk to you. I hid my past and now you've got access to it all, but from other peoples' points of view, not mine. No matter what happens, there'll always be the seed of doubt in your mind about why I didn't tell you. I was going to get around to it. It was more a habit that I'd fallen into, rather than any deep need to be secretive. I had this little fantasy of giving you a copy of my book once it was published, of dedicating it to you for heaven's sake. Like that's going to happen now.

I wrote to you when I was first in here to tell you not to bother with me, to get on with your life. I thought it was only fair. That was before I knew about the press stories. Before I knew that every pathetic arse who's been pissed off by me at some time in the past has sold their 'story' to the paper. You said you wanted to write a book on all of this. Ha – now that's ironic; it really takes the biscuit. If you're still reading this, if you read my manuscript, at least that way you will hear my side of the story.

Who will you believe?

Chapter Twenty-Five

JACK

"Hey, Jack – long time no see."

"Hi Gail, how was Christmas for you?"

"Fine, fine. And you?"

"Fine."

"You look as if you've lost weight. And over Christmas too; what's your secret?"

"Have I?" I looked down at myself. "I hadn't really noticed; it's not like I've been trying or anything. Probably the stress."

"Well, you look good on it anyway."

"Do I? I thought I looked like shit." Gail seemed uncomfortable at this and my mind worked fast, trying to think of something to say to change the subject. I smiled. "How's the new man? Keeping up with your expectations?"

Gail blushed slightly but laughed. "Oh yes. Magnificently."

"Any new members of the writing group?"

"No." Gail squinted at me suspiciously. "Why do you ask?"

"Oh, nothing, only that people keep asking me if I've met that woman, you know the one who's being tried for Fleur whatsername's murder."

"I know the one you mean. People keep asking me too. Seems she's a local celebrity. Well I've not seen her but I've heard they've put her in solitary for her own protection. She'll be on suicide watch too."

"Oh yeah? Christ, I tell you what, I wouldn't want to be an inmate here."

"No. Well thankfully, you and I are not likely to be, are we?"

I smiled again. "Well, must go, see you around."

"Bye."

JIM

"So what time are you picking Josh up tomorrow?"

"In the morning. I told Dianne I'd be there just after breakfast."

"I suppose you'll want the car?" Jack stabbed her fork into her battered fish. Our Friday night fish and chips treat. She hadn't really been eating properly for a while. I worry that I influence her on that.

I raised my eyebrows. "I can drop you off on the way? When's your first client?"

"Ten," Jack admitted. "But it's hardly on the way, is it?"

I shrugged. "I don't mind. So long as you don't mind being in a bit early."

"Hmm. I may as well get a lift with you then." Jack caught the expression on my face and tried to smile. "Sorry, yeah thanks, it'd be great to have a lift, love."

"I wish you wouldn't be so negative all the time."

"What do you mean?"

"Well. Everything I say. You've got a negative answer. You even complained about having fish and chips. For God's sake."

"I didn't fancy it. Is that a crime?" Jack asked hotly.

"You don't fancy anything lately," I countered.

"You're a fine one to talk about that!"

BANG BANG BANG "SHUTUP!!"

I winced. "Keep your voice down, will you? We don't want to set him off again."

"I'm sorry. It's just… I feel like I'm under a lot of pressure lately."

"Well I don't see how. You're working as little part-time as it's possible to work. All you do is lounge around all day on the internet or writing. I mean. What is there to be under pressure about?"

"Oh great. So you want me to get a real job, do you? Is that it? Well, you know you could have just said that."

I sighed an exasperated sigh. "No it's not that. I didn't mean that at all. I said I'd support you while you wrote your book. I just didn't think…"

"What? That it would take so long?"

"No. I didn't think it would feel like this."

"Feel like what? How do you feel, Jim. Come on, I'm interested."

"Well. I'm not likely to tell you. When you ask me like that. Am I?"

"I'm sorry. I didn't mean to start a row. We really need to talk."

"I know we do. We should make some time. To talk properly."

"Tonight?"

"Well. You know I've got a rehearsal…"

"Can't you phone them and tell them you're not coming? Tell them you're on call or something. Jim, this is important."

"I know. And I *am* on call anyway. But I've missed a few rehearsals lately. The Girls'll start to get pissed off with me. Look. Jack," I reached out and held her hand. "Tomorrow night I'll make it special. Jo's on call. I'll make it *really* special." I looked Jack in the eye. "I promise."

Jack smiled coyly. She looked down at her half-eaten fish portion. "I'll hold you to that."

"Well," I said. I rose from the table. My mind was already on the evening ahead. "We'd better clear away. If you're finished?" Jack passed me her plate. "Maybe we should think about getting a cat," I said to myself. Then to Jack, "You don't mind me leaving you with the washing up, do you?"

Jack sighed. "Remember to take that CD with you tonight.

See what they think of my mixing."

"Yes. Of course. Now. Where did I put that mobile?" I looked around for the phone. It was nowhere to be seen. I picked up magazines. I picked up books. I began to panic. "Have you seen it? My Women's Aid phone? Have you seen it?"

Jack stifled a laugh. "Isn't that it dangling from your waist?"

"Oh!" I laughed with relief. I opened the phone pouch. Jack had got me a new one for Christmas. I checked the phone was charged. I maxed up the volume. "I'll get used to it soon enough."

JACK
YOUR INSTANT MESSAGING SERVICE REPORT
To: CrackerJack
From: AmericanPie
Subject: music talent!
Hey girl! Love that mp3 you sent, didn't realise you had such talent! Is that your voice? U sound s x e.

To: Pie
From: Jack
Subject: shucks
Nice to be appreciated. Yes, it's my voice on the rapping. That's The Girlz jamming and i put in a voiceover. U like? I did a whole CD for g/f as xmas present, been working on it for ages. Of course I got her the usual commercial rubbish too, books, choclate, sox, u know. But I like to do something homemade. Thoght I'd show off to you wot I could do. U really like it?

To: CrackerJack
From: AmericanPie
Subject: more?
Love it babe, can hear more? Want me to put some on the web for u?

To: Pie
From: Jack
Subject: music on web
I'd have to ask The Grrlz first. It's their copyright after all. Well,
ours if I include me. They're talking about cutting another CD,
now I've got the technology – hey million dollar woman! We
have the technology. mwaahaha

To: CrackerJack
From: AmericanPie
Subject: million dollar woman
Easy to earn a million when u know how

To: Pie
From: Jack
Subject: what do you know?
Tell.

To: CrackerJack
From: AmericanPie
Subject: re: what do you know?
Ah, now that would be telling

To: Pie
From: Jack
Subject: why do you keep doing that?
nnnnggggg!!!!
INSTANT MESSAGING SERVICE REPORT ENDS

I was already in bed when Jimmie crept up the stairs. "Hey
babe," she called softly from the landing. "Did it all get too
much for you?"

"Mmm, I couldn't write any more and just suddenly felt
really tired."

"Not surprised. After staying up for so long last night."

"Mmm." I didn't tell her that I hadn't actually slept at all. Usually if I had a late night I would sleep in the spare room so as not to disturb her and she must have assumed that's what I'd done.

"Do you mind if I turn the light on? Need to get changed."

"No, go ahead," my voice was muffled as I dived under the duvet before she clicked the light. I squinted out of a tiny gap in the covers to watch her getting undressed. "How was the rehearsal?"

"Oh. Fine," she said pulling off her jumper and t-shirt as one. "They like your CD." Jimmie had her back half-turned but I could see her pert milky breasts as she raised her arms and pulled down the top of her new 'little miss naughty' pyjamas I'd got her for Christmas. *Little miss wishful bloody thinking*, I thought and pushed the duvet cover fully down from my face as Jimmie bent forward to take her jeans over her ankles.

When I get changed I get completely naked and then put the fresh clothes on. Jim is only ever naked in the shower. And even then I think she keeps those damn wristbands on.

"They like it, do they?" I asked, straining my neck to get the full view of her backside. "Did they say anything specific?"

"No. Nothing really. They reckon they might want a couple of tracks on the new CD to be mixed like that. But they're not sure the punters would go for it. If the whole CD was like it." Jimmie jumped into bed and pulled the covers right up to her shoulders. "Christ it's cold tonight."

"Hey, don't take all the duvet!" I complained.

"Cuddle me. We'll be warmer." She turned over and put her arms around me and I responded by laying my head on her arm. We faced each other for a while, Jimmie smiling like an innocent teenager on a sleepover. I felt the familiar knot of desire rising inside me like acid indigestion and swallowed hard, trying to imagine that my saliva was milk of magnesia.

"Are you ok?" asked Jimmie, cupping my chin in her hand. "You look a bit sick. Are you just tired?"

"Yeah, I'm tired." *Tired of this fucking waiting game.* "It's been a long day."

"Better get some sleep then." Jimmie leaned towards me and kissed my forehead chastely and then turned over on her right side and snuggled deeper into the duvet. I reached out and pulled the string above the bed that served as a light switch. I leaned into the contours of my lover's body and slipped my hand over her exposed midriff. The sharp intake of breath made me pause.

"What? My hands aren't cold."

"Tickles," said Jimmie, and held my hand firmly but didn't push it away. I took this as all the invitation I needed and began to kiss the back of her neck.

She gently brushed Jimmie's hair away from her lips with her right hand while her left reached upwards as far as Jimmie's luscious breasts. Jimmie's back arched and she turned her head with a sigh towards Jack, feeling in the dark for her lips. Jack squeezed her nipple between two fingers and Jimmie let out a squeal and tried to turn fully towards her. "No, stay like this, I like it," said Jack and Jimmie leaned forwards again, now allowing Jack's hands to roam downwards with a light touch. Jimmie lay still while Jack stroked her ribs, buttocks and thighs and finally her lower abdomen. Jack's left hand explored the top of Jimmie's pyjamas, skimming back and forth just under the waistband. Her fingers caught the top of Jimmie's pubic hair and she heard her lover gasp again. Jimmie parted her legs slightly and seemed to involuntarily push her hips upward to meet Jack's hand. Jack slipped her right hand under Jimmie's body so that she could caress her breasts while with her left hand she eased Jimmie's legs open wider. With a practiced fingertip, Jack slid...

"Bbbbrrrrriiiiiiinnnnggggg!!!!!"

"What? Holy fucking shit! That fucking phone." I sat bolt upright and tugged on the light switch. The Women's Aid mobile was vibrating itself into a frenzy on the top of the box next to Jimmie's side of the bed.

"Sorry. Sorry. I forgot about the volume. Did it wake you up?" She leapt out of bed and made a grab for her towelling dressing gown before picking up the phone. She shot me an apologetic look and stabbed the green button. Holding it to her ear she was already half out of the room when I heard her speak. "Hello… yes, this is Women's Aid…" She continued to murmur in the spare room while I waited restlessly for her return. After five minutes, I jerked the light string off again and returned to my fantasy.

JACK

We woke with the alarm the following morning. Saturday the sixteenth of January. The date that stays in my mind after a year. The date that will stay in my mind for the rest of my life. The day I became a killer.

"Sorry about last night," said Jimmie over our tea and toast. I had lit the gas fires downstairs while the toast crisped and brought the tray upstairs as we waited for the house to warm up.

"Don't worry," I said. "There's always tonight." I munched on in silence for a while before I spoke again, "What time did you come to bed in the end?"

"Oh," said Jimmie, looking out of the window at the snow, "quite a bit later. I was on the phone for ages. Then I had to go and look for the charger. You were snoring by the time I came back in. You didn't even flinch when I brought the cold into bed with me." She rolled a small piece of doughy toast into a ball between her fingers.

"I must have been out for the count, I can't remember it at all. I remember a nice cuddle before the phone rang though…" I smiled and rubbed my hand along Jimmie's thigh under the duvet. She ducked her head and popped the ball of toast into her mouth.

Soon we were both showered and had towelled down in front of the fire: I hopped around on one leg looking for my other sock, and Jimmie packed a bag with book, phone and emergency rations. The house phone rang and for a moment we stood motionless – me still on one foot – and looked at it. Jim walked over to the phone and hovered her hand over the receiver. She looked at me, I nodded, and then she picked it up.

"Hello?" I watched Jimmie's expression turn from suspicion to relief. "Oh. Claire! Yes. She's here." She held the phone out to me. I hopped towards her and grabbed it.

"Hi, what's up?" I asked, unused to early morning calls from my friend.

"Oh, Jack! Are you ok?" Claire's voice was full of concern.

"Of course I am, why?" I sat at the desk and felt something land on my head. Looking around to see Jimmie laughing, I pulled the lost sock down and lifted my bare foot up to its opposite knee.

"It sounds silly now…"

"Well now you've got me, you may as well say it, whatever it is."

"I had a nightmare."

I stopped trying to pull my sock up one-handed and sat up in the chair. Jimmie looked at me quizzically but I shook my head.

"Jack?"

"What kind of nightmare?"

"One of those kinds, you know."

"What happened, Claire?"

Jimmie shrugged and continued on packing her bag. She was used to me and Claire discussing our dream lives.

"I just wanted to check you were… all right. I just – I'm sorry, it sounds thick."

"No it doesn't. I appreciate you worrying about me. Tell me

about the nightmare."

"You were... something happened – to you and Jimmie. Something bad. Tell me you're ok."

"Yes. Really ok. I mean it."

"Right then. Just... just be careful today, ok?"

"Sure I will. I'm always careful."

"What are you doing today?"

"I'm at work and Jim's having a day in the park."

Jimmie laughed at this and Claire heard her over the line. "Well, you sound ok. I was just worried, that's all."

"No problem. Any time. How are you and Tilley, everything ok your end?"

"Yes, fine. I feel daft now."

"Don't. Thanks for calling. Look, we've got to go – give us a call tonight, yeah?"

"Yeah, ok. Bye then."

"Bye." I put the phone down and looked at it for a moment. "She had a nightmare," I said to Jimmie as I picked up my E45 cream. My hands were getting really sore.

"So I gathered."

"Well, you know how Claire's nightmares are often portents of doom."

"Whooo. I'm really scared. Not," said Jimmie. "Are we leaving or what?"

"Yes, yes. Keep your fanny on."

"I thoroughly intend to."

JACK

The clang of the gates, the familiar smell. There I was walking into Newpark as a counsellor for the last time and, as I leave the prison again at the end of the morning, I am blissfully unaware that the next time I see the gates it will not be as a free person.

***

"Hello?" I called, closing the door behind me and shaking snow off my boots. "Anyone in? Jim?" I had been surprised to see the car at the bottom of the hill as I'd thought Jimmie had Joshua for most of the day. But then my questions were answered when I heard the thudding of feet and a childish giggle from the other side of the door.

"Come here, you little terror!" shouted Jimmie in mock-anger as Josh shrieked and fled towards me. He bumped into my knees before he had noticed I was there and looked up at me with a startled expression.

"Hello, Josh," I said, in what I hoped was a kindly, welcoming voice. He didn't answer but ran back towards Jimmie and hid behind her, wrapping his arms around her legs so she almost fell forward. "Am I that scary?" I asked, raising my eyebrows at Jimmie who collapsed laughing. She sank down onto the floor and grabbed Josh, pulling him over her shoulder so that he landed in her lap.

"I'm going to tickle you now!" she shouted and made him giggle, shriek and writhe around, totally at her mercy.

"Thtop, thtop!" he cried.

"You'd better stop," I said, edging past them towards the kitchen. "He looks like he's going to be sick."

Jimmie pulled him upright and then grabbed him in a huge embrace. "We've had great fun. Haven't we, matey?"

"Yeth, we have," agreed Josh.

"So it seems," I said, as I surveyed the scene of devastation in the kitchen. KFC wrappers trailed greasy crumbs over bubble blowing equipment and finger paintings done using my watercolours. "Are these my...?" I began but didn't finish as I knew the answer. When did I ever paint, anyway? Then I noticed my chess set. She'd only let the little brat play toy soldiers with my pawns. Ok, so it was the old wooden one but I notice that her *Lord of the Rings* set was still in a box on a high shelf. I took several deep breaths: *you're gonna crack, Jack;*

you're gonna crack. I managed to shrug off my annoyance. "So what happened to the park?" I asked eventually, clearing a space in front of the kettle for some mugs.

A cloud passed across Jimmie's face. "Oh. We only stayed for half-an-hour. It was really cold."

"We made a thnowman," said Josh.

"And a snowwoman," said Jimmie.

"And a thnowdog," added Josh seriously, holding his hand up for emphasis.

"And I just. I thought we'd better come indoors."

"There wath a man," Josh informed me.

"Shh," said Jimmie, but I had already caught on to her unease.

"What? What man?" I looked from her to Josh and then back again. "What man."

"There wath a man," said Josh again, nodding.

"What man, Jim?"

"It's ok," said Jimmie, standing up and holding Josh by both hands. "It's ok. Really. It was nothing. I only got a bit nervous. That's all."

"But what man?" I persisted.

"I didn't see who he was. He didn't approach us. It was Josh that spotted him. Didn't you mate?"

"Yeth. I got eyeth like Action Man."

I was looking at Jimmie.

"Tell me," I said. "I know there's more to this."

"Really it's ok," she laughed nervously and looked away. "Go and get your new toy, Josh. Let's try and tidy up, shall we? Now that Mrs Perfect is home."

"Hoy! I'm not Mrs Perfect," I shouted, but I laughed all the same. Once Josh was distracted, I murmured to Jimmie, "Do you think it might have been the E-X?"

"The E...? Oh! No. I don't think so."

"So why...?"

"Just leave it? Will you? I'll talk to you about it later."

JIM

I had been quite freaked out. To see Frank in the park. I was glad to be with Dianne's child. Not one of Donna's. But even so it could have turned nasty. We drove the long way home. Just to be sure. I decided that I would tell Jack about him. But didn't want to say anything in front of Josh. That little boy has enough problems at the moment. He doesn't need nightmares about stalkers.

Jack said she'd take Josh back home. I think she realised that if I'd gone then I would never get away from Dianne. The poor woman was so needy at the time. We wanted to have our evening together. I'd been planning a nice meal. Got the food in ready.

It had started raining again. The snow might melt now. But it could freeze overnight. The weather was so unpredictable. Jack suggested that she would leave the car at the bottom of the hill again. Just in case. I had another cup of tea when they'd gone. Tidied up a bit. Put the telly on. More on Fleur Baker, pitiful soul. Will they ever let her rest?

I turned the TV off and switched on our new computer. I connected to the puzzle site Jack had shown me. There were a few new logic puzzles. I got engrossed for a while. Forgot to put the dinner on. Then suddenly the computer froze. The connection went dead. I tried to reconnect a couple of times but nothing.

When the knock came on the door. I thought it was Jack. Forgot her keys. Or hands too frozen to hold them. I imagined her on the doorstep. Stamping impatiently. Muttering to herself. I remembered the dinner. I ran for the door. Didn't take my stick. Didn't think to use the chain.

It wasn't Jack.

Chapter X

JACK

Still raining on the way back, it is one of those days that make you want to emigrate. Sky the shape of a giant raincloud; outside objects becoming grey and drab, coated in drizzling dampness; inside objects radiant with early-evening lights and TV, emanating warmth and where I'd like to be. The knowledge that a stranger's knock at the door will be met with hostility drives me on home to the place where, if not welcome, at least I am entitled to claim space.

Chill creeping through the big black coat threatens to wrap around my already frozen heart. No hat, only my upturned collar to protect me, so my hair first holds the drips in tiny glittering diamonds, then reacts to the wet and turns into frizzy ringlets until finally it succumbs and adheres to the side of my face like seaweed slime.

I don't know why I didn't call first.

I like to think now, as I remember the last walk back to the place I called home, that I was filled with a sense of foreboding. But it's more likely my dramatic imagination imposing this memory onto my already confused recollection. What I do remember is the cold, wet, damp, dusking afternoon and one buzzing streetlamp outside the house that flicked incessantly on and off, on and off as if it were trying to send a coded danger signal.

If I had called first, would she have answered?

My lips were sore. It had been a few days since Jimmie and

I had kissed on the lips. And the other, well, I don't know how long. When I have chapped lips I make them worse by rubbing them and biting, worrying at them constantly. I can't stop myself, it's a habit.

Had she not answered the phone, would I have known something was wrong?

Habitually, I held my keys in hand as I walked up the street, a habit learned as a teen. Now I selected the necessary key a few paces from the door to speed my entrance into the comfort and safety of hearth and home.

I didn't think it strange there was no light in the front room as we generally used the back room, it being warmer, but something made me pause outside the front door as I held the key up to the lock – a shout or muffled bang just on the edge of hearing. My recollection of events is precise at this point. My mind becomes a freeze-frame slow-motion movie, each take lasting an eternity. I stood transfixed - like someone suspecting a surprise birthday party hovering outside a room of people ready to shout 'surprise'. The door was ajar. I pushed and stepped over the threshold into a world of horror.

Not blood. Not gore. Not severed limbs and cannibalism. Not satellite television horror. Real life horror. The kind of horror that happens every day, in every town, city and village around the world, that has happened since before human beings became human. No less horrific, though, for the fact that it is commonplace. No less horrific for me, standing there witnessing it.

I thought at first that they were having sex, consensual sex I mean. Jimmie, my lover, lying back rigidly on the old sofa we used as a filing cabinet, the pages of my recently rejected novel spilling out onto the floor from underneath her, casually reordering themselves in the process; a dirty scruffy stranger who I now know to be one Francis Little of no fixed abode, humping manically on top of her, his hand over her mouth and not a sound emanating from either of them.

Then her eyes flicked in my direction and I saw the horror reflected there and a silent plea that tore me apart.

I didn't have time to feel rage. I leapt on him as a lion on an antelope, roaring, grabbing, teeth and claws ready to maim and injure. I dragged him from her and flung him across the room. He staggered backwards into the fireplace, his elbow knocking some unpaid bills from the mantelpiece. His trousers slid from knee to ankle and he looked at me bewildered. If at this point I could have stopped myself then perhaps I would not be here now and you would not be reading this. But we both know that I could never have changed the inevitable.

I took advantage of his dazed state and struck again. I went straight for his face: his stupid, ignorant, ugly, hairy face. With one hand I grabbed his dirty jumper and pulled him towards me and with the other I punched hard into his left eye, feeling like my hand could go through to the back of his head. I heard Jim shouting, "No! Jack, no!" as he went down, but it was too late. She could never have stopped me any more than I could have stopped myself. He crashed into the hearth and lay still.

I stood over him, fists balled, knuckles white, waiting for him to try to stand up. But he didn't. He lay there semi-naked, his arms splayed out and legs awkwardly stuck in the tangled trousers, his white skin shockingly pale against the dirty dark clothes. The ugly, turkey-neck prick was flopped to one side and stuck at half-mast. I let out a sharp burst of laughter at the ridiculousness of his position, still expecting him to react in some way, but he didn't move.

I heard a whimper from the sofa and my peripheral vision caught Jimmie shuffling into her jeans, wincing as she did so. I looked at her and she looked back at me. I looked at her feet and where she had placed them on the loose pages of my life and I remember thinking then: *he has done the one thing that she would not let me do*. It was then that the rage came into me, rising up like sickness. It caught me by surprise and gave me a faint, light-headed feeling. For so long I had waited for her to be ready. For so long I had been patient and forestalled my own pleasure until that special time when she would say yes. Then along comes a man and takes it anyway, takes by force what is rightfully mine.

I roared again, the red rage searing fire on my breath. I grabbed the labrys from its place above our mantelpiece, holding the flat side of the axe-head down to smash against his skull. I heard her as if from a distance, "No, Jack." Not screaming this time, but gently, calmly, her hand closing over mine and holding the heavy brass replica back so it could do no harm. "He's dead already. Look at him." I let her take the labrys and hang it on the hooks over the mantelpiece. Then she came back to me and put her hand on my shoulder as if I were the one who needed comforting. I shrugged her off, don't know why but I just couldn't let her touch me.

I looked at him properly then, for the first time. He wasn't that big, I think smaller than me, but it was difficult to tell in his twisted position. He looked like a stereotypical image of a vagrant: unshaven, uncut hair, ingrained dirt, filthy check shirt and torn jumper – had I made those rips? – dark, stained cords and string for shoelaces. His eyelids were half-closed, the left bulging slightly, and his mouth sagged open. If it weren't for the slick red pool emerging from under his head he could almost have been mistaken for a drunk. Dead drunk.

The horror of it struck me again and I sat down heavily. This is where my memory fuses and I must reconstruct the conversation we had from those fragments that remain, like Sapphic poetry. I threw my coat off and sat on the floor because I couldn't go near the sofa. Jim sat back there and looked at me, waiting. I don't know how long we sat like that. Finally she said: "We have to call the police."

I looked at her aghast. "You're joking aren't you? The

police? We have to think about how we're going to get him out of here."

"I'll tell them it was self-defence…"

"Hardly." She's so naïve. "How do you think this looks? A jealous lover stumbles on her girlfriend having sex and…" I saw her flinch. "He *was* raping y-?"

Too late I swallowed the last word. I'd said it; I'd voiced doubt and then the gulf between us became impassable. She was dumbstruck. I saw the shocked indignation in her eyes being replaced by the hurt. When she could speak, the words came out in a hiss. "Yes. Yes, he was."

"I'm sorry, I just… Well, what I mean is that the courts aren't necessarily going to believe that. They'll concoct some story about you luring him here or having an affair or –"

"Stop. Just stop."

"What? What can I say?" I spread my hands in a gesture of hopelessness. "We have to be realistic here. We have to think their way or we won't survive this. Once they know your history…"

"You can claim self-defence. He attacked me. He could have attacked you. I'll back you up."

"It's not that easy. How will they believe that he attacked me?" I managed to turn my face towards the corpse without allowing my eyes to register the image. "I'm twice his size; I've got karate trophies; he's got his trousers down for God's sake." I thought about *Thelma and Louise* 'you don't want to be caught in Texas when you've killed a man with his trousers down' – Claire would have loved that one. "He was defenceless; a poor defenceless boy with his prick out – what jury is going to believe…?"

"What jury? What do you know about juries?" We were shouting now and I held up my hand to quiet her, instinctively looking to the wall that separated us from the neighbour. Jim's head turned as well and we both held our breath for a moment, expecting the banging to begin, but none came. We turned back to each other and she spoke in a calmer tone. "I'm the one who's been quizzed by the police. Treated like a criminal myself. I'm the one who's had to face questions. About my background and my sexual habits. I don't think I could..." Her voice broke. "I don't think I could do that again."

I was tempted to say, "Well, thanks for your support because without you as a witness I'm completely buggered." But I needed her on my side right then. Instead I said, "In that case I think we should get rid of the evidence as soon as possible and forget this ever happened."

She muttered something about not being able to forget an incident that happened twenty years ago and then sat with her head in her hands for what seemed like an age. I knew I had to stir her if we were to get going but I also had to keep calm or she would be no use to me at all. I forced myself to look at the cooling body on the hearth. Seeing his face in profile, I knew what I had already suspected: he was the dead man I'd seen in Claire's tealeaves. The angle of the head and the shape of the pool of blood matched up to the silhouette burned into an age-old memory that when I closed my eyes I could still see.

A shuddering breath and sigh from Jimmie snapped my attention back to her. I sighed too and said, "We have to do something about this."

"Yes," she said, "we have to call the police." She started to stand and winced again, clutching her abdomen.

"Babe!" I jumped up from the floor and grabbed her before she fell. "He really hurt you, didn't he?" She didn't answer but buried her head into my shoulder. I hugged her tightly. I felt a third wave of anger, weaker than the others but keen nonetheless. "Bastard, bastard..." I repeated through clenched teeth, while my chin rested on the top of her head. "Who was he anyway? Was this your man in the park?"

She extricated herself and stepped back, wiping her hand

over her dry face. After a moment, she said, "Yes. At least I think so. It's Frank Little. A guy I used to know at the shelter."

"Right." Well that would make it easier to get rid of him, if no-one would notice he was missing; the downside was that he wasn't a random stranger. "Right. We need to find something to wrap him up in; an old rug or blanket would do." I rubbed my hands together. I distinctly remember doing so and then stopping and thinking, *why have I just done that?*

"What are you talking about?" she said. "You sound like you've done this before."

I spread my hands again, smiling in what I hoped was a winning way. "I've just read a lot of bad detective stories."

"Well, I never wanted to be in a detective story. I'm calling the police," and she strode past me to the back room. I ran to her and tried to block her from the phone on the computer desk but she got there first. She lifted the receiver and looked at me as she held it to her ear. I began to protest but then noticed a change in her expression. She put the receiver down and picked it up again, then jiggled the handset rest. I thought at first she was listening to my protestations but then: "It's dead."

The phone dropping from her hand. "I was on the internet. It suddenly disconnected just before…" She sagged back against the desk. "He must have cut it from outside. When he knocked I thought it was you… forgotten your key." Then the tears began, and great gulping sounds, and I had to hold her again for a while. "It's ok. It's ok," she said, wiping her face on my shirt. "I'm ok. Look. I've got my mobile." She reached into her jeans pocket and pulled out the mobile, flipping it open awkwardly. I put my hand over it and pushed it down. I was getting pretty frustrated now. She just didn't seem to be taking in what I was saying.

"Listen to me. You're not listening. We can't call the police. It's not an option. I'll be arrested and maybe you too. They'll search the place. They'll find anything they can to pin on me.

Besides which…" I had to tell her; it wasn't something I'd want her to hear from someone else. "They know me. I've got previous."

"What? Previous what?"

"You're not the only one with a history, you know. There's a lot you don't know about me."

"And whose fault is that? It's not like I haven't asked you about your past."

"I know, I know. Suffice to say you're not the only one with experience of being in the dock."

"Look, I don't care what it is; it can't be that bad. But this was self-defence and it wasn't your fault."

"No, it wasn't self-defence, Jim. If you'd killed him yourself then it would be but it was me that killed him and it won't matter what we tell them. They have forensics and they can find out everything that happened. Look at what they did to that guy who killed Fleur – they tore his house apart."

"But if they can do that then there's no point in us trying to get rid of the body; we may as well own up from the beginning and explain that it was an accident."

"They won't find out it was us if they don't make the connection. Think about it: we can dump him in an alley, make it look like a mugging. No-one'll care about someone like him; no-one'll come looking for him. If we take his ID they might not be able to find out who he is and he'll wind up just being another unsolved case."

She blanched. "That's horrible. How can you wish that on someone?"

"Jim, he just raped you…"

"Yes, but he was still a human being. He's entitled to…"

"I don't think he was giving much thought to *your* human rights."

She looked at me as if seeing me for the first time and opened her mouth, about to speak again, when a noise came from the front room that made us both jump.

"Hello? Police. Anyone home?" The front door! I hadn't closed it behind me. Jimmie and I looked aghast at each other then rushed towards the lounge but we were too late. Two uniformed officers with fixed professional smiles stood in the doorway. "We've had a report of a disturb-" one began but was interrupted by the other officer who nudged him, nodding towards the body on the hearth. "Well!" they stepped inside and the one who hadn't yet spoken pushed the door shut with his elbow. *Fingerprints*, I thought.

"I was just about to call you," said Jimmie, holding up her mobile. The first policeman put his hand up to silence her as he knelt next to Frank and felt for a pulse. The second policeman began muttering into the radio attached to his shoulder, eyeing me as he did so. I tried to look innocent.

When he paused in the muttering, I said, "As you can see, officers, we've had an intruder..."

"Save it till we get to the station, love," said the first one without looking at me. The second one took a step closer and frowned at me, his head to one side.

"Don't I know you?"

"I doubt it," I said, turning my back on him. Jimmie sat down on the sofa with the expression of a smacked puppy. "Jim, you'll be ok. Don't worry about me."

"That's it!" he said, stepping round and peering into my face. "It's Crackerjack! Bloody hell, where've you been all these years? You've certainly changed."

"Thank you," I said and rolled my eyes at Jimmie, trying a wry smile. But it didn't wash. She just looked at me blankly.

"*I* don't know you anymore," she said, her eyes wide like a child. "Who are you?"

I wouldn't have time to explain any of that now. I'd thought I'd be safe a hundred miles or so from Birwood but it turns out there's always someone who'll recognise you. Just my luck that my arresting officer would be someone from the Pink Scheme.

I heard the sirens in the distance. Jimmie heard them too – I saw her eyes flick to the window and back again. "Look," I said, more urgently, "whatever you hear about me, just remember I love you." I could see the tears lining her eyes again, never very far away. "Just remember that I didn't tell you about my past because I love you."

"Aaaah, aint that sweet?" said the policeman with a laugh.

"Fuck off will you and get a life?" I said and then appealed to the other policeman who now stood next to the sofa, next to Jimmie. "Please, will you make sure she goes to the rape suite?"

"Jack…" she protested.

"Will you just make sure she has a woman police officer with her? If you have any shred of decency then you'll realise that she's the victim here."

"Jack. I want to stay with you."

"They'll split us up anyway. They'll interview us separately and they won't let us see each other." I heard the screech of brakes outside and turned back to the second policeman. "Could I at least pack a bag to bring with me?" He looked at me tight-lipped. There was a loud bang on the door. One of them opened it and five or six more officers walked in, their eyes darting round the room, taking everything in. I was tempted to make a crack about number seven buses or how I hadn't had this many visitors in two years, but thought better of it. Instead I repeated my plea to fetch an overnight bag.

The first policeman looked at another officer, who I presume was his senior because he nodded and called to a WPC to follow me. I went upstairs and got two bags, putting Jimmie's pyjamas into one and mine into the other. I added my quilt and then methodically went through our drawers packing a whole set of clothes for her and a few things for me. I put a couple of books in each bag and in mine I put my diary and puzzle book. I left the Fay McMullins out. All the while the WPC watched in silence. Then I stood up and said to her, "The bathroom's downstairs. I'm going to need a toothbrush and stuff." I could see the look on her face, the unvoiced 'you've done this before, haven't you?' but she nodded and we went downstairs. Once I'd taken the necessary from the tiny damp cubicle at the back of the house, I went back into the crowded front room. I dropped Jimmie's bag into her lap and she looked at me with a bewildered expression. That's how I remember her now, sitting on the sofa surrounded by uniforms, with that pathetic, confused look on her face, and I can only feel irritated.

I noticed polished shoes walking over my novel and, almost as an afterthought, I scooped up the pages and added them to my already bulging bag. Somehow I felt I needed it with me.

I looked around my front room for one last time and said, "Right. I'm ready to go."

Chapter Why

JIM

We weren't allowed to contact each other for quite a while. We were taken to separate police stations. The rape suite is out of the Valley anyway. I don't intend to think about that. I was finally allowed to talk to Jack. I found that she didn't want to talk to me. I wrote a couple of letters. Just notes really. Asking why she wouldn't get in touch.

She didn't reply. Then the stories started appearing in the papers. I didn't know whether she saw them. I'm not sure of the rules in prison about media access. I don't know very much at all about prison. I didn't know very much about Jack either, it seems.

I thought about writing it all down. I had a lot of time on my hands. I was on extended leave of absence. On full pay. I had said I would go back. As soon as I had recovered physically. Dianne suggested I should take time out. She was back at work now, although her children hadn't been found. I spent some time helping her. I spent some time practising with The Girls.

Then one morning. I had a letter from Donna. Sent via Women's Aid.

Dear Jimmie,

I am very sorry to hear about what happened to you. Tell Jackie thank you from me. I am now free at last. I can make plans and have a life now I know that the bastard is not able to get me anymore. You can't imagine how that feels after so long of running away and hiding. I can get a job – I can find somewhere nice to live – somewhere nice for the kids. The possibilities are endless. I'm sorry it happened like that but I'm not sorry he's dead.

Jimmie, I didn't know you was that way but I don't mind. You've always been good to me and the kids. They miss you, by the way. When are you coming back? It's strange without you coming round to take them out.

We've had our fair share of the press camping on the doorstep. Stace was happy cos it gave her an excuse to stay off school. But no-one sticks around on this estate for long. One of their cars got trashed. Ha ha.

Any way Jimmie, I just wanted to be sure you knew there weren't any hard feelings about Frank. I don't care what they say about your Jack in the paper. (did you see what they said about me?!!) If anyone deserves a medal then it's her for getting rid of the scum of the earth.

You know what's ironical? If she gets sent down for killing him then she'll probably have a longer sentence than he would of done if he'd killed me. Is that justice? I ask myself why everyday.

Well Jimmie, I'm not one for writing long letters but I just wanted you to know. That's all.

All the best,

Donna and the kids.

I wrote back to her. To say thanks for the support. I told her that I was planning to write a book. Asked if she minded. She wrote a short note in reply. She said she didn't mind at all. So long as I made sure I told everyone what a bastard Frank was. I hope I've done that.

But you know it's sad. Because he could have been a great man. He was intelligent, I remember. He had some beautiful children. He could have been a success. I know enough to have seen that he was an alcoholic. Jack says he deserved to die. Everyone dies eventually, she says. But I don't think we have the right to bring that date forward.

I have a recurring vision of him falling backwards. The look of surprise on his face. Pitiful. But I have to agree with Donna. In the long run. It's better that he's dead. For everyone except him, of course. That old Utilitarian stuff Jack goes on about, Christians, Romans and lions. I couldn't have gone through another rape trial. Jackie's trial will be bad enough. And if he'd been alive now. It might have got very complicated. So Jack and Donna are both right. He's better off dead. And we're better off without him. All of us.

I wrote to Jack again. I didn't expect her to answer. I thought it was only polite. If I was planning to write a book with her in it. Considering she was already writing one herself. In reply I got a parcel. On top of the manuscript was a letter.

Dearest Jim,

I'm surprised you still want to speak to me. I imagined that you would hate me after all the revelations.. But darling sweet Jimmie you never cease to amaze me with your forgiving nature.

You can't rescue me now, either; I'm done. So you may as well forget about me and move on with your life. It's not so bad in here for me; I actually feel quite at home. You know me and institutions! There's a library and I actually get time to read. I can even go on the internet although it's restricted access. In a way it's a relief. I always knew that something would put me away eventually and it's better not to have it hanging over my head.

As for the book. Yes, you write it. That's a bloody good idea. For a start, you'll probably finish one, whereas I never will. You'll find some interesting chapters on the computer. Look in a folder called 'Breaking'. This is all stuff I meant to show you some day but never got around to it.

Dearest Jim. I'm not going to be around to tell my story so I'm trusting you to do it for me. I know you'll do a good job. Look in other places on the computer – you'll find all sorts of things there that aren't in the manuscript. I'm still writing it, of course, so I'll send you more when I have it.

Meanwhile it's probably better if you don't contact me again. We'll see each other around the trial I'm sure, but I don't want you to be a prison widow. Go and find a life somewhere else. I'm sure Dianne will be happy to have you, and there you have a ready-made family. Sorry, but I couldn't resist that.

Be selfish for once in your life, Jim. Do something where you're only thinking of your own needs and not other people's. Remember to push that CD with The Girls – you could be big!

Just try to remember in all of this that I love you and I always have. I only wanted to protect you and look where that got me.

Take care,
Jackie

So there it is. I have permission for writing this. It took a while to get through all of Jackie's old chapters. She's not the most organised of people. Though she likes to say she is. She gave the chapters letters instead of numbers, for a start. And even then I don't think it was chronological. But I got there in the end. Then she started sending me these revised chapters. She'd seen the newspapers and had rewritten the whole thing in answer to each clipping. I've put it all together in a sort of scrapbook. She's still sending them to me but I've got more than enough for the moment.

I'm finally ready to send it out. I've edited out the personal attacks because I'm not putting my name to that kind of thing. You should see the stuff she's written about Viv Diggen! I've already got an agent. Someone contacted me. I didn't even have to do the chasing. The power of the press.

Turns out that autobiographies of unknowns are all the rage right now. So long as there's enough misery. You want misery, I can give you misery. Layer upon layer of it. But that will be another whole book.

I know what she meant about me being forgiving. But you see I have to believe Frank wasn't evil by nature. I have to believe that violence is something learned not innate. It is important for my baby that there is a clean slate.

I laughed at the bit about Dianne. Jack always was jealous of her. But I can't see why. She is not at all attractive to me. And of course I don't need the 'ready-made family' now.

I refused the morning-after pill. They couldn't understand why at the rape suite. But as I said to Claire Tilley, it is possible for something good to come out of everything. My little silver lining is growing well. I haven't told Jack yet although she's dropped enough bombshells on me to take one back. Although it probably wouldn't do her any favours at the trial. We'll have to see. I don't know how Donna will react.

I've moved now. I've got a flat quite near to The Claires. Although, as it turns out, I'm not sure how long they're going to stay there.

Claire O'Malley came round to see me this morning. Apparently, that 'source close to Jackie' was her own lover and she is furious. I am too. I thought Claire-T was my friend. It looks like their relationship is on the rocks now. Perhaps there is no such thing as the perfect marriage after all. I know a few people who will be annoyed if they split up – no more parties at The Two Claires.

Mum and Dad came and helped me move. I can't do any lifting in my condition. They tried to persuade me to move back with them. But no. If there's one thing I need right now, it's control over my own life.

Jack told me to be selfish. I can't help feeling guilty, though. I've always been insular. But it's not like me to be so self-seeking. It's amazing what being pregnant can do for a person. I remember the last time.

I have to be able to be strong for us both. And as for Jack. Well. We'll see. I have a lot to say to her. A whole lot.

The time for silence is over. Now is the time for screams.

Acknowledgements

The first acknowledgement must go to Tom Chalmers at Legend Press, without whom this book wouldn't be published. I'd also like to acknowledge Emma Howard and Lucy Boguslawski, both Legends in their own right.

I acknowledge every teacher and therapist I've ever had, especially Heather Beck of Manchester Metropolitan University who gave me ideas above my genre, and Miss Unwin, my High School English teacher to whom I promised I would dedicate my first book.

I acknowledge my mother and sisters, for their part in me becoming the person I am. My Gran, for giving me reprieve from home, and for telling me that although she doesn't like swearing in books, she'll read it and let me know what she thinks.

I stand on the shoulders of every lesbian writer that has gone before. I thank them all, from Ann Bannon with 'I am Woman' for paving the way to Guinevere Turner and Elizabeth Ziff with 'The L-Word' for taking it prime-time. I most especially acknowledge Sarah Waters for 'Tipping the Velvet'. Without that novel I would never have conceived of being so direct and explicit, nor considered a mainstream publisher for this book.

Thanks go to the friends I made at university, in Women's Aid, hospitals, internet chatrooms, karate and counselling, and the experiences they shared with me which added to the pot of ideas for this book.